Praise for

'A gripping story . . . Juxtaposing illuminating contemporary accounts of the Wars of the Roses with breathtaking insights into the minds of the principal players, *Succession* puts the conflict into a compelling context whilst exploring the human cost of the bloody, bitter birth of the Tudor dynasty' *Lancashire Evening Post*

'Livi Michael is new to historical fiction and it shows, in a good way. Focused on the earlier years of the Wars of the Roses (about which I knew nothing – and nor did she, by her own admission, before she started), this novel is wonderfully stylistically fresh, making inventive use of contemporary chronicles, which it mimics to blackly comic effect. But it's also a heartfelt account of the eye-opening, hair-raising early life of Margaret Beaufort, mother of Henry VII' Suzannah Dunn, Waterstones blog, 'Author's Books of the Year 2014'

'*Succession* is a powerfully written account of the fifteenth-century Wars of the Roses . . . finely balanced between history and fiction . . . a fascinating, riveting read' *Historical Novel Society*

'In *Succession* Livi Michael engages meticulously with the diverse historical accounts of the Wars of the Roses, but she also invests intimate and poignant humanity into the personal tragedies of an era wrought with conflict and terror' Elizabeth Fremantle, author of *Queen's Gambit*

'Rather refreshing' *The Bookbag*

Praise for *Rebellion*:

'A gripping read full of historical detail' *Woman Magazine*

'Highly recommended' *Historical Novel Society*

ABOUT THE AUTHOR

Livi Michael has published six novels for adults: *Succession* and *Rebellion*, the first two books of her Wars of the Roses trilogy; *Under a Thin Moon*, which won the Arthur Welton award in 1992; *Their Angel Reach*, which won the Faber prize in 1995; *All the Dark Air* (1997), which was shortlisted for the Mind Award; and *Inheritance*, which won a Society of Authors award. Livi has two sons and lives in Greater Manchester. She teaches creative writing at the Manchester Metropolitan University and has been a senior lecturer in creative writing at Sheffield Hallam University.

Accession

LIVI MICHAEL

PENGUIN BOOKS

PENGUIN BOOKS

UK | USA | Canada | Ireland | Australia
India | New Zealand | South Africa

Penguin Books is part of the Penguin Random House group of companies
whose addresses can be found at global.penguinrandomhouse.com.

Penguin
Random House
UK

First published 2016
001

Copyright © Livi Michael, 2016

The moral right of the author has been asserted

Set in Dante MT Std 11/13 pt
Typeset by Palimpsest Book Production Limited, Falkirk, Stirlingshire
Printed in Great Britain by Clays Ltd, St Ives plc

A CIP catalogue record for this book is available from the British Library

ISBN: 978-0-241-97763-7

www.greenpenguin.co.uk

To the memory of Margaret Beaufort, Countess of Richmond,
1443–1509

Contents

LANCASTER

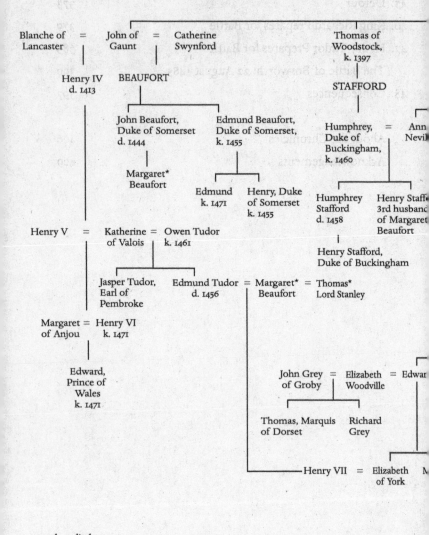

d. = died
k. = killed
* = appears more than once

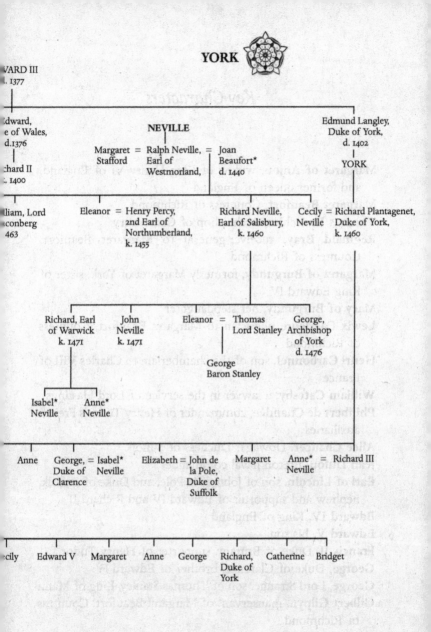

YORK

WARD III
. 1377

dward,
e of Wales,
d.1376

hard II
. 1400

NEVILLE

Margaret = Ralph Neville, = Joan
Stafford   Earl of   Beaufort*
            Westmorland,   d. 1440

Edmund Langley,
Duke of York,
d. 1402

YORK

liam, Lord   Eleanor = Henry Percy,   Richard Neville,   Cecily = Richard Plantagenet,
conberg   2nd Earl of   Earl of Salisbury, Neville   Duke of York,
463   Northumberland,   k. 1460   k. 1460
                        k. 1455

Richard, Earl   John   Eleanor = Thomas   George,
of Warwick   Neville   Lord Stanley Archbishop
k. 1471   k. 1471   of York
                                                       d. 1476

                                    George
                                    Baron Stanley

Isabel*   Anne*
Neville   Neville

Anne   George, = Isabel*   Elizabeth = John de   Margaret   Anne* = Richard III
        Duke of   Neville   la Pole,   Neville
        Clarence   Duke of
                                         Suffolk

cily   Edward V   Margaret   Anne   George   Richard,   Catherine   Bridget
                                                  Duke of
                                                  York

Key Characters

Margaret of Anjou, widow of King Henry VI of England, and former queen of England

Margaret Beaufort, Countess of Richmond

Thomas Bourchier, Archbishop of Canterbury

Reginald Bray, receiver-general to Margaret Beaufort, Countess of Richmond

Margaret of Burgundy, formerly Margaret of York, sister of King Edward IV

Mary of Burgundy, her stepdaughter

Lewis Caerleon, physician to Margaret Beaufort, Countess of Richmond

Henri Carbonnel, son of the chamberlain to Charles VIII of France

William Catesby, a lawyer in the service of Lord Hastings

Philibert de Chandée, commander of Henry Tudor's French auxiliaries

Alice Chaucer, Dowager Duchess of Suffolk

Jean Dufou, Breton naval commander

Earl of Lincoln, son of John de la Pole, 2nd Duke of Suffolk, nephew and supporter of Edward IV and Richard II

Edward IV, King of England

Edward V, his son

Francis II, Duke of Brittany, supporter of Henry Tudor

George, Duke of Clarence, brother of Edward IV

George, Lord Strange, son of Thomas Stanley, King of Mann

Gilbert Gilpyn, manservant of Margaret Beaufort, Countess of Richmond

Richard Grey, brother of Richard, Duke of York, son of Elizabeth Woodville by her first marriage

Thomas Grey, Marquis of Dorset, son of Elizabeth Woodville by her first marriage

John Howard, Duke of Norfolk, supporter of Richard III

Thomas Howard, Earl of Suffolk, son of John Howard, Duke of Norfolk, supporter of Richard III

Lady Maltravers, sister of Elizabeth Woodville

Thomas Millying, Abbot of Westminster

John Morton, Bishop of Ely

Anne Mowbray, wife of Richard, Duke of York

Anne Neville, younger daughter of the Earl of Warwick, married firstly to Edward of Westminster, Prince of Wales, then to Richard, Duke of Gloucester. Later Queen Anne of England

Cecily Neville, Dowager Duchess of York, mother of Edward IV and Richard III

Isabel Neville, sister of Anne Neville, wife of George, Duke of Clarence

Perrin, a Breton squire

John de la Pole, 2nd Duke of Suffolk, son of Alice Chaucer; married firstly to Margaret Beaufort, then to King Edward's sister, Elizabeth

Richard, Duke of Gloucester, brother of Edward IV, later Richard III

Richard, Duke of York, son of Edward IV

Thomas Rotherham, Archbishop of York

Jane Shore, mistress of Edward IV

Henry Stafford, 2nd Duke of Buckingham, nephew of Margaret Beaufort by marriage

Thomas Stanley, Baron Stanley, King of Mann, fourth husband of Margaret Beaufort, Countess of Richmond

William Stanley, brother of Thomas Stanley, King of Mann

Dafydd ap Thomas, Welsh leader and former retainer of Jasper Tudor

Morgan ap Thomas, brother of the Welsh leader Dafydd ap Thomas

Henry Tudor, son of Margaret Beaufort, Countess of Richmond

Jasper Tudor, Earl of Pembroke, uncle of Henry Tudor

John de la Vere, Earl of Oxford, Lancastrian supporter

Roger Vaughan of Tretower, Welsh landowner and Yorkist supporter

William, Lord Hastings, Lord Chamberlain of Edward IV

Anthony Woodville, Earl Rivers, brother of Elizabeth Woodville

Edward Woodville, brother of Elizabeth Woodville

Elizabeth Woodville, wife of Edward IV, Queen of England

Katherine Woodville, sister of Elizabeth Woodville, wife of Duke of Buckingham

Lionel Woodville, Bishop of Salisbury, brother of Elizabeth Woodville

Richard Woodville, brother of Elizabeth Woodville

Joan Worsley, servant of Alice Chaucer

Elizabeth of York, daughter of Edward IV

Prologue

I t came to Margaret Beaufort, in the dead of night, as she lay awake listening to the racing of her heart, that she should marry again.

Like an instruction, but not one she could follow.

Marry. Again.

Why would she want to? She'd been married since she was six years old. Memories of her three marriages haunted her through the night hours. Why would she go through another?

But the answer came clearly. Because of her son, who was exiled in Brittany.

The king and the prince were dead, the queen imprisoned. The Lancastrian cause was lost. Only the Earl of Oxford and Jasper Tudor remained.

And her son who, at fourteen years old, was the last surviving heir of the House of Lancaster.

King Edward had begun negotiations with Duke Francis of Brittany to have Henry and Jasper returned. She knew nothing about Duke Francis. But plied with offers of money and military support against the French, why would he refuse?

Unless he was planning to use her son in his own game.

She had forgotten how to sleep. It was the strain of the last few months, of caring for her husband, who had been wounded in battle; of waiting to hear about her son. She couldn't live through such months again.

Jasper and Henry had never reached Tewkesbury to fight in that fateful battle for the queen. They'd got as far as Chepstow before hearing the disastrous news, then they'd fled to Pembroke and set sail to France, but strong winds had blown them to Brittany.

Margaret received this news late in September and one week later, her husband had died.

And the uncontrollable racing of her heart and nerves began.

Meanwhile, after all the executions, the celebrations started. The infant prince was created Prince of Wales. Everyone who had helped Queen Elizabeth in her confinement was rewarded. Abbot Millying, who had housed her in Sanctuary, was made chancellor of the young prince's household; William Gould, the butcher who'd supplied her with meat, was given his own ship for trading; Margery Cobbe, the midwife, was given a pension for life. And at Queen Elizabeth's behest, the old queen was removed from imprisonment in the Tower to Wallingford, to the custody of Alice Chaucer, who had been Margaret's guardian when she was a child.

Bishop Morton and John Fortescue were also reprieved. It was as though King Edward was holding his hands up to show they were not red with blood. He had pledged himself to peace and the rebuilding of his kingdom.

But he was trying to get her son back into England. And who knew why, or whether he would be merciful? He had saved the queen, but killed the prince and the king. King Henry had *died of grief*, according to official accounts, yet his body had bled in its coffin outside St Paul's. The last Duke of Somerset had been offered a pardon, then executed. King Edward, it was said, had *chosen to crush the seed*.

Her son was the last of that seed.

He was only safe while he was in exile, held hostage by the Duke of Brittany. But Margaret might never see him again.

For the first time in as long as she could remember, she didn't have a plan. She fell asleep intermittently, at odd times of the day, when praying or trying to read, and when she woke up, still exhausted, for a short time she couldn't remember who she was.

In those moments everything fell away from her: all the trappings of rank, of family and place.

She had worn out her knees with prayer and received no answer, no coherent thought at all apart from this one: that she should marry again.

She dismissed it as evidence of her madness. She had been driven to the limits of endurance, only to discover there are no limits.

But the thought didn't go away. It recurred in the dead of night. *Marry again.*

She'd done everything else in her power. She'd tried, so many times, to have Henry returned to her custody. And he was further away from her than ever.

But who could she marry?

She wasn't in favour with the king, so she had to marry someone who was. In order to ensure that, when her son returned – *if* he returned – he wouldn't be killed. So she needed someone close to the court, someone with influence, someone the king wouldn't wish to offend.

She only knew of one man in such a position: Thomas Stanley, steward of King Edward's household. His wife had died weeks before Margaret's husband.

She'd hardly registered it at the time, absorbed as she had been by her own anxieties, but she remembered it now.

Thomas Stanley, King of Mann.

He owned more land in the north of England than the king.

He had a large family: at least ten children from his wife. More, possibly, from his mistress.

His brother, William Stanley, had broken the news to Margaret of Anjou that her son had been killed at Tewkesbury. With great pleasure, she'd heard.

Thomas Stanley hadn't been there. He'd been conspicuously absent from most of the battles between Lancaster and York.

Through all the wars, his role had been ambiguous at best, treacherous at worst, yet he had risen steadily, gaining power and wealth.

He was a survivor. She needed someone like that.

Margaret's eyes were closed. She prayed for an answer, some thread that would guide her, but there was nothing. Nothing that offered her an alternative to holy matrimony. That coercion of the soul.

If she wanted to marry Thomas Stanley she would have to act soon. He was unlikely to stay a widower for long.

Why would he want to marry Margaret?

For her fortune, of course, and her estates, which, thanks to the efforts of her late husband, were untouched. Now she had the Stafford estates to add to them. Her lands in Kendal would make Stanley the supreme magnate of the north, and there were her other estates in the south.

She could make him the greatest landowner in England.

Her barrenness shouldn't trouble him – he hardly needed more family. Since he had a mistress, they would not need to associate in that way at all.

Her son could be his most useful political tool.

But could she do it? Even for her son?

She prayed again for some other solution, but none came.

She would have to write to him and invite him to her home.

He might not come, of course. And then she would have lost nothing. Or he might come – and then –

And then she would have to be equal to the task of marriage. To the task of him.

She pushed back the sheets and crossed the room, taking one candle with her and lighting another on the way. Then she sat at her desk.

Nothing had happened yet; she could still choose not to write.

She picked up her quill and held it, without dipping it in the ink.

Flight

Later, Henry Tudor would remember the flight from Chepstow as one of the best times of his life. A time of smoky fires, quickly stamped out, of poached and roasted rabbit, pigeon or fish. A time of lying silently in the blue-green shade of the forest with its musty scents, rain-water dripping all around.

They'd left most of Jasper's men in Chepstow. Three thousand men could hardly pass through Wales unnoticed. So they'd abandoned them to surrender, or escape if they could, while Henry and his uncle fled with a few companions.

That was after the beheading of Roger Vaughn. Who had been dragged to his knees before Jasper, his eyes darting about like flies in his sweating face. Henry heard the huff of breath as his knees smacked the ground. When Jasper read out the list of his crimes, which included the killing of Owen Tudor, Jasper's father, ten years earlier at Mortimer's Cross, he lifted his face and said, 'My crimes are for God to judge, not you.'

Jasper nodded, then walked round to the rear side of the kneeling man, unsheathing his sword. He lifted it and paused, glancing towards Henry, and Henry understood that his uncle was asking if he had prepared himself. He stiffened slightly and Jasper took this for assent.

The sword moved so swiftly it whistled through the air and took Roger Vaughn's head off at a single stroke.

Henry saw the spurt of blood from the neck; he watched the body slump to the ground and did not look away. Jasper walked towards him and gripped his shoulder.

'That was for your grandfather,' he said, and Henry nodded.

He felt as though he was required to say something, but he didn't know what. Jasper squeezed his shoulder, almost shaking it, and he understood that he'd done well.

He understood also that the execution was partly in revenge for Jasper's own failure to reach Tewkesbury in time to save the queen.

When Jasper heard the news from Tewkesbury his body seemed to buckle, though he was still standing. In Chepstow he'd remained for some time in the church, staring uncomprehendingly at the cross.

Only when the siege began did he come to life again, first beheading Roger Vaughn, then taking the decision to flee. They'd set off in darkness, through wooded copses that thickened into forest, pathless and trackless, darker than night because no trace of sky or star could be seen.

Henry tried to keep up, hacking his way through dense branches, tripping in tangled undergrowth or crawling through mud. He didn't mind stumbling so much, though on at least one occasion he'd hurt his ankle; he did mind holding everyone up so that one or other of the company had to help him through some ditch or tangled thicket. Jasper didn't come back to help him. He barely spoke to Henry at all.

Of course, he didn't complain. When the stitch in his side, the cramping of his muscles, became unbearable he thought of the knights in his favourite stories – Parsifal, Sir Gawain and the Green Knight – who always had to trek through impossible and unknown terrain.

And there was the hour when a small fire was lit, meat roasted and water brought from the nearest stream. The men talked together in low voices, firelight flickering over their faces. And Jasper would sit with him then, usually in silence, but on one damp night he began to talk. Tendrils of hair clung to his sallow face, his long nose was red at the tip, his cheeks hollow. He didn't look at Henry, but he said, 'Do you understand why I beheaded Sir Roger?'

Henry said he did.

'Why?' said Jasper, and now he was looking at Henry.

'For your father,' Henry said.

'Your grandfather,' Jasper said. 'You won't remember him.'

It wasn't a question. 'This was his country,' Jasper said. 'He was born near here. His family – our family – were from the north of Wales.'

And he spoke to him then of his father's father, Mareddud, and his father, Tudur Hen. 'My father was Owen ap Mareddud ap Tudur,' he said, staring into the flames. 'No one in England called him that. In England he was only Owen Tudor.'

The rain dripped like tiny footfalls while Jasper spoke.

The family had come from Abergele in the district of Rhos. They were kin to the rulers of Gwynedd. Over the years they had come to terms with the English kings, even though the first King Edward had made his son Prince of Wales.

Jasper was staring away from the fire, into the trees, '*See you not that the world is ending, Ah God, that the sea would cover the land,*' he quoted. Henry didn't know whether he was talking about the conquest of Wales or the defeat of the House of Lancaster and the loss of its last prince, his other nephew, Edward. Who was, or would have been, Prince of Wales.

He could feel the heat of the flames on his face. In spite of himself, he yawned. Jasper looked at him. 'You're tired,' he said. 'Get some rest.'

But the next night Jasper had spoken to him again, about the Tudors.

Owen's father, Mareddud, was cousin to Owen Glyndwr, who had fought Henry IV and declared himself Prince of Wales. But the rebellion had failed and Glyndwr had mysteriously disappeared. Mareddud went into exile.

He'd married a woman from Angelsey, and Henry's grandfather Owen had been born. Named, as he'd always said, after Owen Glyndwr.

3

Owen had managed to enter the service of Henry V and had fought with him in France. But then he'd served in the household of King Henry's wife, Katherine of Valois. And after King Henry had died, they had fallen in love and secretly married.

The King's Council had pursued Owen for this and imprisoned him; he'd had to escape from Newgate Gaol. After Katherine had died, their two oldest sons, Edmund and Jasper, had been taken into the court of Henry VI, and the king had married Edmund to Henry's mother.

Jasper paused just when Henry wanted him to go on. 'You know what happened to your father,' he said.

Henry did know. He knew that his guardian, William Herbert, had imprisoned his father in Carmarthen Castle, and Edmund had died there, of plague. Then William Herbert had brought Henry up with his own children. But he knew little else about his father, who had died before he was born.

'Am I – like him?' he asked. Jasper didn't smile. 'Not really,' he said. Then, as the light in Henry's eyes faded, he said, 'Though you are fairer, certainly, than your mother. If anything,' he said, 'you're like my younger brother, Owen. The priest.'

Henry didn't know what to think of this. Anyone other than Jasper might have been making fun of him, saying that he looked more like a monk than a warrior, but it was hard to imagine Jasper *making fun* at all. Already he'd withdrawn from Henry and was staring silently into the trees.

There were many more questions Henry wanted to ask, about his father and about his foster brother, William Herbert the younger, who was pursuing them with an army. But maybe he didn't want to know, because knowledge brought pain. The only father he'd known had killed his actual father. How was it possible to know such a thing?

Jasper said, 'I must speak with my men,' and Henry understood the conversation was over. He began to prepare his bed.

But as he lay down he thought about what Jasper had said.

Because he knew so little about himself, he had trained his memory to remember what he could. Now in the darkness he repeated the names he'd been given like a litany: Owen ap Mareddud ap Tudur. He himself was Henry ap Edmund ap Owen.

He had not known any of this family. Not his father, Edmund, his grandfather, Owen, nor Prince Edward his cousin, who'd been killed at Tewkesbury. He'd not even known his mother well. And though he'd spent more time with his uncle, he would not have said that he knew him either. But he could see now that they were all part of a larger story.

Jasper had woven him into this larger story so that he could see his place in it; at the end of every line. Beaufort, Tudor, Lancaster, Valois – there was no other future for all these lines in England but in him. It was a new thought and a strange feeling, because until that moment he had considered himself entirely separate, a cuckoo in the Herberts' nest.

This was the reason for Jasper's assiduous protection of him – not just that he was his only nephew now that the young prince had been killed but that he was the *last of the line*.

It was not a comfortable thought. He felt suddenly burdened by it, by the weight of the past. As if he was no longer free to choose his place or his path – it had already been chosen for him.

Somehow, he'd thought that as he got older he would achieve a measure of free will. When he was a man, he had often told himself after being chastised or set some complicated task of learning that *no one would tell him what to do*. Now he lay on his back in the dense forest, aware of the mist rising from the damp earth, the murmuring of men settling in for the night, and knew he was part of a story that had started long before he was born and would continue long after his death.

It was difficult to sleep on the rough ground. His ankle hurt, and his knee, there was a pain in his shoulder. When he shifted position he could hear all the small scurrying, rustling and crawling noises around him, for the forest was never still. Somewhere beyond the canopy of leaves was the sky, paler than the blackness of leaves, and somewhere in it, paler still, were the stars. And in all that was Henry Tudor.

He was the Henry who did as he was told, absorbed all his lessons, adapted to different schedules and routines, and the Henry who practised certain quiet subversions: reciting a different litany in his head, telling lies so small as to be insignificant and undiscovered, accumulating a secret hoard of treasures stuffed into his pillow that no one else could touch or see.

He was the Henry who had witnessed war and executions, who folded certain memories away in his mind where he did not have to look at them ... and the Henry who lay on the uneven ground with a root digging into one shoulder and a pain like a heat in his knee. And the Henry who would disappear into sleep, to a mysterious, ungovernable land, only to return each morning with no explanation or comprehension of where it had been.

Somewhere of no precise location within him, if the priests were to be believed, was a small spark called *the soul* that belonged to God, which would fly up after death to an infinite existence of either torment or bliss, according to how he was judged.

It existed within him like a star that could not be seen but which illuminated nonetheless, and offered guidance. It would guide him through the story of his life, which had already been written.

He felt as though his mind would crack open on this mystery like an egg.

A smattering of rain began again, tapping on the leaves and making them quiver, so that ripples of disturbance passed through the forest as through a giant pool. The breathing of the men around him altered with sleep. Henry shifted again and stared up into the quivering darkness of leaves until he, too, fell asleep.

After this the journey seemed to end quickly, though it must have taken some days for the vast walls of Pembroke Castle to appear.

'This is where you were born,' Jasper said. Henry knew that he had lived there before being given to William Herbert, but he had no memory of the place at all. It looked like a giant fortress rather than a home.

They were welcomed into the castle, fed and bathed in a proper bath. But the next morning Henry woke to the walls of his tower room shaking so he almost fell out of his bed. The castle was under siege.

It was not the expected siege, led by his foster brother William Herbert, but one led by a Welshman named Morgan ap Thomas. He was the grandson of Gruffyd ap Nicholas, the Welsh leader who Henry's father had fought. He was not fighting for the Welsh, apparently, but because Roger Vaughn had been his father-in-law.

Herbert's army was still advancing from the north, and now they couldn't leave the castle.

Morgan ap Thomas wasn't interested in terms; he wanted vengeance. He sent a herald to say that if the garrison would send Jasper out to him, they could go free. Otherwise, he would starve or bombard them to death.

Jasper's only response to this was to open fire. He told Henry to remain in the inner ward and, though his uncle didn't explain, Henry knew it was because he was now the greatest prize his enemy could possess. So he stayed in his room, thinking about his foster brother, William Herbert, who would arrive soon to capture or kill him. If he was captured, would Lady Herbert plead on his behalf with her son, or with the king?

But the bombardment of the castle walls soon made it difficult to think at all.

By the fourth day the garrison was in trouble. The besieging army had dug ditches and trenches around the castle; it was said they were tunnelling underground and mining the tunnels. Then that they had poisoned the water supply.

The arrival of Jasper's soldiers had already drained the resources of the castle. By the fifth day they had slaughtered the last of the livestock, the well was no longer usable and the men spoke of drinking horse piss or their own urine.

The worst part was the constant bombardment, the noise that battered the inside of the skull. Even when Henry lay still there was the sensation of movement around and under him, tremors and judders in the stone. Much of the time he lay on his bed with his hands clamped over his ears. When he closed his eyes he could see hairline cracks in the walls running together into fissures and greater cracks through which the sea would pour. All that rock crumbling and tumbling into the sea.

He'd heard it said that a siege could break a man's soul before it broke down the walls, until he ran stumbling towards his enemy with outstretched arms.

On the seventh day they ate the last of the food, slowly, carefully, and Henry couldn't even taste it. He could no longer answer when spoken to nor think for the battering sounds inside his skull.

Then on the morning of the eighth day a new sound entered the battle, like a series of discordant notes, an irregular stuttering rhythm. Different shouts rose.

'Dafydd!' cried the men. 'Dafydd ap Thomas!'

Morgan's younger brother, who had been Jasper's retainer, had ridden to help them, bringing two thousand men with him. Morgan ap Thomas' men fled within two hours.

Dafydd stood before the gates of Pembroke Castle as they swung open. Jasper went out to meet him and the two men embraced. Henry left the inner ward for the first time since the siege began, an unfamiliar silence ringing in his ears.

Jasper's men streamed into the town, bringing back what food they could find, and two days of feasting followed. Jasper sat with Dafydd, who said that William Herbert's men were approaching; it was not safe for them to stay either in England or Wales. Henry sat close by but couldn't hear everything that was said. He wondered if his ears had been permanently damaged.

He did hear Dafydd say that they should waste no time, because his brother would never give up. Even now he would be looking for reinforcements to return. It would be bad for them if he joined with Herbert's army. They should leave the castle, go to Tenby and get a ship.

Jasper's face looked even longer than usual. He knew the mayor had a ship, he said, that he would sometimes hire out. And Jasper had spent money on the town of Tenby, reinforcing its defences against attacks from the hills; he hoped the mayor would remember that.

'We'll go tomorrow,' he said.

Henry felt a slow coil of fear uncurling in him like smoke, or like worms in his stomach. Dafydd looked at him.

'You'll need to eat up, eh?' he said. 'Eat while you can.'

Henry looked at his plate. He had hardly touched his food. On the previous day he had eaten so much he'd almost been sick.

'You're going on a voyage,' Dafydd said. 'Like an adventurer – a pirate. You'll enjoy that, eh?'

'I don't know,' Henry said.

Dafydd laughed, unpleasantly. 'Your uncle here is going with you to save your skin,' he said.

'Where?' said Henry to Jasper. 'Where can we go?'

Dafydd started to speak, but Jasper held up his hand. 'You're right,' he said to Henry. 'It may not be safe, wherever we go. But we'll sail to France – in the hope that the French king remembers his kin.'

'He'll remember that he doesn't like the English,' Dafydd said.

France, Henry thought. It was as though his uncle had said they were going to the moon. He didn't want to go to France, even though he could speak French, of course, and his grandmother had been a French princess.

Jasper was looking at him again. 'Do you have any other suggestions?' he said.

Yes, Henry thought. Leave me here. I'll give myself up to

William Herbert and take my chances – hope for the best from my foster brother, who has no reason to kill me at all. Unless –

Unless he was under orders from the king.

'Of course he doesn't,' said Dafydd. 'Anyway – you'll travel, boy – see the world. Many young men would love to go.'

Henry was beginning to dislike this man who had saved all their lives. *You go,* he wanted to say, *I'll be fine,* but he knew that the words would sound childish in the extreme. Reluctantly, he speared some meat on to his knife.

'That's better,' Dafydd said. 'You'll need your strength for the journey.'

The mayor of Tenby could certainly see the sense in not housing any fugitives. Not while two armies were after them. They stayed one night in his house while the boat was prepared. There was enough room in the small barque for Jasper and Henry and a few men, but the rest would have to make their own way home, or go into hiding. Jasper couldn't afford to pay them, either, though he gave them his heartfelt thanks when he addressed them all. Which some of them took right sourly.

The next morning a message came from Henry's mother. Hope flared in Henry as Jasper opened it, that he could return to her household and remain in hiding there, and trouble no one for the rest of his days. But Jasper read the letter, then handed it to Henry.

Do not put your faith in any promises or offer from the king, she wrote. *Remember the Duke of Somerset.* And to Henry she said: *God bless you and keep you, my son. I will pray for you always in my heart.*

And Henry's heart sank – a phrase he had not fully understood before – because a reprieve had not come.

Before noon they set sail, but ran into storms. The little boat was buffeted and tossed, almost upended, and Henry was sick twice, clinging to the side of it. As the men battled with the sails he thought that now he would die after all, at sea. But they managed to put in at Jersey, where their only consolation was that no one else could reach the island, assaulted as it was by gales.

Twice they set out and were driven back. The third time they stayed at sea for several days, running out of supplies and into further storms. Then at last they saw land.

They didn't know where they were until they managed to put in at a small port. Jasper's men discovered this was Brittany, not France, and the small port was Le Conquet.

They couldn't set sail again while the winds were still raging. Jasper decided they would travel overland instead, to the court of the Duke of Brittany, and beg for asylum. After some fierce bargaining, he managed to arrange for them to stay at an inn, a crowded, dingy hovel, where Henry slept like the dead. In the morning his uncle was nowhere to be seen.

Henry got dressed, washing himself at the basin as well as he could, while rehearsing in his mind all the French words he might need to make his way through the country alone.

Then Jasper returned, carrying writing materials. A few of his men would take the ship back to Tenby for him, he said, and would carry a letter with them. He handed the paper to Henry. 'Write to your mother,' he said.

This Earl of Richmond . . . fell into Duke Francis' hands during a storm when he was attempting to flee to France with his uncle, the Earl of Pembroke. The duke treated them very gently as prisoners.

Philippe de Commines

2

Proposal

When Thomas Stanley didn't reply to her letter, at first she was relieved. Then she felt piqued. He could have turned her down politely if he'd already chosen another wife. He might at least have replied.

As the weeks passed, she thought perhaps he was away for the Christmas season, but she learned from her servant, whose brother worked in the court kitchens, that he was still with the king.

Her pique turned to a resentment tinged with fear. His silence might mean she was more out of favour with the king than she'd thought. Or that he had other plans for her. To arrange her marriage himself and remove her entirely from court circles. To dispose of her wealth in his own way.

Unexpectedly, she found she could not stop thinking about Stanley. He was not particularly distinguished-looking, neither overly tall nor handsome. He had a long, clever face and a subtle mouth. He did not attract her; she didn't want to marry him at all.

Then early in February a messenger came. He rode up to her door in the early light and left before she'd finished her prayers.

She pushed her hair into a cap and hurried downstairs, to find two servants looking at her in consternation.

'That was Lord Stanley's messenger, my lady,' her steward said. 'He's on his way. He'll be here before noon, with three of his sons and fifty retainers.

'Before noon?' she repeated. *Fifty?* she thought. 'Send two servants to market,' she said. 'And prepare the Great Hall.'

No time, no time, she thought. And it was Lent. There would be practically nothing in the shops.

'See if there are any fish in the pond,' she told her steward. 'Fetch the grain from the granary.'

How dare he wait until Lent to call on her, practically unannounced?

She went to the kitchens to break the news to the cook, whose face set into grim lines. Oatmeal was brought from the granary to take the salt from the dried fish, wheat and rye for the bread, corn and maize for the sweet courses. Servants were dispatched to strew herbs in the Great Hall and put up trestle tables for Stanley's men. All the wine was brought up from the cellars.

Margaret set about some of the work herself, peeling apples, pounding stock fish with dates. Miniature pastries were made, lamprey and sturgeon were stewed into jellies and a whole carp was garnished with crayfish.

Then she went up to her room to dress.

She was in mourning, so she chose dark blue velvet and one of her ladies scraped all her hair under a wimple. But she put rings on her fingers and a jewelled cross round her neck.

Too soon they could hear hooves shaking the ground. Stanley and his army, as she thought of them, were arriving.

She glanced at the mirror, seeing a tiny, sharp-faced woman who looked older than her years, and went out to meet them.

'Lord Stanley,' she said as he rode forward and grinned down at her with yellow teeth.

'Countess,' he said; then, 'I hope you have plenty of food in – my men are starving.'

She could think of nothing polite to say to this. As he dismounted she indicated that his men should go to the kitchens to refresh themselves, then, without waiting to be introduced to his sons, she walked into the house, clutching the cross at her breast.

There wasn't enough room for everyone in the Great Hall, so makeshift tables were put up in the entrance hall. Stanley's men were wild, shouting, laughing and jeering as they fought for a place. To Margaret's dismay, a dozen or so dogs followed them in and began to fight and bark.

She could feel a headache coming on.

She took her seat at the great table and Stanley sat next to her. On her other side sat Reginald Bray, her receiver, who had been practically running her household since her husband's death. His expression was carefully neutral. On the other side of Lord Stanley sat his eldest son, George, a pimply youth of about sixteen who was nothing like his father but round-faced with prominent eyes.

Further along the same table were two more of Stanley's sons, one called Edward, who was about thirteen years old, and another she thought was called Dickon – a chubby, solid lad of perhaps eleven years. The eldest and youngest brothers looked alike and must resemble their mother. Only the middle boy looked anything like his father, long-faced and with a hint of cruelty about the mouth. And he was a reprobate – sticking his dagger into the food on other people's plates then flicking the sauce at them.

Lord Stanley said nothing about this but glanced occasionally at her with a look of calculated amusement. She kept her own gaze lowered, dipping her fingers into a water bowl, though she seemed to be the only one taking advantage of this particular facility.

Stanley's men thumped their mugs on the table when they wanted more ale, broke into impromptu song, held arm-wrestling matches, spilled the sauces and their drinks and tormented the dogs. Over all this Thomas Stanley presided like some Lord of Misrule, grinning silently and picking his yellow teeth with a bone. He didn't join in the ruckus, nor did he try to stop it, but looked at her expectantly when his men bellowed for more food or wine, as they did regularly, so she feared her larders would be entirely empty before the meal was finished.

Lord Stanley addressed few comments to her, for which she

was grateful, since she might not have heard him. At one point he looked at the food she'd barely touched on her plate and said, 'The beggars at your gate must do well, my lady.'

'We prefer to feed the beggars,' she said pointedly, 'rather than the dogs.'

He merely grinned again before turning his back on her to watch the clowning of his sons.

You are the rudest man I've ever met, she thought. *How will I ever get rid of you?*

Two men were sick on the table and had to be carried out. One dog bit another and then a man. As the meal drew to a close there was so much burping, farting and scratching, they might have been in a menagerie. *Even the beasts in the Tower behave better than this*, Margaret thought.

Not one of them, certainly not Stanley himself, complimented her on the food that had been got together in such haste and at considerable cost. Her staff hadn't let her down. One dish after another came from the kitchens in response to the bellowing of these rough strangers, and each one was elaborately presented. A great, shining blancmange made from white fish, almonds and aniseed was followed by a series of small dishes that were shaped into the form of the Stanley arms. Yet no one thanked her for her hospitality.

By the end, men lay sprawled across the tables or slumped against the walls. One or two had staggered outside to relieve themselves in the gardens. Even the dogs had quietened, sniffing through the remains. Only Lord Stanley remained fully conscious. His son George lolled over the table with reddened, watery eyes. Reginald Bray had excused himself nearly an hour ago. Margaret hoped he was arranging for the mess to be cleared.

Thomas Stanley turned to her. 'Well, my lady,' he said, dabbing at his beard. 'Shall we dispense with the formalities?'

She could hardly bear to look at him, or at the carnage around them.

'I thought you'd already done that,' she managed to say, but Stanley only grinned; like an ape, she thought. He turned to his son and clapped him so hard on the back that he gave a terrific belch.

'Well, my boy,' Stanley said, 'what do you think of Lady Margaret?'

George's red eyes rolled in his skull before veering towards Margaret. 'She is rather short, Father,' he said, and Thomas Stanley gave a bark of laughter.

'That she is, son. But height on its own is no recommendation.'

Margaret rose abruptly, begging to be excused. She picked her way through the debris, the bodies on the floor, then hurried upstairs.

The pounding of her heart seemed to be affecting her vision as she paced around her room. The objects in it were jumping and flickering. She made herself stand still and closed her eyes, aware for a few moments only of the drumming of her blood.

An image of her third husband rose in her mind. *Henry*, she thought, with a terrific pang. If Henry were here – patient, long-suffering Henry – he would know how to make her calm again. But he wasn't here, and this thought alone made her want to weep.

But it wouldn't help. She made herself sit on the window seat, facing the room rather than the gardens, because she didn't want to see what Stanley's men were doing outside.

She'd seen enough of Stanley himself to know that she never wanted to see him again, let alone marry him. She just wanted him to leave.

Yet he was the only person she could think of who had any influence with the king. And it was rumoured that the king was planning to send his brother-in-law Anthony Woodville to Brittany, to negotiate the return of her son.

If the king chose her husband, he might pick someone equally obnoxious (though that was hard to imagine) and further removed from the court. Someone who would agree to give the king a large portion of her wealth in return. Whereas Stanley, she was sure, would know how to keep it all.

But the thought of it, of what she had to do, made her moan aloud.

Blessed Lady, help me, she murmured. *Mother of Christ, deliver me.*

And she listened as well as she could, but the only voice she heard was her own mother's.

Marriage is nothing but strategy and negotiation, it said. *Men do it on the battlefield, women in the bedroom. You make one deal after another until one of you is dead.*

Margaret didn't want to do any deals with Thomas Stanley in the bedroom. When no other answer came she pressed her fingertips into her eyes, then pushed the flesh of her forehead up and back.

Make a deal. Negotiate. That, after all, was what she knew how to do.

You had to be clear about what you wanted. And she *was* clear. She wanted to help her son. And to be left alone.

She remained in her seat for several more moments, eyes still closed, feet not quite touching the floor. Then she slid to the floor and went downstairs.

He was holding on to his son, who had just been sick, by the hair. She didn't approach but waited in the doorway until he glanced up, then said, 'When you're ready.'

Thomas Stanley let go of his son's head. It fell with a smack on to the table. Then he rose and followed her.

Before he could speak, she began: 'Your wife has died,' she said, 'as has my husband. An agreement of some sort might be advantageous to us both – that's why you're here. But I will not enter into it without certain conditions, and my conditions are these.

'Firstly, I will expect you to use whatever influence you have with the king to help my son, who is at present in exile. I would like him to return safely to his home and his inheritance. In return for that you will receive one fifth of that inheritance upon my death, or his, if he should die first.'

Thomas Stanley looked at her. It was a look full of insolence, she thought, and arrogance. He drew up a chair and sat in it, pressing the tips of his fingers together.

She said, 'That part is not negotiable.'

Thomas Stanley settled back in his seat, fixing her with his hooded stare. But at least he wasn't smiling.

'You will have a life interest in all my estates,' she said, 'from my father and from my husbands. The manors inherited from my mother's family I will keep in my name, but you will have a share in Kendal, Lincolnshire, Berkshire, Cornwall, the West Country and the Midlands. In return, you will provide me with a yearly income of five hundred marks from your properties in Cheshire and North Wales.'

He said nothing, but she thought she saw him reappraising her. *Good*, she thought.

'I will retain some estates in the West Country for my son, should he return from exile. You will act as guardian for these while he's away. He will also receive some lands from my mother, on her death. If he does not return' – she paused, her lips dry – 'these lands and their revenues will be divided between us.'

Finally, she stopped, not looking at him.

'Is that all?' he said, with a touch of sarcasm.

'No,' she said. 'The final matter is this.'

For a moment her nerve failed her, but she knew it would have to be said.

'I've had three husbands. If circumstances were different, I would not choose to marry again, or to enter into any further arrangement. But I will do so on condition that we keep separate households, lead separate lives and . . . interfere with one another as little as possible.'

She had clasped her hands together to stop them trembling.

Thomas Stanley gave a short, incredulous bark of laughter. 'Will you so?' he said, and she looked at him steadily.

He lowered his eyes for a moment, rubbed the side of his nose, then pulled it. Then he looked at her again. His eyes were grey, she saw, and cold as stone.

'Well, madame,' he said. 'You may be sure that I will not *interfere* with you, as you put it. I have other interests, as I'm sure you are aware. Besides' – he flicked a spot of food from his sleeve – 'you are not to my taste.'

She smiled warmly at this rudeness. 'Then we understand one another,' she said. She had not expected it to be so easy, but she remembered to say, 'I will instruct my lawyers to draw up the contract.'

Thomas Stanley stood up. His face was a little flushed. *From drink*, she thought, yet he walked towards her steadily enough.

She stood up also and did not flinch as he drew close. Though not overly tall, he towered over her. But she stood her ground.

'You may instruct your lawyers as you like,' he said, 'and I will instruct mine. But I will tell you now that I will not have it discussed by them, or put in writing, that my wife will not sleep with me.'

Wife, she thought, momentarily distracted by the word. But there was no point arguing with him. When it came to a woman refusing to sleep with her husband, no agreement would stand up in court. So she hesitated only for a moment before saying, 'Well, then, I must depend on your word.'

There was no man in the country who did not know he could not depend on Thomas Stanley's word. This was a man who had betrayed kings. Perhaps something in her face conveyed that she knew this, because there was a flicker of amusement in his eyes.

'That you may have,' he said.

'Then it only remains for our lawyers to communicate,' she said, extending her hand. Adding, as he took it, 'Your men may need some time to recover. Before you leave.'

'The air outside is fresh,' he said. 'They'll wake up on the ride. Perhaps your men will get them together. I'll wait in the fore-court. Unless that is too much interference for you.'

She would not be wrong-footed. 'I'll instruct my steward,' she said, turning away from him.

When he'd gone, she sank down on a seat. There was a trem-bling sensation in her legs. She felt as though she had passed through something irrevocable and irremediable, like an earth-quake, or a flood.

It seemed she was engaged to be married.

3

Lady Alice Receives a Guest

She'd had the original tapestry – Judith holding the head of Holofernes – taken down, and replaced by one of the Virgin. Then she'd decided that was tactless, perhaps; the image of a mother holding her child and wearing a serene expression as though it were the supreme joy that the world had to offer.

So now there was an older tapestry, of inferior quality, depicting Ruth and Naomi: *whither thou goest I will go*. Lady Alice didn't think there was anything too controversial in the story of Ruth and Naomi. Although she had not gone with the queen, of course. And now the former queen was coming to her, though not of her own volition.

Apart from the tapestry and a crucifix, the room was bare. Lady Alice believed in the value of simplicity when it came to nursing the broken spirit. Plain pale walls, simple furnishings, a view over the garden because it was good to see growing things, to be reminded that the cycle of life goes on.

Also, the former queen should not get the idea she was no longer in custody.

Lady Alice lingered in the room, mentally running through the things she should provide: books, paper, ink, one of her own ladies to attend her. The list of things she could say to a deposed queen who had lost everything was more difficult to compile. They could talk about the weather, of course; the garden, possibly her health.

She found she was nervous at the prospect of meeting her again. How did one even address a former queen?

She hadn't asked for this commission. Her son, who was the king's brother-in-law, had presented it to her.

'You'll be paid, of course,' he'd said. 'And I don't suppose you'll have to see her at all if you don't want to. You just need to monitor her correspondence. Any messages she receives from her own country must go directly to the king.'

Queen Margaret, as Lady Alice persisted in thinking of her, would have said this was her country, of course.

So she was to keep her out of the way and spy on her. 'Anything else?' she had enquired. Her son had stared at her. 'His majesty has entrusted you with this,' he'd said, 'as a reward for our faithful service.'

Don't jeopardise my relationship with the king, he hadn't said. So like his father. Lady Alice wondered whether she'd not had enough of the diplomatic manoeuvrings of men to last her a lifetime. And if there was one thing she'd learned about kings, it was that one should try to avoid being rewarded by them.

Still, it wasn't as though it was possible to refuse.

'How much money should I spend on this – honour?' she'd asked. She couldn't help it – she hadn't liked his tone. After a stern pause she'd been told that the sum of eight marks a week had been allocated.

'So much?' she'd said, and he'd frowned. But did he expect her to put the former queen up in the stables?

'You will write to the king at the end of each year for your remuneration,' he'd said.

'Fine,' she'd replied.

Hostility seeped from him, almost like a smell, no matter what she said or did. Some unspoken blame, for the death of his father perhaps, though she could hardly be held responsible for that. Or possibly for all the wars that had happened since. Someone had to take the blame – why not her?

Lady Alice was inclined to blame her daughter-in-law Elizabeth for the distance between her and her son. The king's sister did not seem to like her, despite Alice's efforts. The feeling was mutual, though Lady Alice had negotiated the match herself. And it seemed to be successful, or fecund at least. Five children in ten years, and another one expected in spring.

She had ensured that her son was married to the winning side, but he didn't appear to be grateful. Once the purpose of his visit had been established, he'd been anxious to leave.

Stay, she could have said to him. *Stay a little while and talk to me.* But he'd left.

And so here she was, considering what might be done for the former queen for eight marks a week.

This was the third reason for the simplicity of the room. Still, it must be an improvement on the Tower, where the queen had been imprisoned since Tewkesbury.

Lady Alice pressed her hands to her back, which was aching. A problem attendant, her physician had told her, on having such a long and elegant spine. Meaning she was unreasonably tall for a woman; such an unnatural anatomy was bound to cause problems. And so it had. She'd had difficulty both in conceiving and giving birth. She was arched like a bow after years of bending over her books. Her scholarly proclivities might also have affected her fertility, according to her physician; draining the necessary humours away from her womb.

She could have chosen another physician, of course, but over the years she'd seen a great number of them and had not been impressed by any. She preferred to make her own diagnoses, reading the great medical treatises of Galen or Hippocrates in the original Greek.

She'd put three books on the small table in the queen's room: the Bible, Christine de Pizan's *City of Ladies* and a specially commissioned edition of her grandfather's book, *The Canterbury Tales*. Whether the queen would read them or not she didn't know.

She was putting off the moment when she would have to greet her guest. She remained in the room, feeling a slow infusion of melancholy at the thought of everything that had brought them to this point. She'd lost three husbands, either in or because of war; the former queen had lost her husband, her son and her nation.

Well, she thought, with the twist of irony that never entirely deserted her; they should have plenty to talk about, after all.

Margaret of Anjou arrived by boat along the river. She seemed to have some difficulty getting out of the boat, and at first no one helped her. Then one of the guards extended his hand. She walked unevenly, leaning on him, towards the castle gates.

If Lady Alice was shocked at the sight of her, she didn't show it. Some change was to be expected of course. She stepped forward with a practised smile, not curtsying, since it was no longer necessary and besides, her knees wouldn't take it.

'Welcome to Wallingford Castle, my lady. I hope you'll be comfortable here.'

The former queen stared at her in confusion. For a moment, Lady Alice thought she hadn't recognised her, then the look sharpened to hostility. She said, 'So you are my gaoler now.'

'I hope you'll come to think of this as your home,' Lady Alice replied. But she said it briskly, with no display of sentiment, and was rewarded with a look of contempt. Then the former queen walked past Lady Alice unaided, so that Alice was forced to observe her from behind.

Whatever was affecting her walk, her back was as straight as it had been nearly thirty years ago when they had first met. All those years ago, Lady Alice had thought, upon first seeing the fourteen-year-old girl who would be England's queen, *she will not bend, that one, she can only break*. Astonishingly, she was not broken yet, and she had certainly not bent, though there was little enough to keep her upright.

Lady Alice spoke to the guards, dismissing them, then went to her ward, who stood motionless before the door. Adopting the impersonal mode she reserved for any patient, she said, 'Your room is prepared. Shall we go in?' And without waiting for a response, led the way.

She had to wait for her guest to catch up because she was walking so slowly. Lady Alice found herself considering the symptoms – rheumatism? Gout? She didn't think Margaret of Anjou would have suffered any physical abuse in prison. Though it was hard to say, of course. And certainly, she would not enquire.

She talked instead about the castle itself, and the ways in which she was altering it to make it less like a fortress.

Lady Alice's room was also on the first floor, so they could be sociable, she'd thought, in a moment of optimism, and because Alice had painful knees. So fortunately, there was only one flight of stairs, which they both negotiated with some difficulty before arriving on the tiled landing.

'Here we are,' she said.

A woman opened the door to the queen's room. 'This is Joan Worsley,' Lady Alice said as the woman dropped into a curtsy. 'If you have any particular needs, she'll let me know.'

Margaret of Anjou made no response and Alice was suddenly aware of how the room looked to her eyes: sparse and neat, like a hospital room. But there was a fire and a tray of food by the bed.

'The window is new,' Lady Alice said. 'I had it put in last year.'

Margaret of Anjou limped across the room to the window, which in spring and summer showed the gardens off to their best advantage. At this time of year, however, they were bald and bare.

No tree grew close enough to the window to facilitate either escape or attack; the queen wouldn't kill herself if she leapt through the glass. It was an altogether satisfactory window. Margaret of Anjou, however, made no comment about it but remained staring out, beyond the garden to the river and the land she'd once ruled.

'I trust the bed will be comfortable,' Lady Alice said. 'And the view will improve with the season. Would you care to eat something?' she added, indicating the tray.

No response.

'Or to read? We could play a game of cards if you prefer.'

Silence.

It was an attempt to embarrass her, perhaps, in front of her servant, or to redress the imbalance of power. But Lady Alice was not going to be wrong-footed so easily.

'Very well, then,' she said. 'If there's nothing you need –'

'You may go.'

It was said in such a low tone that for a moment Lady Alice thought she must have misheard. But she had not; the former queen had dismissed her. She could feel all the muscles along her spine contract, straightening its curve. *Who do you think you are?* she might have said, or *Where do you think you are?* Instead, she looked at Joan Worsley, who stood with lowered eyes, a linen cloth over one arm.

'Joan,' she said. 'Come with me.'

She left the room, Joan following and closing the door silently behind her. Once outside, Lady Alice issued several instructions to her servant. The former queen's room was not to be locked unless it proved necessary, but Margaret was to be attended at all times either by Joan or by the little maid in her charge, and each day they would report to her. She was to be allowed no visitors except for a priest, if she requested one, to hear her confession. Which would also be reported to Lady Alice. The king had been thorough in his extermination of rebels, but the Earl of Oxford, for instance, was still hiding somewhere, and the earls of Richmond and Pembroke were in Brittany. His majesty would certainly want to know if any messages arrived from other countries.

Then, though she'd already said all this, she issued further instructions about reporting on the former queen's diet, and on the passing of water and stools, because it restored her sense of authority.

You may go, she'd said, and Lady Alice had simply allowed herself to be dismissed. Her heart was beating quite erratically; her face felt as though it was flushed. As soon as Joan had gone she attempted to see herself in the window-glass, to straighten her hair.

She would not allow such rudeness in future; she wouldn't be denigrated in front of her own servants. If her visitor – or prisoner – did not respond to kindness, then other tactics could be tried. Though she would have to think of them when she was less unsettled.

At least, she thought with a little twist of her mouth, the question of who Margaret of Anjou thought she was had been answered. Obviously, she thought she was still queen.

For a few days after that first encounter Lady Alice didn't approach her guest. She turned her attention to her accounts, to raising the rents on her properties, as she did assiduously each year, and sending notices of eviction to those tenants who claimed they couldn't pay. The weather changed from a dull rain to a hoar frost that froze all the land to stillness. Those birds that hadn't already flown south disappeared into bracken or were occasionally found stiffened beneath a tree. Cattle and sheep stood motionless in the fields. From time to time, men were sent out to break the ice forming around their nostrils.

Inside the castle, ice formed on the inner walls and much effort was expended on keeping the fires going, though the heat from them didn't travel far. Lady Alice spent most of the time in the room she had come to think of as her *withdrawing* room, or study, sitting as close to the fire as possible without hazard and trying to keep her cramped fingers warm. She was making her own translation of the odes of Horace:

Ask not – we cannot know – what end the gods have set for you and me.

It was hard to concentrate with the heat from the fire reaching only one leg, its flames drawing her attention. She was sixty-eight years old and had already outlived most of the people she knew. She hadn't known she would have to cope with all the discomforts of old age. Something inside her still didn't know she was old, was surprised when she had to stop writing because her fingers were swollen and there were shooting pains in her wrist. Or when she fell asleep at unexpected moments, gazing into the fire.

When she woke, the light had faded and her heart was racing inexplicably. She could hear a series of small sounds coming from the hearth. At first she could make out only that the embers of the fire were smouldering, but then she saw a figure bending over it.

'What is it?' she asked sharply, though she had meant to ask *Who is it?* but as the figure straightened she saw it was Joan.

'Beg pardon, my lady,' she said. 'I didn't want you to catch cold.'

She'd been trying to re-ignite the fire, and now she started to light the candles.

Lady Alice did feel cold, and stiff. Her feet were numb. And her spectacles had slipped from her face. She patted her dress and was relieved to find them in a fold of her skirts.

Gradually, the room came into focus. 'What time is it?' she asked.

'Past four, my lady. Shall I bring you a tray of food?'

But Lady Alice had a mild feeling of nausea, a sensation of burning in her gullet. She adjusted her spectacles and wondered whether there was enough light left to continue her annotations. If Joan hadn't been there, she would have liked to rub some feeling back into her feet. 'A little hot wine, perhaps,' she said.

'Yes, my lady,' Joan replied, but didn't move.

'I'm worried about her ladyship,' she said, referring to the former queen.

'Is she ill?'

28

'She's hardly eaten anything since she came.'

Fasting, perhaps, Lady Alice thought, but as if she'd heard her, Joan said, 'I know it's Lent, but she should be eating something.'

'Perhaps her stomach is delicate,' Lady Alice said, aware of the discomfort in her own. 'Have you tried soup?'

'We've tried everything – soups, jellies, cake. Nothing tempts her.'

'I see,' said Lady Alice, after a pause. She closed her eyes. So the queen thought she would starve herself to death. In Lady Alice's care.

Why hadn't she seen this coming? Why would she not try to starve herself? Why, in fact, had she not done so before? Had she been forced to eat in the Tower?

There were those who would say, perhaps, that Lady Alice should allow her to die. Her son, for instance. And certainly, the king wouldn't object. There were few people in the country who wouldn't welcome the news that the former queen had died. It would be said of her, as it had been said of her husband, King Henry, that she had died *of pure displeasure and melancholy*.

'I've tried telling her she needs to keep up her strength,' Joan said. She did not say that Lady Alice had been negligent, had put off visiting her guest, or eating with her. 'You could go to see her, my lady,' she said.

'I'm not sure what good that will do.'

'She might listen to you, my lady – she won't listen to me.'

Lady Alice rubbed her forehead, then took off her spectacles and rubbed her eyes. 'She's not noted for listening to anyone,' she said.

The next morning she went to the queen's room.

'I thought we could keep one another company for a little while,' she said. She didn't expect a reply and she got none. But at least her guest wasn't lying in bed. She was sitting in a chair, looking out of the window.

Lady Alice indicated to Joan that she should pull up another chair so she could sit facing the queen. Then she told her to bring some soup and a little strained fruit.

'I'm not hungry,' the queen said, without looking at her.

'Well, I'll eat,' said Alice, 'and you can keep me company.'

She adjusted herself in the chair before looking at the queen.

A white light fell on her face. It wasn't flattering. Her skin had a crinkled texture like old paper, and already the bones seemed more prominent than before. Since she was squinting, Alice couldn't see her eyes clearly but she could see the shadows beneath them.

'It's a good view, is it not?'

Silence.

'It will improve, of course, with the season.'

Silence.

'You may as well speak to me, my lady. I'm not going to leave.'

'Why?' said the queen, without turning her head. 'Are you so desperate for company?'

'We were good company once,' said Lady Alice.

The queen looked at her for the first time, her eyes smudged by shadow. 'That was a long time ago,' she said.

Lady Alice chose not to answer this. Instead she said, 'You look tired. Are you not sleeping?'

'I sleep,' said the queen indifferently, turning away again.

'Do you have a headache?'

'Is this a medical examination?'

'Do you require a medical examination?'

The queen only sighed, as though Lady Alice's presence was an intolerable burden. Alice felt a prickle of irritation. She was the one being inconvenienced. But the queen had never cared about the trouble she caused to other people.

'I see you don't want company,' she said. 'And yet it's difficult to see what you do to pass the time. It must be tedious for you.'

The queen shot her a look that was heavy with irony before returning her gaze to the window.

'I should think your thoughts are not pleasant,' continued Alice. 'The past – being what it is, and the future – well – who knows what the future might bring.'

Ask not – we cannot know – what end the gods have set for you and me.

The queen's look turned hostile. 'Are you trying to torment me?'

'No, my lady. Not at all.'

Alice understood – of course she did – what it was like to live with a foreshortened perspective. At her age she had considerably more past to contemplate than future, although much of it did not bear contemplation. In any case, she was impatient of those people who preferred to live in the past. So she confined herself to thinking about the present and immediate future. It was a little restricted, perhaps. But that was where books came in, she thought. And then she thought she was losing the thread of her argument.

'I merely meant that it's not good for anyone to spend so much time with their own thoughts.'

Once again the queen turned her head to look at her, slowly and wearily. Alice could almost hear the bones in her neck creaking.

'At least they are mine,' she said. 'They're all I have left.'

There were many things that Alice could have said to this. *Do you think you're the only one who's suffered?* for instance. The whole country was still reeling from the impact of the wars.

But the queen had never been inclined to consider any perspective other than her own.

Alice was saved from marshalling further arguments by the arrival of the soup.

'It's chicken soup, my lady,' Joan said. 'But there's no meat in it, because of Lent. So it will be easy to digest.'

'Thank you, Joan,' Alice said, as her servant set out the bowls and a basket of bread. A look passed between them and Joan left the room.

31

'Now,' Alice said, 'perhaps you'll eat a little, to keep me company.'

'I will not,' said the queen.

Lady Alice had some experience of dealing with the broken in spirit; with those paupers in her hospital who turned their faces to the wall. But the more time she spent with the queen, the more it seemed her spirit was alive and well. Something was feeding it, though she didn't know what.

Alice took a spoonful of soup. 'It's good,' she said. She dipped a crust into it. 'And the bread is excellent,' she added.

The queen gave an exasperated sigh.

'I don't intend to leave,' Lady Alice said, 'until you have tried a little.'

'Do you think you can force me to eat?'

Lady Alice had once seen a man force a rag dipped in broth in a patient's throat despite the gagging and reflux action. She wouldn't want to do that to the queen. She put her spoon down.

'Some people might consider it a kindness of the king to send you here. Instead of returning you to the Tower.'

The queen looked at her with a mixture of incredulity and scorn. 'It's not *kindness*,' she said, 'to hand me over to the custody of one who used to be my friend.'

Again, there were many things that Alice could have said. *Did you not dissolve the marriage of my son to Margaret Beaufort? If my son is now brother-in-law to the king, whose fault is that?* But all she said was 'Think what you like. I don't plan to see you starve.'

For the first time the queen smiled at her. 'No,' she said. 'I can imagine that would be inconvenient for you.'

Finally, Alice saw what was feeding the queen's will. *Ah*, she thought, sitting back.

'So I can't persuade you to eat,' she said.

'Don't keep up this pretence – this charade of hospitality. We both know why I'm here.'

'I would rather we did not quarrel. I would rather we broke

32

our bread in peace. But I'm not going to force you. If you want to give up so easily, there is little I can do.'

Again the queen turned on her that bitter smile. 'Now you're going to tell me I have many reasons to live.'

'I am not,' said Alice. 'I should say, rather, that life does not owe us any *reasons to live*, as you put it. And yet we go on living,' she added, as though to herself. 'I am, however, a little surprised that you would make things quite so easy for your enemies. Do you think, when you've starved yourself to death, the king will throw up his hands in horror and regret? The king and all his court will be relieved that he no longer has to consider what to do with you. He might have to come up with some explanation for the French king – or he might use it as an excuse to start the war he has been hoping for. As for the people, if they hear of it at all, they will hear that you passed away quietly, of natural causes, and they will not care. No one will be surprised. It's what they expect. It is probably what they hope.'

A series of expressions flitted across the queen's face: anger and outrage, then a stricken look. When she spoke finally it was as though the muscles of her throat were not quite working. 'Why –' she said, then tried again; 'why do you care?'

It was a good question, and one Alice hadn't fully fathomed. It came as some surprise to her to realise that she did, in fact, care. Was it because of her interest in the mechanisms of healing? Or the professional capacity of the role – at least her interpretation of it – which did not include simply watching her patient die?

Maybe, in the end, she didn't care to be manipulated, either by the king or her son. She looked at the queen with her faded blue eyes. 'I don't know,' she said.

The queen seemed to accept this. She sat back and looked out of the window once more. Alice looked at the soup, which, now that it had cooled, had developed a viscous appearance.

'Shall I have it taken away?' she said, with a certain resignation.

The queen's voice came as though from a distance. 'You may leave it with me,' she said.

After this, Alice was pleased to note that small amounts of food were being eaten each day. Evidently, the queen had decided to stay alive, if only to be a thorn in King Edward's side.

Although she never actually finished anything. Sometimes the trays of food were returned substantially untouched. And she wouldn't eat at all if anyone was watching her. But Joan swore she wasn't simply pretending to eat.

'I've checked, my lady – there isn't anywhere she could be hiding it. And she can't open the window.'

More importantly, small stools began to appear irregularly in the queen's pot. They were yellowish and inclined to float. Alice deduced from this she was eating just enough to stay alive.

Yet she still showed no sign of wanting to leave her room.

'She doesn't do anything to perk up her appetite, that's the trouble,' Joan said.

A change of air would do her good, Alice thought, but the weather was still too cold for the queen to venture outside in her weakened state.

The next time she visited the queen's room Lady Alice suggested they might sit in her study.

The queen treated her to a stare. She continued to act as though Alice's presence was an unnecessary inconvenience; as if she shouldn't be there at all.

'I thought you might like a change of scene. And I want to show you something I've been working on.'

'It's not necessary,' the queen said, turning away.

'I've been translating some of the odes of Horace,' Alice said. 'I thought I could read them to you and you can tell me what you think.'

'Why?' said the queen. It was unclear whether she was questioning the act of translation or the necessity of offering her opinion.

'No reason,' said Alice. 'It keeps my mind occupied,' she added, glancing at the books she had left in the queen's room, which didn't seem to have been touched. 'And it would pass the time.'

For a moment she thought the queen would ask *why?* again, but after a pause she said, 'I have a headache.'

'Tomorrow, then,' Alice said briskly. 'After you've eaten.'

She left before the queen could object.

The following afternoon, Alice arranged for the fire to be lit in her study and two seats placed either side of it. A tray of warm wine and cakes was set on the table. She spent some time rejecting the odes that referred to warfare, shipwrecks or mortality. And the one she had most recently translated wouldn't do at all:

Power the God does have. He can interchange the lowest and the highest, the mighty he abases and exalts the lowly. From one man Fortune with shrill whirring of her wings swiftly snatches away the crown, on another she delights to place it.

She tucked that one away. Then she selected a pair of spectacles. She had several pairs, of varying degrees of efficiency. Eventually, she chose ones that clipped on to the bridge of her nose by means of a small spring, though if she wore these too long they aggravated her sinuses.

She was as prepared as she could be. There was no reason to feel nervous. It was a gesture – that was all. She would reach out to the queen through the medium of fine literature which stated common and universal truths.

She could hear the queen being led along the corridor by Joan.

'That's it, my lady, take your time.'

Such slow, shuffling steps. When the door opened, the queen didn't look at Alice but crossed the room slowly, like an effigy of old age.

She wasn't old; barely in her forties. 'Is your back troubling you?' Alice asked, but the queen, of course, didn't reply. Alice made a mental note to ensure she got more exercise from now on.

Joan took some time to arrange the queen in her seat, tucking a coverlet around her, adjusting the cushion. Alice shuffled her poems. When finally she glanced at the queen she saw that her attention had drifted to the portrait that hung over the fire.

It was a portrait of Alice's third husband, William de la Pole, Duke of Suffolk. It had hung in this room for so long she'd forgotten to notice it. It had been painted some time after their marriage but showed him as he had been when he was younger, in France. He wore armour and was leaning on his sword.

It was not even very like him, but when she saw the expression on the queen's face Lady Alice realised she should have taken it down.

But could she be expected to remove everything that might provoke the queen's memory?

'Shall I begin?' Alice said, and at the same time the queen said, 'How many of them are gone, now.'

'Yes, my lady.'

'But I am still here.'

Alice didn't know how to steer them back to the subject of Horace.

'If you like,' she said, 'I could take the portrait down.'

'Why?' said the queen. 'He was my friend.'

And my husband, Lady Alice thought. But some people always believed they suffered more than others.

Of course, there had been rumours about the queen and the duke. But it was hardly the time to bring that up.

'Shall I read, my lady? While it's still light?'

The queen twisted the coverlet in her hands but did not speak. Lady Alice adjusted her spectacles.

'*Remember to settle with tranquil heart the problem of the hour. All else is borne along like some river, now gliding peacefully into the Tuscan sea, now rolling polished stones, uprooted trees and flocks –*'

'Do you miss him?' the queen asked.

There was a question. Lady Alice didn't know if she did miss him, not any more.

'Do *you* miss him?' she asked, and was surprised to detect a note of jealousy in her voice, even after all these years. Before the queen could respond she added quickly, 'It was all so long ago.'

'Yes,' said the queen, 'and yet more vivid than anything that's happening now.'

Horace had said something similar, in fact. But it seemed the queen was not engaged by Horace.

'Memory fades in time,' said Alice.

'Not mine,' said the queen. 'I remember them all – all their faces – how bright with hope they were – how proudly they rode into battle. And where are they now?' she ended bitterly.

Where are they who lived before us, who led hounds and carried hawks and owned field and wood? The great ladies in their chambers who wore gold in their headbands and whose faces shone?

That wasn't Horace. Alice couldn't remember who it was.

'You didn't think of marrying again?'

'No, my lady.'

Three husbands were certainly enough. After the death of the duke her main concern had been to secure what was left of his property for her son – not to hand it to some other man.

The queen was still looking at the portrait.

'I think – if I could have my life again – I wouldn't marry at all.'

There was nothing to be said to this. What could Alice say: *but then you would not have had your son?*

The experiment had taken an unfortunate turn and she wasn't sure what to do about it. Because it had been her husband, of course, who had brokered the queen's marriage. And that, arguably, had been responsible for all that followed; all the wars. The queen herself could hardly be held responsible – she'd been fourteen years old. Not too young in terms of royal marriages, yet too young, and ill prepared for everything that had happened since.

They were terrible – how terrible – these reversals of fortune, that turned on a single incident here, a chance there. Who could fathom the outcome of a simple action, or bear the weight of the consequences?

Alice turned back, with some determination, to the pages she'd assembled, but even before she could focus her eyes clearly the queen said, 'Will you be buried with him?'

Alice sighed. But it was a fair question, since she'd had three husbands. 'I don't know, yet,' she said. 'I haven't decided.'

And probably she should decide, she thought, given her age. But the queen didn't say this. She continued to look at the portrait.

'I don't think I will marry again,' she said.

No one will ask you, Alice thought, not uncharitably; it was the simple truth. Who would marry an imprisoned queen who had lost everything? And the question of where she would be buried, with her husband or her son, wouldn't arise either, since it was up to the king. Probably he would send her to France.

'Though, my husband –' she said haltingly, 'he . . . was a good man.'

It was impossible not to be afflicted by the mood of mourning. Lady Alice could feel it trembling in herself.

Yes, King Henry had been a good man. And that goodness had brought the nation to ruin. Yes, he'd had to die, and die horribly, since he'd failed to die of natural causes. Countless other men had died also, of course.

Sometimes Alice thought privately that it was easier to believe in the old gods, Horace's gods, who were wilful, amoral and capricious, if not actively malevolent, than in the Christian God who was perfectly and consistently benign.

'I think,' she said, and her voice was not quite steady, 'I should read now.'

And when the queen said nothing to this, she adjusted her spectacles once more and began.

'*Whatever the day's fortune gives, don't spurn sweet love, my child, and do not be neglectful of the choir of love and the dancing feet.*'

This verse, too, seemed inappropriate, but the queen was listening, at least. Perhaps she was remembering how she'd loved to dance.

Neither of them would be dancing now, Alice thought. So that was something else they had in common. Neither of them would marry and neither of them would dance.

No one told you marriage was such a perilous game. It was like stepping on a ship in a storm, not knowing where it would take you or whether or not you would survive.

But they'd put all that behind them, Lady Alice and the queen; the flames of desire would not burn again for them. And that was a good thing; although sometimes she thought that only in the fire of attraction, of that ugly word *lust*, was there enough power to combat those other forces that drew you down. The glowing spark of it rejuvenated like the spark of life itself; its absence turned everything to ashes.

She was too old for such thoughts, yet they haunted her like the ghosts of her old loves.

She didn't mention any of this to the queen, who was apparently content now, and quiet. So Alice read on as the rose-grey evening light that had entered the room gradually deepened into shade.

The next time she read in the queen's room, where neither of them could see the portrait. The passage she'd selected was from *The Book of the City of Ladies*.

'*Not all men, and especially the wisest, share the opinion that it is bad for women to be educated. But it is true that many foolish men have claimed this because it displeased them that women knew more than they did.*'

The queen didn't object to this, or interrupt, so Alice read on, about the necessity of having women in government. At this the queen said, 'Certainly if there were more women in government there would be no war.'

Just in time, Alice remembered not to laugh. Who had been more warlike than the queen?

'Certain women,' she said cautiously, 'have been very involved in war. Eleanor of Aquitaine, for instance. Jeanne d'Arc.'

The queen stared at her. 'That's because men took from them what was rightfully theirs,' she said. 'Or their sons',' she added.

'But women have led armies,' Alice said, 'and provoked war.'

The queen was dismissive of this. No woman, she said, would go recklessly to war, knowing the great cost to everyone. And especially to those they loved. Warfare, she went on, warming to her theme, was a product of man's endless struggle for precedence and self-aggrandisement; his greed. Women, if left to themselves, would not disturb the peace.

Lady Alice suppressed all the things she could have said to this, taking it as a good sign that the queen had engaged in a discussion. Over the next few days she continued to read from Christine de Pisan's book, while instructing Joan to ensure that the queen took some exercise every day.

For a while this plan seemed to be working. The queen's walking improved; she had twice been along the corridor and even up the stairs to the turret, where she could see out. She was eating more and was definitely stronger. When the weather changed, becoming mild and sunny, Alice suggested they should walk together in the gardens.

'I can see the gardens,' the queen said.

'Not all of them,' said Alice. 'And the weather is so good – I thought we would both benefit from a change of air.'

She stood up, holding one of her own cloaks out to the queen. 'It will do us good,' she said.

The queen looked at the cloak and Alice braced herself for an argument. But slowly, clumsily, the queen began to manoeuvre herself out of her chair.

She was surely exaggerating the difficulty, Alice thought. Joan had reported that her movements were much improved. But she straightened and allowed Joan to drape the cloak over her shoulders.

They descended the stairs carefully, the queen leaning on Alice and making an occasional small gasping noise. Alice had not questioned her yet about her aches and pains or suggested she should see her physician. She felt sure the queen wouldn't want to discuss any physical weakness, and anyway she wanted to see the effect of taking the air upon her condition.

There was not a living thing, she believed, that did not benefit from being outdoors once the weather improved. And it had improved. A little spring had occurred in late winter, like a herald. Pale sunlight summoned shoots from the soaked earth, buds from the wet branches. There was a pungent quality in the air; sharp with new life. Alice could feel her bones responding as they always did to this incipient spring; the furred spokes of the willow, the trembling heads of snowdrops nodding like so many nuns.

Surely the queen would feel it too?

In fact, the queen's breathing was not quite regular and she clung to Alice's arm as if she was frightened.

Of course, this was the first time she'd been outside, apart from her journey to the castle. It wasn't so surprising she was finding it difficult to walk. But Alice wanted to take her at least as far as the little bridge, for the view over the river.

A gentle, tender haze had settled over the water. White birds flashed and dipped. The reflection of trees formed a shadowy mass with wedges of pale water between.

This was one of Alice's favourite viewing places. Soon, when the spring came fully, ducks and swans and other birds would populate the waters, followed by their young.

See, she wanted to say to the queen, *there is still so much beauty in the world.*

But it seemed as though the queen couldn't get her breath, even after such a short walk.

'I would like . . . to go back now,' she said.

And without waiting for Alice, she began to hurry back the way they'd just come.

'Are you not well?' Alice called. She felt obscurely annoyed. The queen was moving faster now, unaided, and Alice had to put in some effort to catch up with her.

'I only thought,' she said, finally reaching the queen, 'that while it is so spring-like –'

But the queen turned to her, her face a perfect mask of fear and revulsion.

'You think I want to see the spring?' she said, and Alice had a sudden apprehension of what spring would mean to the queen.

'I'm – sorry – if I've grieved you,' she said, forced to hurry after her again.

The queen stopped. 'What do you know of my grief?' she said.

'Well –' began Alice, but the queen interrupted her.

'How can you know?' she said. 'No one can.' And she began walking rapidly away again. When Alice caught up with her she said, breathlessly, as if the words hurt, 'Each time I wake up I think, *today will be better; it will not hurt so much*. But it isn't better, and it does hurt – if anything, it gets worse.'

Her head was nodding or shaking, Alice could not tell which. Then she clasped her hands to her heart. 'It hurts here. I don't know how I can live with such pain.'

Without waiting for an answer, she set off again, towards the castle doors.

Lady Alice followed in a silence that was tinged with both remorse and resentment. It had not been her purpose to remind the queen of her grief. She'd wanted, rather, to take her out of herself, to make her forget for one moment her suffering and regrets and see that, however substantial they were, they were insignificant when set against the larger context of nature. For what did the birds know of the queen's grief? Or the river, or the trees?

So she felt a little aggrieved as the queen ascended the stairs to her room unaided, then paused before the door.

'I'm tired,' she said. 'I think that tomorrow I will rest. I would like not to be disturbed.'

Lady Alice was left speechless outside the door.

It was her own fault, she thought, returning to her own room, for making such assiduous efforts for the queen, who was by nature ungrateful.

Of course she had suffered. She'd lost her only son, while Alice still had hers. Perhaps there was no point in making any effort while that fact stood between them.

Thinking of her son reminded her that she was expected to report to him and to the king. She took out some paper from her desk and considered what she should write. That the queen was an intolerable burden to her, perhaps, and they should find another host. That eight marks a week was certainly not enough.

Finally she wrote: *she is improving daily, and I am well.*

Unexpectedly, she received a reply from her son within a week. It commended her on her diligence, issued further instructions and warnings, then said, towards the end, that her grandchild had been born. A little girl, called Dorothy.

There had been some difficulty with the birth. The baby had come early and did not appear to want to feed. But he was sure this was a temporary problem and would be quickly resolved.

Lady Alice sat holding the letter. Her granddaughter had been born three weeks ago, yet the letter contained no invitation to visit.

She didn't screw the letter up. She folded it neatly and put it to one side, to give herself time to think.

Two days later she decided that she would visit, anyway, with or without an invitation.

She didn't tell the queen she was going. Communication between them had been minimal since their excursion, but Joan said there was no deterioration in her condition. So on the following day Alice set off, without notifying her son either.

A little more than a week later she returned.

She sent a message to the queen the next morning, but the queen kept her door shut, saying she wasn't well.

Joan had said the queen was perfectly well. But Alice wasn't inclined to argue. She felt unusually weary after her trip. Perhaps it was the weather, which was inclement once more. Great draughts blew through the corridors, rain and hail battered the walls.

'How is your little granddaughter?' Joan asked, setting down a tray. Lady Alice paused before saying that she was somewhat small and not feeding properly yet, but she was sure she would improve once the weather turned. Joan said that was doubtlessly true, she'd seen it herself, many times.

'And my lord the duke?' she asked.

In fact, her son hadn't been there. Even though he couldn't have known she was coming, he'd left the day before to be with the king.

'If we'd known you would be visiting –' her daughter-in-law had said.

But you didn't invite me, Alice didn't say.

'He was with the king,' she said to Joan, who, apparently satisfied by this, left her in her study.

She'd held her little granddaughter, of course, held her and felt a shadow cross her heart. She was so small and still; she didn't respond even when there was a noise behind her. And she took forever to feed; the nurse's nipple kept slipping from her mouth.

But what struck Alice more was the way her daughter-in-law's attention was given not to the baby but to her older, thriving children. Four fine sons and a little girl who could already read and write in French.

At first Alice stayed mainly with the baby and the wet nurse, prescribing syrups and ointments full of herbs, rubbing them into the baby's feet.

When she'd asked where the name came from, her daughter-in-law had merely said that they'd both liked it. At least they hadn't called her Cecily, after the other grandmother.

'Has your mother seen her yet?' she'd asked casually, and her daughter-in-law had said she had. Cecily Neville had stayed for a week after the little girl was born.

Alice said nothing to this, allowing it to burn within her like a live coal.

She, too, began to devote more of her time to the other children, especially Elizabeth, who was six years old, sweet and eager to learn. She had put it to her daughter-in-law more than once that little Elizabeth could come and stay with her. Who better than Alice Chaucer to, oversee her education? But this offer had not been taken up.

She watched the older boys learning to ride and manage a falcon, played boules with the younger ones and tried not to wonder when her son would return.

Then at the end of the week she'd taken a wrong turn somehow along one of the many corridors of the castle and found herself near the servants' quarters. She could hear men speaking through a partially opened door and resolved to ask them to direct her. As she drew closer, however, she could hear what they were saying.

'It's a wonder his lordship's staying away so long with the little one so poorly.'

'He'll be back when his mother's gone,' the other one said with a short laugh.

Alice stepped away from the door. She should have gone in to reprimand them, perhaps, but she couldn't speak. She hurried away before anyone realised she was there.

She couldn't raise the matter with her daughter-in-law. There were all the preparations for the churching, and the anxiety over baby Dorothy. And once the churching was over she decided she would leave immediately. No one pressed her to stay.

All the way home she thought about her son, remembering him as a little boy. She didn't understand what had gone wrong between them, or when they had grown apart.

And now she was home, still feeling displaced; unwelcome even here.

She didn't want to engage with someone else's pain. But she remembered what the queen had said about the spring. Soon it would be the anniversary of her return to England, of the first fateful battle.

And then she recalled also that it was the queen's birthday, at the end of March.

Now she'd remembered, she couldn't forget it again. But was it something she should acknowledge?

In the end she went into her garden, cut some early flowers and leaves into a posy and, bracing herself for the usual outpouring of bitterness and ingratitude, approached the queen's room.

But the queen was quiet and distant, in a sombre mood.

'Thank you,' she said, as if preoccupied. She wasn't preoccupied. No book lay open, the writing materials weren't touched. She was gazing out of the window.

'I remembered the day,' Lady Alice said. The queen looked at her blankly.

'Your birthday,' Alice prompted.

The queen's face cleared. 'Yesterday,' she said.

'Oh, I see. In that case, I didn't remember. I'm sorry.'

'Why should you remember?'

I'm not keeping so many queens in custody, Alice could have said, but she didn't want a discussion about what the former queen had to celebrate. 'I've brought you a different book,' she said.

Silence.

'A copy of some myths. I commissioned it myself.'

46

Nothing. Was she so put out that Alice had left her? Or because she'd not told her in advance?

'A few of the old stories: Narcissus, Orpheus, Persephone.'

The queen continued to look out of the window, frowning slightly, as though trying to solve a problem of some complexity.

'You can choose which one I read,' said Alice. 'Or I could leave it with you.'

The queen looked at her, still frowning. 'As you like,' she said. Just as if Lady Alice's presence, all her efforts, counted for nothing.

Of course, she'd underlined the difference between them by leaving when the queen could not. Still, she hadn't expected it would set them back so far.

'Are you well, my lady?'

The queen's frown deepened. Alice leaned forward. 'You know, I'm sure if you wrote to the king, he could arrange for you to be looked after by someone else. Duchess Cecily, for instance.'

The queen sighed. Naturally, she would not wish to be looked after by Cecily Neville. But she didn't acknowledge that she would be better off here.

Alice tried a different approach. 'Sometimes, you know, I will have to go away,' she said. 'I'm sure Joan told you I was visiting my son.'

As soon as she said this, the atmosphere changed between them. Now she would say, *at least you have a son to visit.*

But she didn't say anything.

'Well, something has upset you. If you don't like the book I can take it away.'

The queen looked at the book with that perplexed frown. Then she turned away again as if it was a matter of indifference to her, either way.

'Well,' Alice said, 'if I can't entertain you –' She began to manoeuvre herself to the edge of her chair.

'Was he well, your son?' the queen asked suddenly, and her voice was constricted and remote.

47

For a moment Alice didn't know what to reply. 'He is well, my lady, but very busy. He was away much of the time.'

She didn't say, *all of the time.*

'And your grandchildren – they are well?'

Alice began to wish she had not brought the subject up. 'They've had a new little daughter,' she said, 'and she's had some difficulty feeding. But with God's grace and the warmer weather, I'm sure all will be well.'

'Yes,' the queen said, with hardly any bitterness. 'God is good like that.'

Alice opted to change the subject. 'Shall I read to you, my lady?'

The queen seemed to be about to speak, but paused. Then she said, 'He used to like me to read to him. When he was small. He could never have enough of the old stories. I had to read them again and again. And he knew them all. If I missed something, he would tell me.'

There wasn't much Alice could say to this. 'Children are like that,' she ventured.

'There was never enough time to read everything he wanted. There was never enough time at all.'

Alice did not want to deal with an outpouring of grief. 'No –' she began; but the queen went on: 'Do you think the time we have is allocated to us at birth?'

Well, who knew the answer to that one? If it was, who had allocated less than eighteen years to the prince?

But the queen seemed to be waiting for an answer. Alice said, 'The Greeks thought so, my lady. The old stories say it's the Fates who spin the thread to a certain length, then cut it.'

'It's not the Fates.'

Now they were moving on to dangerous territory. If the queen started to blame the House of York, they would soon reach the subject of her son's affiliation. Or the queen would say something treasonable that Alice would feel obliged to report.

'It depends what you mean by fate, my lady. We're all of us affected by circumstances beyond our control.'

The queen nodded slowly. 'Perhaps God will take account of that,' she said, 'in His great reckoning.'

Alice didn't want to pursue this line of enquiry either. 'That's what I like about the Greek myths, my lady. They do not pretend to justice, or that anything in life is fair.'

'It's not fair.'

'No,' said Alice, thinking of her own family. 'And there's more than one way to lose a son.'

The queen looked at her. Alice looked at her book. For a moment its embossed cover quivered in her sight. Then she opened it. 'I think I'll read now,' she said.

And she read about Pandora. Who had opened the jar (which was so regularly mis-translated as 'box') and released all the evils of the world.

It was always a woman who released evil into the world.

But at the bottom of the jar there was hope. Most of the Greek myths ended badly, but in this one, at least, there was hope. '*God's great gift to man*,' she concluded.

The queen said, 'Hope is not a gift.'

'That's what it says here.'

'It's not a gift. It's the last and greatest evil.'

Alice was tired of attempting to offer comfort while the queen repudiated it.

'Well, it's the gift we have,' she said, closing the book.

The queen didn't ask her to stay.

All that day, Alice felt out of sorts. She wrote letters to her tenants, serving notice to those who hadn't paid the increased rates. She prepared a physic for herself to counteract the acid in her stomach, took a brief walk around her gardens alone and went to bed early. And the following day she didn't visit the queen at all.

The day after that, she received the not unexpected news that her little granddaughter, Dorothy, had died.

In the early morning, peacefully, in the arms of her nurse.

She read the letter twice then tucked it away.

It wasn't unusual, of course, she thought, returning to her accounts. Most families suffered the loss of more than one child.

Nature was manifestly wasteful; any observer could see that. The number of ducklings on the river decreased daily. So many seeds were planted that didn't take root; so many tiny tadpoles didn't survive.

She took out the letter and read it again.

I thank God our other children are well.

Five children were certainly something to be thankful for.

Lady Alice took off her spectacles and pressed the bridge of her nose.

She shouldn't have left her little granddaughter. The image of her, so quiet and still, returned powerfully to her. Even when she'd rubbed her feet, there had been no response.

The undersides of her feet had felt like crinkled silk.

She should have stayed and prised life back into her somehow. She, Alice Chaucer, with all her medical knowledge, could have tried harder to save that child.

But that was nonsense. She couldn't coax life back into the body of a creature so small, who wasn't determined to live.

She was five weeks old. It would be possible to count the number of breaths she had taken; the number of times her small lungs had unfolded like tiny wings.

Do you think the time we have is allocated to us at birth?

She'd said something glib in reply, about the Fates. She was sixty-eight years old, and all the answers she had came from books.

I'm sorry, she said to her tiny granddaughter. *I'm sorry I didn't keep you alive.*

She would have to write to her son.

She spent the rest of the morning composing the letter, enquiring tactfully about the funeral, because he hadn't mentioned it, then writing to one or two other relatives who might not know, and who might write expressing their congratulations, or breach the delicate wall of grief in some other unintentionally monstrous way. Then she made arrangements to leave once more because, even though she'd not been invited, there was no question that she would not attend the funeral. She would leave as soon as possible in case they forgot, in their distraction, to tell her.

She made herself a sleeping draught, to get her through the night.

But in the middle of the night she woke anyway. Her heart was beating rapidly and in her mind was one great question: *Why?*

Which was the one question that was never answered.

She couldn't begin to answer it now, nor could she go back to sleep because of the pressure in her bladder.

When she stumbled out of bed, cold struck upwards from the soles of her feet, even through the thin hose she always kept on at this time of year. She crouched awkwardly over her pot.

With the split consciousness of the very frightened, she could see herself – an old woman pissing in a pot. And when she got up, clumsily, she almost knocked it over; piss spilled on her chemise. For a moment she stood there, mortified. She was an old woman, staining herself with piss.

She didn't want to summon a servant now, she didn't want them saying she'd been incontinent in the night. But she didn't know where her clean chemise was.

Finally, she stripped off her chemise and put on the gown she had worn that day, then got back into bed slowly. But she was unable to get comfortable because her hip pained her. When she drifted towards sleep another pain shot through her fingers and wrist.

She was an old woman with arthritic fingers, so swollen she

doubted she would be able to write again that week. And kept awake, to be visited by all the grief and torment that visited those who lay awake at night.

But she was alive, while her tiny granddaughter was not.

She could remember a moment when she'd held her, and thought that Dorothy had registered something; the pattering of rain against the window.

Who, after all, could quantify life? Her granddaughter had opened her eyes, however briefly, and seen the light. She'd heard the rain, known the sensations of heat and cold, and the mystery of sleep. She'd known what it was to be held, and fed.

She thought, perhaps, she should try to pray for her. She waited for the words to come, listening for them, but nothing came. Instead, she heard a sound.

It was the soft step of someone trying to be quiet.

Lady Alice was instantly alert. All her anxiety returned. But there wasn't likely to be an intruder in the castle.

There was only one person it could be. The queen, creeping from her room, at this unearthly hour.

For the second time that night Alice got up. She opened the door to her room quietly, and peered out. She thought she saw a shadow, disappearing into the greater darkness at the end of the corridor. For a moment she stood uncertainly, then set off after it.

She'd ordered the door to the viewing tower to be kept locked at all times, yet here it was, open. How did the queen know it would be open? Or was she just trying her luck?

With some difficulty, for her feet were stiff, Alice ascended the curving stairs.

The queen stood on the parapet, looking down. Lady Alice knew at once what she intended to do; she felt almost as though she shouldn't disturb her. Then she stepped forward and spoke softly, because she didn't want to startle the queen into sudden action.

'My lady?' she said.

The queen didn't answer.

'The view is better in daylight.'

A ridiculous thing to say. But the queen didn't respond. Was she sleepwalking? If so, Alice knew it would be dangerous to wake her. But she felt she had to take charge.

'It's cold, my lady, I think you should come in.'

The queen moved a little, and Lady Alice knew she was awake. She said, 'I was dreaming about my son.'

There was nothing Lady Alice could say to that.

'I see him sometimes,' the queen said, 'from the corner of my eye. Or in my dreams. Then I think, *you haven't gone at all, you're playing a game.* He loved to play games.'

Alice knew she should speak. 'He wouldn't want you to catch cold,' she said, sounding ridiculous again to her own ears.

'Tonight I dreamed he was wading through water, through the little stream near where we lived in France. He was a child again. And he reached down into the water, like this' – she mimed the action – 'and pulled up a fish. He looked so pleased with himself. "*Voilà, maman,*" he said.' She laughed a little.

Alice had been going to say something sensible, bracing, but what she said was, 'He was a handsome boy.'

'He was,' the queen said. 'He was my handsome boy.'

'But all this grieving for him, all this dwelling on the past, won't bring him back.'

'I don't want to bring him back,' the queen said faintly. 'I want to go to him.'

'Oh, my lady –'

'You see, when I dream,' the queen went on, just as if Alice hadn't spoken, 'I think it's real. I don't know I'm dreaming. It seems more real to me than waking. Sometimes I think I'm really in that other world, just dreaming that he's gone. All I need to do is to wake up out of that dream. Do you see?'

She turned to Alice for the first time, but her face was in shade.

53

Alice did see. She saw there was no reason or purpose for the queen to live; no underlying, deeply buried hope that would fly out after the other evils of the world.

No one would blame Alice, if she did die. The king would even be grateful. She closed her eyes momentarily.

'My lady,' she said, 'I wish you would come in.' When the queen said nothing, she added, with a touch of asperity, 'I should like to go in at any rate – I'm cold.'

'Then go,' said the queen. 'What keeps you?'

Alice felt a spark of irritation. She said, 'Do you think you're the only person in the world to have lost hope? Do you think I have hope? I'm sixty-eight years old. I can only wait for death, but it will happen when it happens – and I'll face it alone. Do you think you're the first person in the world to find yourself alone?'

The queen looked at her. 'You have your son,' she said.

There it was: the core of everything that stood between them. Lady Alice closed her eyes again. 'My son,' she said. 'Yesterday I heard from my son. His little girl – the baby Dorothy – has died. He didn't invite me to the funeral, as he didn't invite me to the birth. But I shall go, nonetheless.'

She could feel the atmosphere between them changing. The queen turned towards her. 'That's terrible,' she said.

'It is terrible.'

'No – I mean it's terrible for you.'

Alice couldn't bear the note of shocked sympathy in her voice. It threatened to set something loose, something that would spill incontinently from her. Her throat had tightened, but she spoke as steadily as she could. 'I'll set off tomorrow. I would rather take the news that you are alive and well. But – if there is something you must do' – she paused – 'you will have the good grace not to do it while I'm watching.'

And she began to turn away. She couldn't fight this battle any longer. She no longer even knew what she was fighting for.

'Alice,' the queen said softly, and she paused. It was the first time the queen had used her name. 'It's not your fault. You loved your son.'

The words hung between them like a banner raised by all the grieving mothers of history. *I loved my son. I did my best.*

'I don't know whose fault it is any more,' Alice said. 'I'm tired of thinking about it.'

'Yes,' said the queen. 'There's no virtue in thought.'

Alice tried again. 'Will you come inside, my lady? I would prefer you not to die.'

It was true; she didn't want the queen to die. She held out her hand and felt a pang of surprise when, after a long moment, the queen took it. Her fingers were icy.

Still holding the queen's hand, Alice turned back to the stairs.

They didn't speak on the way down, except for once, when Alice murmured, 'Usually this door is kept locked.'

'I know,' the queen said. 'I've tried it before.'

An accident, then, Alice thought. Or she might as well think of it as such. She would not get any other truth by interrogating the servants.

The queen's hand was barely any warmer, and by the time they reached her room she was shivering uncontrollably.

'Get into bed, my lady,' Alice said. She lit two candles, even though the sky was paler now.

One for Dorothy, she thought, *one for the prince.*

The queen watched her from her bed, *like a child*, Alice thought. And just as she would not have left a distressed child alone in the dark, Alice sat down at the table and picked up a book.

It was her grandfather's book, *The Canterbury Tales*, written years before Alice had been born. The language had changed since then; everything had changed.

She didn't have her spectacles, but it didn't matter. She knew most of the prologue by heart. And it was the prologue she wanted to read, for were they not now on the cusp of April?

So she cleared her throat and began as if reading, rather than simply reciting the words that had been read to her since childhood, which she hoped would transport both her and the queen back to a simpler time; that quintessential spring.

> *Whan that Aprille with his shoures sote*
> *The droghte of March hath perced to the roote*
> *And bathed every veyne in swich licour*
> *Of which vertu engendred is the floure . . .*

4

The Wedding

The marriage settlement had proved so complicated that Dr John Morton, King Edward's newly appointed Master of Rolls, had been called in to determine the legality of certain clauses, without which neither of them would proceed. Now he was present at the ceremony, which took place in June, in Stanley's house. Margaret's mother and her half-brother Oliver St John, Reginald Bray, her receiver, and two of her ladies were also present. On the groom's side were four of his children, his brothers William and James and their wives.

Perversely, Margaret's mother seemed to have taken to Stanley. She clung to his arm, laughing, as if everything he said was enormously witty. There were few signs of the illness she'd claimed to have, apart from a certain stiffness, so she had to be helped in and out of her chair.

Margaret wore a robe of pewter silk trimmed with black lace, which her mother said was funereal in the extreme. It was not cut in the new style, immodestly slashed at the bosom and leg, but high-necked and decorously draped. Her mother said she looked as though she was entering a convent rather than getting married.

Good, Margaret thought. She didn't want to give any other kind of message to her groom. After the vows he lifted her veil with that mocking expression with which she was already so familiar and pressed his dry lips swiftly to hers.

At the banquet Margaret was relieved to see that her husband's party behaved themselves. The good wishes of King Edward and Queen Elizabeth were read out and applauded, then Stanley turned to her and said he would not be keeping her company that night, he had to leave on some official business. She was welcome to stay in his house, of course. There were enough rooms for all of them.

Margaret felt her spirits lifting for the first time that day. All morning she'd suffered from a headache that gripped her skull. Dread sat like a stone in her stomach. What if Stanley should refuse to honour their agreement? All their agreements, but especially the one not written down.

She was twenty-nine years old, as her mother would have pointed out, and no virgin. If the worst happened, she could lie on her back and pray.

But he was going away. She smiled at him genuinely for the first time. It was not like God to take her side so openly.

Her mother couldn't understand this arrangement.

'That's no way to keep a husband,' she said. 'Mark my words, if you let him fly, he'll find a different nest.'

Margaret couldn't be bothered to argue. She became animated with the rest of the party, until he pressed her arm.

'Of course,' he said, 'I'll visit your room before I leave. For appearance's sake.' He smiled his yellow smile, and her heart turned to lead.

In her room her ladies took off the high shoes she was wearing, and the veil and gown. Underneath she had on a chemise of fine cambric, silk hose and a close-fitting cap that pressed her hair to her head. She wouldn't let them remove this.

'At least let me brush out your hair,' Edith said.

'No,' said Margaret. She saw them exchanging glances in the mirror, then Marie said, 'Ah, the husband likes to have something to take off,' which set them off laughing and joking as they proceeded with her toilette.

Margaret looked at herself in the mirror. The tip of her nose was flushed from wine, her cheeks had a raw, scrubbed look, but she wouldn't have them powdered, nor her lips reddened. She wondered fleetingly if her life would have been different if she had been beautiful, whether it would have saved her from this moment now. *Probably not*, she thought.

She allowed Marie to dab perfume behind her ears and sprinkle it on the chemise, but when she made another attempt to take off Margaret's cap she put her hand up quickly, almost knocking the candle over.

'Oh, my lady – your pretty hair,' Edith mourned.

It wasn't pretty, it was thin and brown. Already grey threads stood out against the darker strands. But Edith meant she would look better with it down around her shoulders rather than stuffed into the cap. It would at least soften the sharp contours of her face.

Edith was undoubtedly right, but Margaret wouldn't relent. She stood up abruptly, tired of looking at herself, as her ladies lit the candles around the bed. She felt too small without her shoes, like a lost child.

And then they heard him: his footsteps, his voice talking to his manservant. Her leaden heart began to pound. She'd thought many times about what she would say, and what he would say in return, and what she would say then, but now these rehearsals seemed pointless. The door was opening and there was Stanley in his shirt and breeches. His shirt was open at the neck, revealing a cluster of hair. She could only blink at him as her ladies sank into their deepest curtsies with an air of suppressed excitement and mirth.

He was drunker than she'd realised; swaying slightly. She dropped her gaze as he looked at her, then spoke, clearly enunciating his words.

'Are you not going to dismiss your ladies?'

She nodded at them, then foolishly went on nodding as they left. They were actually giggling now, like girls rather than grown women.

The silence seemed bigger once they'd gone. Stanley stepped forward until he was close enough for her to smell the wine on his breath. She wouldn't look at him.

'Are you tired, my lady?' he said softly. 'Are you ready for bed?'

She couldn't answer him. All her breath seemed to be stuck in her throat.

He put out one finger and touched her cheek, tracing the line of her jaw and throat. Then in a swift movement he inserted it into the neck of her chemise and tugged it open.

Reflexively her hands flew up and twisted it away from him. Why had she ever thought he wouldn't want to claim what was his?

'Come now, *Lady Stanley*,' he said. 'We are married, after all.'

She wouldn't resist him, she thought, in grief and terror. She would offer up her suffering to God.

'What's that you're saying?' Stanley said as her lips moved. 'You'll have to speak up. Desire must be making me deaf.'

She gave him a reproachful stare. 'I'm praying,' she managed to say, 'that whatever you do to me the Lord will forgive you and forgive us both.'

Unexpectedly, Stanley laughed. He stepped away from her, then sat on the edge of the bed, shaking his head. 'Congratulations, Countess,' he said. 'You've managed to quench even my ardour.'

She didn't reply; she was concentrating on her prayer. *Make him go away*, she prayed.

'But you know, for appearances' sake, I should stay a little while. It won't do to disappoint the servants. Perhaps we can make the bed creak a little' – he bounced on it gently – 'and ruffle the sheets? You could shout "Hallelujah!" at intervals.'

Her fear was leaving her; she felt a spark of annoyance. 'I'm tired,' she said. 'I would like to sleep now.'

'Sleep?' he said in exaggerated surprise. 'What am I meant to do while you sleep?'

'You may do what you like,' she said, 'in your own room.'

'But if I leave now, everyone will know nothing happened between us on our wedding night. They will say I'm not man

60

enough, or that you're so repelled by me you sent me away. You wouldn't wish the servants to say such things, surely.'

She could have said, *what does it matter what the servants think?* But she knew it did matter. Because they would communicate with other servants, and in no time at all most of the aristocracy of England would know about the state of their marriage. But Henry hadn't worried about it, she thought, feeling a powerful pang for her lost husband, who had been her friend. The man who sat in front of her now could never be her friend.

He was actually holding out his hand, inviting her to join him. She was not such a fool as to take it and let him pull her on to the bed.

'It won't take long,' he said, 'we'll go for speed rather than delectation. Two, three minutes at most.'

When she didn't take his hand he swung himself fully on to the bed and lay with his hands clasped behind his head, saying, 'Suit yourself. But I'll make myself comfortable.'

She couldn't make him leave; her only recourse was to ignore him. She turned her back on him and walked over to the window. Through the pane she could see a single, quivering star. She fixed her eyes on it, thinking, *I can wait as long as you, my lord.* She could still hear the sounds of revelry below. Possibly they would go on all night, keeping the servants up. And she would have to stay in her room, for the sake of the servants, and of the wedding party, who were still celebrating the union of man and wife.

5

The Portrait

King Edward being . . . determined utterly to destroy the remnant of his enemies . . . sent George, Archbishop of York, the Earl of Warwick's brother, to pine away in prison . . . Many moreover, were, upon little suspicion . . . committed to ward or grievously fined.

Polydore Vergil

After this, King Edward reigned peacefully in England . . . although not without some anxieties and a disturbed conscience.

Philippe de Commines

He dreamed that his cousin, the former king, was still imprisoned in the Tower. And he, Edward, had to get rid of him – there was no one else who could do it. So he crept up on the old king as he knelt at prayer and dealt him three blows to the head and neck. But the king didn't die; he went on praying. And he wasn't like a king any more but a child; his hands on the rail were a child's hands. King Edward could hear his whimpering breath and was filled with horror. For he should have protected this man-child, but there was nothing he could do.

He woke groaning and sweating from this dream. He had kicked off all the bedclothes, but his wife didn't stir. She was used to his sleep being interrupted. For a moment he considered waking her, but she didn't appreciate being disturbed and wouldn't be sympathetic.

'You should eat less,' she would say. She attributed all his unease to the casual violence he perpetrated on his gut – gorging himself until he vomited, then eating again. She herself ate only the first mouthful of the forty or so dishes that were provided each night, in an attempt to preserve the figure that was a little distorted by childbirth.

In fact, his stomach was hurting, and his mouth felt like a cave full of dead things. When he'd returned from exile to depose him the old king had said, '*My cousin of York, you are most welcome. I know that in your hands my life will not be in danger.*'

His face had actually lit up, as though Edward was his deliverer. Edward had held him in his arms, and his flesh had slid over his bones; there had been that stale, decaying smell.

But he had not been the one who'd killed him; he'd merely given an order. If Henry had been a horse or a dog, he would have done the same.

But he was a king.

With a stifled moan Edward got up and went to the window, where he could look out over the sleeping world of London. It was his world now.

But the people – his people – seemed to be turning against him. In their collective memory the old king appeared no longer as a madman or a fool but a saint. They were making pilgrimages to his tomb.

How rapidly they forgot what it suited them to forget. A year ago they were saying that Edward's two great victories were a certain sign that God was on his side. Now they were saying he'd murdered a holy man who was God's anointed. They had forgotten that this same holy man had brought the nation to its knees.

Not one of his advisors had thought he should leave the old king alive, to be a focus for future rebellions. How many more men would have died if he'd let him live?

He'd done it for the nation. The people wanted a king who would defend them. After Towton, when the bodies of men lay strewn along the road to York, they had feted him.

But it was one thing to kill a man in battle and another as he knelt at prayer. And no ordinary man, but his cousin and a king.

That's what they were saying, at home and abroad. The foreign rulers who wanted to see him fail.

He had tried and failed to have the two earls, Jasper and Henry Tudor, returned to England. Duke Francis wouldn't give them up; not while the French king also wanted them.

Louis of France was playing his own game. Aiding the Earl of Oxford, keeping in touch with a network of spies and dissidents. Not for nothing was he called the Spider King, spreading his webs across Europe. He'd already caught the Archbishop of York in them. Some said they'd reached even further, into Edward's own family, to his brother George.

He should have his brother investigated, but he didn't want to open all the old wounds, which were barely healing, to start the strife again.

His brothers had been wrangling over the Neville inheritance all year, each petitioning him to take their side. In the end, Richard had married the younger sister, Anne, and taken her to Middleham, along with her mother, the Countess of Warwick. The quarrel seemed to die down. But Richard had stayed in the north, so only George was in London, and Edward could not trust George. It was Richard he trusted.

His brothers hated each other, and one of them hated him. They both hated his wife, as did his mother. And his wife hated all of them, and all of his friends. Especially his greatest friend, Lord Hastings.

But he still had his kingdom. And his children. A new child had been born to him that April. Another little girl, named Margaret, after his sister. She was blue-eyed and golden-haired and beautiful, as all his children were. Like the new Golden Age he wished people to believe had begun.

He'd spent the year of his exile in Bruges, that centre of culture and opulent display. Where great painters and composers flourished and the illuminated manuscripts were the glory of the western world. He'd stayed in the manor house of Louis of

Gruthuyse, who owned one of the finest libraries in Europe. And then with his sister and her husband, Duke Charles of Burgundy, at their dazzling court.

He, too, could have a dazzling court. He could resume work on his palaces, commission new books, create his own memorials.

It came to him then, as he gazed out over his dreaming city, that he would have a portrait painted of his family, which was surely the finest family in Europe. What did King Louis have to compare to it? Or Duke Francis? Or Duke Charles? He would have his wife and family immortalised, in the Flemish style, for the world to see.

And they would see it, because he would invite foreign dignitaries to come and stay. They would report back to their kings and countries that England was no longer poor and ravaged by war but a wealthy, powerful nation.

The first person he would invite was the Lord of Gruthuyse, because Edward had gone to him as a penniless exile and had been the beneficiary of his kindness. Now it was time to redress the balance.

He began to pace at the thought of it and came to a halt by the bedside. Looking at his sleeping wife, he decided that he would disturb her after all. For with the stirring of hope in his body, another part of him had stirred. And besides, he liked the way she responded to him when she was sleeping, before she had recalled all the discord between them.

In the next weeks he spent lavishly on tapestries and ermine, on gold and silver plate. Work began on the chapel of St George, and on five of the palaces. The portrait was commissioned and an invitation extended to Louis of Gruthuyse.

Queen Elizabeth seemed less pleased by this than she might have been. She was indifferent to the building projects, even the refurbishments, and actively hostile to the portrait.

'Will you have all your whores on it as well?' she said.

Which was unreasonable of her, since she knew that the presentation of their marriage, strong, fecund and blessed by God, was at the core of all this effort and expense. Yet the queen, who was usually as keen to impress as the king was, seemed reluctant to find time to sit for the painter.

'I have enough to do,' she said. She visited their youngest daughter, Margaret, frequently, because she was worried about her persistent crying and tendency to fever, which the king attributed to the normal growing pains of infancy.

He attributed her anxiety to melancholy following the death of her mother, for Jacquetta had died just six weeks after the birth of the baby. And the queen had been stricken to an extent that had surprised him. Had she not constantly complained about her mother in private? He'd tried to comfort her, remembering his own grief at the death of his father, but she'd pushed him away.

He didn't miss Jacquetta himself; if anything, he felt moments of relief that the duchess, with her interfering, acquisitive ways, had gone. But the queen was acting as if she was the only one to have lost a parent. Obviously, it was a reminder of mortality, and of her age, about which she'd always been sensitive. So he'd tried to be understanding, but his suggestion that his own mother, Cecily, should be included in the portrait had provoked an outburst of rage.

'You don't need to give her a greater sense of her own importance!'

There was some justice in this, since Cecily undoubtedly enjoyed her new status as the only royal mother and grandmother.

'She's not my mother,' the queen said. 'Nor is she likely to be.'

So eventually it was agreed that the portrait should be of Elizabeth and her children. The king would be painted separately.

Still she was uncooperative; obsessively worried about her

youngest child when, as far as the king could see, there was no
cause for concern.

Sometimes women were afflicted by such moods following
the birth of a child. They were afflicted in any case by mysterious
fluctuations of humour, just like the common people, who were
governed by the moon.

So he gave way to her again, and the painter agreed to make
his preliminary sketches in the nursery. But even here there were
difficulties, for the little prince could not be made to keep still,
and the infant Margaret could only be sketched while asleep,
because the rest of the time she was mewling and squirming in
her nurse's arms.

And when the king saw the artist's first impressions of the
queen, he had to tell him to start again. 'Make her smile more,'
he said. 'She should be serene – like the empress of the world.'
And so the artist painted her from this instruction, since the
queen refused to sit for him again.

Finally, the king pronounced himself satisfied and the portrait
was hung in the Great Hall at Windsor for everyone to admire. In
time for the state visit of Lord Gruthuyse, who came with his son
John and his envoy, Bluemantle Pursuivant, and many nobles
from his court. Hastings took them to meet the king and queen
and the portrait was liberally admired.

It transpired that the envoy had been brought specifically for
the purpose of recording this historic visit. The king was
delighted, since this accorded perfectly with his own plans. He
requested that a copy of the record be made for his own court.

It was difficult to refuse the king, who was pressing down so
heavily on his shoulder.

And so, Bluemantle Pursuivant wrote his account:

After he had supped, the king had my Lord of Gruthuyse brought
to the queen's chamber, where she sat playing with her ladies at
the mortealx [bowls] and some of her ladies and gentlewomen at

ninepins of ivory and dancing . . . also the king danced with my Lady Elizabeth, his eldest daughter . . . In the morning, when Matins was done, the king heard, in his own chapel, Our Lady Mass, which was melodiously sung, the Lord Gruthuyse being there present. When the Mass was done, the king gave Lord Gruthuyse a cup of gold, garnished with pearl. In the midst of the cup was a great piece of unicorn's horn, and on the cover a great sapphire . . . [Later] the queen ordered a great banquet in her own chamber . . . and when they had supped, my Lady Elizabeth, the king's eldest daughter, danced with the Duke of Buckingham . . . and about nine o'clock, the king and the queen, with her ladies and gentlewomen, brought Lord Gruthuyse to three chambers of Pleasure, all hung with white silk and linen cloth, and all the floors covered with carpets . . . There was ordained a bed for himself, of as good down as could be obtained, the sheets of Rennes cloth and fine fustians, the counterpane cloth of gold furred with ermine, the canopy also shining cloth of gold and the curtains of white sarsenet . . .

The Record of Bluemantle Pursuivant

When Parliament opened Lord Louis was created Earl of Winchester and many other honours were distributed. The Speaker praised the king as *saviour of the Nation* and thanked the queen in a special speech for her courage and constancy during the king's exile, when she'd had to go into Sanctuary, where she'd given birth to the prince who would inherit the realm.

The visit was judged to be a great success, although when the party had gone there was a general exhalation of relief. Only the king felt regret, already wondering who else to invite.

But the sense of triumph did not last long, for on the eleventh day of December that year, baby Margaret died of paroxysms in her sleep.

The king wept inconsolably, but the queen was dry-eyed;

seeming to feel a sense of vindication. Had she not said the child was ill? She wouldn't attempt to comfort the king nor be comforted by him. The king felt wounded by her resistance, and when they returned to Windsor he wept again at the portrait in the hall.

There she was, his little Margaret, blue-eyed, golden-haired and laughing (the painter having taken the liberty of invention). The king was temporarily overcome, but the queen looked at him with a mixture of contempt and disgust.

'Perhaps you could have her painted out,' she said.

And so the Christmas season that year was somewhat bleak, alleviated only by the news that the queen was once again expecting a child. And by the news that the Duke of Gloucester would visit, which made the king happy, if not the queen.

6

Parting

[King Edward's] mind was not free from fear or inward trouble, for news was brought to him that the earls of Pembroke and Richmond were highly cherished, well-fostered and entertained by the Duke of Brittany ... [and so] he secretly sent messengers to the duke to promise him great and sumptuous rewards [if] he would deliver both earls to his possession. The duke willingly heard them that were sent, but when he knew that the two earls were of such great value he determined not to deliver them but to keep them more diligently than before ...

Hall's Chronicle

They were playing chess when the knock came. A short, lugubrious man entered. Behind him was a posse of guards who hovered in the hallway with an air of anxious anticipation that was almost comic. Their captain coughed twice.

'His excellency the duke says you are to be removed to a new accommodation.'

Jasper stared at him. 'Tell his excellency we're happy here.'

Another cough. 'My lord the duke regrets this inconvenience very much, but you are to be immediately removed. I'm instructed to wait until you're ready.'

Jasper put down the chess piece he had been holding. 'You must be mistaken,' he said. 'I've had no notification of this.'

The captain didn't shrug, but he raised his eyebrows and pulled down the corners of his mouth.

'Where does he propose to move us to?' Jasper asked.

The captain smiled, in a pained kind of way. 'The young man, your nephew, is to be taken into the household of Jean de Rieux, Marshal of Brittany – to the Château of Largoët. You will like it there,' he said, addressing Henry directly for the first time. 'It's a marvellous building, with towers that are crowned with stars and mist. They're known as the Tours d'Elven.'

Then he turned to Jasper. 'You are to be housed at the Fortress of Josselin, near Vannes. It's very luxurious,' he added. 'I've stayed there myself.'

'Out of the question.'

Henry had never seen his uncle lose his temper, but now he was glaring at the captain as though he would run him through with his sword. But the little man seemed regretful rather than afraid. 'My master instructed me to give you this letter,' he said.

Jasper's long features lengthened even further as he read. Henry thought, *it's true, it's happening – we will be separated*.

He had not been apart from his uncle since arriving in Brittany. At first they had even shared a room. He was accustomed to letting Jasper take all the major decisions for them both. So he was surprised when Jasper finished reading then held out the letter to him. He hesitated before taking it then started to read.

Cher ami, it began, because the duke liked, when it suited him, to abandon all formalities. *I regret to cause you this inconvenience, but I am threatened by two great kingdoms, at least one of which wants war. My little duchy is as a small ship, bearing precious cargo, that is being assailed by two great galleons – pirate ships – which will do all they can to seize that cargo.*

Henry could imagine the duke, who was fond of poetry, smiling to himself at the cleverness of these words.

I am besieged by two kings who will stop at nothing to obtain you, or to prevent the other from obtaining you first. The best I can do is to keep you under stricter confinement than before. It is not for them that I do this, but for your own security . . .

'We can't just pack up everything and leave now,' Jasper was saying. Henry looked up again as the captain bowed.

'With your permission, of course, my men will help you to pack.'

Jasper shook his head in disbelief, then paced from one side of the room to the other. Henry glanced back at the letter.

I know, of course, that you will not want to be separated from your nephew, to whom you have been as a father. But he is a young man now, and I trust and pray to Our Heavenly Father that it will not be for too long. But if anyone plans to attack you it is better that you are not kept in the same place. And your current abode is too easy of access to the sea . . .

The rest of the letter consisted of graceful expressions of regret. Henry put it down and looked at his uncle, who was glaring at the wall.

'I'm not happy about this – not happy at all,' he said, turning back to the captain. 'There's been no discussion – nothing. Why have I not seen the duke?'

The captain sighed and said that Duke Francis wasn't well. 'It's nothing,' he added, as if Jasper had asked. 'Just a chill of the heart.'

'What if we refuse?'

'I do not think you should do that.'

Henry thought about the letter. *Two kings*, it said. He knew King Edward had put pressure on the duke. He'd sent his brother-in-law Anthony Woodville with some soldiers to help the duke against the French, and more reinforcements were promised if Henry and his uncle were returned. But Duke Francis had stood by his promise to the English exiles.

The other king could only be Louis of France.

He opened his mouth to ask why this was happening now, but no one was listening to him.

'How long is this likely to go on?' Jasper asked. The captain looked at the floor. 'It's not convenient at all,' Jasper said. 'I expected something in the way of consultation. I do not, for one moment, give up my guardianship of my nephew – you will tell the duke that – do you hear?'

The captain said he would certainly take that message back.

Jasper hunched his shoulders, looking momentarily like a crow. 'Tell him it's only under protest that I go. Tell him I hope to see him at his earliest convenience, to discuss the terms of this new – accommodation.'

The captain said his master had already expressed his intention of visiting Jasper as soon as he was well again.

Jasper sighed and shook his head. 'Give us one hour,' he said. 'We'll pack our own things.'

The captain bowed and left.

As soon as he'd gone, Jasper walked over to Henry, who stood up. His uncle clasped him by the shoulders. 'I don't like this,' he said, 'I don't like it at all. I promised your mother –'

'Why now?' Henry asked; and Jasper said, 'Louis.'

Jasper told him that King Louis had recently sent his own envoy to order the release of Henry and Jasper. He was outraged, apparently, that the duke should still be detaining Jasper, who was of Louis' own blood royal. He'd said the detention of Henry and Jasper was tantamount to a declaration of war against France.

Since England was also petitioning him, the best Duke Francis could do was to promise not to surrender them to either king but to keep them in stricter confinement than before.

'And now look,' Jasper finished bitterly. 'See where all these dealings have got us.'

Henry ventured the opinion that it might be better if the duke did send them to France.

Jasper glared at him.

'That's where we were going,' Henry said.

'Louis would send us back to England the minute he'd secured a treaty against Burgundy,' Jasper said.

So there they were, at the heart of an impossibly complicated web.

'It's good of the duke to keep us,' Henry offered.

'The duke will keep us as long as we're valuable,' said Jasper. 'Pack your things.'

Sometimes Henry resented the way his uncle spoke to him as if he was still a child. *He is a young man now*, the duke had said. He was seventeen, an age when many men had fought battles, fallen in love, or married. In the kind of stories he read, they had conquered kingdoms.

But Jasper had always protected him. Soon after their arrival at the Château de Suscinio, Jasper had heard a noise outside the door. He had flung it open, thrusting his sword out and narrowly missing the maid, who stood with a bundle of laundry, looking amazed.

Now he would have to learn to think like his uncle and sleep with his sword at his side. He could feel the familiar crawling anxiety in his stomach.

'I don't know what I'll say to your mother,' Jasper was saying. 'She entrusted you to me. Perhaps,' he said, looking back at Henry, 'she doesn't need to know straight away. Not until I've spoken to the duke.'

Privately, Henry considered that his mother would probably find out, whether he told her or not. She seemed to have her own sources of information.

Jasper gripped Henry by the shoulders again. 'You must write to me every day,' he said. 'Tell me everything that happens. If I don't hear from you, I'll know something's wrong.'

Jasper's eyes had reddened, and his voice shook. Tentatively, Henry put his arms up, and his uncle hugged him roughly. 'They won't keep us separate for long,' he said. 'I'll speak to the duke.'

Henry could feel his uncle's tense, thin frame through his shirt, the agitation of his heart. He began to disengage himself, politely withdrawing as he had since childhood. Jasper released him, turning away. 'Finish packing,' he muttered.

Because they were exiles they didn't have much – everything had been provided for them. So the few things they did possess were rapidly rolled up into two bundles, and then the captain was knocking again.

'I see you're ready,' he said.

'We're not ready,' said Jasper, 'but we will go with you. Since the duke is so anxious to appease his master.'

The captain looked at him.

'The French king must be the true ruler of Brittany,' Jasper said. 'Whatever he says goes.'

The captain moved his head slowly from side to side. 'If that were true, you would already be in France,' he said. When Jasper didn't answer this, he added, 'Besides it is the English king, not the French king, who has become impatient again. Now that he has the Earl of Oxford.'

Jasper looked up quickly. 'What?' he said.

The captain seemed surprised, as if he'd expected them to know. The Earl of Oxford had been captured recently – but not executed, he assured them. He was being taken to the Fortress of Hammes, where he would be imprisoned, just as George Neville had been, until the king decided what to do with him.

Henry could see hope draining from his uncle's face. The last pocket of Lancastrian resistance had gone. The Earl of Oxford, George Neville and Margaret of Anjou were all imprisoned. Now only Henry and Jasper were left. And their value had gone up accordingly.

'So you see, King Edward is keen to have you,' the captain said. 'And my master is going to considerable trouble to protect you.'

Jasper's face had set as still as stone. He glanced towards Henry. 'Pick up your things,' he said.

They set off together with their escort, riding for several miles through open countryside. Then they came to a place where the road divided, and the company came to a halt.

'Wait,' Jasper said. He dismounted and Henry did too. Then,

before all the company, his uncle embraced him, hard, murmuring into his hair.

'Make sure you write to me,' he said.

Henry was afraid his uncle would burst into tears in front of them all, but Jasper released him. 'God keep you,' he said, and got quickly back on his horse.

Then he was riding away without looking back. Henry remained looking after him, until one of the guards touched his shoulder. He got slowly on to his own horse, and the guards closed around him.

He was a man now; the duke's letter had said so. He didn't feel like a man, unless this peculiar, hollow sensation was characteristic of the state. If he was a man, surely he would be taking charge of the situation, deciding his own destination, instead of allowing himself to be led, childlike, into the unknown.

Edward IV was called by the Duke of Burgundy to the enterprise of a foreign war against the French king. The king could not choose but to join in that war . . . because King Louis was his enemy as he had armed the Earl of Warwick in France against him; [and] because besides the affinity he had with the Duke of Burgundy, he was also singularly in debt to him for the manifold benefits bestowed on him when he was driven out of England . . . During the Parliament [1474–5] the principal concern was to arouse the interest of the Lords and Commons in the French war . . .

Polydore Vergil

Finally all approved the king's decision [to go to war against France] and tithes and fifteenths were granted . . . In addition all heirs and owners of property freely granted a tenth of their possessions. Since all of these measures did not appear adequate however a new and unheard-of tax was introduced . . .

Crowland Chronicle

7

Freedom

After a season of rain, spring had arrived like a pageant in Lady Alice's garden, spreading its processional colours over trees and shrubs. Even the lawns were spangled with yellow.

That was all she could see, since her eyesight had deteriorated: massed bands of colour. The white of hawthorn, a series of pinks on the other trees, blue and lilac on the shrubs. She could smell them of course, though her sense of smell was not what it used to be either. Her fingers were numb with arthritis, she couldn't walk far because of her hips and the shortness of breath, yet still the spring called her like birdsong.

Last night she'd lain awake during the inhospitable hours when all the old pains and grievances returned. So she'd come out early, to catch that moment when the light changed like a soft breath on the world, to remind herself she was blessed.

The former queen was never awake to see this moment when the world miraculously renewed itself. It was as though captivity, however lenient (and Alice prided herself on her clemency), had made her sluggish. She didn't rise until after eight o'clock, then adjusted slowly to the few demands of her day. The most animated she'd been recently was when they'd spoken of the coming war. Lady Alice could not believe the king would embark on such a foolish undertaking, that all the country had fallen for his persuasive rhetoric.

'What happens if he doesn't win?' she'd said.

'He won't win,' the queen said, and even with her inadequate eyesight Alice could see she was rigid with satisfaction. 'Louis will win,' she said.

'Well – and what will happen then?' demanded Alice, but the queen only smiled that vindictive smile, and a suspicion crossed Alice's mind that maybe she knew more than she was saying. But how could she know more than Lady Alice? And what did she think would happen to her in this war? Did she think Louis would restore her to the throne?

No. It was simply enough for her to contemplate the fall of the House of York. That was what had kept her alive all these years.

Still, it occurred to Alice that she should increase her vigil over the queen, which she'd relaxed in recent months. It was simply not possible to maintain a strict custody for so long. Besides – where could a former queen go? What was she likely to do? There was such anti-French feeling in the country that if she tried to leave it was quite likely she'd be killed on sight.

However, it could do no harm to monitor her activities more closely, keep her company more frequently. She thought this after their conversation about the war and, as with so many things these days, had forgotten it instantly. Until the letter arrived from her son.

It remained unanswered on her table. She couldn't trust herself to make a polite response.

He'd asked her to keep a strict watch over the queen because of the coming war. *Do not forget to pass on any communication to or from her,* he'd instructed. Then he'd gone on to ask for money *for the king's cause.*

But he'd not visited her, even for the money. He'd passed within four miles of the castle, extorting money for the king's 'project' or 'quest', as it was called, because no one would give it its proper name. He'd made several visits to wealthy citizens or minor nobles, but not to her. She'd received the letter instead. Urging her to consider whatever amount she might *freely and willingly give to this most noble cause.*

Nothing, she'd thought. She would freely and willingly give nothing at all to this catastrophic plan. If the king was so foolishly set on it, he would have to come in person and take money from her.

But that wouldn't happen, and her son would not come either, unless explicitly ordered by the king. He would say he was pre-occupied with the king's business. Or with his burgeoning family, for he'd had two more children since baby Dorothy had died, and a third was on the way.

And still she was mysteriously excluded from his life.

It was an old pain now, and she should have grown used to it. But it had kept her awake last night and, even now, in her beloved garden, it caused her heart to throb erratically, sending short stabbing pains between her ribs.

She should go back inside, to pass on her instructions to her staff before she forgot them again.

She didn't want to return while she could still hear the birds and smell the dew. But how often these days did she enter a room purposefully, only to forget why she'd gone in? She should do it now while she remembered.

Even the short walk back almost defeated her. She had to stop several times to catch her breath. Her breathing had worsened, it was an act of will to pump the air in and out of her lungs, to make her joints move. There was a weakness, or inertia, in her legs, as though they would not support her, a sheen of sweat above her lips. She had to stop while her heartbeat slowed and the pain in her ribs subsided. And still she would have to negoti-ate the stairs to her room.

But it was just another of the inconveniences of old age. She was past seventy, but not past caring, it seemed.

At the door she turned to look at her garden.

Of her many accomplishments, it seemed to her that the creation of her garden was the most worthwhile. No wonder that man's earliest imagining of Paradise had taken the form of a garden. Ever since his expulsion from it, he'd tried to recreate it on earth.

She opened the door and went into her castle.

Instantly, all was dark and cold; a partial light slanted through the slits in the wall. The stairs seemed more daunting each time she came to them. But it was nonsense to think there were more of them, or that they were any steeper. And there was no choice but to begin.

She was surprised, but not startled, to see her third husband at the top of the stairs. When she looked up directly he wasn't there, but when she concentrated on climbing there he was, smiling down on her. Not helping her, of course; he was never what you might call a practical man.

What are you doing here? she thought, but was then too preoccupied by the transference of weight from one foot to the other to notice whether he replied. First, her hip would not allow her to lift the leg then put her weight on it, but eventually she managed, with an uneven movement, to shift herself up one step. She paused before starting the next.

She thought she saw behind him the outline of two more figures, shadowy and indistinct, but with a jolt of recognition she realised they were her two previous husbands.

The thought did come to her, as she made a complicated sideways manoeuvre up the next step, that it was odd they should all be there together – all visiting at once. That had never happened before.

It was to do with the war in France, she thought. All of them had been killed either in or because of war with France. So they were here now to see her about it. Though what they expected her to do she didn't know.

And still none of them was making a move to help her up the stairs. Though she could see, after negotiating another two steps, that her third husband couldn't extend his hand out to her because he was holding something in his arms.

When she realised what it was, she missed her footing then tripped on her gown. She stumbled sideways, tearing her skirt, then backwards. All the breath was shunted out of her so that she couldn't even call for help. The last thing she saw was her third husband, William de la Pole, advancing towards her with a look of concern on his face, carrying baby Dorothy in his arms.

They told the queen she hadn't fallen far – five or six steps – but had lain there for some time before a servant had found her, and she had not regained consciousness. When the queen asked to see her, Joan told her, in her usual implacable way, *when her lady-ship comes round.*

This went on for four days. On the fifth day the former queen picked up the Bible Alice had given her and rapped smartly on the door of Alice's room.

'I should like to read to her,' she said when the little maid opened the door fractionally. The little maid looked over her shoulder towards Joan, then let her in.

She could sense at once the presence of death in the room. There was a medicinal scent from various phials, and something else, sickly, like decay.

Joan was adjusting the pillow behind Lady Alice. As the queen approached she could see the gaunt face, its pallor and sheen. When had she grown so thin? Her long frame barely disturbed the bedclothes, apart from her breathing, which came in erratic gasps.

'You can see, ma'am, she's not in a fit state,' Joan said. 'I don't want you wearing her out.'

How would she do that? the queen wondered.

'I will sit with her,' she said, and repeated it until Joan gave in.

'Just while the doctor comes,' she said, and brought a chair. Then she busied herself about the bed, folding a cloth here, emptying a bowl there, conspicuously not leaving them alone.

Did she think she would try to poison or smother Alice?

She wanted only to speak but couldn't think how to go on, unnerved by the stale smell that came from the corpse-like figure, and by the watchful presence of Joan. She couldn't think what she'd wanted to say.

What were those lines of Horace Lady Alice was so fond of?

Ask not – we cannot know – what end the gods have set for you and me.

She didn't know what she should feel. Lady Alice was her gaoler, after all, not her friend, whatever she'd said. And she couldn't cry any more. It was as though she'd offered up her tears to God: *here, take them – are they enough for you? Have I cried enough?* At any rate, she was dry-eyed now.

Still, there was this stick-thin figure on the bed. One of the few links she had left to the world.

She remembered the book she was holding. How often had Lady Alice read to her? Not in recent months, because her eyes had been too bad. But she would recite from her considerable memory. She had recited passages from Christine de Pizan's book about the Amazons of Scythia who had beaten the heroes Hercules and Theseus. Then about the scholarly ladies Sappho and Nicostrata who had learned all there was to know in the ancient world. And she'd said that the warrior ladies were like the queen, and the scholarly ladies were like herself.

It was true that the queen was no scholar. Left to her own devices she wouldn't choose to read. Yet because of Lady Alice she knew so much now, about so many books.

There were also the ladies of constant love and great virtue, Lady Alice had said, but they were very dull. Neither she nor the queen was like them. And she'd smiled her secret, amused smile which was almost sly.

Remembering this, the queen could feel a tightness in her throat. But she wouldn't cry, because there was no reason for it. Lady Alice was old, after all. And no friend, as she had already reminded herself. Yet there were the bonds of daily companionship. And the old friendship that had existed once.

The Bible she'd brought with her lay heavily in her lap. Lady Alice had preferred to read classical works.

The queen looked down at it. There was a silk thread in it, marking the story of Ruth.

'Go on,' Joan said. 'She can hear you, you know.' Then she went to fill the basin with water.

How did she know? the queen thought. It was always said hearing was the last sense to go, but how could anyone actually know such a thing? All those men lying on the battlefields – what was the last sound they heard? What was the last sound her son had heard?

Margaret of Anjou blinked hard and looked up, at the phials and bowls, the towels, the sheet of paper on the small table with the magnifying glass Lady Alice now used rather than her spectacles.

All that knowledge and learning, what would happen to it now? Where would it go? Lady Alice wasn't famous like the scholarly ladies in Christine de Pizan's book, or like her grandfather, the poet. She would pass, and all her knowledge would pass with her, like rain into the sea.

Just as she thought this she glanced back towards Alice and was startled to find that her eyes had opened. She was staring directly at the queen.

There was a peculiar blankness in them, as though her soul had already left.

The queen couldn't speak. Then she said, 'Joan?' and, more urgently, 'Joan!' and Joan hurried over. She took one look at her mistress then ran to the door to give instructions to the little maid.

In moments the room was full of people. Margaret of Anjou moved away from the bed as they surrounded it: Lady Alice's steward, the doctor, the priest. A surgeon had come also, with the express intention of cutting Lady Alice's veins, and a quiet but fierce argument ensued with the doctor, who didn't think this was necessary.

When the queen caught Joan's eye the serving woman said, 'I should go, my lady. We'll deal with this now,' in her definite, unfrightened tones. And the queen didn't object, nor argue; she withdrew.

She went back to her own room and stood in the middle of it, as though waiting. She didn't want to sit or lie down; she couldn't think of anything she wanted to do.

Then she thought she would go into the garden.

There was no one to accompany her, no one watching her as she left, though she wasn't allowed out on her own. Usually, Lady Alice would accompany her. She felt a sense of unease as she turned the handle of the door and it opened, easily.

The garden was in brilliant motion. Light shivered from the leaves, glanced from the blades of grass.

Blow on my garden that its fragrance may spread abroad.

That was from the Song of Solomon. Which she knew, because Lady Alice had read it to her.

Even as she stepped into the garden, she could feel layers of apathy and numbness peeling away from her. She could feel the keenness of fear: *what would happen to her now?*

Her father had written to her. The fact that the letter had come through at all showed the extent to which the vigil over her had relaxed. He'd said everything was in turmoil in the French court, no one knew what to do. *But whatever happens, know you are always in our thoughts. I will keep sounding your name into your cousin's ear.*

She knew from long experience that Louis could turn deaf when it suited him. In any case, what could he do? She had no son for him to put on the throne. The people would never accept her as their queen.

In all probability, she would be kept by the English, but in closer custody than before. Perhaps she would be returned to the Tower.

She didn't want to go back to the Tower.

She passed through the garden, touching a flower here, a leaf there. It was May, and the blossom was at its most profuse.

She came upon a blackbird, bathing itself in a pool of light. Actually, of course, in a small pool of water on the path. Light skittered from its wings. At her approach it cocked its eye at her then flew off. And such a song poured from its throat that the queen knew without any doubt that Lady Alice had died.

She shouldn't be afraid. To all intents and purposes she'd been set free.

She stood absolutely still for a moment then, as the bird disappeared, apparently absorbed into the sky, continued her slow progress towards the river.

There it was, full of lights and shadows.

Sometimes small boats were moored there, for the servants' use. What was to stop her taking one of them, and rowing away?

No one was there. Everyone was preoccupied with Lady Alice. She could take one of the small boats and leave.

But go where? Do what? Would she row herself to the open sea, all the way back to France? Or follow the tangled banks back to London, where she would declare herself queen?

Or would she row to some unknown part of the country where no one knew her, and live a different kind of life? One in which she was no longer queen, had no history nor heritage, had never suffered the appalling pains of marriage or warfare, had never had her son?

She stood for several moments, gazing down at the swiftly flowing water. She was more than usually aware of her breathing, of the expansion and contraction of her lungs.

Four years ago she'd lost everything she had to lose. Often, she'd thought she'd died herself then, with her son and her husband and her cause, because what was left?

But who would she be without it all, without all the drama and disaster of her reign?

She realised at that moment that she wasn't free, not because she was in custody but because of who she was. Who was she if not the queen?

A long shudder passed through her body. She could see once more Alice's dead gaze, which seemed to bore straight through her, summing her up in a single stare.

She could give herself up to the river, to the fast-flowing currents of water, feel the suction of them pulling her under: *whither thou goest, I will go.*

For so long she'd felt herself close to death, wrapped in a cocoon of despair. Now here she was, keenly and terribly alive. She stood close to the banks of the river, aware not only of her own heartbeat but of the pulse of the world, how a single beat could alter everything.

Even as she stood there, she knew she would return. Freedom, with all its terror and joy, was not for her. She would go back to her room in the castle and wait for news of the war.

We hear that the king of France has bought, for 24 or 30 thousand crowns Queen Margaret of England, daughter of King Rene, widow of King Henry and prisoner of King Edward of England and has fetched her to France.

Milanese State Papers, 21 April 1476

8

The King's Heart

During May and June the king transported his whole army to Calais in splendid and impressive array.

Crowland Chronicle

At Picquigny the two kings met on a bridge over the river Somme, had a long talk together and finally concluded a truce for many years . . .

Polydore Vergil

Some at once began to cavil at this peace . . . others resorted to theft and pillage as a result of which no road throughout England was safe for merchants or pilgrims . . . Following his return the king himself was compelled together with his judges to journey round the kingdom sparing no one . . . from being hanged if they were found guilty of theft or murder . . . there is no doubt that there was deep anxiety in the king's heart over this state of affairs . . .

Crowland Chronicle

Overall, he was not dissatisfied with the outcome. He'd secured an income for his country, and a truce between his nation and its ancient enemies, France and Scotland, that included the marriages of two of his daughters. On his return that autumn his seventh child had been born, and he had immediately negotiated a match for her with the son of the Archduke of Austria, who would pay him the largest sum ever offered in such negotiations.

But the people didn't seem to understand what he'd achieved.

He'd had to suppress attacks on foreign merchants made by ignorant persons who couldn't see they were vital to the economy of the country, and to punish those who had resorted to theft or murder by way of protest. Presumably because they'd not been slaughtered in their thousands in France.

'You promised them one thing and delivered another,' his wife said. 'That's so unlike you,' she added.

But he hadn't deliberately set out to deceive them. If matters hadn't gone his way, he would have waged war. It was rather that his own private agenda was more complex than he cared to reveal.

'It won't come to war,' he'd said to his wife.

'You're taking twenty thousand troops to France, but not to war? You must be very sure of your welcome there.'

The king didn't answer. He preferred his wife not to ask political questions.

When he returned, she said, 'Congratulations, my lord, you've pulled the wool over everyone's eyes.' And he didn't bother to explain that this hadn't been his intention. Sometimes it seemed to him that his full intention – his secret heart – was hidden even from himself.

Still, he wasn't unhappy, though not wholly happy either. He didn't trust Louis for one thing. And there was all the unrest in the country for another. And, of course, there was Burgundy. His brother-in-law the duke was furious about the truce. Even his sister was angry with him. Now Duke Charles was waging his own war with France, but Edward had promised Louis that he would stay out of it. Or lose the pension and the truce.

So there was no pleasing everyone, it seemed. His experience of kingship made the process of winning the crown look simple by comparison. Now he had to win back the people.

He toured continuously. Whenever he was with the people, listening to their complaints and grievances, he could sense the restive quality in them calming. He tamed them as he would a young horse.

When he wasn't touring the country he was in the Westminster courts, sitting in judgement on a long train of complaints: land disputes, theft, drainage issues, trespass. All the surprising and wearing trivia, the anxieties and grudges that flourished whenever people were made to live together. They poured their complaints into the Great Hall and the noise increased steadily as the day wore on, to a cacophonous babble.

It was there he first met Elizabeth Shore.

She was known as Jane, in order, as he later discovered, to distinguish her from her mother and mother-in-law, both of whom were called Elizabeth. He was glad he didn't have to call her Elizabeth – there were more than enough Elizabeths in his life. He called her Jane. A single syllable, but imbued with such tenderness.

Jane.

Her petition had been presented unsuccessfully by her lawyers, so she'd turned up herself as witness. But the Dean of Arches was unsympathetic. Annulment, he told her, was granted only when the marriage had occurred between persons who were within the forbidden degree of affinity, or when there was known coercion, which was not the case here. And he told her further that hers was an impudent and immodest plea, and then he walked away from her. And so she followed him, all the way into the Great Hall, where few women went, past the Court of Common Pleas and Chancery, protesting that she only wanted a child, as was any woman's right. And the Dean of Arches turned on her finally in exasperation, saying that she could not put herself forward as witness in this brazen and presumptuous way. He would consider her case only if her husband himself came and bore witness, or at least was prepared to offer a statement witnessed by honourable persons who would testify that the document had been written by him in person with his own quill and ink.

And Mistress Shore, quite out of temper, replied, 'But, my lord, I have just told you his quill *has* no ink!'

And at that precise moment the cacophony in the Great Hall ceased, so that Mistress Shore's words reverberated around the walls, penetrating and shrill.

After a heartbeat's pause there was an eruption of laughter. Everyone present shouted with mirth, apart from the Dean, of course, who glared at Mistress Shore, and Mistress Shore herself, who reddened prettily and looked as if she didn't know whether to laugh or cry.

The king had just left the Great Hall, but he wanted to know the cause of the uproar. So Lord Hastings, who was familiar with the case, apprised him of the details.

And the king, who found it impossible to believe that a man would not bed a pretty woman, added his own guffaw to the general mirth and insisted on meeting the protagonist of this unusual case.

So Mistress Shore was escorted from the Great Hall, alarmed now and protesting that she'd done nothing wrong, into an inner or privy chamber, where the king awaited her.

Even as she sank to the floor in a curtsy, she was uneasy. She knew she should not be alone with the king.

The king himself felt that the occasion called for a degree of delicacy. Partly because of the information given to him by Hastings – that this lady was the daughter of John Lambert, who was one of the richest men in the city. The king knew him well, for Lambert had on several occasions loaned him money, most recently for the French expedition, and like the dutiful citizen that the king wished more of his subjects were, did not appear to expect it back. He'd lost his cloak of office in 1471, for supporting the king against the Earl of Warwick, so now he was one of the Four Wardens of the Holy Fellowship of Mercers, whose interests controlled the City of London. His wife had taken to calling herself Lady Lambert.

He'd married his daughter to William Shore, a mercer with whom he wanted to do business, when she was ten or eleven years old. She was certainly a virgin then and, if reports were true was still, though it was hard to believe a pretty woman in her mid-twenties would have no lovers. Still, it was another cause for delicacy, and so when the king raised her up from her curtsy he didn't lead her directly to his own couch but to an adjacent one, and suggested courteously she should put her case to him in person.

No one could listen so attentively as the king when he chose. He assisted her tactfully through the moments of difficulty caused by the intimate nature of the problem, while assessing the level of resistance he might have to overcome.

There was not usually much resistance. It had been all he could do, on his progress around the country, to prevent some women from breaking into his rooms. He was not averse to such behaviour; in fact, he took up as many of these offers as was practical. But it would be fair to say that over the years his attitude to such women had coarsened. Now he was rediscovering the charm of formal courtship, which led to the same outcome while protracting the enjoyment of both parties along the way.

Naturally, he didn't wish to protract it indefinitely. When Mistress Shore finished her account he told her there was nothing he could do about the judgement of the court, for not even the king was above the law. But about the other matter of her neglected bed, there was something he could do.

There was a certain kind of woman who routinely affected a show of virtue. He bedded one of them, whom he described as the *holiest harlot in the realm*. So he prepared himself now, with a degree of resignation, for the customary display of modesty. But Jane Shore's forehead crinkled attractively; the king could see she was thinking. When he asked her what she was thinking, she said, 'I'm thinking if there is something you can do, my lord, you should do it.'

Which made the king laugh for the second time that day, because it was going to be so simple, after all.

He made his first moves routinely enough, drawing her to him, loosening her gown, but then something else came over him. It was as though he was becoming more naked than she was, shedding layers of himself with his clothing.

So enchanted was he by this experience that he found he could not abandon William Shore's wife, as he'd abandoned many others. Indeed, for several weeks he could not get enough of her. In between encounters he pressed his lawyers to find some way out of her marriage settlement and then to dispose of her husband, not violently, but in some way that would enhance his professional standing and make it difficult for him to refuse.

For many he had but her he loved.

Thomas More

She was no more beautiful than his other women, there was no measurable difference in her skin, her hair, her female parts. It was perhaps only that she did not ask anything of him he could not give, but responded always to his presence with a simple joy.

Where the king took displeasure she would mitigate and appease his mind; where men were out of favour she would bring them into his grace. For many that had highly offended she obtained pardon, of great forfeitures she got man remission . . . Proper she was and fair, nothing in her body that you would have changed unless you would have wished her somewhat higher . . . yet men delighted not so much in her beauty as in her pleasant behaviour, for a proper wit had she and could both read well and write, merry in company, ready and quick of answer, neither mute nor full of babble . . .

Thomas More

9

Strategy

The king had been accumulating great riches and he spent a great part of them on the ceremonies accompanying the re-interment of his father Richard, late Duke of York [July 1476] . . .

Crowland Chronicle

As soon as possible he sent ambassadors [to the Duke of Brittany] laden down with a great weight of gold and to impart a more honourable face on his demand [King Edward] bid them declare to the duke that he was asking for Henry so he might join him to himself by kinship.

Polydore Vergil

I n October a letter arrived from his mother, instructing him not to return to England, no matter what offers were made. At least, that's what she seemed to be saying, but she expressed herself in such convoluted terms that he couldn't be sure:

I hope and pray daily that we will soon be reunited by the king's grace; prithee put your trust in this, yet be not persuaded by uncertain proposition into leaving your present secure abode . . .

But no one had asked him to leave his present abode. He'd been here for nearly three years now, without his uncle, and there was no sign of him ever leaving.

Then a few days later a letter arrived from the Breton court. It was so peremptory as to be almost an order. He was to be transferred under close guard to Saint-Malo.

He studied this letter while the woman in his bed got up and put her clothes on. The signature was not that of the duke, who had been ill, but of his treasurer, Pierre Landois, a pushy and scheming man.

Saint-Malo was the port.

He considered the reasons why he might be transferred to the port while the familiar qualms began in his belly.

He'd heard nothing from Jasper.

How did he know that the duke even knew of this plan?

The woman, Jeanne, paused in her dressing and asked him if he was all right. She had to ask him twice before he responded. Then she came and stood by him.

His guardian, Jean de Rieux, had taken care of his education in every sense.

One day he'd come back to his room after fencing, expecting to give the manservant instructions to prepare his bath. But it was a maid instead, stocky and short, with abundant dark hair.

She's not wearing a cap, he thought, as she smiled at him and fanned herself.

'It is hot in here, no?' she said, but he was too surprised to reply. He was more astonished when she undid the bodice of her gown, revealing her small breasts, which were pointed and brown-tipped. She came towards him and put a hand on his arm.

'My name is Suzanne,' she murmured into his ear. 'You would like me to prepare a bath for you, I think.'

Then she kissed his ear softly and put his hand on her waist, and in the following moments the sense of unreality faded from him. His life became vivid to him again.

But Suzanne had been sent away for stealing just two months into their liaison, if it could be called that. For a while he'd been attended by a large, raw-boned woman called Marie, who was probably twice his age but generous and good-natured. She'd disappeared one day, and no explanation had been offered. He would have protested more vigorously but, in the same week, Yvette had arrived.

He'd felt differently about her from the start. He liked her neatness, the way she would smooth her long hair back into two shining rolls after their lovemaking had disturbed it.

There was a quality of stillness in her face, something graceful in her collarbones or the small bones of her feet. He felt protective of her, though she was at least five years older than he was. For a while he thought about nothing and no one else.

He didn't ask her directly about herself but began to press the brothers Rieux for information. Which was how he discovered she was married.

The pain he'd felt on learning this surprised him. It was the most intense feeling he'd ever had.

Her husband was a builder who'd broken his back while trying to mend someone's roof and had not walked since. They had one child, a little girl called Charlotte, who was now looked after by her husband's family, while Yvette, in order to earn money, had gone into the household of Jean de Rieux.

They told him this, Jean de Rieux and his brother, over backgammon, and he'd suffered his unreasoning, intense pain. Yet he needed to know more. He asked François, casually, how he found her in bed, and François awkwardly shrugged. Of course, both brothers had had her.

After this he didn't feel the same way about her. Ever since he was a small boy he'd withdrawn instinctively from anything he felt was soiled or corrupt.

He knew that it was not, strictly speaking, her fault. He tried, out of a sense of justice, not to make his withdrawal too plain. And he went on using her, of course, since she went on presenting herself and no one else appeared to take her place. (And there was the sex itself, of course, that powerful hook, drawing him under, almost to the point of drowning.)

Then one day she'd gone, and did not return, and was replaced by this woman, Jeanne, who had paused in her dressing to ask if he was all right. And when he didn't answer she came and stood by him, without touching.

She, too, was not forward, not demanding. And she understood him well enough after all these months to know that he needed to be alone. 'What is it?' she said, and when he didn't reply she gathered up her remaining clothes and left.

He compared the two messages. His mother had added her usual expressions of affection to hers, saying that she lit a candle for him every day and kept one alight in her heart.

He couldn't remember her face. His time in England seemed so far away – even his time in Wales seemed remote, as though seen through the wrong end of a telescope. He walked over to the window, gazing at the view that was so familiar to him. The forest was in perpetual motion, like a small sea. He was almost able to predict which of the trees would go russet in turn, how the mood of the lake changed with the weather. In summer he'd swum with the brothers in the lake, and François had even taken him hunting through the forest.

He lived in an octagonal tower surrounded by forest, where Tristan and Iseult had fled together as lovers, where the Lady of the Lake had made her underwater home.

But it was an impregnable fortress, despite the fairy-tale setting. It was impossible to imagine anyone breaking down the doors or scaling the walls.

Once he'd had a dream that he'd stood at the base of the tower and shouted up the long, grey walls that seemed to go on for ever, into the sky.

But all that was about to change. And he didn't like change. In particular, he didn't like the change that was being proposed now. The wrongness of it struck him like an arrow in the throat.

Who could help him? The marshal was away, and in all probability would be able to tell him no more than the letter. François would know even less than the marshal, and he'd not heard from his uncle – had Jasper not received the same command?

No one could help him. He could only wait.

But he didn't have to wait long, because a few days after the letter the soldiers arrived.

Getting their hands on their prey, the ambassadors went happily to the seaside town of St Malo so that there they might board ship and sail to England. During the journey, Henry, well aware that he was being taken to his death, feigned illness.

Polydore Vergil

It was true that he didn't feel well.

He'd spent the whole journey in great agony of mind, wondering what manner of death awaited him; whether he would be secretly murdered en route like the Duke of Exeter, who had drowned on his way home from France, or whether he would be officially executed by the king. And if they did try to drown him, would he be able to hold his breath underwater while freeing himself from any ropes that bound him with his secret dagger?

He'd swum many times with the brothers in the lake, but he didn't know how far he could swim in the open sea.

But perhaps they would poison him. Or it could be a sword in the night.

They would have to make it look like an accident.

As he stepped on to the jetty he felt a sense of prohibition so strong he actually stumbled. Then he fell, clutching his head with a great cry, much to the consternation of his guards, who could only assume he'd been attacked.

Henry rolled upon the ground in apparent agony, and the guards drew their swords. Robert Stillington, Bishop of Bath and Wells, attempted to push through, crying, 'What is it?' and 'Stand clear!' And in the next moments a furious row broke out.

The captain of the ship said he wasn't paid to carry contagious persons on board, and Bishop Stillington, who'd been entrusted with this mission by the king, abused him roundly. Several men bent over Henry, but then more men ran up behind shouting, and in the chaos that followed Henry got to his feet.

Meanwhile Jean Quelennec ... a favourite of the duke ... returned to court ... He presented himself to the duke ... [and] said, 'Illustrious duke ... lately, heedless of your pledge, you have handed over Earl Henry of Richmond, an innocent young man, to butchers for the ... killing ... those who love you are not able to restrain their grief when they see that your famous name will forever be besmirched by such treachery.'

The duke, moved by these words, immediately sent his treasurer, Pierre Landais, to intercept Henry ...

Polydore Vergil

'This way! This way!' the men cried out to him, and Henry, recognising the duke's livery, ran. Through narrow, twisted streets and stinking alleys, through a labyrinth of close passageways, he ran with the guards, finally emerging into a great square, wherein rose the imposing façade of the Cathedral of St Vincent.

One of the men accompanying him pounded on the great doors, crying, 'Sanctuary!' The priest let them in with a furrowed expression because, for all he knew, they might be murderers. They followed him into the cool darkness of the interior, and he barred the doors behind them.

The townspeople, disturbed by all the shouting, flocked to the cathedral gates, bearing such weapons as they could carry. For the laws of Sanctuary were clear and, while they might be broken in England, that Godless country, in Brittany at least they would be upheld.

Such was the situation when Pierre Landais finally arrived. The English envoys and guards had stationed themselves outside the cathedral, Henry Tudor and the duke's own guards were locked inside and all the townspeople were gathered round.

Priests passed among them with communion wine and bread. Masses were sung. Food was smuggled in to the fugitives by a secret entrance. By which they could have left, of course, if the negotiations had not gone their way.

Bishop Stillington was aggravated in the extreme as Pierre Landais relayed his message from the duke. For the King of England had been seeking this prize for years, and he, Robert Stillington, had temporarily achieved it. He'd looked for an archbishopric at least.

But Landais stood firm, though he'd previously agreed to surrender Henry, and at last the English envoys realized they were beaten. They set sail from Saint-Malo without the precious cargo they had so nearly obtained.

The doors of the cathedral were opened and Henry and his guards came out. Everywhere he looked people were smiling and cheering. He felt moved, almost to tears, and relieved, for had he not been reprieved from certain death? He'd acted on his own instincts for the first time, and the outcome had been good.

Not long after, Pierre Landais brought him back to the duke . . . and King Edward . . . was exceedingly chagrined . . .

Polydore Vergil

King Louis sent his own envoys to Brittany to urge for the release of the Tudors in response to the news of Henry's narrow escape. King Edward at once sent a strongly worded message to Duke Francis, reminding him of his promises to England and the danger of breaking them. For if the hostages went to France Louis would use them for his own purposes and this would almost certainly mean war.

He almost felt inclined to declare war in any case, out of sheer frustration. But soon he was distracted by the conflicts in his own family.

10

Brothers

A fresh dispute arose between Edward IV and his brother Clarence, severely disrupting the glory of this most prudent king.

Crowland Chronicle

Clarence's wife, Isabel, gave birth to their fourth child that autumn, and swiftly went into a decline. She died on the Sunday before Christmas, her infant son soon following, and Clarence took this as badly as a man could.

She was buried in a vault in Tewkesbury Abbey. Her husband wept throughout the ceremony, though people said he was never as fond of her in life as in death. But in Clarence's mind this wasn't true; he'd always loved her. Until the last moment, he'd believed she would recover.

Clarence blamed his father-in-law, the Earl of Warwick, for the wreckage of his life, and his own brother, the Duke of Gloucester. Anne Neville had, earlier that year, given birth to a son who had survived. His brother and sister-in-law were now one step closer to the Warwick inheritance; they stood in the vaulted gloom of the abbey like two vultures, or effigies of avarice.

Their son was named Edward, after the king.

More than anyone, he blamed the king. Who was also present, with his wife, who was pregnant yet again. She wore a veil because she'd become somewhat swollen about the fingers and face and didn't like to be seen. People said she was too old for this new pregnancy, being now in her fortieth year, but Clarence had no doubt she would survive, like the breeding sow she was.

Veiled and hooded, she seemed to him like one of the Fates who presided over life and death. Beneath the shroud she was rejoicing, he was sure, at his misfortune. She had never liked him, or Isabel; had taken every opportunity to poison the king's mind against them both.

Not that the king had taken much persuading. He'd never forgiven Clarence for the rebellion with Warwick.

Or for being the next son in the family and his mother's favourite; younger and fitter than the king, who had run to seed.

They stood together in this sacred place that was itself tomblike and oppressive, with its massive pillars, its censorious angels peering down from the roof, the grotesque faces carved into the stone, while the priest expressed his regret at the passing of one so young, who had lived such a troubled life.

He glossed over what troubles there had been, but Clarence knew what people were saying, or thinking: that Isabel's life had been marred by the arrogance and discontent of two men, her father and her husband; that since the sins of the father fell on successive generations, no good would come of Clarence's line.

That was what he heard, while the priest spoke of Isabel's youth and piety and learning.

No one said of her that, as a child, she had loved to listen to Aesop's fables, and later had read the works of many poets, including Chaucer and Boccaccio. She was an accomplished lutenist and sometimes composed her own madrigals, though she could rarely be persuaded to sing them. She had always loved the colour lilac, but did not like eggs, and could not be made to eat them even when they were beaten into other foods to disguise them by her nurse.

Once, looking out of a window at a bird that was trilling its song, she thought she'd discovered the mystery of life: God's own secret purpose pumping through its tiny veins. But she kept this secret to herself, having learned to be demure.

Clarence was too overcome to vent his rage at the funeral, but soon afterwards he began to behave in a way that would inevitably provoke the king.

He sent back dishes ostentatiously, as though he feared they had been poisoned. In the privacy of his own home, he said there was nothing natural about his wife's death. She was only twenty-five and all through her pregnancy had been well, right up to giving birth. And even then she'd been healthy and happy in the first days, slipping only gradually into a decline.

It seemed to him obvious that a poisoner's hand was in this. Or was he to believe that God Himself had played a cruel trick, that his Heavenly Father had turned His back on him? Because Clarence was widowed, while the king, who spent so much of his time whoring, was still married. The king did not love his wife, for who could love such a malign vixen, who had more than once been accused of witchcraft?

Those who were with him would try to calm him when he spoke these words, ascribing them to drink. But he was like a man who walks perpetually with a sharp stone in his shoe, who might forget it intermittently, but not for long, because the pain only worsens over time.

Still, his grievance might have abated, if not for another event that rekindled it.

[After the Treaty of Picquigny] duke Charles [of Burgundy] waged war on the duchy of Lorraine, besieging Nancy . . . in the depths of winter with a few badly armed and ill-paid soldiers, many of whom were sick, while many leading officers were scheming against him . . . When the two armies met the duke's was immediately defeated and everyone was killed . . . [including] the Duke of Burgundy. This took place on 5th January 1477.

Philippe de Commines

Duke Charles had left only one daughter, Mary, and French law was plain:

Daughters should not inherit the kingdom in order to avoid it falling into the hands of a foreign prince ... for the French people would not tolerate it ...

Philippe de Commines

So the question of Mary's marriage now arose.

The duchess [of Burgundy] ... who was fonder of her brother Clarence than anyone else in the family devoted all her effort and attention to uniting in marriage Mary, only daughter and heiress of Charles, and the Duke of Clarence, whose wife had recently died.

Crowland Chronicle

Clarence was delighted, for it meant that he would have a new wife who was the greatest heiress in Europe, and he would rule his own nation, which occupied a position of strategic power between England and France. Furthermore, his sister was fulsome in her praise of her stepdaughter, saying that she was wise beyond her years and excellent in her disposition, with no false affectations or pride.

She didn't say she was beautiful, and Clarence had no clear memory of the duke's daughter, yet he didn't remember that she had a hump, or was disfigured in any other way, and she was in her twentieth year, which seemed to him to be an excellent age for marriage. He had discovered that he liked being married, that he missed the fact of it almost as much as he missed his wife. His mercurial spirits began to rise at this new prospect.

But King Edward had other ideas.

So exalted a destiny for an ungrateful brother displeased the king who therefore threw all possible obstacles in the way of such a marriage; rather he urged that the heiress should be given to Maximilian, the emperor's son ...

Crowland Chronicle

Neither would he consider an alternative match for Clarence, to the sister of the Scottish king, James III. It was plain to see that the king didn't want his brother to have any political power or status, except that which he gave him, in England.

Not even his mother could persuade him.

'George will marry someone,' Duchess Cecily said. 'If you won't let him choose, you had better choose for him.'

'There's no rush,' said the king. 'His wife has only just died.'

'If you don't want him to marry Mary of Burgundy,' his mother said, 'or Margaret of Scotland, you had better propose a different match. And explain to your sister why he can't marry her stepdaughter, who is the most eligible heiress in Europe.'

'You know who is behind this plan? Louis – as usual.'

'Why would Louis want to bring his two enemies together?'

'You've forgotten, Mother, that Louis doesn't think of Clarence as his enemy but as his pawn.'

'I have forgotten nothing,' his mother said sharply, for her son had hinted before that her faculties might be failing. '*You* have forgotten what caused all the previous trouble with the Earl of Warwick – that you wouldn't allow your brothers to marry his daughters. And look how that ended,' she added.

But Edward wouldn't be coerced into agreeing to a marriage that would give Clarence control over England's trade, her relations with France and even (possibly) the pension that Louis currently paid him. He was sure Louis was secretly in favour of a match between Clarence and Mary, even though he had recently proposed his own son as a husband for the Burgundian heiress.

This was despite the Treaty of Picquigny, which had agreed the betrothal of the Dauphin to King Edward's eldest daughter. And despite the fact that the Dauphin was only seven years old, Mary of Burgundy was obliged to consider the proposal. But the card Louis wanted to play was never the one on the table, and Edward was convinced that Clarence was Louis' hidden card.

Accordingly, King Edward dispatched his brother-in-law,

Anthony Woodville, whose own wife had recently died, as suitor to Mary of Burgundy, in a move that enraged Clarence.

Then he set about increasing his revenues against the possibility of war. He levied customs duties with such rigour that even the merchants who loved him complained. He resumed possession of many royal estates that had been granted to various nobles, including certain properties belonging to his brother, Clarence.

Clarence reacted so vehemently to this that people began to say he'd gone mad. He made open accusations against the queen, saying she had proposed her own brother for this marriage to Mary of Burgundy because of her great malice and jealousy of Clarence. He also said she was not the true wife of the king, because English law didn't permit kings to marry widows. Further, he alleged that the king was no true son of his father, and therefore he and all his brood were bastards.

Once the queen learned what was being said about her, she urged her husband to act, but he was loath to drag such scandalous accusations into the public sphere. He wouldn't acknowledge them by openly reprimanding his brother but waited for Clarence's overheated emotions to cool.

But they didn't cool so much as fester. For though Clarence was still one of the richest men in the country, he could see only what he had not. He had inherited half of the Warwick fortune, but only half, the rest of it being held by his brother Richard, and he had no prospect of marriage. So he was gratified when Mary of Burgundy rejected Anthony Woodville because he was only an earl, and when she turned down the proposal of the seven-year-old Dauphin, saying that what her country needed was not a child but a man who was capable of giving her children.

Then the Duke of Guelders was killed in an attack on Tournai, but still King Edward wouldn't consider Clarence as a possible suitor for the heiress. So Clarence chafed and brooded over his grievances. And when bells rang out across the nation and cannon were fired to celebrate the birth of a new prince in the king's household who was named George, in an attempt to appease him, he was not appeased. In fact, his feelings erupted with such acrimony that the earlier rumours of insanity seemed justified.

That year, the queen took into her service one Ankarette Twynyho, who had previously been in the service of Clarence's wife. The suspicion flared in Clarence's mind that the queen might have used this lady to accelerate his wife's death. And so he took action that was as vicious as it was prompt.

On Saturday, 12th April 1477, divers riotous persons to the number of four score came to Ankarette Twynyho's manor of Cayford about two o'clock in the afternoon, entered her house and carried her off . . . to [the Duke of Clarence in Warwick]. They took from her all her jewels money and goods and the duke kept Ankarette in prison until nine o'clock the next morning. They then caused her to be brought before justices of the peace and indicted of having at Warwick on 10th October 1476 given to the said Isabel, Duchess of Clarence, a venomous drink of ale mixed with poison of which she sickened until she died. The judges arraigned Ankarette and a jury appeared and found her guilty and it was determined that she should be drawn through the town to the gallows and hanged till she was dead . . .

Chancery Patent Rolls

This particular outrage so touched upon the queen's honour and reputation that she couldn't let it pass.

The queen remembered the insults to her family, and the calumnies with which she was reproached, namely that . . . she was not the legitimate wife of the king. Thus she was persuaded that her offspring by the king would never come to the throne unless the Duke of Clarence were removed.

Dominic Mancini

The king didn't want to aggravate her while she was recovering from the birth of their son, yet he still didn't want to prosecute Clarence directly. So in May he ordered the arrest of an Oxford clerk, Master John Stacey, together with John Burdet, who was a squire in the household of the Duke of Clarence, on suspicion of necromancy.

After rigorous examination Stacey confessed to casting the horoscopes of the king and the Prince of Wales in order to determine when they might die. And that the two men had moulded leaden images of King Edward and his son with murderous intent.

> Sentence of death was passed upon both by the King's Bench at Westminster in the presence of almost all the lords temporal of the kingdom, as well as the judges. They were drawn to the gallows at Tyburn where they were permitted briefly to say anything they wanted before being put to death. They protested their innocence, Stacey indeed but faintly, while Burdet spoke many words with great spirit, finally exclaiming 'Behold! I die, though I have done none of these things.' Next day the Duke of Clarence came to the council chamber at Westminster . . .
>
> *Crowland Chronicle*

He burst in with a preacher, Dr William Goddard, who read Burdet's statement of innocence aloud.

They were ushered out, of course, Clarence denouncing the judges and crying fiercely that the king meant to consume him *as a candle consumeth in burning, whereof he would in brief time requite him.*

Fortunately, the king was not present, having left on the previous day for Windsor. But when he heard the news he returned at once to Westminster and summoned his brother to appear.

Clarence didn't obey immediately, but ordered all his retainers to be ready within an hour's notice to wage war against the king.

So when his brother finally appeared before him the king's rage was terrible to see.

> There in the presence of the mayor and aldermen of the city of London the king from his own lips began to inveigh forcefully against the duke's conduct as if he were in contempt of the law of the land and a great threat to the kingdom . . .
>
> *Crowland Chronicle*

He kept up his tirade for more than twenty minutes, and Clarence's famous eloquence did not avail.

'Can I not speak?' he said. 'Can I not be heard?'

But the king's words rolled towards him like boulders, crushing all resistance. At the end he was silent as the formal indictment was read out. And he was taken directly from Westminster to imprisonment in the Tower.

II

Cecily, Duchess of York, Seeks Audience with the King

'Edward,' she said, and he waited, knowing full well what she wanted to say.

'Edward – he is your brother.'

'Perhaps you could remind him of that.'

'He knows – Edward – he knows he's acted wrongly.'

'Wrongly? Or treasonably?'

'He . . . is grieving . . . he's not been right since the death of his wife.'

'He's not *been right* since I took the throne.'

'Yet he has served you well on many occasions.'

'He's served me ill on many more occasions. And you know this.'

'I know he's done wrong, but –'

'But yet you speak for him. You've always spoken for him, Mother, though God knows he can speak for himself.'

'I told you,' she said, nodding. 'I told you he needed to marry again.'

Edward stood swiftly, in a surprisingly agile movement for a man of his size.

'You told me,' he said, advancing towards her, 'your king, to defer to my brother, who would be king. His words in your mouth.'

'That's not *true*,' she said. 'I've only tried to heal the rift between you.'

'Why do you not speak to him?' the king said, circling her. 'Why not speak to your other son, Clarence, who started this?'

'I have spoken to him,' she said, clasping her hands. 'When he rose in rebellion against you I went to him and begged him not to do it –'

'And yet he didn't listen,' the king said softly. 'Why do you think that is?'

The duchess twisted her hands together as if she would pull the ligaments apart.

'You mustn't destroy our family,' she said. 'Your father –'

'Don't bring my father into this,' Edward said, his voice rising. 'Do you think he would put up with this sedition? Do you not think he would see its cause – and stamp on it?'

Duchess Cecily could feel herself becoming short of breath. Her son stood so close that she could feel the heat of his rage, like a live coal that would burn through the fabric of her family and everything she had. Her joints were stiff, but still she got clumsily to her knees.

'Do not do this,' she said.

Edward reached down and took hold of her arm, exerting pressure so that she was raised again, irresistibly, until her face was close to his own.

'One of your sons will destroy the other,' he said softly. 'Who will it be, Mother? You choose.'

But the duchess couldn't find enough breath to reply.

Yet it could not but affect him to see his mother, who had once defied an entire army at Ludford Bridge, leaving the room like an old, bent woman. So for a while he did nothing about his brother, leaving him to contemplate his crimes in the Tower. But this didn't please his wife. The queen said he was weak, or spending too much time with his whore to attend to the insignificant matter of the kingdom.

He said, of course, that it wasn't true. And if he was spending more time with another it was because she asked nothing of him but gave all freely. To which the queen said it was easy to give something of so little worth, and in a moment it seemed as though the ground had shifted beneath them. They faced one another like wild beasts, glaring and panting, as though each were the other's enemy, and the king's face was congested as though it was the queen and not his brother he wished to kill.

But he wouldn't budge, and so the matter of Clarence was unresolved. And in the meantime Mary of Burgundy married the Archduke Maximilian of Austria. This didn't please the French king, Louis, who immediately waged war against them both. Which distracted the English people from the strife within their own royal family; and to distract them further the king arranged for the marriage ceremony between his second son, Richard (now Duke of York) and Anne Mowbray, heiress of the Duke of Norfolk, to take place in St Stephen's Chapel, Westminster, on 15 January 1478.

The little bride, aged six, and the groom, aged four, smiled sweetly at one another throughout the ceremony. The bride wore white cloth of gold embroidered with seed pearls and was led from the Queen's chamber at Westminster by the queen's brother, Anthony Woodville, Earl Rivers, then into St Stephen's Chapel by John de la Pole, who was married to the king's sister, and Henry, Duke of Buckingham, who was married to the queen's sister.

(Margaret Beaufort, who had once been married at a similar tender age to John de la Pole, was also there. She stood, very neat and erect, next to her husband, Lord Stanley, and did not catch the eye of John de la Pole, and he did not catch hers.)

After the ceremony came the jousting and feasting, and the Duke of Gloucester cast gold coins among the common people so that they quite forgot the long shadow caused by the absence of the Duke of Clarence.

But the following day, while all the celebrations continued, King Edward opened Parliament and Clarence was brought in.

He looked thinner and shabbier after six months of imprisonment, yet still handsome and still with that defiant air. There was the suggestion of a smile on his lips, which faltered when he saw the number of his enemies who were ranged against him in that room. Then his gaze was drawn irresistibly towards the king.

> The mind recoils from describing what happened next . . . so sad was the dispute between two brothers of such noble character. For no one argued against the duke except the king, no one answered the king except the duke . . . [who] denied all charges, offering, if it were acceptable, to uphold his case by personal combat.
>
> *Crowland Chronicle*

No one laughed, but the silence that greeted this proposal seemed imbued with contempt, as if he had just said the most foolish of all the many foolish things he had ever said. The king barely paused, but went on with his pronouncements, saying

> He had ever loved and cherished the Duke of Clarence as tenderly or kindly as ever creature might his natural brother . . . giving him so large a portion of possessions that seldom hath been seen. The duke for all this no love increasing but rather growing daily more malicious, conspired new treasons, falsely and traitorously intending the destruction and disinheriting of the king and his issue, and the subversion of all politic rule of his realm . . . fully intending to exalt himself and his heirs to the regality and crown of England . . . For which . . . causes the king . . . ordains, enacts and establishes that the said George, Duke of Clarence, be convicted and attainted of High Treason.
>
> *Rotuli Parliamentorum*, January 1478

There was nothing he could say, nothing he was allowed to say. It seemed to him that his words, however eloquent, had never had any substance with the king, who, by the simple act of not listening to him, had rendered him less than human, like any dumb creature braying out its pain. So he gave up the attempt to speak and the petulant expression on his face was replaced by a wary, haunted look.

The king's voice, by contrast, conveyed an implacable finality. When he had finished, the silence in the room was palpable, and the only answer Clarence made was to clap his hands over his ears in a symbolic gesture as he was led away.

12

Richard, Duke of Gloucester, Seeks Audience with the King

He stood stiff and erect, as was his habit when nervous. For while he was famously brave on the battlefield, nothing there had terrified him as much as the situation he was facing now.

The king sat before him impassively, but it was plain he'd been drinking. He invited his younger brother to join him in a goblet of wine.

'A toast,' he said, 'to our family.'

A small contraction passed over Richard's face. He neither accepted nor refused but allowed the wine to be brought in then did not touch it.

'Brother,' he said, renouncing all formality, 'I am almost out of words.'

'Wine will help,' said the king.

Richard didn't like the mood his brother was in. It had a feral quality, as though it could be tipped over rapidly into rage. But while he knew his brother wouldn't be receptive to what he had to say, he knew he had to speak. 'You've asked me to pass sentence on my brother,' he said. 'But I can't do it.'

'Of course you can,' said the king. 'You are Steward of England, are you not?'

'No,' said Richard. 'I mean, I will not do it.'

'You will not?' said the king.

'I can't be the one to pass sentence of death on my brother.'

He waited for the eruption, but the king began to laugh. Tears of mirth came into his eyes, while Richard looked at him, unsmiling.

'Do you think – if you don't say it – it won't happen?' sputtered the king. Then, calming himself, he said, 'You've been listening to our mother.'

'I've been listening to no one,' Richard said. 'It's obvious to me, as it should be to you, that I cannot do this.'

Now the king was serious, his eyes narrowing until they almost disappeared in the folds of his face.

'It's obvious to me that you should stand with me,' he said. 'Do you think you can save him?'

'No,' said Richard, 'you can.'

'Why would I do that?'

'You could grant him a reprieve – commute his sentence to long-term imprisonment – it's been done before. The people would approve.'

'The people? Yes – he has a way with them.'

'They know he's acted badly – many times. But they will not approve of one brother killing another.'

The king nodded. 'You are quick to forget your injuries,' he said.

'I forget nothing,' said Richard. 'For all I care you can keep him in prison until he dies. But you should not commit fratricide. Leave him in there,' he said. 'Let him rot.'

'And let my enemies gather round him? Let him conspire with the king of France once more? Let them say he is the rightful king – when has that happened before? Ah yes,' he cried, clapping a hand to his forehead. 'When Clarence and Warwick freed King Henry!'

'That won't happen –'

'No, it won't,' said the king. 'Because I will have him executed – whether you stand by me or not. But remember,' he said, wagging a finger, 'if he doesn't die, you'll have all the longer to wait for your inheritance.'

Richard of Gloucester stood rigid with hostility.

'You are my brother,' he said, 'and I will stand with you, as I have done before. But you can't expect me to do this, or approve. You've been listening to other persuaders, and not your own family.'

The king knew the young duke was referring to his wife, and to the rest of the Woodville clan, but he didn't speak, because it was enough that he'd accused one brother of treason without falling out with the other. He turned his bloodshot eyes away.

'I'll see what I can do,' he muttered, and the Duke of Gloucester left the room.

Parliament formally condemned the Duke of Clarence, the sentence being pronounced by the mouth of Henry Duke of Buckingham, newly created Steward of England for the occasion. Afterward, the execution was delayed for some time.

Crowland Chronicle

In the end the Speaker at Parliament demanded that *what was to be done should be done at once*, and a deputation of ministers went to the king to request him to act.

The king had just received a letter from his mother, begging him once again to commute the sentence or, if he would not, to change it from the full horror of a traitor's death, if he had any love or respect for his mother, his family or God. She further exhorted that the execution should take place in private to avoid some of the scandal that would attach itself to fratricide.

She made him angry, his mother, by her refusal to take his side. In this extraordinary situation many things had become exposed, like the bones of a carcass exposed to the elements. It was obvious to him which side his family were on, and which side his wife's family were on. And he was strung between them like a man tied to wild horses. No one considered his feelings, that he had been put in this impossible position by a brother who would never be content while he was king.

If Clarence was king, would his mother take Edward's side? He didn't think so.

So he pressed the quill into the paper heavily, then restrained himself, and wrote, with commendable formality, that Clarence could choose his own method of execution, but it would take place that week.

13
Duchess Cecily Visits Her Son

The words fell like hail on her heart. She sat holding the letter for a long time, not looking at it, staring at the wall.

So it has come to this, she thought, and then she could think nothing else. All she knew was that she would take the message to her younger son herself.

Clarence had started drinking early. He had a bright, hard air like a diamond when he greeted his mother, and was mocking and witty in the old way. But Cecily made him sit down and held his hands as she delivered the king's message.

His mouth twisted momentarily. Then he said he would like to be drowned in a cask of his favourite wine, so at least he could take some pleasure from his death.

He said this as a joke, but his mother closed her eyes and began to weep.

His mother, who was as stern as a rock.

As he stared at her his heart began to pound erratically and his mouth went dry. He tried to free his hands but she was holding them too tightly. And at last, in a kind of bewilderment, he leaned forward and laid his head on her shoulder. And there they stayed for a long time, too overcome by grief to speak.

[On 18 February 1478] George, Duke of Clarence, brother to the king was . . . put secretly to death within the Tower and as the fame ran, drowned in a barrel of malmsey.

Great Chronicle of London

He was given a noble funeral and a beautiful tomb in Tewkesbury Abbey, surmounted by effigies of the young duke and his

118

wife. The king paid for this, and his brother Richard set up chantries so that prayers could be said in perpetuity for Clarence, and for all his dead siblings.

Clarence's two children were taken to Sheen to be brought up in the royal household. Custody of his young son, Edward, was given to the queen's son Thomas, Marquis of Dorset, who received several of Clarence's more lucrative estates, including Tewkesbury. The rest of Clarence's estates, and the Warwick inheritance, went to his brother Richard, whose son was created Earl of Salisbury, though this did not appease him.

> Thereafter he came very seldom to court, but remained on his own estates.
>
> *Dominic Mancini*

Duchess Cecily secured the custody of Clarence's little daughter, Margaret, but afterwards retired, suffering from an unspecified illness, to her rooms at Berkhamsted for the rest of the winter.

> As for the king himself, he very often repented privately of what he had done.
>
> *Crowland Chronicle*

Sometimes he woke, moaning in distress from the old dream, in which he had killed his cousin, King Henry, by creeping up on him from behind. The third blow would cause him to cry out and wake.

He couldn't speak of this to his wife, who would react with scorn, but if he was with Mistress Shore she would hold him and comfort him in the way she knew, with her body. She would tell him it wasn't his fault, he'd only done what he had to, what any king would do. And the king listened to her and was soothed, not only by the words themselves but by the sound of them murmuring in his ear. And by the closeness of her, the distinctive smell of her body, the feel of her flesh.

14

Repercussions

Following this deed many people deserted King Edward . . .

Crowland Chronicle

Just as a rock striking glass causes fractures to spread away from the centre of impact, so Clarence's death caused fissures throughout the nation. Such a rift had appeared in the House of York that people wondered whether it might not fall apart. Whichever way you looked at it, one brother had killed another and the third had absented himself from court.

King Edward ate and drank even more excessively than before and his appearance became bloated rather than merely corpulent.

> He was prone to violent outbursts . . . [and] was wont to cry out in a rage 'O unfortunate brother, for whose life no man in this world would once make request,' affirming that [Clarence] had been cast away by envy of the nobility . . .
>
> *Polydore Vergil*

Many, he said (meaning his wife), had urged him on in order to further their own ends, with no regard for his own suffering or the consequences of such an act.

In one of these moods he had Robert Stillington, Bishop of Bath and Wells, suddenly arrested on no particular charge, other than that it was said he had *violated his oath of fidelity by some utterance prejudicial to the king.*

No one knew what this utterance might have been, and the bishop himself vigorously protested his innocence, yet everyone knew he had failed to deliver Henry Tudor to the king. Also, his diocese bordered on lands belonging to the Duke of Clarence, so some said he was accused of intriguing with the duke, others that he was one of those who had urged the king to kill him.

Whatever the case, Stillington remained in prison for some months and was only released on payment of a large fine.

But an attack of plague sweeping through London that winter drove this episode from people's minds. They said it was retribution for the death of Clarence, for it pursued the royal family into the country, striking the king's youngest son, George, who followed his uncle into the Fields of Asphodel. Much to the distress of the queen, who, as everyone knew, had been the primary instigator of Clarence's death. It was widely rumoured that the king's two remaining sons would be picked off also, one by one. Then in August 1479 the queen gave birth to another daughter, which seemed to confirm God's displeasure.

But the plague passed and the princes survived. France did not invade Burgundy. And the House of York, which had been so severely rocked, was to all intents and purposes stable once more. Until the war with Scotland began.

> The Scots shamelessly broke the thirty years' truce we had made with them, in spite of the fact that King Edward had long paid a yearly sum of one thousand marks by way of dowry for Cecily, one of his daughters who had earlier been promised in marriage to the eldest son of the king of the Scots. In consequence of this, Edward proclaimed a terrible and destructive war against the Scots and the entire command of the army was given to Richard, Duke of Gloucester.
>
> *Crowland Chronicle*

Rumours grew that the French king had provoked this war and was in league with the Duke of Albany, brother of the Scottish king.

It continued throughout the year. And nothing was achieved on either side. But towards the end of that turbulent year 1480, Queen Elizabeth gave birth once more.

15

Margaret Beaufort Receives an Invitation

S he broke the seal in the presence of the messenger, who waited with a neutral expression on his face. Then she read the words twice.

She was invited to the christening of the king's youngest child.

She could feel heat in her face; all her blood seemed to have rushed to her head.

The messenger was looking directly at her. God only knew what he was thinking.

But he was a messenger; it wasn't his place to think anything.

She sent him into the kitchen to eat then sat down at the table to read the message again. She was being invited not only to the christening but to carry the child during the ceremony.

She'd thought it would be another message about her son, but this was an honour, a definite mark of favour. She'd been invited to other occasions, of course, as Stanley's wife, but this invitation was for her alone.

The letter went on to say that the child wasn't born yet, but would be christened immediately after birth. So she was required to stay near the queen at Eltham, to be ready for the ceremony.

She would have to pack and leave.

What should she pack? Who else would be there?

Suppose something happened at the birth?

Birth was always a risky procedure, especially at the queen's age. But she'd had enough practice. If anything, she seemed to be getting more fertile with age. Her previous child, Catherine, was barely a year old.

But perhaps she should pack mourning clothes, just in case.

She couldn't risk anyone seeing she'd packed mourning clothes.

Her mind was running on. And she had to reply to the invitation. She rose and got herself some paper and a quill.

It is a very great honour, she wrote, then crossed it out. *I am overwhelmed*, she wrote, then crossed that out also.

She would have to spend some time in close proximity to the queen. Would the queen try to speak to her about her son? Surely she would have other things on her mind.

I am most sensible of the honour bestowed upon me, she wrote, and considered crossing that out also. But she would go through a whole sheaf of paper at this rate. And she couldn't keep the messenger waiting for ever. All she had to do was accept.

So she wrote a few lines and gave them to the messenger and then summoned her steward and her ladies to tell them to prepare for a move to her London home. Her earlier feelings of excitement and relief were replaced by a sense of apprehension. It was never safe, after all, to be at court.

In London she received news that the queen had given birth to yet another daughter. She travelled at once to Eltham for the christening, and as soon as she arrived she was summoned to the queen. Apparently, she was to see the new baby before the ceremony.

As she entered the room Margaret could smell, beneath the lavender and rosewater, the faint odour of carnage from the birth. The queen sat up in her bed, wrapped in a shawl of fine cambric and lace. She looked exhausted; there were purple shadows beneath the hooded eyes. But her voice was steady enough.

'Countess,' she said as Margaret rose from her curtsy, 'I have another daughter to christen.'

What was she supposed to say to that?

'Your majesty has been blessed with many children,' she said, approaching the bed. *Unlike some of us*, she might have added.

Just for a moment she thought she saw a flicker of humour in the queen's eyes, but she couldn't be sure because the queen shifted uncomfortably and one of her ladies hurried to adjust the covers.

'The child,' she said, without looking specifically in any direction, and another lady handed Margaret a tiny bundle.

Black hair, was her first thought, because all the king's children were fair. But then babies often lost their hair, there was nothing so unusual in that. At the queen's nod, she sat in the chair vacated by the child's nurse, adjusted herself and prepared to make all the usual comments. Then she looked down into the tiny, wizened face.

Margaret knew that newborn babies could not focus properly. Yet in that moment she could have sworn that the baby's eyes looked directly into hers. Her mouth formed a tiny 'O'.

'Oh,' Margaret said.

It all came back to her: holding her own baby, those filmy eyes that still seemed to be underwater, the pink ridge of gum.

She felt a tugging sensation in her stomach and at the same time a peculiar hollowness. She saw the miracle of this baby girl, who had budded into herself in the confinement of her mother's womb, then emerged into the immensity of the world.

Anything at all could happen to her.

She'd seen babies before, of course; all the new arrivals in her own family, or her husbands' or her tenants'. But now, when she needed to speak, she couldn't.

Everyone was waiting for her.

'It's a miracle,' she whispered.

'Hnnh,' said the queen, and Margaret knew that, for her, this twelfth child was nothing of the kind. Because she wasn't a boy.

'She's beautiful,' Margaret said, and the queen said, 'Yes,' in a dispirited way, but Margaret meant it. She'd not held anything as beautiful since her own baby son.

'She will be christened this afternoon, in the chapel,' said the queen, and Margaret remembered to enquire about her name.

'Bridget,' the queen said.

'Brigitte,' said Margaret, thinking of the Swedish saint.

'Bridget,' said the queen.

She seemed tired by the meeting already, and Margaret prepared to rise, to hand the baby back, then felt compelled to say, 'It's a great blessing to have a child.'

'Yet you didn't have any more,' said the queen.

'I've not been as blessed as your majesty,' Margaret said.

'Still, you have a son. And he is well, is he not?'

Margaret hadn't intended to draw attention to her son.

'I – do not see him –'

'No,' said the queen. 'It's a pity he's still in exile. The king, my husband, would welcome his return.'

'As would I, your grace.'

'How old is he now?'

'He will be twenty-four in January.'

'And still not married?'

The queen knew perfectly well that he wasn't married. She continued, 'That's why my husband would like to bring him back. To discuss a marriage for him.'

'Yes, your grace.'

All her muscles had stiffened. She looked down at the infant Bridget so that the queen wouldn't see the look of extreme wariness in her eyes.

'Still – he's away. And I have so many unmarried daughters.'

Margaret's heart quickened. But all the king's daughters were betrothed. Surely she couldn't be talking about the baby?

There was the war with Scotland, of course, which would affect the betrothal between the third daughter, Cecily, and the King of Scotland's son. And since that war was said to be instigated by King Louis, where did that leave the oldest daughter, Princess Elizabeth, who was betrothed to the Dauphin?

But how many times had this question of her son's marriage come up? Always with hints and innuendoes, never promises or contracts. She murmured something inconsequential about how they could all only wait for God's plan to unfold.

'Or the king's,' said the queen, but Margaret was wary of further discussion. Bridget's nurse stepped forward, and Margaret rose.

'I don't want to tire you, my lady,' she said. 'You're doing so wonderfully well.'

For a moment she thought the queen would say something else. But she had other people to see, so she nodded, and Margaret was able to curtsy and leave.

The ceremony was as grand as England had come to expect from the king. A hundred knights carrying torches were led by the Earl of Northumberland, who had temporarily returned from fighting the Scots. The queen's brother-in-law Lord Maltravers carried a basin, and the Earl of Lincoln, oldest son of Margaret's first husband, John de la Pole, carried the salt.

Duchess Cecily stood with the queen's eldest daughter and the Bishop of Chichester by the font.

Margaret carried the infant Bridget. There was no reason at all why she should drop the baby or trip up. She approached with slow and regular steps, beneath a canopy of cloth of gold. *I will not stumble, I will not fall.*

She passed her husband, Lord Stanley, who stood with Lord Hastings and Lord Dacre, and progressed safely to the font, standing between Lady Maltravers and the Earl of Lincoln.

How many children did John de la Pole have now? Lady Maltravers had at least as many as her sister the queen. Lord Dacre and Lord Hastings both had large families. And Duchess Cecily, of course.

The Bishop of Chichester was holding out his arms for the child. And for one moment Margaret didn't want to give her up, this small, unwanted girl. But the bishop took her and Margaret let her arms drop, empty.

He placed salt in the baby's mouth to preserve her soul, wet her ears and mouth with saliva, smeared oil on her breast and back then dipped her three times in the water, on the right side, then the left, then face down. By which time, of course, she was no longer asleep but squealing.

The bishop raised his voice over the child's cries, pronouncing the holy words, and all the torches were lit.

At the feast Margaret sat between Lady Maltravers and Duchess Cecily.

'It's such an honour,' she kept saying, especially to Lady Maltravers, who might have thought she should be the one to carry the baby.

'It's a great honour,' Margaret said to the duchess, who treated her to her dismissive stare. 'It must be wonderful for you to see your family growing,' she went on, then remembered the Duke of Clarence. But Cecily only said, 'My daughter-in-law is famously fertile.'

There are worse things to be famous for, Margaret thought, and just prevented herself from saying the words aloud.

Many dishes were brought in, and she carefully sampled each one. It wouldn't do to refuse the king's food, as Clarence had done. But she couldn't manage more than a spoonful of each.

'Are you watching your figure?' the duchess enquired with some irony, since Margaret was the thinnest person there.

'No, my lady – it is just . . . such a very great honour.'

Cecily stared at her. 'I know. You said.'

Margaret felt a tinge of heat in her face. She sounded like a parrot; *such an honour, such an honour*.

Still, it was the safest thing to say.

'Another daughter, another marriage to arrange,' Lady Maltravers said; and Margaret said, 'There are worse problems.'

What was happening to her? Had she forgotten how to behave?

Diagonally opposite to her was the Princess Elizabeth, whom she watched surreptitiously. She was pretty, of course, with long, gilt-blond hair. Her face had already acquired that mask-like qual-ity common to courtiers, though she was only fourteen. Or courtesans, she thought, watching her smile at the Bishop of Chichester. She tilted her head archly at him, laughed a practised laugh.

Then when she thought no one was observing her she became closed and secretive again, almost sullen, her eyes hooded, though not so heavy-lidded as her mother's.

Would this girl marry Henry? Margaret thought, and, in the same instant, *I don't like her.*

She hadn't liked Maud Herbert either, but at least she'd been more transparent.

There would be no point refusing such a match, of course. It would enable her son to return. It would make Margaret one of the first ladies of the land.

Doubtlessly, the girl would breed well, like her mother.

But in any case it wouldn't happen – she was only dreaming.

Duchess Cecily rose between courses, leaving the seat next to Margaret vacant. And Margaret was roused out of her dream when her husband sat next to her.

'You're unnaturally quiet,' he said. 'Have you forgotten how to flatter everyone?'

She straightened, moving slightly away from him. 'Ah, Thomas,' she said. 'I see you've managed to avoid fighting the Scots.'

'And will continue to do so,' he said, gesturing for more wine, 'for the king needs me here.'

'Still, you might want to protect your estates in the north.'

'Luckily, the Scots have not found them yet.'

'How fortunate for you,' she said. Then added, 'I spoke to the queen today.'

'That must have been enlivening.'

'She mentioned my son.'

'Yes,' said Thomas Stanley, smiling at the bishop.

'She said he should be brought back, to marry one of her daughters.'

'Yes,' said Stanley again. Margaret felt a prick of annoyance.

'What do you think?'

'Obviously, that would be a desirable outcome.'

'Not,' she said, lowering her voice, 'if it's a trap. Like last time.'

He said nothing.

'Well?' she said.

He helped himself to the platter of meat with his fingers, and chewed.

'Princess Elizabeth must marry someone,' he said, still chewing. 'They say the king may betroth Cecily to the King of Scotland's brother, who is fighting for the Scottish throne. And we are likely to fall out with King Louis. So Elizabeth will be free.'

They both looked at Elizabeth, who was smiling sweetly at her half-brother, the Marquis of Dorset.

'Will you speak to the king?' Margaret asked.

'Probably not.'

'Why?'

'The king will ask if he wants my advice.'

'But –'

'Certainly he's worried about Brittany,' her husband said. 'That's why he's arranged the marriage of his son to Duke Francis' daughter. And they say the duke is ill. So if the marriage goes ahead, the Prince of Wales will succeed him.'

'If the Prince of Wales becomes ruler of Brittany, there's no reason at all why the king wouldn't have my son executed.'

Stanley pulled his mouth down. 'I think he would rather find another solution,' he said, 'after Clarence.'

'You don't know that.'

'No,' he agreed. 'I don't.'

Impatient outbursts never worked with her husband. 'That's why we must act.'

'Or wait,' he said. 'If Louis sends more of his envoys there, the king will be forced to act. Surely you're used to waiting, by now,' he said.

She started to speak, but the duchess returned and he gave up his seat to her with all the usual pleasantries, and left.

She considered following, but it was pointless to press him. She would never know whether he would act on her behalf or not. If it wasn't to his advantage, he wouldn't act at all.

At such times she missed her third husband, Henry Stafford, who had at least been on her side. And Edmund, of course. If her son's father had still been alive, how different his life might have been. She remembered her son's birth, almost twenty-four years ago. The days of agony, the sense that she was splitting apart, passing beyond some threshold that her body could stand. And then what? Darkness and absence: that was all she remembered. It had haunted her ever since.

She would like to have said she'd seen or heard something to sustain her through the years of loss and deprivation that had followed. All the hours she'd spent on her knees – for what? That same darkness and absence that had failed to respond to her many pleas for her son to be returned.

You're used to waiting, her husband had said. She resented him saying it, but it was true. She'd spent her life waiting. And now, once more, there was nothing she could do but wait.

16

Waiting

She didn't appear to be waiting. She was perpetually busy, managing her husband's estates in the north and her own in the south, prosecuting her claims to land, supervising the building of bridges and walls and mills. She was present with her husband when his brother was made warden of the collegiate church in Manchester and donated handsomely to its repairs. She sent presents to the king's daughters Mary and Cecily when they were betrothed again that year, Mary to the King of Denmark and Cecily to the Duke of Albany, brother of the King of Scotland. And when at the end of 1481 little Anne Mowbray died just three years after her wedding to the king's son, she was one of the most conspicuous mourners.

That year the harvest was the worst she could remember. She had to open up her granaries and visit her tenants, who were afflicted by illness or bereavement, misfortune or despair. She listened to their supplications, their complaints, gave them bags of grain and medicines she'd concocted herself. She gave them messages of hope from the Bible; *not even a sparrow falls to the ground apart from the Father's will*, etc. though she was no longer sure she believed in the individual attention of God.

She left them, she believed, in a better condition than she'd found them, comforted or reconciled; *waiting for better things*, though it occurred to her that if we did not, as a species, wait, we would not despair. She herself prayed and waited, waited and prayed, nurturing her own despair.

Her tenants saw only a fine lady dispensing charity, which was what most people saw. She'd grown used to her solitary grief. Her heart had grown harder, perhaps, or shrunk. *Hope deferred maketh the heart sick.* Possibly her heart was sick; how would she know? Certainly, it had altered. Her face had altered also; aged, obviously, in the ten years since she'd seen her son. It was thinner from fasting, and lined. The bones of her skull showed through her flesh, which was sallow; on her worst days she looked like an effigy of death-in-life. She had long ago given up the thought that her features might mutate into beauty, but they had a certain distinction, she'd been told; intelligence, at least.

Her son, too, would have aged. Would she even recognise him now? And was the king too preoccupied by the murmurings against him, because of the war and the bad harvest, to remember what he'd said about Henry's return?

She couldn't know the answer to these questions. She could only fend off a brooding sadness, that wasn't despair, she told herself, but a response to the weather. She had to wait for the spring, when there would be some news, surely, some word from the king, because nothing else, she believed, could relieve her state of suspension.

And then her mother died.

She sat down suddenly on receiving the news, as though she had been winded. But swiftly she got up. There was so much to do.

The letter, which was from her half-brother Oliver St John, said that her mother would be buried in Wimborne Minster, next to Margaret's father.

Of course she would. She could not be buried with her third husband, who had been attainted. And her first husband had been buried in Rouen, Normandy. Whatever scandal was attached to her second husband, Margaret's father was the duke and Margaret's mother would be buried with him.

She made arrangements to travel south immediately.

Perversely after so much rain, the day of the funeral dawned bright and clear. Margaret stood with her family in the church.

Her head was bowed so no one could see she wasn't weeping. She focused on her knuckles and the grain of the wooden pew.

She felt alone. Her husband couldn't be there; he'd finally been sent to the Scottish war. Her son was in exile. Her brothers and sisters had their families around them; only she was alone.

The will had been read and Margaret had inherited more than any of her sisters; her son was specifically mentioned. Anyone would think she'd been specially favoured. Only she knew the truth. She'd spent so much time trying to win her mother's approval, win her heart. It wouldn't happen now. She'd lost her mother and she'd never known her father.

Thirty-eight years ago, her father had been buried here quietly, without ceremony. There was little to commemorate him apart from one small window depicting the Beaufort arms. A priest had been paid ten pence to say prayers for his soul. And the manner of his death had been kept secret so he could be buried at all.

She had never allowed herself to speculate about what he'd gone through, what had driven him to take his own life. Or what her mother had suffered afterwards. She had lost his second child, a son, who would have been Margaret's only full sibling.

How different Margaret's life would have been if her brother had survived. For one thing, he would have inherited the dukedom and all the estates.

She might not have been given away.

I didn't give you away, her mother said in her querulous voice. *It was the king who gave you to the Duke of Suffolk.*

They'd never discussed how she'd felt about that. Whether she'd felt ripped apart, as Margaret had when her own son was taken from her. But Margaret doubted it. Probably, it had been a relief – one less thing to think about.

It was the best possible outcome at the time, her mother said. *And you still stayed with me regularly – I made sure of that. As your father wished.*

She had all of eternity to complain to her second husband, and justify herself to him. But Margaret felt mortified that all the family could see how little there was here to commemorate them. She resolved to have a grand tomb built here, for the parents for whom she couldn't grieve.

When they arrived at the castle she'd inherited, rather than speak to the servants or tour the property she went straight to the rooms she'd stayed in as a child.

Various items were laid out for her there: some rings in a jewelled box, a parcel of tapestries that had belonged to her father and a book of hours from her mother. Her own birth was recorded in it: 31 May 1444. And almost exactly a year later, on 27 May 1444, her father's death.

John, Duke of Somerset, d. was all it said. Not in her mother's hand.

Who had recorded it? Had her mother been too stricken to write? That was something else she would never know.

Out of all of us you are most like her, her sister had said. Margaret hadn't said she was mistaken; she was nothing at all like her mother.

Her mother had once said she resembled her father. But that wasn't true either: she did not resemble him.

This book of hours had been commissioned by her father's father, apparently, and had passed to her mother on her father's death. She would keep it with the one she'd been given by Margaret of Anjou.

There was a woman who had suffered and lost. How could anyone bear such loss? At least she wasn't like Margaret of Anjou. Her son was alive.

But what did he have? His family line was blighted by disgrace, illegitimacy, suicide, execution. He was still known as the Earl of Richmond, but actually that title belonged to the Crown, to King Edward, who would sell it to the highest bidder. And while he was in exile he couldn't inherit anything from her mother.

But he wasn't dead yet, and neither was she. Their lives would carry on. They would carry on waiting.

Even as she thought this she had the strangest sensation that time was simultaneously rushing past and standing still. Thirty-nine years of her life had passed. Both of her parents were dead.

She felt a constriction in her chest. With an effort she made it to the open window, pressed her face against the cool stone, made herself breathe. All her waiting, all her preparation and planning, had led her to this. Nothing she'd wanted had come about.

Nothing would ever change, unless she changed it.

Not God, not that silent absence that had never responded to her prayers, but she, Margaret Beaufort, would have to change it.

She would get her son back, whatever it took.

17

Mediation

She wrote to the king and he wrote back. He would grant her an audience at Westminster on 3 June.

She was gratified but not surprised. She'd made her resolution and was shaping things according to it. She hadn't even prayed.

But before the meeting could occur, tragedy struck the royal family. The king's second daughter, Princess Mary, died at Greenwich of an unspecified illness. She was not yet fifteen years old.

Margaret was invited to the funeral, as was her husband, Lord Stanley, who returned from Scotland for the occasion. They were to meet the funeral train at Windsor, where Princess Mary would be buried in the chapel alongside her little brother George.

Neither the king nor queen was present. All close family had shut themselves away with their grief. Lord Dacre and the queen's sister, Lady Grey, represented the queen; Lord Stanley stood for the king.

Margaret knelt over her prayer book as though reflecting upon the young life wasted, the pretty girl so recently betrothed to the King of Denmark who would now know neither marriage nor motherhood.

Actually, she was praying that the king would keep his appointment with her.

After the service her husband took her arm. 'I believe you're hoping to see the king,' he said.

'I have an appointment,' she replied.

'His majesty may not be able to keep appointments now.'

Her stomach lurched. 'He hasn't cancelled it.'

'He's in mourning. And has other business to attend to.'

Margaret was briefly, intensely silent. Then she said, 'Has he said he will not see me?'

Thomas Stanley pursed his lips.

'Well, then,' she said, 'I'll stay in London until I hear otherwise.'

'I think you should return to Woking.'

Margaret tried to free her arm, but he was holding it more tightly than she liked.

'It would be better if you did not press your business upon him at this time,' he said. 'If you showed you were prepared to wait.'

She managed to disengage her arm. 'I've been waiting for more than twenty years,' she said, 'since my son was first taken from me. He at least got to see and know his daughter.'

'I hope you're not planning to say that.'

'Have you spoken to him?'

'No.'

'No, of course you have not.'

'I will speak to him if you like – to see if he feels able to have this meeting.'

'To put him off it, you mean.'

'I will advise the king in his best interests. As I always do.'

With some difficulty she reined in her rage. 'If I hear that the king won't go ahead with our meeting, I'll know who to thank.'

Why did I marry you? she thought.

Stanley's face didn't change, but there was a flicker of amusement in his eyes. 'I'm just saying that now might not be the best time to presume upon the king's favour.'

'When is there a good time?' she said. 'And when have you ever felt moved to speak on your stepson's behalf?'

The flicker of amusement had gone. 'I'm not your messenger,' he said. 'I speak to the king when he chooses. Do you think he wouldn't notice if I were merely the mouthpiece of my wife? He needs to know that I'm loyal to him, despite my marriage.'

He was referring, of course, to her history of opposition to the House of York, but she didn't flinch.

'Since you're not my mouthpiece, you have nothing to worry about,' she said. 'I will speak to the king with or without you.'

Stanley's face was expressionless now. 'Do as you please,' he said. *And take the consequences*, he did not add.

Outwardly calm but inwardly seething, she returned to her London house. And waited every day for the news that the king had cancelled their meeting. When it didn't come, she presented herself at Westminster on the morning of the third day of June.

As she neared the king's chambers her husband stepped forward.

'His majesty has sent me to escort you,' he said. The guard fell back.

'Lord Stanley,' she said, and did not add, *what are you doing here?* But he said, smiling, 'I thought it best to advise you before your meeting'; and she said, equally pleasantly, 'I don't need your advice.'

'Accept it, anyway. As a gift. I wouldn't like you to speak out of turn in the king's company.'

She looked at him with a measure of scorn. 'Is that it?' she said.

'It might be better if you allowed me to speak for you.'

'Why would I do that?'

'The king is used to dealing with me. He trusts me. I know the case better than anyone.'

'Except for me.'

'And the king.'

'The king does not know the depths of my grief – how often I have wept – how my heart has been tortured by fear and longing – how many hours I have fasted and prayed –'

'That's not relevant here,' Stanley said.

'Yes, it is,' she said, her voice rising in a whisper. 'It's relevant to me!'

'If you're not careful,' said Stanley, 'you will ruin any chance you have of seeing your son again.'

To her horror, she felt tears threatening. And she was just a few feet away from the king's door. It was so like Stanley to try to ruin this meeting even before it had begun. She blinked her tears back and controlled her voice.

'Why are you not in Scotland? Surely there's some trouble you can cause there?'

'Because I'm here, on your behalf, to speak for you.'

'To say what?'

'I will remind his grace that it's in his interests to welcome your son back into his family – for he *is* his family, and there's no Lancastrian cause now to threaten him. And even if there were, the best way to suppress it would be to marry your son into his own household.'

She said nothing, silenced by this unexpected reasoning.

'And I will say that, as a gesture of good faith, he should restore at least part of your son's inheritance – to prove that he will be treated well on his return.'

'I can say that.'

'But it would be better coming from me.'

It infuriated her that she couldn't find a flaw in his argument. Then she said, 'What about his father's legacy – that passed to the Duke of Clarence?'

'For God's sake, do not mention Clarence.'

'If I don't, who will? Clarence had Edmund's estates and title – and now he's dead. They should be returned to my son.'

'You see,' said Stanley, 'that's precisely what the king will not wish to hear.'

'I'm sure there are many things that the king does not *wish to hear*,' she said. 'So no one will say them – and nothing is ever done.'

They stood facing each other, she glaring at him, he with his usual inscrutable expression. Then he sighed. 'All I'm saying,' he said, 'is that you should not open old wounds; the king has had enough grief with the death of his daughter.'

Briefly she closed her eyes, then said, 'If there's one thing you might have learned about me during our years of marriage, it's that I'm not entirely stupid.'

'Well, then,' he said, 'let me speak to the king.'

And he took her arm and steered her to the door.

She felt a throb of fear as a groom opened it and said, 'My lady, the Countess of Richmond,' but she lifted her chin and walked in on her husband's arm.

At first she could only see the king, massive in his purple robes. She had last seen him at the funeral of Anne Mowbray, a little more than six months ago, but she was shocked by the sight of him now. At her funeral his great frame had seemed sufficient to carry his bulk, but now he'd turned into a mountain of flesh, sliding downwards into tight hose that seemed likely to burst.

She curtsied, lowering her eyes, because it wasn't permitted to stare at a king, but not before she'd seen him appraising her similarly, with those small eyes that had almost disappeared in their pockets of flesh.

He extended his hand to her. On each finger there was a jewelled ring, which must, she considered, have been specially enlarged for his fingers.

'You come at a difficult time, Countess,' he said. '*My heart is spent with sorrow and my years with sighing.*'

She knew the psalm, of course. It went on: *my strength faileth because of mine iniquity*, so she could hardly finish the quote for him. Instead, she said, '*The heart of the wise is in the house of mourning, but the heart of fools is in the house of mirth.*'

'Then I must be wise,' said the king, 'for I'm certainly in a house of mourning.'

Emboldened, she lifted her eyes and saw how puffy and swollen the king's were, still reddened. In a voice full of suppressed emotion she said, 'Your majesty – I beg you to allow me to offer my deepest condolences to you and to her majesty the queen. There are no words to express the pain of losing a dearly beloved child.'

A look of emotion passed across the king's face, but all he said was, 'Kind words, Countess. Perhaps we should concentrate, however, on more material affairs.'

And for the first time she noticed the other occupants of the room, who sat at a table in an alcove.

She was surprised to see Giovanni Gigli, the papal legate, John Alcock, Bishop of Worcester, and John Morton, Bishop of Ely, who gave her his brief, economical smile as she sat down.

There was a pile of paper in front of him. Behind them at a writing table, there was a clerk, preparing to take notes.

She could feel her heart thumping. This was indeed an official meeting; something of the greatest significance was about to occur.

Bishop Morton adjusted his spectacles, then placed one hand on the papers in front of him. 'Sire,' he said, 'I have all the documents here. If it pleases you, we can proceed.'

Two hours later she left the palace.

She climbed into her carriage, sat back and closed her eyes.

Many things had been agreed. The king had said many things.

The principal being that Henry would inherit all his grandmother's estates in full and a share of Margaret's other lands worth up to four hundred pounds a year on condition that he would return home from exile.

At this point she'd said, 'Ah, if only that could be!'

And the king had turned to her with a look of mild enquiry, while the clerk stopped taking notes and Stanley gave her a warning glare.

'Why should it not be?' said the king.

'There is nothing I desire more in the world.'

'Then our desires are one. It's my dearest wish that your son should be restored to my service.'

'He would be a good and faithful servant to your grace.'

'I believe it,' said the king. 'I know it to be true.'

'Your grace is so benevolent, so kind,' she said. 'Yet – there have been certain false and malicious rumours . . .'

'My lady wife speaks from a mother's susceptibility to groundless fears,' Stanley said.

'What rumours?' asked the king mildly.

'Oh, my lord,' she said, lowering her gaze, 'monstrous lies have been whispered into the ear of Duke Francis – that you intend to harm my son.'

In the pause that followed it was possible to hear a fly buzzing about the room. *She'd said too much*, she thought. She would get herself arrested and her son killed. But the king said, in the same mild tone, 'How could that be? Your son is of my own family, my own blood. How could I wish to harm my own household?'

There was a short pause, during which no one mentioned Clarence.

For God's sake, her husband had said, *do not mention Clarence*. She bowed her head. 'The Duke of Clarence holds the rest of my son's inheritance – his title, the honour of Richmond.'

'That is a different matter,' said Stanley, but Bishop Morton said, 'In fact, we could discuss it – the papers are all here.'

She sensed Stanley's surprise and was herself momentarily struck dumb. Then she said to the king, 'My son's father was never attainted. You yourself agreed as much when we met in Woking. His estates were never forfeit, though they were taken away. If they could also be restored to my son, then the rumour-mongers would be silenced.'

'His majesty does not have to justify himself,' Stanley said, and they glared at one another.

The king said, 'You may trust my good intentions towards

your son, Countess. Everything will be done for him on his return. But he must return.'

He went on to say that France was even now concluding a treaty with Burgundy, so Duke Francis had begged him to help. He was more than willing to grant assistance to Brittany but each time he had requested the return of her son and his uncle as a small gesture of goodwill, there had been no response, nothing. So now the king was turning to Lady Margaret. Because once the treaty was concluded, both Burgundy and Brittany would be trapped as flies in the French king's web, and surely she did not want her son to be trapped with them?

She was mesmerised by him, by his eloquence, and by the intensity of his gaze, which was fixed upon her as though she was a morsel of food on his plate he had neglected to devour.

'How many years has your son been in exile?' he murmured. 'Ten? Eleven?'

He knew, of course, exactly how long. 'You must miss him very much,' he said, 'and he you. And his own country. Is it not truly said that every man has two mothers – the woman who bore him, and his native land that has nurtured him?'

She had the measure of him, this overblown, scheming king. She raised her hand to her heart as if overwhelmed. 'Your grace is as wise as he is merciful,' she said. 'I know my son is only too anxious to return, to be restored to your favour and his full inheritance. And then, perhaps,' she said, 'he will be able to marry.'

'Again – that need not concern us here,' said Stanley.

But this issue had been raised in private between herself and the king; she wouldn't miss the opportunity of raising it publicly now.

'Of course he must be married,' said the king. 'We've discussed this before.'

She waited.

'Your son will be married into my household once he has come into his inheritance,' he said. 'Unfortunately, my daughters are already betrothed, of course. Apart from Bridget. But I doubt he would want to be married to an infant.' He laughed a brief, unamused laugh.

'Betrothals are not set in stone,' Bishop Morton said, and she glanced at him gratefully. Princess Elizabeth was betrothed to the Dauphin, but the French king could not be trusted.

'That is so,' said the king. 'Contracts may be broken. Or unexpectedly terminated.'

A look of grief crossed his face, and everyone knew he was thinking of the death of his young daughter Mary, which had cost him, among other things, an alliance with Denmark. They lowered their eyes in respect, and only Bishop Morton dared to speak.

'If the Dauphin were to die, for instance,' he said; and Margaret held her breath. It was the first reference to the unratified agreement between her son and the princess.

'In that case,' said the king, 'different arrangements would be made.'

'There are too many obstacles,' her husband said. 'The blood relationship, for one.'

She couldn't look at him for fear that her fury would be plain.

'But that isn't insurmountable,' Bishop Morton said. 'That's why we have our good friend the legate here.'

And Giovanni Gigli, who hadn't spoken at all, bowed in his seat and smiled.

Then the Bishop of Worcester began to read out the genealogies of her son and Princess Elizabeth, demonstrating that the degree of kinship between them was no greater than that between the princess and the Dauphin, since all three were descended from Edward III.

Margaret sat with her head bowed as her son's descent was read out, his royal status confirmed, and his eligibility as a potential husband for the princess. None of this had been proclaimed in such company or so formally before. She felt moved by a kind of gratitude as well as vindication; she could feel tears threatening again. Here, in this room, everyone was looking at her differently.

After the recital, at Bishop Morton's suggestion, the draft of a pardon was made. It was written on the inside leaf of the document that had granted Edmund the title of earl in November 1452.

So much had happened since then.

They would have to wait for it to be ratified by the king's lawyers, since the king said he would be setting off to the Scottish war. Thomas Stanley would ride with him, and his brother the Duke of Gloucester.

Margaret felt stricken. *Another delay*, she thought; but the king said, 'Don't worry, Countess, I will be gone only a short while. My fighting days are over.'

Everyone wished the king well, of course, and expressed their concerns for his safety, and assured him that his fighting days were not over; indeed, if he were to fight, the war with Scotland would soon be ended. But, of course, he should not take unnecessary risks.

'I won't be taking any risks,' he said. 'And when I return, this business will be concluded.'

Then he turned to Margaret and said, 'So you will write to your son?'

She didn't mention that other time when her son had been forced to escape. 'I will, your majesty,' she replied.

'Good,' he said. 'And I'll write to the duke.'

There was nothing else she could say except to express her gratitude. This meeting amounted to a public declaration of intent regarding her son's pardon, inheritance and possible marriage.

It was more – much more – than she could have hoped for. And there was something else. She'd looked at the king and she'd begun to believe that this cunning man and ruthless killer didn't want to execute her son, to bring any further scandal down on the House of York. He wanted to welcome Henry into that house by marriage.

It made perfect sense to her. It was exactly what she would have done.

Her spirits rose as her carriage rattled through the London streets.

The king would go to the Scottish war, but he would return soon; he wouldn't take any part in the fighting. And when he returned the discussion about her son's pardon, his inheritance and his marriage could be resumed. Thanks to her persistent efforts.

No thanks to Stanley, who was too busy trying to dissociate himself in the king's eyes from his wife. He had made himself a hindrance, in fact. Whereas Bishop Morton had taken her side, as far as he could.

It had been one of the major revelations of that meeting: that this unobtrusive, impressive man might be Margaret's ally and her friend.

18

Decline

The curé Jean-Luc had a young man's pleasant openness of face, a pink colour on his cheekbones and a somewhat lengthy nose, which was no bad thing in a scholar or man of God. But his eyes were fine, bright with hope; they gave the impression that he was about to break into a smile. Despite his youth, he had recently been appointed confessor to the exiled Queen of England, Margaret d'Anjou, a woman of notoriously uncertain temper. His abbé had shaken his head when he heard.

'I would have said she needed someone more experienced,' he said, thinking, perhaps, of himself. But the former queen had heard the young priest preaching on a day when the older priest was ill, and he was the one she had asked for. She wanted him to visit her personally, because she so rarely went out.

Queen Margaret ('You must always address her as if she is still queen,' his abbé told him) was famous for picking arguments with her confessors, pouncing on any loopholes in their knowledge. Now she was retired, so to speak, she'd become something of a scholar. She had nothing to do all day apart from scour the pages of her books – the Bible, and the great philosophical treatises of Aristotle, Augustine or Boethius. She was investigating the possible source and cause of her misfortunes, she said, but she had found nothing in either pagan or Christian belief that accounted for them.

It was certainly the source of her priests' misfortunes that they had not come up with an adequate explanation. She poured scorn on notions of free will (what choice did I have?), was dissatisfied by theories involving the world, the flesh and the devil (was he so much more powerful than God and, if so, did that not make him God?), and she had chased one priest out of her house for citing Job.

It was with some trepidation, therefore, that Jean-Luc approached the small château. It was surrounded by a maze that was encircled by water that was in turn surrounded by forest. Statues of mythological creatures stood at intervals on the approach, and it came to him, as they stopped at an ancient door, that he would not be surprised to find an elderly fairy or witch at her spinning wheel inside.

The servant knocked, stood as if listening to something just beyond the range of human hearing, then pushed the door open.

The curé stepped inside.

It was an oddly shaped room, all angles, containing only a bed, a table, two chairs, a bookshelf and a small, sputtering fire. A worn tapestry depicted the martyrdom of St Christina who'd had her tongue cut out for singing the praises of the Lord. And when she'd continued to sing, using the stump of her tongue, she was beheaded and her head was boiled in pitch and then sent to sea in a barrel, from which ghostly hymns could still be heard as it bobbed forlornly on the desolate waves.

The former queen sat at a table wrapped in a woollen cloak, for though it was August the evenings and mornings had been cold. Most of her face was in shade. Once she'd been a famous beauty; now, however, she was past fifty and her sufferings had taken their toll. He thought that one side of her face was swollen, or that it had simply dropped with age. What he could see of her hair was white, but her eyes were bright and severe.

'What?' she said, in a hoarse, not unmusical voice as he approached. 'What do you see?' and when he didn't reply, she said, 'Sit down – you will see it more clearly.'

As he pulled out a chair she said, 'So – you've come to discuss my salvation.'

He had prepared only one short passage for discussion: *Blessed are they who mourn, for they will be comforted*. Now he thought it might have been better to pick something celebratory, perhaps, that didn't directly address the question of grief.

'If – you're not well –' he began, but she waved a hand in a gesture that revealed all the old elegance.

'I have a toothache,' she said. 'Begin.'

He read his brief text, sensing the inadequacy of the words as he spoke them, and as he finished she said, 'When?'

'Pardon?'

'When will they be comforted? Does it say?'

The curé advanced the idea that comfort was always there; the difficulty was in perceiving it.

'That is not the difficulty,' she said. 'The difficulty lies in accepting the fact that there is no comfort anywhere to be found.'

The curé perceived that the former queen needed to talk, or to recite, rather, her narrative of despair.

It was a dramatic tale, the true story of how she'd been sent as a girl of fourteen to a grey and bitter land where she was treated with unremitting hostility because she'd come without a dowry. And her husband had been a good man, but an innocent, no match for the treacherous cunning of his lords. So she'd been abandoned to the internecine plotting of the English nobility, who fought like wolves and whose savagery was unsurpassed. She'd been mocked, reviled, slandered and abused all through her marriage, and the king was so poor they could afford neither clothes nor food. Meanwhile, their coffers were plundered, their characters defamed by lying knaves who had pretended, at first, to serve them.

'They smile with their knives, the English,' she said.

The curé would have interrupted her, but she would not be interrupted. Her voice rose and quivered with emotion. She had been decried for having no child, she said, which was not her fault. For the king, her husband, was a holy man, a kind of saint, but it was almost as though he didn't know how to be a man, or a king. He wasn't fully of this world.

'What kind of God,' she demanded, 'would take a man like that as an innocent babe and make him king? It was cruel beyond all cruelties. Only a monster would do such a thing.'

She looked at him defiantly and he saw her hands were trembling and her eyes wet. But before he could speak she carried on. When she did have a child, a beautiful boy, they said he wasn't the king's son – no accusation was too bad for them. Her husband had never said such an iniquitous thing, no – but he had collapsed from nervous strain, and the wolves had taken power.

And then what was she supposed to do? she wanted to know. Abandon the kingdom to them? Let them disinherit her husband and her son? No! She'd fought, and would not give up. She'd been forced to flee, hunted down, made to live as a vagabond in the forest, to beg for food and shelter. She'd led armies into war. And for what? For a final defeat so bitter it was wonderful she had survived without going mad. Her husband, that good man; her beautiful son – both murdered; herself imprisoned in the Tower then sent back to her old country like an unwanted package. She'd tried repeatedly to have their bodies sent to her, but to no avail. She'd tried to seek audience with her cousin, King Louis, but he wouldn't see her. He'd forced her to give up the lands of her inheritance after her father had died, in order to pay her keep. Which cost him nothing – she was kept here on a pittance. Growing old alone – the only one left to live and to endure it all. And why? What had she done that was so wrong, so hateful to God, that he had abandoned her to be persecuted in this way?

She was leaning forward now, fixing him with her tragic luminous gaze, her mottled skin. Her voice was hoarse with grief, but no tears fell.

She'd never run away, never shirked her duty. She'd faced the worst alone. A strong woman surrounded by weak men (for all she'd ever had from her father were pledges and promises that came to nothing). So what she wanted to know from the curé, she said, leaning still further forward, was what exactly she could have done differently, to have earned God's favour.

The curé was lost for words. He could see the terrible picture exactly as she had painted it, and more besides. He saw she was trapped inside that picture, and the story she had told over and over again. He saw she was exhausted by it, it was consuming her, but she couldn't escape. The sun had risen and set many times since these events, she lived in a different country now, but in her mind nothing had changed. She was still fighting her own bitter war.

She was like a donkey tethered to a post that must always trudge around the same track.

He wanted desperately to find the words that would free her, yet nothing he could think of to say seemed adequate.

'It's a mystery,' he began, but she only made a sharp, impatient movement.

In that moment he saw, or thought he saw, something that afterwards he couldn't explain and was perhaps afraid to try. He was no mystic, and left miracles to the saints. And perhaps, after all, it was only the light playing on the wall. But he thought he saw the shadow of an older and a younger man, on either side of the former queen. Both of them were wearing crowns and smiling, or at least looking towards her with delighted love.

It was only a momentary impression, yet when he closed his eyes it remained with him, imprinted on his eyelids in light. When he opened them again the impression had gone and there was only the queen, still waiting expectantly for his response.

On impulse, he dropped to his knees and took her hand and kissed it. 'Your majesty,' he murmured. 'Your grace.'

She looked at him in mute surprise and then, for the first time, an astonished smile trembled on her lips. He remained kneeling before her and, when he released her hand, she placed it momentarily on his head.

Then she lifted her hand and he sat back in his seat and looked at her in silence. Finally, she turned away from him with a sigh, saying, 'It was no life for him; no life at all for a little boy.'

He understood she meant the prince, her young son Edward, cut down so cruelly in the first battle he'd ever fought. The curé bowed his head.

He expected her grief to burst forth in a deluge that would drown them both. But she didn't weep. He saw her lips moving soundlessly, her face contorting, but she only said, with some effort, 'You may go.'

Perhaps he should have argued then, but instead he rose and bowed, promising to come again. Yet when he did come, three days later, he was told she was ill and unable to see anyone.

And then she died.

Arrangements were made for her body to be buried at the cathedral in Angers. The coffin was covered in blue cloth of gold, and accompanied by four attendants wearing white and silver. It was followed by a train of monks and nuns. The curé Jean-Luc walked behind them, feeling a sense of unease because of that moment he'd witnessed when the former queen's anger had changed to sorrow. Which was a dangerous thing, because a mortal being might be sustained by rage but cannot bear too much sorrow. He felt almost as though he'd ended her life, and the thought had kept him awake at night. So he prayed for the former queen earnestly as he walked, that she was released from her trials and reunited with her husband and son, and that he had not been the cause of her demise.

On 25 August 1482, at the cathedral at Angers, he maintained his solitary vigil while what was left of Margaret of Anjou was buried next to her father in her ancestral home.

The King of France received letters saying that the Duchess of Austria [Mary of Burgundy] had died as a result of a fall . . . [from] a fiery little horse . . . this was a bitter blow to her subjects and friends . . . [but] King Louis was overjoyed . . . and from that moment began to intrigue with the leading men of Ghent for the marriage of his son the Dauphin with Marguerite, the daughter of the Archduke [and Mary of Burgundy].

Philippe de Commines

King Edward was very worried and aggrieved when he saw how, in the end, he had been duped by King Louis, who not only defaulted on the promised tribute but also refused to allow the solemnly agreed marriage of the Dauphin to the king's eldest daughter.

Crowland Chronicle

Therefore he called an assembly together [in January 1483] and . . . exhorted his noble men to defend the honour of their realm . . . They answered that . . . every man would be desirous to fight with the French whom they had so often vanquished and for the honour of their country they were ready at his command to avenge so great an injury with sword and fire . . .

Polydore Vergil

19

Fishing

One day he was taken in a small boat with those whom he had
bidden to go fishing . . .

Dominic Mancini

They told him not to go, of course. Edward's physician,
a long-faced, sallow man who looked as if he'd never
breathed fresh air in his life, begged him to take into
consideration the effects of the damp and cold.

'Your lungs will be overwhelmed,' he said. 'They will cling
together like damp cloths. And then where will you be?'

But it was the end of winter and spring was thrumming in the
fields and hedgerows, in the tiny, swollen buds. Beasts were suddenly restive in the fields. There were still frills of snow on the
hills, but the sky was rinsed blue and the birds were calling insist-
ently. And the king's own flesh, the hairs on his flesh, were
answering that call.

'It's the court that won't let me breathe,' he said, and William
Hobbes, who for many years had tended his majesty's physical
condition, was obliged, as he always was in the end, to agree the
change might do him good. But he insisted the king took all possible care, wrapping up warmly and staying out of the water at
all costs. He might watch the fishing from the bank, but not par-
ticipate. He was suffering from an excess of watery humour (a
cold on the chest that had failed to clear), and he shouldn't stay
out at all.

The king bore all these instructions with as much patience as
he could, for he was fond of his physician, who had performed an
unrewarding task for many years, nursing his overworked bowels

and cock, poring over his urine and faeces with as much absorption as a navigator studying a map. He liked him and was irritated by him in equal measure, mocking him and playing cruel tricks on him, such as when, after one particularly heavy banquet, he had pretended to be dead. And he'd sent him to the Scottish war with his brother's army when the poor doctor had no desire to leave even his own room. The king liked to think of him being suddenly exposed to the rigours and horrors of the battlefield, or being jolted around in the back of a wagon, looking as oppressed as it was possible to be.

So now he accepted these restrictions after only mild abuse, promising he wouldn't stay out long, and would keep away from the water itself, and would wrap up as warmly as any old woman – or even the doctor himself. He set out with a few companions on the morning of the thirtieth day of March, wrapped in furs like a bear and travelling in a carriage rather than riding a horse, because it was hard to find a horse that would carry him.

Still, he could feel the clean air on his face, burning the inside of one nostril then the other. It seemed to him there was a new note in the song of the birds, and it was a good note. And a wonderful world that renewed itself so diligently. No matter what occurred, it put on this display in which not a blade of grass or a budding leaf had ever been seen before.

When they got to the small lake in the centre of a wood, he wanted to laugh aloud in triumphant joy. For it was not, as his physician had predicted, entirely frozen over and the fish all dead under three feet of ice. The ice had substantially melted and the water was as still and pure as glass; here and there softly webbed into a crystalline pattern but otherwise perfectly reflecting the trees and sky.

His men carried his chair to the edge of the lake. He found, though he'd had every intention of defying his doctor, that he was wary of trusting his weight to the boat, but neither did he want to sit in the chair like an old man or an invalid. So he walked up and down at the water's edge, even splashing in it a little and getting his feet wet, shouting out instructions and suggestions and laughing uproariously when one of the little boats capsized.

But soon his laughter changed to wheezing. He was out of breath and his back ached, so he sat down to watch, after all.

Sadness tinged his joy. What had happened to the young man he had been? Twenty-two years ago, almost to the day, he'd won his great victory at Towton and the world had changed. Certainly, his world had changed, for ever.

On that day there had been a whirling snowstorm. Images of it came back to him in dreams; men's faces contorted in agony and fear, blood on the snow. *It begins like this*, he'd thought, *in blood*.

But he'd put a stop to all that now. In the years since Towton he'd gone to battle as little as possible. His brother Richard had fought and won the Scottish war for him. He, the king, had returned home, to his business of promoting the interests of merchants and trade, rather than the lords with their feudal fiefs. He'd made alliances with other countries rather than waging war; though, because of the duplicity of the French king, his relations with Burgundy, France and even Spain were now under threat.

He couldn't even think of the French king without feeling a pain in his chest. He'd undone so much of what Edward had tried to achieve, making him seem inept and foolish in the eyes of his people.

He would have to look elsewhere for a marriage for his eldest daughter.

The Countess of Richmond had written to him, of course: *I hope you will remember our former agreement*. But he didn't want to commit his daughter to an exiled earl. Not while there were any princes left.

And he didn't trust the countess, though there was an intelligence in her he'd come to respect.

Who could he trust? His closest friends had gone, or he was separated from them because of the rifts and divisions in his household.

Before Christmas his wife's family had accused Hastings of trying to sell Calais to the French. Or at least of having keys copied so French troops could get in.

He hadn't believed them, not really. But because of the situation with France, he'd had to take it seriously. As they'd known he would.

He'd summoned Hastings back from Calais. Hastings, of course, had been outraged at the accusations, and had produced allegations of his own: that his wife wanted Calais for her brother Anthony. And somehow – he could hardly remember how – he'd ended up shouting at Hastings as if possessed, or senseless, with rage. Until he couldn't draw breath.

Hastings, in some terror, had called his physician. Between them they'd got him into bed. Where he'd been forced to lie still. Whenever he'd tried to speak he'd been told, *do not exhaust yourself, sire.*

The first words he'd spoken were to his friend. *Go,* he'd said. *I can't bear to look at you.*

He could still see the look on Hastings' face as he left.

Meanwhile, during his illness his wife managed to have the witnesses produced against them hanged for libel. Hastings by that time had fortunately returned to Calais.

It had never ceased to rankle with her that he'd appointed Hastings Captain of Calais.

You will allow me to fill one post with someone other than a Woodville, he'd said to her. Obviously, she'd not forgiven that. While his brothers hadn't forgiven him for allowing Earl Rivers to have control of the prince.

'He's of the House of York, not the tribe of Woodville,' Clarence had said.

That was Clarence, who was dead now. His wife hadn't rested until he'd had his brother killed.

That was his wife's method: to strike at those who came between her and the king. Hastings, too, had suggested that the young prince should learn kingship from his father rather than Earl Rivers. And had been sent away.

But Edward stood by the appointment of his wife's brother as guardian for his son. The earl was the greatest scholar in the country. No one else was better suited to supervise the training of the heir to the throne.

He wanted so much for his son. He wanted him to be a better scholar, a greater knight, than he had ever been. A better king.

Yet it was true that he hardly saw him. The young prince spent all his time at Ludlow, where he was subjected to a routine of stupefying rigour. He hardly saw his brother Richard either. He was away, ruling his *empire of the north*, as his wife called it, because he'd been richly rewarded at the last parliament with lands along the Scottish border.

'They'll say there are two kings in this country,' his wife had said.

She had driven a stake through the heart of his family: Clarence was dead, Richard stayed away from court, his son was in Ludlow. And Hastings didn't dare show his face outside Calais.

It wore him out, this strife. It seemed to him that always where he most loved, he was most betrayed. Though his wife would be astonished to hear she had betrayed him. Yet why had she married him, really, if not to promote her family?

So he sat, an ageing, overgrown king, on the edge of a lake. None of his close friends was with him, only some of the younger men of the court. And he was unable to join in their sport, because of his ruined body.

Twenty-two years ago he had won the kingdom and wooed his wife. It was not easy to see which had brought him the greater grief.

Then there was the loss of his daughter, Mary, which he dared not think about. That was a dangerous pain.

But he shouldn't be thinking like this on his day of freedom. He'd come here to leave the court behind him, not take it with him – what was the point of that? He was here now, in the midst of so much beauty it made his heart ache.

It was not too late; he was only forty. Surely he could renew himself, begin again, as the earth did each year. He could become, if not the young man he'd once been who had ridden and hunted, loved his horses and his dogs, then something better than he was now, a massive ruin. He could get up, work what was left of his muscles, attempt to put his court to rights.

And he should do this for the sake of his nation, and his son.

In that moment the king felt an impulse to rise so powerful it was almost as though wings had unfurled from his spine. At the same time he experienced the strangest sensation, as though part of himself was indeed getting up and leaving. His younger self, not yet nineteen years old, was leaving this massive carcass by the lake and heading into the forest. Where it would pursue some alternative life, running wild and free. There it went, leaving all the rest of him, the kingship and the state behind.

He opened his mouth, to call it back perhaps, or perhaps it was only to call for help. But whichever it was, he couldn't do it. The muscles of his throat wouldn't work, and he was dully surprised to find he couldn't move.

20

The King's Will

The king, although he was not affected by old age or any known
kind of disease . . . took to his bed around Easter time.

Crowland Chronicle

Each of his attendants in turn denied they had neglected
the king, or left him too long in the cold, though none
of them could remember the exact time of his col-
lapse. And the physicians couldn't account for it. Some
said it must be an apoplexy, while others said it was a fever caused
by the cold striking into his vitals. William Hobbes pressed the
king's stomach and, noticing a spasm of pain on the royal face,
proposed gallstones or appendicitis, though the king, who was
intermittently conscious, complained of a pain in his left lung
which argued for pneumonia. So the fires in the bedchamber
were kept burning day and night, while all the windows were
open and bowls of steaming water were brought to the king's
bedside to help him breathe. Blood was let from his temples and
his stomach, an evil-smelling poultice was applied to his chest
and a pigeon split and tied to his feet.

But his majesty showed no sign of improvement. William
Hobbes did his best to persuade him to lie alternately on either
side, but the king turned back whenever he could to his right
side, because the pain on his left was worsening.

On the third day, William Hobbes announced to the Council
that it might be best to notify *all significant persons*. The queen
came first.

She arrived in an unhurried way. All she'd been told was that
the king had taken a chill, but as soon as she saw her husband she

forgot the reproving speech she'd been going to make and simply sat at his side.

He tried to speak, but couldn't. Then she, who never publicly showed emotion, turned her face to one side and wept, which everyone took as evidence of grief. But in fact, the queen had seen, suddenly and clearly, how things might be for her if her husband died.

She took his hand, which rested limply in hers. Still he couldn't say the things he might have said, that he was sorry for the way things had turned out between them, and perhaps after all he shouldn't have married her, though he couldn't regret their children. And seeing her for the first time beneath an oak tree that spring so long ago remained the most perfect memory he had.

Above all, he wanted to say that he forgave her, for he could see now that none of it – the quarrels, the machinations, the growing coldness between them – was her fault. He was sorry now, he could have said, that he had ever tried to make her what she was not, or ask of her what she couldn't give.

But these words would have been wasted on the queen, who had never for one moment considered any of it was her fault. She'd always laid the blame squarely on her husband and his family, and being forgiven now would simply have aggravated her. So they remained together in silence until the king indicated to Bishop Morton that he wished to see him and his lawyers alone.

'Why?' said the queen, and Bishop Morton said it was possible he wanted to speak about his will.

'But I'm one of the executors of his will,' the queen said. 'I should stay.'

Bishop Morton said there were many other affairs of state that the king might wish to discuss, but it was only under protest that the queen allowed herself to be led into an adjacent chamber. Where Thomas Rotherham, Archbishop of York, suggested they should notify the Duke of Gloucester and perhaps Lord Hastings in Calais.

'Why?' she said.

'Well – because – they would wish to know.'

'They don't need to know,' she said. 'I will notify anyone who needs to know.'

'Well –' said the archbishop, but the queen turned the full force of her glare upon him. And because he found it too difficult to suggest to a distressed woman that her husband might not recover, he didn't press the matter further.

Meanwhile, the king was attempting to tell Bishop Morton about a dream he'd had, but the effort exhausted him and the bishop begged him to rest. He persisted, however, though the bishop could hardly make out what he was saying. Something about a good man, too good to rule, and how he wished he'd visited his shrine.

Then the bishop exhorted him not to speak. He hoped when the time came for his last confession the king wouldn't say too much, for it was a delicate thing to be confessor to a king.

But most of that day he said nothing at all. He flickered in and out of consciousness, and only when the lawyers came did he become lucid and start to speak.

Long before his illness, he had made a lengthy testament . . . and had appointed many executors to carry out his wishes. As he was dying he added several codicils to it.

Crowland Chronicle

He also expressed a wish to see his stepson, Thomas, Marquis of Dorset, and his friend Lord Hastings.

The next morning, several Woodvilles arrived – Lionel, Bishop of Salisbury, Edward and Richard Woodville and the marquis. As yet, of course, there was no sign of Hastings, who had to travel all the way from Calais. When he arrived he hurried to the bedside of his king. His face was grey, his jaw shook when he tried to speak. 'My lord,' he managed at last, 'what is this foolishness?'

The king held out his hand. Hastings took it and chafed it and gazed earnestly at him, looking much older than his fifty-odd years.

Then the king said, 'Where is my stepson, Thomas?'

The Marquis of Dorset approached the bed reluctantly and the king gestured to him to come closer. He continued to hold Hastings' hand, so the older man couldn't retreat. His mouth worked strangely so they had to lean forward to hear the words. And when they did, they were not sure they had heard them correctly and he had to repeat himself. 'Embrace – each other – for love of me.'

It was all he could say. He hadn't energy to explain the politic nature of his request. For he didn't want to leave his son to the mercy of a court so dominated by rival factions that he would be pulled and torn between them.

Lord Hastings blanched visibly and Dorset scowled. Neither of them made a move.

Then the king, making a heroic effort, grasped Dorset's hand also.

> No longer able to sit up, he lay on his right side, his face toward them. And no one there present could refrain from weeping. Then in his presence the lords forgave each other and joined their hands together [even though] . . . their hearts were far asunder.
>
> *Thomas More*

That night the king took a turn for the worse, and yet refused, or was unable to make, full confession. Those magnates within easy reach were sent for, including Lord Stanley. Everyone wondered why Richard of Gloucester hadn't arrived. On the following day Bishop Morton administered the last rites, and before morning, as the first birds sang, that most liberal, genial and (in his youth) handsome of kings delivered his soul to almighty God.

[On 9 April 1483] died the excellent King Edward at his palace of Westminster, after he had reigned a full twenty two years . . .

Great Chronicle of London

Bells rang from more than one hundred churches throughout London, from Westminster to St Paul's to St Martin-in-the-Fields, and St Mary-le-Bow in Cheapside to St Olave's in Southwark. Through the four gates of London, to all the alleys and cobbled streets and marketplaces the news spread:

The king is dead, the king is dead!

And all the work of the city, the clanking and hammering and sawing, the loading and unloading, the haggling and crying of wares, ground to a halt. People clustered in the streets and clutched one another and wept. For most of them had only just heard he was sick, and who had been more hale and hearty than the king in his prime, more impressive in his stature and his strength? Certain people began to talk of poison, and others of witchcraft, because the king was not an old man and had shown no signs of an early demise, and everyone knew the queen was a witch, like her mother before her. Others, however, could only ask themselves what they should do: what could be done? For there was only a young boy to take his place, and a boy king was always a danger to the land.

As they murmured, the aldermen in their fur-trimmed gowns made their solemn way to the Guildhall. On the river splendid barges moved upstream as lords temporal and spiritual were rowed to Westminster. People thronged the banks to watch, feeling a loss of direction and hope like a physical blow. Overnight it seemed King Edward's reign was transformed into a Golden Age, and the king himself from debauched and corpulent sluggard to a valiant and noble prince. Just as twelve years previously, the death of King Henry had transformed him from witless fool to saint.

21

Eight Days

eanwhile, in the Chapel of St Stephen the dead king lay upon a board, naked apart from a cloth which covered him from his navel to his knees, so all the lords spiritual and temporal, the mayor and the aldermen, might look upon him for the last time and see he was indeed dead and no violence had been done to him.

The sheet covered his modesty; that part of him which had led him to conquests in both armour and amour. While he lay in the chapel a stream of people visited, from magnates to squires and valets and cleaners, and more than one of them, left unattended for a moment, lifted the cover quickly, ostensibly to check for wounds, actually to peek at the royal member, wondering if its dimensions were proportional to his stature. Of these some were disappointed, others mystified, but at least one went back to the kitchens and entertained all the staff there with his description of the royal rod, which was like the worm Erebus, he claimed, prodigious and unvanquished, even in death.

As for Edward himself, there was no way of telling whether in the darkest chambers of his brain all sparks of life were indeed extinguished or whether an intermittent flickering played over again scenes from his life. Or which scenes they might be – from his childhood, perhaps, when the sky was a more vivid blue, or from the morning of Mortimer's Cross, when three suns appeared in the heavens and he knew he would be king. Or when, in the course of Warwick's rebellion, all his men had deserted him and he had stood beneath the stars and known himself alone.

Equally, they could have been scenes of violence and bloodshed, or sexual excess. No one would ever know, any more than they could know that all life in that great body was truly extinct, leaving nothing more than a heavy mortal shell.

But for the eight days he lay in the chapel the rain fell steadily, persistently, on the roofs of London and on the Thames, where it made circular patterns in the water that grew and spread.

From Baynard's Castle, Cecily Neville gazed out at the river as the bells tolled. She didn't weep, but her face settled into lines of a peculiar heaviness. There was a part of her that was unsurprised, that had already adapted, since her husband's death, to a life of mourning. She waited with a tragic acceptance for the arrival of her younger son, feeling no need to write to him, for surely he would already be on his way.

Further along the Thames, Margaret Beaufort closed her eyes against the rain and tried to comprehend the impact of this death.

All she could see was an image of the king as he had been, larger than life, shouting with laughter. That was the first thought she had, that he had always seemed so vital, bursting with an energy that was too much even for his gigantic frame. She was one year younger than him but had always felt much older, ancient and shrivelled in his company.

Her second thought was an impulse to send for her son, because now, surely, she could present him at the new king's court, rather than waiting for the interminable negotiations to begin again.

But the wary part of her said her son should stay where he was; the political situation was bound to be unstable. If the queen's faction ruled and had control of the new king, there should be no reason to fear. Henry Tudor was no threat to them and the queen might be prevailed upon to uphold the king's offer of marriage to the Princess Elizabeth or another of her daughters.

But Richard of Gloucester would arrive soon and change the balance of power. He wouldn't want the queen's family to have control of the new king. Margaret didn't know what Richard of Gloucester's attitude to her son was, or what would happen if a regency government was formed and his faction prevailed. The duke was an unknown quantity.

Once again she would have to wait, while the country was suspended between opposing forces.

She felt an unbearable tension, amounting almost to vindictive rage, as though the king had died purposefully to thwart her. *Why now?* she thought. She'd been so close. But it was pointless to wonder why God had sent yet another obstruction to her cause. She could only bear this new delay in silent agony, as other players in this drama acted for good or ill.

The Queen

She'd spent more than twenty hours arguing in Council over the king's will, reaching that point of fatigue where the room quivered around her and lights flickered in the corners of her eyes. So now she sat at her window seat without even seeing the rain that rattled the pane or formed into great pools in the courtyard below, and wondered if she was going mad.

Her husband of nineteen years was dead.

She was so angry with him that she'd had no time even to take this in.

He had made a new will.

As soon as she'd been told this, she'd sent for her lawyers.

The terms of the old will were plain. He had entrusted everything to her; to *his dearest wife, the queen*. She was to have the care of the Prince of Wales and his younger brother; the rule and guidance of all their daughters; power of disposal over his treasure and goods. She was the chief executor.

But on his deathbed, in the last moments of his life, he'd revoked all that. So she'd been told, but she couldn't believe it.

She'd refused to believe he could have done something so deceitful and destructive.

'Even you, Edward,' she whispered. 'Even you.'

The new will named Gloucester Protector of the Realm and the king's children. The queen's brother was to be removed from his office of governor to the prince; Thomas Stanley had been awarded custody of Princess Elizabeth; different executors had been appointed. The queen was left with no power at all.

'No,' she'd said. 'He was not in his right mind.'

And Hastings, her husband's philandering sidekick, said, 'There was nothing wrong with his mind, madame.'

'Then why should he change it – at the last moment?'

'Perhaps because he wished to avoid any further division in the land.'

'What division?' she'd demanded, looking round at them all: Thomas Stanley, Bishop Morton, Bishop Russell, Archbishops Rotherham and Bourchier. 'What division?'

And the arguments had begun.

Her brother Lionel, Bishop of Salisbury, had consulted his own lawyers, who said a dead king's wishes had no force in law. In 1422 the King's Council had rejected the wishes of the late king Henry V regarding his choice of Protector for his son. Only the King's Council, in fact, had the right to decide who should govern the realm.

'This is the King's Council,' Hastings said, 'and it has decided.'

All they could agree was that a coronation date for the new king should be proclaimed. And the funeral of her husband should take place as soon as possible so the new king could be crowned.

But Hastings (again) had said the actual date should be decided by the Lord Protector. Once he'd arrived.

'What?' he'd said, into the silence that followed. And the Archbishop of York, somewhat uncomfortably, said it probably was time for the Duke of Gloucester to be notified.

'What?' said Hastings again, with a different emphasis, and he followed the direction of Rotherham's glance towards the queen.

Then a furious row had erupted.

Hastings leapt to his feet. He'd actually jabbed his finger towards the queen.

'You – madame – have concealed this vital information from the Protector of the Realm?'

She had only been able to respond, palely, that he had not been Protector then.

'And is not now, as yet,' her son Thomas had said.

Hastings rounded on him. 'He is the king's brother!' he roared.

'Late king,' said the marquis. 'He is brother to the late king. I am brother to the new king. And Lord Rivers is his uncle.'

She'd thought for a moment that Hastings might suffer an apoplexy as her husband was said to have done. He leaned over the table towards the marquis, his face congested with rage.

'How dare you speak of him thus!' he bellowed, while Thomas turned to the rest of the Council, spreading his hands. 'You who are no one – you shouldn't even *be* here! Do not think to dictate to this Council. Your origin is too low and your blood too base for you to rule England!'

At one time, just recently, she could have had him hanged for such words.

The marquis' smile froze. 'Says the dead king's lapdog,' he said. 'The Squire of Burton Hastings.'

Then everyone was on their feet, shouting at once, but one voice was raised above the others.

'ENOUGH!' bellowed Thomas Stanley, and everyone looked at him, startled. Into the silence he said, 'This is getting us nowhere.'

It was an *unconscionable omission*, he said, that the Duke of Gloucester had not been notified, but that error could be rectified immediately. 'Perhaps you will see to it, Lord Hastings?'

Hastings said he would certainly do so, since no one else could be entrusted with the task.

'Your majesty,' Thomas Stanley said, addressing her for the first time, 'I believe you have not as yet notified your own brother, Lord Rivers. Or your son?'

'That was what I was going to say, if I'd been allowed,' she said. 'No one has been notified yet at *all*. I wished to consult the Council first.'

'To see which way the land lay, you mean,' Hastings said.

'Do I have to listen to these insults?' she asked Lord Stanley, but Hastings replied, 'Madame, if we followed your suit, nothing would be said and the king's death would be kept secret from the world.'

'For God's sake,' said Stanley, and it occurred to the queen she had never seen him angry before. '*Keep your peace* and let's make some progress here.'

And temporarily, at least, Hastings was silent.

Still the debate went back and forth, about the day of the funeral, the day of the coronation, until finally, 20 April was proposed for the funeral and 4 May for the coronation. That should give time, Stanley said, for all the peers to come to London. And then a parliament could be held.

'But my brother, Lord Rivers, will have to arm the garrison,' she'd said, 'and equip them with supplies.'

'Are you preparing for war?' asked Hastings.

'My son will need suitable protection on the journey from Ludlow,' she said to Stanley.

'He won't need an army,' Hastings said.

'My son, the king,' she said clearly, 'cannot travel through two hundred miles of country where anyone might attack him. Or try to abduct him,' she said, glancing at Hastings.

'If you are referring to the Protector,' Hastings said, 'he would have every right to take the prince – his ward – into his custody.'

'He's not the Protector yet,' the marquis said again. 'Furthermore, the office of Protector is purely an interim one – its purpose being to secure the realm until the sovereign is crowned. In 1429,' he said, as Hastings attempted to interrupt him, 'the king's uncle Humphrey, then Duke of Gloucester, relinquished his office immediately after the king's coronation.'

Hastings made a sound very like a snort. It came as some surprise to him, he said, that the former reign of the House of Lancaster was being cited as precedent by those who should, by all instincts and honour, be loyal to the House of York. It was even more of a surprise, he continued, overriding the marquis, that the king's own wife would attempt to undermine her late husband's will and betray his wishes before his body was *even cold*.

And the meeting had degenerated into uproar once again.

At one point Hastings had thundered that if they wanted an army they could have one – he would send for his own garrison at Calais. The marquis had reminded him that he had all the armoury of the Tower at his disposal, and his uncle Edward Woodville had control of the fleet. And the queen had seen that they would come to the brink of civil war.

It took the combined efforts of two archbishops, two bishops and Thomas Stanley to bring them back from that brink.

'Gentlemen, my lady – I beg you –' Bishop Morton said, raising his own voice for the first time. 'This is no way to proceed. We're here to secure the future of this realm, not tear it apart. Your majesty – surely some compromise can be found?'

She rose, feeling terror inside, but spoke coldly. 'I've lost my husband. I do not intend to lose my son. He must be escorted by as many armed men as is necessary.'

'Necessary for what?' said Hastings, but Bishop Morton raised his hand.

'What number of armed men,' he said, 'do you think will suffice?'

'Two hundred at most,' Hastings said. The marquis had laughed, and she'd said that was not enough.

They couldn't agree on a number, though they had argued far into the night. Then, because everyone was exhausted, they had adjourned the meeting. They had managed to agree only that the new king should be proclaimed throughout London and the bells rung.

There were many other things to be decided, but it was nearly dawn. And so she'd left the meeting with her son, who'd said he would tell his uncle to mobilise the fleet and blockade Calais, if need be. Meanwhile, he would take charge of the ordnance at the Tower. Then they'd parted, and she'd made her own way to her rooms, refusing all offers of assistance from her ladies.

And now she sat here, as exhausted as she'd ever been in her life but unable to sleep.

Perhaps she would never be able to sleep again, without her husband.

She could feel a heaviness in her chest that could only be grief. Yet what was she grieving for, really? In the last year there had been only coldness between them.

He had changed his will, excluding her, his *dearest wife*.

She wasn't his dearest wife, she'd known that for some time. But that he should humiliate her so thoroughly at the very end was almost more than she could endure. Had he hated her so much? At first, at least, he'd loved her.

Had she ever loved him?

Not when he'd strained and grunted over her like a great beast at toil. After all the gorging and the vomiting so that his breath stank and he farted almost continuously through the night. The massive weight of him made it difficult to breathe, so that she was forced to try new and whorish positions to accommodate him.

Still, it was hard to believe she wouldn't feel that weight again.

She'd borne him ten children, put up with all the other women, all the lies, the slights to her and her family.

Once, after he'd bucked and grunted himself into unconsciousness, rolling off her, she'd got up naked but covered in

173

his sweat and stood in the breeze from the window. She'd glanced back at him and thought, *how easily I could kill you now.*

Then something had happened; the light had shifted or he had stirred, and she'd seen the young man he'd once been. Who had ridden past her that spring morning as she stood waiting for him, and checked his horse and looked again.

It seemed to her she could see the innocence of the child in the grotesque beast he'd become. There were echoes of that same face in the faces of all her children.

She'd had to turn away quickly then, unprepared for the piercing pity she felt for him. She could almost have cried because of it – she who'd long ago stopped crying. In that moment she would have spared him all of it – everything that had happened since that May morning – all the rows with his family, Warwick's rebellion, the death of Clarence, the trouble with the French and the Scots and the old Lancastrian lords. Often she'd felt it was an evil trick that had brought them together that morning in May.

But it wasn't a trick – she'd planned it, as she'd planned so much of her life. And now she'd been abandoned to the wolves, she needed a different plan.

One that dispersed Gloucester's power so that he was only one member of the Regency Council, not head of it. Her son was not an infant; he would be thirteen that year. At fourteen he could rule alone, without any Protector, and would not be dominated by his Council.

But he would still have his mother.

All she had to do was to steer them both through the next eighteen months.

Elizabeth Woodville smoothed back a strand of hair, then removed her headdress and folded it neatly, orderly even in grief. As she put it away she felt as though she was putting away her old self, wife to the king.

Now she was mother to the king.

In his will Edward had dealt her his final injury. He couldn't hurt her any more, now he was dead. And she hadn't killed him, even after nineteen years of marriage.

Was that love? She didn't know.

Lord Hastings

In one of the darker passages of Westminster, lit only by a single torch, Lord Hastings intercepted Lord Stanley. They had left the Council separately to avoid any charges of confederacy. As Hastings stepped out from the shadows, Stanley started violently. 'For Christ's sake,' he said.

'How is it possible,' said Hastings, 'that Gloucester has not been notified?'

Stanley brushed his sleeve as though Hastings had grabbed him, though in fact he hadn't touched him at all. 'You heard what was said. No one told him.'

'But surely the bells have been rung?'

'I heard no bells have been rung outside London.'

Even in the dark, Stanley could tell Hastings was staggered by this news. 'What?' he cried in a hoarse whisper. 'Half the nation doesn't even know their king is dead! But you knew it – and you didn't write?'

Stanley shrugged. 'I was told I was temporarily relieved of my duties.'

'Relieved? You? Who has the power to relieve you of anything? What were you thinking?'

It was Stanley's turn to get annoyed. 'I was thinking that some-one would already have written. Lord Dacre told me everything was being taken care of.'

'Lord Dacre –'

'And in any case, I trust you are going to write now.'

'Indeed I am,' said Hastings. 'Before we are both temporarily, or permanently, relieved.'

Stanley was silent. In the darkness Hastings could see the glitter of his eyes. He was aware of Stanley's reputation as a man who would go to any lengths to preserve his own skin. Yet Hastings had seen him fight in battle with a lethal speed and calculation that took the ground, literally, from his enemies' feet. And for this Hastings cautiously admired him. He didn't trust him, but for some reason Edward had trusted him. And his brother Richard, with whom Stanley had fought against the Scots.

And here in Westminster there were few other people he could trust.

'I'll write,' he said. 'I'll tell him he must come to London with all speed, and as many men as he can arm.'

'No,' said Stanley.

'Did you not hear the queen?' Hastings demanded. 'Her brother will come with his army.'

'We will try to prevent that,' Stanley said.

'And if we don't prevent it?'

'We don't want a coup.'

'What coup? Gloucester's or the queen's?'

'Let us at least try to negotiate with the queen.'

'She's not negotiating,' said Hastings. 'Nothing speaks so clearly of her intent as this secrecy over the king's death. She will have her son ruled by her Woodville tribe, and she will rule through them.'

'Even so,' said Stanley.

Hastings felt a deepening outrage on the dead king's behalf. Yet he knew they should try to avoid war. 'What do you suggest?' he said.

'Write to the duke, but advise caution. Let him know the prince will be arriving with only a few men. Tell him the situation here is under control.'

Hastings noticed that Stanley was not proposing to stick his own neck out and write to anyone. 'Whose control?' he said, then he shook his head. 'For God's sake.' He would do it, because it had to be done.

The two men looked at one another without smiling, then each bowed slightly and went their separate ways.

Alone in his room, Hastings was uncomfortably aware of the shadows and silences. The absence of the king, who would have clapped his shoulder and laughed at him and told him he worried like an old nurse. What would he not give to hear that laughter now? Despite the quarrel they'd had, Edward had been his greatest friend. How many people could say that of a king?

He went to pour himself a glass of wine then stopped. Poison was a woman's trick. Who knew how far the queen would go to be rid of him?

His mouth felt suddenly dry and his hands shaky. He felt more powerfully than ever the loss of his king. He could see how that solid, massive presence had bound them all together. Edward had been fearless, even in the darkest hour.

What, Hastings? he would say. *Afraid of your own shadow?*

Hastings wondered if that great laugh would be heard now on the shores of hell, since, as the king had been fond of saying, there was no fun to be had in heaven.

He sat with a sheet of paper, trying to find the right words to say to the king's brother, who was bereaved, though no one had thought to tell him. Who should come at once, but not armed for war. He sighed over this impossible task. Perhaps he should try to sleep. There was only an hour or two till morning, and he could give it to his servant then.

But he didn't want to spend the night in that room. He didn't want to be alone. He rose and went to the window.

There was someone he wanted to see; someone who had loved the king as he had. He needed the comfort of seeing her now, even if it was only for a moment, even if she sent him away.

And outside in the night air he might feel better, perhaps, more able to breathe.

Jane Shore

She lay in the bed given to her by the king. It had a canopy depicting Venus and Mars in erotic embrace. Although she was gazing up at it, she was not observing the artwork (done after the new style in Florence, he'd said – he'd been so proud of it and she'd never liked it at all). She seemed to be staring into an impenetrable darkness, as though her eyes, like the king's, had opened on to death.

She had retired to bed early for the past two nights, using a different excuse each time – headache, indigestion – and undressed herself, because the sight of her maid's eyes upon her in the goldleaf mirror he had also given her was more than she could stand.

Alone in her bed, she contemplated her situation.

She was no one and had nothing. Each day she expected to be evicted from her house. And she didn't know where to go. Or perhaps, as the old mistress of a dead king, she didn't want to go anywhere.

There was her husband, William, who had been set up in business in Antwerp. She'd heard he was doing very well but had never married again. Poor William – he was hardly likely to offer her shelter now.

It was hard to understand how she had come to this situation of abandonment and despair.

There was no curse like the love of kings.

She had no friends; she dared not take a lover. She spent her time fending off advances from those reckless enough to try and occupied herself by reading and needlework until such time as the king needed her. Which might sometimes be only once or twice a month.

But at those times she was transformed by his heat, blossoming furiously like an exotic flower. Only then did she know her own power.

Women wondered what Edward saw in her. She was by no

means the most beautiful of the ladies at court, and was certainly the lowest born. Men wondered what she kept between her legs that exercised such power over the king. They were pleasant to her face, charming even, while behind her back they called her whore and beggar maid.

Perhaps she should have asked for more. Court mistresses were notoriously rapacious about securing their position. But she knew the charm she exercised over Edward was due partly to the fact that she never asked. He had given her this house, but she doubted it was his to give. He had nothing, not really, he'd always had to beg or extort funds.

Those who thought she wanted the things he gave her were mistaken; she wanted to feel powerfully and vividly alive. That was what he'd offered her after so long in a dead marriage.

Then at some point, she didn't know when, she'd begun to pity him. He'd grown so heavy, in body and spirit, and correspondingly less capable. It had been her job to comfort him, to appease his sudden rages and, at the same time, to make him feel desired.

Exhausting. She'd begun to feel relieved when he didn't call. Yet each night was a preparation for his visit, dressing her hair, applying perfume. There was little to do when he didn't come. And when his absences were protracted and she didn't know when he would call again, she could detect a cooling in the manner of those around her, a willingness to erase her from their lives.

And the queen, of course, hated her. Jane was surprised she hadn't taken action already. She woke with a dull sensation of surprise that she hadn't been evicted or imprisoned; then a sense of disappointment that she was, in fact, still here. Because she couldn't think where else to go. She couldn't think at all beyond this great vortex in her life that made her flesh shrink and her lips turn dry.

If she could have had his child – that would have made a difference. The king was not ungenerous with his bastards; he would have provided for their child in his will, and it would have given her someone to love. If there was anything she'd learned from her years of solitude, it was the necessity not of being loved but of having someone to love.

Although, increasingly, the king hadn't wanted her attention to be divided; he'd wanted it focused on him. And he didn't see how monstrous that was. Because now she was here alone, retreating from the eyes of servants, in a bed that wasn't hers, where she was unable to sleep.

She was like a flake of soot or a snowflake in the wind: borne up and carried along, then dropped into the flames of the hearth, or on to the earth or the sea, silently, unobtrusively, to disappear. No one had come to tell her that the king had died; no one had visited her at all.

But that night there was a soft rapping on her door.

She got up at once, her heart pounding. Would the queen's guard come for her in the middle of the night? She stood by the window in her chemise and saw that it was, in fact, a solitary figure, wearing a hat. She couldn't make out who it was.

But there was no mistaking the Lord Chamberlain's voice as he spoke to her maid.

'Tell Mistress Shore I'm sorry to disturb her . . .'

She withdrew from the window as if it had grown suddenly hot and slipped a loose gown on over her chemise. There was no time to pin up her hair or cover it. She stood for a moment, heart quickening with awareness of the impropriety, how scandal was wreathing itself around her like smoke.

Then her maid came in, eyes bright with curiosity. 'Shall I tell him it's too late, my lady?'

'No,' she said quickly, smoothing her hair. 'I'll come down.'

He was standing in the reception area, admiring her as she descended the stairs. If she hadn't felt so fraught she might have laughed. But he came up to her and clasped both her hands and kissed them, then kissed her lips, as was the custom – but it was not the custom to linger over the kiss. In the end, Jane had to withdraw.

'My lord, you do me too much honour,' she said.

'Jane, Jane,' he murmured, still clasping her hands, 'don't be formal with me. You look marvellous.'

'I don't feel it.'

'Of course not – we are both bereft – that's why I came. Here,' he said, turning towards one of the downstairs rooms, 'may I sit with you a while? It's been such a terrible strain –'

He was leading her towards the couch. 'Let me place the cushions for you – so –'

'You shouldn't be here,' she said; but he only said, 'Sssh.' Already his fingers were loosening her gown.

She resisted being pressed back on to the cushions, pushing his hands away.

'Jane,' he said reproachfully.

It was outrageous really, yet she was also amused, as she had not been amused for several days. This was Lord Hastings, senior statesman. One of the courtiers who had repeatedly waylaid her as she went to and from the king's rooms, pressing her hands, kissing her, but doing no more, either out of fear of his sovereign or love of his friend.

She'd learned quickly to assess the men who approached her. This one was arrogant, certainly, as they all were, but more likely to withdraw offended than to force himself on her.

She didn't want to offend him.

So she allowed him to open the front of her gown before taking his hands and saying, 'My lord, you forget I'm grieving.'

'You think I'm not?'

'I think you have other things on your mind.'

'No, no,' he said. 'We're both in need of comfort, are we not?'

She laughed aloud, and his wide mouth curved into a smile, then immediately he looked crestfallen. 'Ah, Jane – you laugh at me.'

'No, not at all,' she protested, still laughing, and his mouth curved once more.

'I thought I would never hear that sweet sound again,' he said.

Instantly, she stopped laughing. There was still between them the shape of the absent king. She was conscious suddenly of her loneliness, the difficulty of her position, and her eyes filled with tears.

'My poor, sweet lord,' she said, and Hastings' own eyes filled.

'Ah yes,' he said. 'Yes.' His features seemed carved into a mask of sadness. Then he recovered. 'But, my dear, he has died, and we must live.'

He kissed her shoulder, where her gown had slipped, and she pushed him away again, not hard.

'You're very eager to step into his place.'

His face was close to hers; she could smell the scent of him, of sweet, subtle decay. 'If I am, Jane, it's because I see how you miss him, as I do. And because I've held myself in check all these years. And because I know that all this time you've had some kind of *tendresse pour moi* – hmm? Did you not beg the king to reprieve me when certain other persons would have had me executed? Admit it, Jane – I know it was you.'

She lowered her face. It was true she had begged the king to reconsider during those terrible weeks before Christmas, when he had ranted about Hastings and his wife's family and the court as though he would have had everyone put to death.

'That was because it would have hurt him too much,' she told Hastings. His smile turned tremulous.

'Would it not have hurt you, too?' he said.

'Not as much as it would have hurt you,' she said sharply, and his eyes registered the humour.

'But it would hurt you a little,' he said. 'For one thing, you would have lost a friend. And at court you need all the friends you can get. Especially now. You need a guardian, a protector.'

'Who can protect me?' she said.

'I can! I have my garrison, my retinue, my wealth – and today

I will send for the king's brother. He'll come and sort out this wolf-pack and see that the queen does not rule. She mustn't rule. She should go back to the smallholding she came from! I will look after you, Jane!'

She shook her head. The Duke of Gloucester was no friend of hers. He wasn't openly hostile, in the king's presence at least, but when he passed her by chance, his eyes were cold. If he had little love for the king's wife, he had none for his concubine.

She could see that Hastings was making the same error as the king had, in persistently underestimating the queen. Edward had always shrugged off suggestions that the queen might be behind any conspiracy. He saw her only as a woman taken from her rightful place by him, to a place where others wronged her.

Hastings could see she had a will to power, but thought it could be easily checked. Sometimes she wondered if either of them knew the queen at all.

'It would be better for England if the Duke of Gloucester ruled for now,' he said, 'until the prince is of age. And then he can continue to guide him. And I will help him – I will be his right-hand man, as I have been his brother's. Stanley, Northumberland and Howard will stand with us. And many others.'

'And the queen?'

'She will be given some house or other, I suppose. But you and me, Jane – we'll be safe. We could live together openly – why should we not? I will continue to play my part at court and I'll come home to you, Jane – to your arms.'

She didn't even ask about his wife, who lived her own life in the country and must long ago have given up all thought of her husband returning to her. For a moment Jane envied her fiercely. She pushed Hastings away once more and stood up.

She was tired. Tired of all the game-playing, the jostling for a perch that was secure only as long as nothing shook it. She had been the king's concubine and was now to be the chamberlain's whore. What alternative was there?

At the same time, something in her was responding to this new challenge. 'This is not my house,' she said quietly, as if to the wall. 'I don't know how long I'll be able to stay here.'

At once he said he owned a house in Cheapside, where she could stay if necessary. She would not regret allowing him into her affections, he told her. He might be older, but he had much to offer.

She turned back to him, smiling. 'Well, my lord,' she said. 'Let's see what that is.'

He didn't sleep in her bed but left early, in a great hurry, because of the letter he had to write. Then, in case she thought he was too eager to get away, he added that he should have written it last night but he had been too ardent for her, too overwhelmed by love. And she didn't say she was relieved to see him go but kissed him and made him promise to return. Then she waved to him from her bedroom window, and he bowed with mock-gallantry. And when he was gone, finally, she didn't go back to her bed, where she'd said she would wait for him, but on a sudden impulse dressed herself and went out, to see the sun rise over the Thames, the water igniting slowly, changing from brownish-grey to gold.

She loved the mutability of the world; the way one moment could so swiftly change into another. Life was so unpredictable, it could not be defined or determined by any concept so narrow as God's will, or Fate. Some people said she was one thing, some another – who could actually say *what* she was? She couldn't be contained any more than life itself.

Smoke rose from kitchens, there was a meaty smell from the markets. A variety of birds dipped and flashed on the water, their shadows angled into fleeting shapes. Men unloading barrels called out to her and she laughed back at them, but she didn't stay out long; too many drunks were reeling through the streets. She made her way back home and let herself in. The house was dark and quiet, her maid, she supposed, asleep.

So she was startled when a man's voice spoke to her.

'You took your time,' it said.

It was the queen's son, the Marquis of Dorset.

'Who let you in?' she said, recovering rapidly, removing her cloak.

'I told your maid you were expecting me.'

'She knows I was not.'

He shrugged and moved forward suddenly, with that lithe, impressive grace. 'She didn't need much persuading. Aren't you pleased to see me?'

'Of course,' she said warily, as he moved closer.

'You don't seem it.'

'I am – surprised, that's all. And a little tired.'

'Hastings wearing you out?' he said. 'With his limp dick?'

She didn't answer, and he laughed softly, putting his hand on her shoulder, stroking her neck. 'I knew I wouldn't have first pickings,' he said, 'but I don't mind.'

Her silence took on a mutinous quality, but she didn't push him away. She felt a little afraid of him, this dissolute boy, as she was not afraid of Hastings.

'Surely you would prefer someone younger, for a change?'

'I would prefer to be left alone.'

'No,' he said, 'you would not prefer that.'

He stood between her and the door, feral, intent. 'You've been drinking,' she said.

'Of course,' he replied. 'Haven't you?' He indicated the jug of wine on the table then moved his hand swiftly to her face and hair. 'What's the matter, Jane?' he said.

'I think you should leave.'

'Come on, Jane,' he murmured. 'You know you want to.'

He was leading her towards the couch on which she had just been with Hastings. And when she protested he pressed his lips to hers, silencing her. She didn't resist him; it would be too undignified. She only thought with a certain resignation as he pushed her down that he was the queen's son, so at least he could protect her from the queen.

The New King

In word and deed he gave so many proofs of his liberal education in polite, nay scholarly achievements far beyond his age . . . his special knowledge of literature enabled him to discourse eloquently, to understand fully and to declaim most excellently from any work, whether in verse or prose that came into his hands . . .

Dominic Mancini

It had rained that morning, but now sun shone through the rain, glinting on the swords and helmets of the men below, who were practising their daily routines. The prince was thinking of the words of the philosopher Menander:

I call that person happiest who has the chance to look upon the sun that lights us all, to gaze upon the stars, to see the clouds and water, the fire of lightning in the sky . . .

He was trying to remember the full verse when his uncle Earl Rivers tapped on the door.

He seemed unusually hesitant, entering only after the prince told him to come in.

'What is it?' the prince asked, already apprehensive.

Earl Rivers looked taut, as if his mouth was tightly sealed. Then he opened his lips minimally. 'Your father,' he said, 'has been very ill.' He stopped, and looked away, then back at his nephew. 'You must be very brave,' he said. 'You must remember everything you have been taught.'

'I do remember,' said the prince.

'You mustn't be afraid.'

The young prince could see his uncle was afraid. 'I don't understand,' he said.

Earl Rivers crossed the room suddenly, then knelt and took his nephew's hand and pressed it to his forehead. 'Sire,' he said, without looking up. 'Your majesty.'

No! the prince thought.

His uncle was telling him that everything had been done for his father but he hadn't recovered. That in his will he had stated that he, Prince Edward, was to be his heir. Which he had known already, of course.

'No one expected it,' his uncle said. 'He was so strong.'

Vividly, the young prince remembered riding on his father's shoulders when he was very small. Despite the protests of his nurse, the king had got on a horse and ridden around the courtyard with the prince.

Never be afraid of your horse, he'd said, finally putting him down. *He will be your best and closest friend.*

And the sun had streamed behind him so he couldn't see his father's face.

'Say something,' his uncle said.

The prince withdrew his hand. He moved his mouth as if he would speak. A fractional irregularity in his lower jaw meant that he had to move it forward slightly before he spoke. 'When –'

'Five days ago,' his uncle said, then he wept.

He'd never seen his uncle weep before, but he didn't embrace or touch him. After a moment he got up and went to the window, looking at the men who were still practising their manoeuvres with what now seemed meaningless repetition. It was the fourteenth day of April. His father had died. He was king.

Who has known such joys
Can go quickly as he came
To that dispersion where we are all formed.

187

How strange that he'd been trying to remember that verse just before his uncle came.

He'd not seen much of his father; he had been too preoccupied by state affairs. But the king had come recently to Ludlow, in order to see the progress his son was making in his lessons.

He had excelled himself that day, in Latin, geometry and Greek, but when it came to horsemanship and archery he'd been less impressive. His father hadn't been pleased.

But he hadn't said so, he'd waited for the prince to criticise his own performance, which he'd done, saying that his posture had not been good, his wrist not strong enough and his aim erratic.

He'd recited this catalogue of faults then looked up nervously at his father.

'I'm not like you,' he'd said, then, in case his father was displeased again by this, he added, 'I don't think I will be a great warrior.'

His father had placed a hand on his shoulder. 'There's more than one way of being a king,' he'd said. 'There is the old way, and the new.'

And he'd walked with him then, saying that the new king would be more learned than any of his subjects, whether they were doctors, lawyers or philosophers. He would need the wisdom of Solomon, rather than the strength of Samson, to keep his enemies at bay and to enrich his nation by means other than warfare.

It was the longest time his father had ever spent talking to him. He'd felt proud and anxious at the same time, wondering whether he should take the opportunity to display his knowledge again, which everyone said was prodigious.

But the moment passed, and his father, once he'd finished speaking, seemed preoccupied. 'Well,' he said, and it was almost a sigh. 'In the end we do what we can.'

And they'd carried on walking together in silence, the prince uncomfortably aware of his father's weight still pressing on his shoulder.

Now that weight was gone. And in its place was the weight of the Crown and the nation. Even though he'd not seen his father often, he felt as though some massive support had vanished, or the sky had lifted suddenly, leaving him vulnerable, exposed. For all his training, he didn't know how to be king. A nation seemed to him to be a vast, unwieldy thing.

All this time, his uncle had been watching him, waiting for him to respond. He had risen from his knees and was sitting on a low stool. He knew his nephew well enough not to rush or press him. Besides, his mind was preoccupied with other questions.

That morning he'd received two letters, one from his nephew the Marquis of Dorset telling him the king was dead and his will had designated the Duke of Gloucester Protector of both the nation and the young prince. The prince had already been proclaimed King Edward V in London. That news had been startling enough, but the second letter had been from his sister Elizabeth, telling him to come directly, bringing only the garrison he had at Ludlow. *But see they be well armed and measurably accoutred.* Gloucester was coming from Middleham, she wrote, to rule as he thought. She, however, was determined he should not rule unaided, but *as one among many.* She'd said as much to the Council.

The Council, of course, consisted mainly of his own family and affinity. He didn't suppose that Hastings, for one, would support this decision. According to his nephew, his brother Edward Woodville had already blockaded Calais to prevent Hastings from summoning his own garrison.

So he, Earl Rivers, was to bring the prince to London for his coronation, accompanied only by his small garrison.

They were afraid of Gloucester, of his hostility to their family, but he was not afraid. It seemed clear to him that some reasonable compromise would have to be made with the duke, and that he, as the oldest of the Woodville family, should be the one to make it. After all, they were both uncle to the young king; both of them should have his interests at heart.

It did occur to him, however, to wonder how many men the duke would have with him.

But his nephew was looking at him again, moving his jaw. 'What will happen now?' he said.

'Nothing,' said Anthony Woodville. 'We're not expected in London until the first day of May. You'll be crowned soon after.' He saw a look of uncertainty in the young prince's eyes and went on quickly, 'We need not set off straight away. We'll celebrate St George's Day here, with a special ceremony, to commemorate your father. But from now on,' he said, 'you will speak and act as king.'

'But – you will help me?' his nephew said.

'Of course,' said Earl Rivers. 'I will always help you. But the first thing we should do,' he said, standing suddenly, 'is to go to the chapel, to pray for your father's soul.'

He waited for his nephew to leave the room, because now that he was king all the rules of precedence had changed. But as they went into the corridor, he placed his hand gently, briefly, on his nephew's shoulder. Because he was his nephew, and still a boy, king or not. And he, Earl Rivers, had brought him up. He was closer to the young king than to any other member of his family. The previous king had renewed his commission to look after the Prince of Wales. And he had no intention of relinquishing that commission – whatever Gloucester had in mind.

Meanwhile, in London, the body of the dead king was moved from the Chapel of St Stephen at Westminster to the Chapel of St George at Windsor.

He had been wrapped in cerements and waxed linen, and clothed with robes of state. Shoes of red leather were on his feet, so that he might walk easily through Purgatory. A life-sized effigy of him with a crown on his head, a sceptre in one hand and an orb in the other stood on top of the hearse, and above this was a fringed canopy of cloth of gold. When the people saw this effigy they wept and groaned in grief.

The procession was led by fifteen knights and squires of the body, followed by ten bishops and two abbots and a long line of paupers carrying torches. The body went to Charing Cross, where it stayed the night in the Chapel of Sion, guarded by nine lords and one hundred men, then the next day to Eton, where the bishops of Ely and Lincoln censed the corpse and, finally, on the twentieth day of April, it arrived at the Chapel of St George, where lay the bodies of the king's little son George and his daughters Margaret and Mary.

Masses were said by the Archbishop of York, Thomas Rotherham, Bishop Russell and Bishop Dudley of Durham. The queen's son Sir Richard Grey, her other son the Marquis of Dorset, Sir Edward Woodville and the Bishop of Salisbury, her brothers, knelt together with the lords Hastings and Stanley, and made offerings of cloth of gold.

The chief mourner was the Earl of Lincoln, son of John de la Pole. The new king remained at Ludlow with his uncle Earl Rivers, and the queen herself remained in her rooms at Westminster.

Offerings were made of the dead king's helmet, shield and swords, then all the officers of his household and his heralds cast their staves of office and their coats of arms into the grave. So many candles were lit that the church reeked of tallow and the doors had to be opened because of the choking smell. The company departed, leaving the body in the tomb, where chantry priests would sing masses for as long as it would take to purge the dead king of his sins.

Which some said would take for ever, although already the people at least had forgiven him. They remembered him now as brave and good, heroic and handsome, full of that love for life that life repays with love. Many men had stories of how he had been familiar with them, raising them from their knees and walking with one arm about their shoulders as if they were old friends. Many women also had tales of their familiarity with the king, but didn't speak so freely of this if their husbands were around. In their memories now he was larger even than his effigy.

> King Edward was very tall of personage, exceeding the stature of almost all others, of comely visage, pleasant looks, broad-breasted . . . of sharp wit, high courage, passing retentive memory, diligent in his affairs, ready in perils, earnest and horrible to his enemies, bountiful to his friends and acquaintances, most fortunate in his wars . . . he left a wealthy realm, abounding in all things . . . and so bound to him the goodwill of the people that they mourned him long after he was dead.
>
> *Polydore Vergil*

> When the body of the dead king had been taken for honourable burial . . . everyone looked forward to the eagerly desired coronation of the new king.
>
> *Crowland Chronicle*

22

Northampton

The young king rode his white palfrey in silence, accompanied by his uncle Earl Rivers.

They were going to Northampton, to meet his other uncle, Richard of Gloucester. He had several uncles, but he hardly knew that one. He'd heard tales of his bravery, of course, but had met him only once or twice. His uncle Rivers told him that, since they would be passing Stony Stratford, it would be a pity if he could not see his grandparents' home. It would be a pleasant interlude for him there, while the old men got on with discussing affairs of state.

Instantly, the new king knew the earl didn't want him at these discussions. He'd spent so much time with his uncle that their minds were perfectly attuned.

Now the earl reached over and pulled the young king's reins so he had to slow down.

'You're not listening,' he said sternly.

'But I have heard.'

'What have you heard?'

The boy fixed his unearthly blue eyes on his uncle and said, 'I've heard that you don't trust my uncle of Gloucester and don't want me to meet him for reasons that you will not say.'

Earl Rivers knew better than to deny what his nephew had said, or to try to reassure him. Instead he began telling him about Stony Stratford, where he'd grown up. It was also, of course, where the young king's father had met his mother.

His father, who had been king.

It was impossible to think of anyone being king other than his father. Every night since hearing the news the young king had woken with his heart pounding in an uncertain rhythm, *you are king now, you are king now.*

He didn't feel like a king, though he'd spent his whole life preparing for it. He felt like a young boy with an aching jaw that no amount of tooth-pulling by his surgeons seemed to relieve. Also, he had poor eyesight, caused, they said, by an over-burdening of knowledge, and his headaches were fearful.

People said he was handsome, like his father, but he'd already learned that no one spoke the truth to a king.

Sometimes he thought his younger brother, who was in fact like his father, would make a better king. But he was the eldest and would soon be crowned. He wondered if the coronation itself would make a difference.

His uncle Rivers was speaking again, and once again he'd not been listening. It was as though he'd forgotten how to listen since hearing the news. He tried, and then that voice said, *you will be king,* his heart began to pound and all other words were lost.

But his uncle was saying, 'Here's your brother now.'

And he saw Sir Richard Grey, coming to meet them before they reached the town.

'At your service, sire,' he said, taking off his hat and making an exaggerated bow.

The young king didn't smile. 'I expect there are things you will want to discuss with my uncle,' he said, 'and don't want me to hear.'

Sir Richard looked at Earl Rivers, and the older man shook his head slightly as if to say, *don't ask.* The young king spurred his horse forward.

'If anyone wants me, I'll be just out of earshot,' he said.

Richard Grey pulled his horse closer to his uncle's. 'The plans have changed,' he said.

At Northampton, Richard, Duke of Gloucester, was met by Duke Henry of Buckingham.

Polydore Vergil

*

'I'll bet you anything you like,' the Duke of Buckingham said, 'that the king is not at Northampton. The queen has no intention of letting you anywhere near her son.'

Richard of Gloucester said he had no reason to doubt the letter sent to him by Earl Rivers.

'It's not Earl Rivers you have to doubt,' said Duke Henry, 'but the queen and her son. They've already begun plundering the treasure of the Tower. They've appointed their own commissioners. And your name was nowhere on the list.'

Then, when they arrived at Northampton, the streets were empty.

'It can't be easy to hide an army,' said the duke.

Richard's gaze narrowed as he scanned the square. He said, 'We should wait.'

'What – so they can reach London without us? We could at least send out some scouts to find out where they are.'

There was something underneath Buckingham's usual bombast. Years of resenting his wife's family, perhaps. But Richard didn't want to be deflected from his plan. He'd already found an inn for the night, he said. He was tired, his men were tired and so were the horses. Besides, they couldn't be sure that the king wasn't on his way to them, even now.

And just at that moment they heard the sound of horses' hooves.

But it was only Earl Rivers, with a few men.

He rode up to them then dismounted swiftly. 'My lords,' he said, 'I'm glad I've not missed you.'

Buckingham looked at Richard as if to say, *now let's hear what tale he tells.*

'I must apologise,' the earl said. 'His majesty the king has had to ride on to Stony Stratford. There was not enough accommodation here for all his men.'

'Is there more accommodation at Stony Stratford?' queried Buckingham, and the earl said at least the king had a place there. 'And there's more than enough room for you and your men here,' he added, repeating that he was glad he hadn't missed them.

'You wouldn't have missed us if you'd waited here, as promised,' Buckingham said.

Earl Rivers spoke only to the Duke of Gloucester. 'His majesty very much regrets not being able to meet you,' he said. 'He suggests we could meet him tomorrow at Stony Stratford, and ride to London together, if you will. He is indeed sorry that he couldn't be here.'

'But you are here,' said Richard.

'I've taken a room here for the night,' Earl Rivers said. 'Because, as you know, there are many things to discuss.'

For the first time, Richard smiled, suddenly and briefly. 'Then we should go to my inn,' he said, 'and dine together.'

> So was there made that night friendly cheer between these dukes and Lord Rivers.
>
> *Thomas More*

23

An Honourable Man

Earl Rivers wore a hair shirt beneath his costly garments, spent several hours a day in prayer, fasted more frequently than was required. And he went on pilgrimages when he could, bringing back wisdom and knowledge from afar. He'd produced the first book ever printed in England.

That, he believed, was his real work, to make available the wisdom of the ancients. Somewhere in the confluence of Christian and pagan philosophy he thought might be found the *pearl of great price*. What these ancient scholars left behind them was indeed like a pearl. A residue of perfection from their mortal toil, the essence of everything they had learned.

But his sister Elizabeth had assiduously sought promotion for him. He was Lord of the Isle of Wight, High Sheriff of Caernarvonshire; he had been Lieutenant of Calais and Admiral of the Fleet. He owned land in Norfolk, Cambridge, Hertford, Sussex, Essex, Wales and the Marches. He was Lord Scales in right of his wife. And of course he was Earl Rivers, head of the Woodville clan.

He had turned down many other offices, saying they would leave him no time for his studies. Because with each role came responsibilities: repairs and maintenance, lawsuits and administration. It amounted to an absolute burden of care.

What did it mean, then, to *be in the world but not of it*, as Christ had once proclaimed? In his more jaded moments, Anthony Woodville thought Christ had not come from a large family of brothers and sisters, all of whom were jockeying for position. If he had, he might have remained a carpenter.

Of course, he didn't know how many brothers or sisters Christ had. But he did know that none of them was queen.

He had accepted the office of governor to the young prince, however, with a wary optimism. It seemed, unlike all his other commissions, to offer him the chance to be removed from court, legitimately immersed in his studies.

His sister had obtained this for him, finally acknowledging his needs. Terrifyingly acquisitive, she was also conscientious in her duty of care. Sometimes she was like a magpie, at others like a brooding hen, and if she or any of her family was threatened she became as savage as a swan. She had submitted her son to his guidance, however, knowing they would flourish together.

And they had flourished, because the prince's mind was, it turned out, remarkably similar to his own. He had the same serious intent and thirst for knowledge. If he could have had a son, he'd often thought, he would choose this one. He could not have been happier in his role.

But in March his sister had written to him, saying the king was ill and the earl should send for a copy of the royal patent that had made him governor to the prince.

He knew she wouldn't rest until he'd done as she asked.

Then came the shock of Edward's death, which had precipitated further letters from the queen.

He had responded sympathetically, expressing his sorrow for her great loss and his own, agreeing to summon an army, then not to summon an army, but to escort the young king to London as quickly as possible.

Do not hold any conference with the Duke of Gloucester, she'd written. *Do not, under any circumstances, allow him to take custody of my son.*

He had agreed again, sensing in this latest drama the end of all his hopes of pursuing a peaceful, scholarly path. For if his sister had her way a Regency Council would relegate the Protector to a minor post, while he himself, doubtlessly, would be expected to take the lead. He would be immersed again in all the sordid squabbles of the court.

And yet Gloucester, so far, had shown no sign of hostility. He'd written cordially to the earl and they'd agreed to meet at Northampton, to escort the young king into London for his coronation.

Nothing could be more reasonable.

So when his other nephew, Richard Grey, had approached him outside the town with a new message, he'd felt that sinking of the heart that had lately accompanied all exchanges with his family.

'Don't wait at Northampton,' he'd said. 'My mother wants you to press on to London with all speed.'

He'd argued, of course, that he'd already agreed to meet the Protector and it would not do to fan the flames of that particular fire.

His nephew had responded with that peculiar barricading of all alternate points of view that was so common in their family. Those were his mother's wishes, he'd said, and she was queen. It was not right to flout her, given the current state of affairs. It would precipitate a crisis.

Are you with us or against us? his eyes had said.

And Anthony Woodville, feeling the age-old resentment of all those who have ever been compromised by their families, had finally agreed, against his better judgement, to bypass Northampton and go to Stony Stratford with his nephews.

But his better judgement nagged at him all the way there, until, having found a room for the young king at the Rose and Crown inn, he said, 'I'll ride back to Northampton and meet the Duke of Gloucester, as I promised.'

Richard Grey had looked surprised by this, then contemptuous that his uncle would put the Protector before his own family. But at least the young king was safely in his care.

So Anthony Woodville rode back, taking only a few retainers with him.

He'd not been pleased to find the Duke of Buckingham with Gloucester. And Buckingham had made things harder for him, casting doubt on the explanation he'd offered. Gloucester, however, had responded with courtesy, inviting him to his inn.

Where he'd unexpectedly enjoyed himself. The food was good, the wine average but plentiful; they drank many toasts to the new king and the new world that was to come. Buckingham was especially merry, telling stories of the late king with wit and zest, so that the three of them were united by their memories.

They had even asked him about his studies. And managed to look interested when he replied.

After much wine he'd begun to relax, to view the future with an expansive glow. This was how it should be – there was no necessity for conflict and division. He drank some more, then, realising how late it was, he excused himself, saying they should make an early start in the morning, and made his way to his own inn, feeling vindicated. He'd been right to try to mend the rift in the new king's family and to avert disaster for them all. Sometimes it was given, he reflected as he stripped to his shirt, to the man who is *in the world but not of it* to say or do something to amend that world. Once in his bed, he fell peacefully asleep with the mellow conscience of one who has drunk much and forgotten more.

Which was why, when his servant woke him the next morning with the news that his inn was locked and barricaded, he reacted with incomprehension and disbelief.

> Now had these dukes taken into their custody the keys of the inn so that none should pass forth without their approval. And besides this, on the highway toward Stony Stratford where the king lay, they had ordered their men that they should compel to return any man who were gotten out of Northampton . . .
>
> *Thomas More*

He ran down the stairs in his nightshirt, shook and rattled the door to the inn. 'Where is the landlord?' he demanded of his servant. 'Where are all the people of the inn?'

His servant could only say he didn't know, but there were guards outside both doors.

The earl banged on the door with the flat of his hands. 'You out there – what's the meaning of this?'

But there was no reply.

Suddenly conscious that he wasn't dressed, the earl ran up the stairs again and began pulling on his clothes while looking out of the window.

The square was full of armed men. Guards were posted at all the exits to it, at all the streets that led away from the town.

His servant pointed out they were all wearing the livery of the Duke of Gloucester.

Still he couldn't make sense of what was happening. But as he fell back from the window a horrible awareness pressed on him. With one part of his mind he was reviewing, or attempting to review, everything he'd said on the previous night; with another he was planning his escape.

'There must be another exit through the cellars,' he said. 'Or we could break a window.'

His servant said only there were too many guards outside.

Earl Rivers returned to the window. He could see a servant of the Duke of Gloucester crossing the square indifferently, as though nothing very much was happening. He hammered on the window to attract his attention. 'HOY! YOU THERE!' he shouted, but the servant didn't even look up. Earl Rivers managed to prise the window open with his knife and leaned out as far as he could. 'YOU!' he barked so loudly that he could see the servant start. 'Let me out of here now. AT ONCE!'

The servant said he couldn't do that, he wasn't allowed.

'Where is the Duke of Gloucester?' the earl demanded. 'Let me speak to him!'

With aggravating slowness, the servant turned and went back to the inn he'd just left. And after what seemed an interminable amount of time, the two dukes came out.

'What is this?' he shouted to them. 'What's going on?'

[Gloucester and Buckingham] arrested Earl Rivers . . . and certain others . . . and ordered them to be taken to the North in captivity. Immediately after . . . they went to the place where the youthful king was staying . . . The Duke of Gloucester did not refuse to offer to his nephew the king any of the reverence required from a subject . . . uncovering his head, bending his knee . . . he said that he was only taking precautions to safeguard his own person because he knew for certain that there were men close to the king who had sworn to destroy his honour and his life.

Crowland Chronicle

The youth, possessing the likeness of his father's spirit, replied to this saying 'What my brother Marquess has done I cannot say, but in good faith I dare well answer for my Lord Rivers and my brother here (Grey) that they be innocent of any such matter.' . . . He believed that they were good and faithful ministers, he could see nothing evil in them and wished to keep them . . .

Dominic Mancini

Richard Duke of Gloucester, brother of the dead king, and by his ordinance Protector of England, took the new king into his governance. Anthony, Earl Rivers, brother of the queen, Richard Grey, brother of the king on his mother's side, and Sir Thomas Vaughn, were removed from their office, arrested and sent to be imprisoned at Pontefract.

John Rous

At which dealing [the young king] wept and was nothing content.

Thomas More

24

Archbishop Rotherham Hears the News

Now came there a messenger not long after midnight from the
Lord Chamberlain (Hastings) unto the Archbishop of York, to his
place not far from Westminster and he showed the servants he
had tidings of so great importance that his master had charged
him not to tolerate their master's rest . . .

Thomas More

Even as a child the archbishop had disliked the first
moments of waking more than any other. His nurse
had said he used to cry inconsolably, as if anticipating
all the harm a day might bring. Still, now, the first
moments of waking felt to him as though he was deeply lost in
that otherworld of sleep. It was difficult to place a foothold on
the shore of consciousness.

At one time he'd wondered if this was a sign of saintliness, or
at least virtue; proof he didn't belong fully in this troubled world.
But as the years advanced he'd come reluctantly to accept that it
was a failure in his body. He woke regularly to the sensations of
heartburn and despair, a kind of limpness and reluctance in his
limbs. He had coped with the rigours of clerical life only by retir-
ing very early to bed and by snatching a few moments of sleep
during meetings or prayer.

All his servants knew not to disturb him, certainly not to wake
him by bending over him and imploring him to put on his robes.

'Whh–,' he said.

'I'm sorry, my lord,' his servant's voice said. 'I couldn't stop
him – we couldn't keep him out –'

'Get up now,' said a different voice; and his servant said with

203

rising agitation, 'You must wait outside – my master cannot see you here!'

'He will see me,' the intruder said. 'He'll want to hear what I have to say.'

The archbishop struggled with competing sensations. His eyes were still closed but the darkness had taken on an orange glow. Someone was lighting candles; his nostrils were assailed by the smell of tallow. 'Whmff,' he said.

'You must forgive me, your grace,' the strange voice said. 'My master, Lord Hastings, said I must not leave until I had imparted urgent news that you, above all others, should know.'

The archbishop tried to rise, but failed. He was too old for this, he thought. It was not for him, this political knife-edge, this endless drama. He could feel himself being sucked back into unconsciousness, but then someone actually shook his shoulder, and his servant cried, 'Now this is too much! You must leave at once or I'll call the guard!'

The archbishop clutched the bedclothes to him in a defensive manoeuvre. 'Wh– Who is it?' he managed to say, then, peevishly, 'I cannot see you.'

'You must open your eyes, your grace,' the voice said.

With some difficulty, the archbishop managed to squint. A long, unshaven chin came into his line of vision and, for the first time, he felt a pang of fear. *Murderer*, he thought sadly, for ever since being awarded his high office he had anticipated a violent end. Or robbery, at least. 'Who is it?' he said; and the man spoke a name he didn't recognise or fully hear, then said, 'Servant and messenger to my Lord Hastings.'

'Shall I send him away?' his own servant said.

At last the archbishop understood that something was required from him. His heart began to thump erratically; there was an unpleasant taste in his mouth. He struggled into a sitting position, clutching the bedclothes to his chest, and squinted again, because his blurred vision would not clear. 'Do I know you?' he said.

'You've seen me before,' said the face, and the archbishop realised that he had, in fact, seen this young man before, at Council meetings. He would think the archbishop was witless with age.

'What is it?' he asked irritably.

'My master, the Lord Chamberlain, sends you greetings, and offers his apologies for disturbing your rest.'

The archbishop closed his eyes once more, then opened them. 'That's surely not why he sent you,' he said.

'No, my lord. He says to tell you that something of the utmost consequence has occurred.'

'Am I to guess?' said the archbishop, then realised the intruder was gazing meaningfully at the archbishop's servant. But the archbishop didn't want to be alone with the intruder. 'Speak,' he said. 'What you have to say can be heard by both of us.'

The messenger glanced doubtfully at the servant, but said, 'Well, then. My master said to tell you the Lord Protector is coming towards London with the king.'

The archbishop thought he couldn't have heard correctly. Everyone knew the Protector was coming to London with the king. 'Is that all?' he said.

'No, your grace. My Lord Protector has taken the king into his custody.'

The archbishop shook his head. It failed to clear his brain. 'You've woken me up, at this hour, to tell me that the Duke of Gloucester, who has been awarded custody of his nephew, has taken him into that custody?'

'Yes, my lord. And he has sent his other uncle and the king's brother into prison.'

Now at last the significance of what the messenger was saying struck home. The archbishop's heart set up its characteristic knocking complaint. 'Earl Rivers –' he said.

'Prison, sir.'

'And – Sir Richard Grey?'

'Prison – and Thomas Vaughn with them.'

'How –' said the archbishop, meaning, *how was it possible?* then he said, 'Where?'

'No one knows, your worship, though I daresay my master will soon find out. He's already written to the Protector at Northampton, where he waits with the Duke of Buckingham and the king.'

The archbishop stared at him helplessly. 'Why – why has he done this?'

'My master didn't say.'

'But – there will be war!'

'My master said there will not be war, nor any trouble of that kind.'

'Does the queen know?'

'I imagine so, your grace.'

The archbishop sank back. Not only his heart but his head was pounding. He felt weak with realisation. 'This is very grave news,' he said. 'Very grave news indeed.'

'Notwithstanding, sir,' the messenger said, 'my lord sends your lordship word not to fear. He assures you all will be well.'

'I can assure him,' said the archbishop, 'it will not be well. It may never be well again.' Then he looked around the room, as if he had lost something. 'The queen,' he said. 'I must go to the queen.'

When the news of so outrageous and horrible a fact came to London all men were wondrously amazed and in great fear, but especially Elizabeth the queen . . .

Polydore Vergil

In great flight and heaviness, bewailing her child's ruin and her own infortune, damning the time that she ever dissuaded the gathering of power about the king, [the queen] got herself in all haste possible with her youngest son and her daughters out of the Palace of Westminster into the Sanctuary, lodging herself and her company there in the Abbot's place . . . [The Archbishop of York] caused in all haste all his servants to be called up and so with his own household about him and every man weaponed, he took the Great Seal with him and came yet before day to the queen. About whom he found much heaviness, rumble, haste and business, carriage and conveyance of her stuff into Sanctuary, chests, coffers, packs, fardels, trusses, all on men's backs . . . the queen herself sat alone on the rushes all desolate and dismayed . . .

Thomas More

It took a moment for him even to recognise the queen, who sat alone, head bowed, dressed not with her customary splendour but in a simple cloak and gown. As soon as he had recognised her, however, the archbishop went up to her, then knelt, somewhat clumsily, among the dust and rushes.

'Your majesty,' he said. 'I've just heard.'

She didn't lift her head.

'I came as soon as I could. I'm so sorry.'

She expelled a breath, as if she had been holding it. 'He's taken my son,' she said.

'Yes, your majesty – but he's bringing him here, to London.'

'He has imprisoned my brother – and my other son.'

'But not for long, your majesty. Your son will be crowned and then –'

'And then Gloucester will rule,' she said, turning on him a look of terrifying bleakness.

'No, my lady – not so. The people – and the lords – know who is king.'

'The lords,' she said bitterly. 'They're all on his side.'

'Your majesty' – the archbishop made a move as if to clasp her hands, but restrained himself – 'the lords want to see your son crowned as much as we do.'

'He will not be crowned,' she said.

Archbishop Rotherham protested. Of course he would be

crowned – it was unthinkable that he would not. The coronation would be held in three days' time.

'And where is he?' she said, turning that bleak stare on him again.

The archbishop began to talk rapidly. 'He's on his way here, now, for the coronation. My Lord Hastings said so.'

'*Hastings,*' she said, with such venom it was almost a hiss.

Ah woe worth him! quod she, for he is one of them that labours to destroy me and my blood.

Thomas More

The archbishop didn't know what to say. He could only repeat what Hastings' messenger had told him: that there was nothing to fear and all would be well. The queen made a small movement with her head, not quite shaking it, and closed her eyes.

Then the archbishop withdrew a silver casket from his robes. 'I've brought the Great Seal for you,' he said, holding it out towards the queen. She looked at it wonderingly. 'Nothing can be done without it – keep it as surety for the king.'

The queen opened the casket. There lay the Seal in its silken wrap. The archbishop felt a qualm at his own daring. The queen touched the Great Seal with her finger, then rapidly shut the lid again. She glanced around. The flames from the torches guttered in the gusts of wind caused by the movements of men fetching and carrying, loading and unloading, shouting orders. Crates and boxes, trunks full of tapestries and plate, were being passed from one man to another. Two men were hacking a hole in the Sanctuary wall so that larger items could pass through.

'This – is not the place,' she said, and at the same time he said, 'I thought you should have it.' He wanted to say it was a gesture of faith but felt suddenly tongue-tied, overwhelmed. The Protector would be furious with him. But he would say he'd done it to reassure the queen that she need not be afraid, all would be well. Which he hoped was true.

She tucked the casket beneath her own cloak, then said, 'It's no use without the king.'

'No, my lady,' he said, 'but the king cannot act without it.'

She looked at him without speaking, so he said, 'Where are your other children?'

'They are here, with me,' she said, and he told her there was no reason, therefore, to despair.

> For I assure you that if they crown any king other than your son whom they now have with them, we shall on the morrow crown his brother whom you have here with you.
>
> *Thomas More*

He didn't know whether he was trying to reassure her or himself. 'So you see,' he finished, when she didn't respond, 'you have the Seal, and your other son, and the king is on his way here to be crowned.'

She closed her eyes then. The archbishop thought she might weep. He didn't know what to do with weeping women, especially queens. One could not hold them, or pat their shoulders. So he said quickly, 'Where's the marquis? Is he here?'

She opened her eyes, but he couldn't read her expression. 'The marquis,' she said slowly, 'is busy – elsewhere.'

It was the archbishop's turn to bow his head. 'Ah,' he said. The marquis would be intent on resisting the Protector. He would try to rouse the other lords against him. There would be war, and Richard of Gloucester would win. Which would make his own actions seem like a betrayal.

But there was no point thinking the worst.

'*Honi soit qui mal y pense*,' he said, quoting the words on the Great Seal, attempting to smile. The queen didn't smile. Nor did she tell him he could get up, but his knees were hurting. Slowly and stiffly he began to rise, apologising, brushing bits of sawdust from his robes. 'Well, your majesty,' he said, 'I must leave you now, but I will return. And rest assured, I'm not the only one who wants to amend this – situation.'

When she didn't move he held his hand out to her, but she didn't take it. Archbishop Rotherham felt a momentary awkwardness – he wouldn't normally turn his back on the queen. But he felt a strong impulse to return to his own rooms. So after a moment he bowed and left, and the image of her sitting there, like an effigy in stone, remained with him all the way home.

By which time he might in his chamber window see all the Thames full of boats of the Duke of Gloucester's servants watching that no man should go into Sanctuary nor none could pass unsearched . . .

Thomas More

The dukes brought the new king to London [on 4th May] to be received in regal style . . . and they compelled all the lords spiritual and temporal and the mayor and aldermen to take the oath of fealty to the king [which] was performed with pride and joy by all . . .

Crowland Chronicle

The Protector removed the Archbishop of York from the office of Chancellor, and Master John Russell, Bishop of Lincoln, replaced him . . .

John Rous

25

The Queen's Audacity

At the next meeting of the lords of the Council the Protector proposed to them that it was a heinous deed of the queen's proceeding
from great malice toward the king's councillors that she should
keep in Sanctuary the king's brother from him . . . as though they
were not to be trusted . . . It was pure malice, audacity or folly that
caused her to keep him there . . .

Thomas More

She'd already received several letters from the Council, saying her children could not receive the bequests left to them
by their loving father while they remained in Sanctuary.

She'd replied that she would consider coming out
when and if her brother and son were released from prison and
she had proof they were safe and well. No explanation had been
offered to her for this untoward and unlawful imprisonment;
there had been no plot against the Duke of Gloucester. Earl Rivers and Sir Richard had only been conducting her son the king to
London, as requested by the Council.

In another letter they said if she kept the younger prince and
the rest of her family in Sanctuary it would seem that she did not
trust the Council. She replied that since the Duke of Gloucester
had taken the king her son into his custody so precipitately, using
unnecessary force and removing him from everyone he knew, she
was necessarily concerned for the welfare of her other children.

She derived a certain satisfaction from rebutting their arguments, but there was no progress, no foreseeable end to this
situation. The most that could be said was that it gave her something to do. Life in Sanctuary had become a tedious routine. She

rarely left the abbot's house, in order to avoid being accosted by one of the thieves or beggars who clustered around it. She recoiled from the noise and squalor of the surrounding streets so remained cloistered like a nun, taking mass, listening to the younger children read. On certain days she felt overcome by lassitude, and as if she was looking at the world through a dark tunnel.

Thirteen years ago she had retreated into Sanctuary after her husband had fled the country. That time it had been Warwick who had usurped power and had executed her father and her brother. All she'd been able to do was await the birth of her son and pray daily for her husband to return.

Now her husband could never return and her son had been taken captive by Gloucester. She could taste the bitterness of it in her mouth; the bitterness of loss against which she had striven all her life. This was where her striving had got her, trapped like an animal in a hole.

Her son the marquis was less confined, mingling freely with the Sanctuary rabble. She didn't reprimand him for this, because Sanctuary had changed things between them. He had assumed the role of head of the family.

It irked her, however, when he was late for meetings, which were the chief focus of her day. They met at ten in the Jerusalem Chamber, where the abbot conducted his official business, to discuss any developments. Already half an hour had passed. Her daughter Elizabeth sighed pointedly, while the abbot wore his usual expression of good cheer in the face of adversity.

She remarked that her son must be on some important errand.

'Drinking and gambling,' her daughter said, but the queen said there might be news in the city.

'He can't go to the city,' her daughter said. 'He can only go to his whores in Thieving Lane.'

'I apologise for my daughter,' the queen said to the abbot. 'Evidently, she has something more important to do.'

'Apologise for your son,' her daughter said, while at the same time the abbot said, 'Not at all,' and she wasn't to worry, he didn't mind waiting. The princess shot a sour glance in his direction. She'd grown more waspish with the passing weeks. The marquis had said her presence wasn't necessary at these meetings, since she was only a girl, but the queen had replied that she would one day be a wife, to some prince or courtier, and who needed to be more politic than a wife?

Nobody said there was no prince or courtier on earth who would marry the princess now. Not unless, *until* her brother was crowned. She was seventeen years old, beautiful and the daughter of a king, but her prospects had never been lower. So the queen didn't speak sharply to her daughter but said merely that whatever company her son kept gave him valuable information, which they depended on now.

Over the past few weeks he'd brought them news of the changes Gloucester had made in Council. The Protector had rewarded all those who had supported him, such as the Earl of Northumberland and the Duke of Norfolk. The greatest awards had been given to the Duke of Buckingham, however, who was now Constable of England, Chief Justice and Lord Chamberlain of Wales. It was said Gloucester would marry his son to Buckingham's daughter.

A new date had been fixed for the coronation and, more worryingly, Gloucester had extended the terms of his Protectorate until the young king attained his majority. Her son had been moved to the royal apartments in the Tower, where preparations for the coronation were going ahead.

Also, the marquis had told them her brother Edward had fled to France, with Gloucester's ships pursuing him. He was making his way to the Earl of Richmond in Brittany.

She received these messages avidly, like a starving animal driven to eat poisoned meat. She didn't know where the marquis got his news from and didn't care, so long as it came.

The princess shifted restlessly. 'He won't come, Mother,' she said. 'He's found some new washerwoman to woo. All we do is wait, wait, wait for him,' she said, getting up, and as if this was his cue, he arrived.

He'd been drinking, she could see that at once. His face and eyes were reddened; his clothes looked as though they'd been slept in. Her daughter shot her a look as if to say, *see*, and the queen said, 'Well, Thomas, you've kept us all waiting. I hope it was worth it.'

The marquis looked around the room with sullen eyes and the abbot offered him his chair. Which he accepted at once, slinging one leg over the armrest.

'Well?' said the queen, but he appeared to be studying a cherub on a tile.

'Gloucester has called another Council,' he said finally. 'He's put it to them that, since your younger son is no criminal, he doesn't need Sanctuary and can't claim it. Therefore, it would be no crime to take him out by force if necessary.'

The princess gave a little cry of protest, and even the abbot looked aghast. 'But – it is *Sanctuary* –' he said. 'It may not be violated.'

'That's what the Archbishop of Canterbury said, apparently,' her son replied.

'Because it's true!' said the abbot. 'No one has come uninvited to Sanctuary for more than five hundred years. Since St Peter himself descended on it with all the angels!'

The marquis looked at him with dislike. 'Just so,' he said. 'However, it's a legal point. If a child doesn't need Sanctuary, he can't claim it.'

The queen remembered that the latest letter from the Council had made special mention of her youngest son. It was the opinion of them all, it said, that Sanctuary was no place for him. He should not be surrounded by thieves and murderers.

Each time they wrote they advanced their argument methodically, by a single point, like an army advancing relentlessly to siege.

'What can I do?' she said, and her son shrugged.

'If they come with an armed force,' he said, 'you'll have to give him up.'

'No!' she said; and in the same moment the abbot cried, 'But this is monstrous – I will write to the archbishop!'

'Aye, do,' her son said; then, less laconically, 'he is our only hope. And the bishops will stand with him, I suppose. And the people, of course – they won't like it either.'

'I'll write to him at once,' the abbot said, leaving the room.

'Maybe he can write to St Peter as well,' the marquis said; and the queen said, 'This is no joke!'

'I'm not laughing,' her son said, turning his reddened gaze on her.

'I won't give him up,' she said. 'They'll have to cut me down first – on sacred ground!'

'It won't come to that,' her son said, but the queen had begun to pace.

'Do they think I'm stupid?' she said. 'Do they think I don't know they want to destroy me? Destroy all of us? How do they think I could trust them?'

'They have only said my brothers should be together for the coronation,' the princess put in timidly. They both glared at her.

'Yes,' her brother said, 'and of course we believe them.'

The queen stopped pacing and stood still, biting her lip. 'I'm so tired of this game,' she said.

'Aren't we all?' said the marquis. 'There is nothing so wearying as confinement. They hope it will break our spirit.'

'You come and go as you please,' said the princess.

'No, sister, I do not,' said the marquis. 'If I could *come and go as I please*, I would be in France now, looking for my uncle.'

'And leave us here?' the princess said.

But the marquis went up to his mother and put his hands on

her shoulders. 'Write to them,' he said. 'Tell them your youngest son is sick. Nothing dangerous, but infectious, perhaps. Something they wouldn't want to be passed on to the king.'

The queen struggled to keep her voice steady. She could feel tears threatening. 'And then what?' she managed to say.

The marquis let his hands fall. 'And then – we'll do whatever we can. But nothing can be done from here. I'll have to leave.'

The princess gasped and the queen said, 'Leave? How?'

'I've not decided yet. But think, Mother – I can't stay here if they are going to break in. I have to go.'

'To save your own skin,' said the princess.

'Look what's happened to my uncle and my brother. We can't all end up in prison.'

'But you don't mind if we do,' his sister said.

'They won't imprison you,' said the marquis to his mother. They won't imprison the late king's wife and the new king's mother – even Gloucester won't go so far. I am a different matter.'

The queen could see some sense in this. She said, 'But where will you go? To your wife?'

'Of course not,' the marquis said. His wife was the stepdaughter of Lord Hastings. He would give her no opportunity to pass on information to the Lord Chamberlain, who was so close to the Protector. Although, interestingly, Hastings had not been honoured by the Council with the Protector's other friends. Nonetheless, his wife's house would be the first place they looked.

'Then where?' said the queen; and her daughter said, 'Will you be smuggled out by your washerwomen?'

The marquis shot her a warning look. 'I will go,' he said, 'to find supporters, and make new ones if I can.'

The queen turned away from him. *Must I lose everything, everyone?* she thought. 'How can you leave us?' she said.

'Mother,' he said, 'I'll be more use to you in hiding than in prison. I'll find out what I can. I'll raise people against the Protector. And I will stay in touch.'

'I'll go with you,' said the princess. 'I'll dress as your page.'

'I don't think so,' said her brother.

'When?' said the queen. 'When will you go?'

But the marquis said he didn't know yet. Not that night, certainly – he had some business to settle first. But soon.

The queen took a long, quivering breath. Soon she would go to mass with the abbot, who would spend some time convincing her not to give in to despair, which was the chief evil in the heart of man. It was the crux of his ministry, he said, to battle against despair. When she'd said she could see no hope, he'd said hope didn't depend on being seen. He'd given her a treatise on the subject, which lay unopened by her bedside.

She'd stopped arguing with him, stopped pointing out that the nobles who would have done anything for her husband would do nothing for her, that most of her family were imprisoned, exiled or dead. And now her eldest son was leaving.

There was something inevitable about it; the process of stripping away. She said, 'Go then,' and her son took her in his arms. 'God go with you,' she said, and her voice shook.

'I'm not going *now*,' he said gently. 'At least – I do have to go now – but I'm coming back.'

She nodded, unable to speak.

'Mother,' he said.

She shook her head.

After a moment he lowered his arms. 'I'll write to you,' he said.

The queen expelled another shaking breath, remembering the abbot again.

Despair, he'd told her, was only a means of bringing her to God. And she hadn't rebuked him, because she was completely dependent on his hospitality. She could hardly tell him to go away and leave her alone.

Her daughter came up to her, pressing her shoulder, touching her hand. They embraced briefly, and the queen felt the difference between her daughter's warm pliancy and her son's tensile strength.

'Mother,' she said, 'you still have us. We won't leave you.'

'I know,' said the queen.

Her son looked away from them. 'Something has to be done,' he said. 'We need to make people aware that they're threatening us with force.'

The queen separated herself from her daughter. 'As to that,' she said, 'you should let them know – let everyone know – I will never give in. I don't care what they threaten me with – I will never, voluntarily, give up my son to that man.'

Bishop Stillington

The Bishop of Bath, who had previously been King Edward's chancellor before being dismissed and imprisoned . . . revealed to the Duke of Gloucester that King Edward, being very enamoured of a certain English lady, promised to marry her provided he could sleep with her first, and she consented. The bishop said that he had married them when only he and they were present . . . later King Edward fell in love again and married the daughter of an English knight, Lord Rivers . . .

Philippe de Commines

There was a protracted silence when he'd finished. The bishop could feel everything hanging in the balance: his future, the long-awaited archbishopric; or imprisonment, even death. He knelt before the Protector as though bowed with fear. Indeed, he was afraid, but also tense with expectation.

The Protector walked away from him, towards the back of the room.

'You say you married them?'

'I did, my lord.'

'And this was before my brother married the queen?'

'Some months before, my lord.'

'Who was this lady?'

The bishop was on safer ground now. The lady herself could not be questioned, since she'd been dead for fifteen years.

'Lady Eleanor Butler, my lord, widow of Sir Thomas Butler and daughter of the Earl of Shrewsbury.'

'You're sure of this?'

'Quite sure, my lord.'

'You're sure they weren't merely betrothed, but married?'

'I married them myself.'

Now the Protector went to stand by the window. Without looking up, the bishop followed his movements anxiously.

'What evidence do you have?' he murmured.

The bishop assured him he could produce evidence of an incontrovertible kind.

... instruments, authentic doctors, proctors and notaries of the law with depositions of divers witnesses ...

Philippe de Commines

'Yet you said nothing of any of this,' the Duke of Gloucester said, 'for nineteen years.'

The bishop's heart pounded. Everything depended on the Protector's acceptance of this part of his tale.

'How could I, my lord, when your brother was king and I was no one – a lowly prelate?'

The Duke of Gloucester looked up at the ceiling for a long time. 'Married,' he said, and the bishop's heart began to beat rapidly, with a kind of joy.

Lord Stanley

The Duke of Gloucester had welcomed his wife into Crosby Place, a house he'd leased some years ago. It was not surprising, perhaps, that he preferred this more splendid residence to Baynard's Castle, yet it gave Thomas Stanley cause for concern. He had observed, he said, that those members of the Council who had courted the Protector's favour (Buckingham and Howard, in particular) had visited Crosby Place, while the rest of the Council had not been invited.

He said this to Hastings, who only shrugged. 'He's allowed to see who he wants in his own home, I suppose.'

But Lord Stanley was not persuaded that these were merely social visits. 'We don't know what they're saying,' he said.

Hastings told him he worried too much. 'If anything important was being discussed at these meetings,' he said, 'someone would see that I heard about it.'

This 'someone' was a lawyer named William Catesby; a man whom Hastings had promoted steadily and who had also found favour with Gloucester. But Hastings, whose first gift was not subtlety, thought Catesby's loyalty still lay with him, whereas Stanley thought Catesby gave loyalty to no one but himself. He'd tried to warn Hastings about him, but the Lord Chamberlain was still basking in the glow of the new love that had come to him so late in life, and the new regime, free from the Woodvilles, and wouldn't listen. 'Catesby is my third ear and second mouth,' he said.

And yet Catesby had recently sounded out Hastings about the coronation. How would it be, he'd asked, if the Protector himself ruled for an interim period?

Hastings' response had been forthright – he would serve no prince but the late king's son and rightful heir. Certainly, he would see no other man crowned – he would muster all England against any man who tried.

And Catesby had laughed and said it was only a fanciful notion on his part – the Protector had no such plans.

But Hastings had reported this to Stanley, Morton and Rotherham at a secret meeting in his own house. There had been some discussion, then, of deposing Gloucester by force and proceeding immediately with the coronation, but it came to nothing, because, as Morton said, it was plain to see that the business of the coronation was proceeding. Everything was being done to ensure it went ahead.

Hastings seemed satisfied by this, but Stanley was not.

'I don't like the way the Protector looks at us,' he said, but Hastings only laughed and said that was his normal expression, etched in acid. 'It's hard to believe he and his brother issued from the same womb,' he said.

Stanley said, 'Does Catesby know we're meeting here?'

Hastings looked discomfited for a moment, then said he might have mentioned something. 'What?' he said, at Stanley's expression. 'We're doing nothing unlawful. And Catesby will report to me.'

'He should not have to *report*,' said Stanley. 'We should be invited.'

'Seriously, do you want to go to more meetings?'

'You put too much trust in Catesby.'

'I put my faith in the new king, as you should. In a little over a year he'll attain his majority, and then where will Gloucester be, for all his plotting? Besides, we're meeting the Protector tomorrow, are we not? Perhaps he'll tell us then what's on his mind.'

There was no arguing with him. And it was true that the four of them had been summoned to a special meeting in the Tower early the next morning. So Stanley left Hastings' house still dissatisfied, and went to bed just after nine. He had a sensation of burning in his gut. It might have been the wine, though Hastings swore by the wine he brought over from Calais, or it might be his ongoing anxiety and suspicion. There was something in this situation with the Protector and Buckingham and Howard that he was failing to see, like something in the corner of his vision that disappeared when he tried to look at it directly.

Hastings would only have said that was because it wasn't there; that Stanley trusted nothing but his suspicion. So he continued to ensure that his doors were double-locked at night, then went to bed early and had troubled dreams.

On this particular night he had a dream so terrible that he woke from it sweating. He wasn't comforted when the bells chimed twelve, for it was midnight, the witching hour, on Friday 13 June.

He wasn't usually superstitious or cowardly, though more inclined to use strategy than force. Yet he didn't fear a fight so much as a situation in which he was rendered powerless, unable to defend himself, so his dream continued to haunt him as he got up. He found paper and a quill and, though his hands were actually shaking, he wrote a message to Hastings. Then he gave it to his servant, telling him to take it to the Lord Chamberlain with all speed.

The servant looked at him in some astonishment and said, 'Now?'

'Yes, now!' said Stanley. 'Wake him up if you have to – wake up the whole street!'

Lord Hastings

'Stanley has lost his nerve, or his wits,' he said, climbing back into bed.

'Stanley?' said Jane. 'What does he want?'

They had both been wakened by repeated knocking on the door. Hastings' servant had answered it, then a heated exchange had taken place, before Hastings had got up and pulled on some clothes.

'I will see to it, whatever it is,' he muttered, and Jane called softly after him, 'Be careful!'

His manservant met him on the stairs, holding a letter in his hand. 'I beg your pardon, my lord,' he said. 'This is from Lord Stanley. His servant refuses to leave.'

Hastings opened the letter, which had been roughly sealed.

I have dreamed that a wild boar slashed us both, it said. *We cannot go to the meeting. Leave with me tonight.*

Hastings stared at it as though it was written in some foreign tongue. When he looked up he saw that Stanley's servant had slipped into the hall. 'What's this?' he said. 'Is your master ill?'

'He's worried, my lord. He has bad dreams.'

Hastings glanced back down at the sheet of paper. The boar was Gloucester's emblem, of course, so the symbolism of the dream was plain. But it was only the result of Stanley's obsessive concern.

'My master says I am to wait for your reply,' the servant said.

'Tell him it's plain witchcraft to believe in such dreams,' Hastings said. 'They tell us nothing – unless we make them true by acting on them.'

Stanley's servant bowed, and Hastings, thoroughly irritated, made his way back upstairs.

He told his mistress about Stanley's message, expecting her to share his indignation, but Jane was silent. It had never seemed to her that Stanley was of a nervous disposition.

'Can't you get out of this meeting?' she said. Hastings' eyebrows rose.

'How? If the Protector wants to see us, he will see us, one way or another. Stanley can't complain he's not keeping us in his counsel and then refuse to attend a meeting! What's more likely to arouse suspicion?'

'But – the dream –'

'If we are to take notice of dreams,' Hastings said, pulling the sheets up, 'then I should have sailed to sea in a pumpkin by now, with a talking cat and a bear.'

He laughed, because she had told him about this dream a few nights ago, and he'd found it funny, but Jane wasn't amused.

'Why is this meeting in the Tower?' she asked.

'Well, probably because he wants to discuss the business of the coronation,' Hastings said. 'I told you that's where the preparations are going on.'

And when she still didn't look reassured, he kissed her on the mouth, then undid her chemise and kissed her breasts; tenderly, because she was more dear to him, this mistress, than anything in the world.

Yet as soon as light came she insisted on leaving, as she always left before he was ready for her to go. She kissed the top of his head and told him he should get some rest before the meeting.

He didn't like that either; he was sensitive to any reference to his age. He said he wouldn't sleep now, but she was insistent. So he watched her leave, fearing that she wouldn't turn as she usually did and blow a kiss; his heart lifting when she did.

Then he got back into bed and fell instantly asleep.

Soon after, on the Friday, the 13th day of June, certain lords assembled in the Tower and there sat in Council, devising the honourable solemnity of the king's coronation, of which the time appointed so near approached that the pageants and subtleties were in making day and night at Westminster ... The Protector came in among them, first about nine of the clock, saluting them courteously and excusing himself that he had been from them so long, saying merrily that he had been asleep that day. And after a little while he said to the bishop of Ely, 'My lord, you have very good strawberries at your garden in Holborn, I would like you to let us have some of them.'

'Gladly, my lord,' said he, and he sent his servant for a mess of strawberries. The Protector, praying them to spare him for a little while, departed thence and soon, between ten and eleven, he returned into the chamber among them, all changed, with a wonderfully sour, angry countenance . . .

Thomas More

The room itself seemed to darken. Stanley's face turned quite grey, but Hastings sat with an arrested smile on his face as the Protector turned to him.

'Can you tell me,' he demanded, 'what men deserve who have plotted my destruction?'

Lord Hastings looked around the room in mild astonishment, but when no one spoke he said, 'Certainly, if they have done such a thing – they deserve to be punished – but –'

'Do not serve me with "if"s and "but"s!' roared the Protector. 'I tell you they have done this!'

And therewith, as in great anger, he clapped his fist on the table. At which token given one cried treason outside the chamber . . . a door slammed and in came there rushing men in armour . . . and the Protector said to Lord Hastings 'I arrest thee, traitor!' 'What, me, my lord?' said he. 'Yea, thee, traitor,' said the Protector. And another let fly at Lord Stanley, who shrank at the stroke and fell under the table, or else his head had been cleft to the teeth . . .

Thomas More

Stanley, Morton and Rotherham were hustled from the room, but Hastings was surrounded by armed men. 'My lord – what is this?' he said, but the Protector told him he had better confess his sins.

For by St Paul I will not to dinner ere I see thy head off.

This only deepened his incomprehension. He stared round, at Howard and Buckingham and Gloucester. Only Buckingham was smiling. Something in that smile made Hastings grasp what was happening, and he started to protest. He was hauled from the room shouting that he was innocent, this was wrong – he could not believe the Protector would suspect him of any mischief against his person. His disbelief didn't leave him, even as he was dragged across the Tower Green.

In the centre of the green there was a log of timber which lay there for the purpose of repairing one of the beams in the lower hall. The branches had been lopped off; it was honed to smoothness. Hastings was pushed down to his knees before it now.

He could see the hem of a priest's robe and the tips of his shoes. Then he heard Buckingham's voice, telling him to confess his sin.

'I have nothing to confess,' he said, still with that note of incredulity in his voice. 'Nothing at all.'

In his last moments Hastings saw the pattern of bark on the log, tiny beads of dew still clinging to the grass. It struck him with wonder, so that he was silent and amazed as the first blow fell.

The first jarring pain was followed by another, so intense it caused an explosion of light and colour in his mind, before his head rolled across the grass.

> Thus fell Hastings, killed not by those enemies he had always feared, but by a friend whom he had never doubted.
>
> *Dominic Mancini*

The King

In his apartments, some way above the green, the young king wanted to know what the commotion was. His tutor, gazing out of the window, didn't know what to say. He could hardly believe what he'd just seen: the spray of blood, the green grass turning red. But to forestall the young king getting up and joining him at the window, he said, with a qualm in his voice, 'It's nothing, sire – a quarrel has broken out between some guards,' and he went back to sit with his pupil at the table, to encourage him to read his text.

But he didn't hear what the king was reading. He rubbed his fingers across his forehead and closed his eyes.

When he opened them again he could see the gold and vermilion angels on the walls, the floor tiles decorated with royal leopards, which were the emblem of Richard II.

That doomed king.

The young king had always been transparently pleased to see Hastings; he was a reassuring presence, full of optimism and good humour. They had walked together around the Tower walls and gardens, and Hastings had talked of how his father had been a great king, but he would be still greater. He could hardly wait, he'd said, to see the new world the young king would bring about.

And now his head had rolled across the Tower Green.

The king was looking at his tutor with those disconcerting eyes. 'What is it?' he said. 'What's happened?'

The tutor opened his mouth, then closed it again. He said, 'I – don't know.'

Another boy would have got up to see for himself, but the young prince sat silent and still. He'd asked many questions about his mother, and his uncle Rivers, and had grown used to the way men looked when he asked them; how the light in their eyes died and their glances slid away. Sometimes he could hardly bear to look at them, so tired was he of reading the movements of thought across men's faces.

It wasn't hard to read his tutor's face now, to see that some catastrophe had happened. After a moment he said, 'Shall I go downstairs?' and his tutor closed his eyes.

'My lord,' he said, 'I would give it some time.'

Thomas [Rotherham] Archbishop of York and John [Morton] Bishop of Ely, saved from capital punishment out of respect for their order, were imprisoned in different castles in Wales . . . In

this way, without justice or judgement, the strongest supporters
of the new king were removed.

Crowland Chronicle

Jane Shore

As soon as the deed was done they cried Treason, Treason
throughout the Tower and throughout the city the citizens began
to cry out likewise.

Polydore Vergil

When she heard the criers Jane knew at once that something had
happened to Hastings. The marquis put his arms around her, but
she shook him off. In that moment she couldn't bear to be comforted by him.

'Something terrible has happened,' she said.

'Something terrible is always happening.'

'You must go.'

'Go?' he said. 'Go where?' but she was already gathering his
clothes.

'Back to Sanctuary if you must.'

'I can't go back to Sanctuary –'

'Then go somewhere – anywhere – it's not safe here.'

'Jane –' he said, catching her hand.

'Please – I know it isn't safe.'

To his surprise, he saw tears in her eyes. He was about to say
something reassuring or argumentative, but there was a thunder-
ous knocking at the door and someone called out, 'Open in the
name of the Protector!'

'Go!' she cried.

He was at the window, opening it, climbing through, but he
hovered for one moment.

'Jane!' he said. 'Come with me.'

'I can't!' she cried softly. Then the marquis dropped out of sight and Jane ran from the room. She could hear the door bursting open, several guards pounding up the stairs. Thomas Howard, that sharp-faced man, led them. He came to a sudden halt as he saw Jane, standing pale and straight at the top.

'What is it?' she said to him. 'What do you want?'

The Protector sent into the house of Shore's wife and spoiled her of all that ever she had, above two or three thousand marks, and sent her to prison. And . . . he laid accusations unto her that she went about to bewitch him and was of council with the Lord Chamberlain to destroy him [but] when no pretext could fasten upon these matters then he laid heinously to her charge the thing that she herself could not deny, that all the world knew was true and nevertheless every man laughed at, that she was wicked in her body. And he caused the bishop of London to put her to open penance . . .

Thomas More

Once the proclamation had gone out that William Shore's wife, mistress of Edward IV (deceased), and Lord Hastings (deceased) and of Thomas, Marquis of Dorset (vanished), was to do public penance, the crowds poured into the streets. She could feel waves of anticipation rolling towards her as she stood before them, barefoot, dressed only in her shift.

She'd had time, in the days since her arrest, to weep a little for the loss of Hastings, who was a kind man, to wonder where the marquis was now and to fear for herself. It was not in her nature to despair, but she'd wept for herself also, for the vicissitudes of fortune. She'd lost both her patrons, the Protector was accusing her of many things, even treason, and there was no appeal. She held a lighted taper that guttered in the breeze.

'Give us a smile, sweetheart,' one man called out, while another cried, 'Give us a kiss!' and another, pointing to her chemise said, 'Wait till the wind blows up!' and there was a general laugh.

She wouldn't look at them; she looked at her feet. This gave the impression of modesty, but actually she was looking where she placed them, at the sharp stones on the path. She took one small step, then another.

The priest moved in front of her, carrying the cross, and the crowd fell silent.

She stepped after him, picking her way delicately, looking neither to the left nor right, feeling the gaze of the crowd like a heat on her skin. But gradually the atmosphere changed.

Her shame won her much praise among those that were more amorous of her body than curious of her soul, and many good folk that hated her living and were glad to see sin corrected pitied her penance more than they rejoiced therein . . .

Thomas More

It began with one woman, a flower-seller, who pushed her way forward and scattered some flowers in her path. 'Step on these, dearie,' she said. And a young man snapped a flower from a bush in the churchyard and held it out to her, and a second woman held out a posy of herbs 'to preserve you from the stink of your enemies!'

Then one man put his cloak down for her to step on, and a young boy gave her an apple. Jane Shore looked up at them and laughed and blushed, and they laughed with her and clapped as she blew kisses into the crowd. For she'd loved the men they'd loved, who had been cruelly taken from them.

And so she proceeded to the doorway of St Paul's, stepping on fine cloth and scented flowers.

The Queen

The following day [16 June] they came by boat to Westminster with a great crowd armed with swords and clubs and compelled the lord cardinal of Canterbury to enter Sanctuary with many others to call on the queen to allow her son Richard Duke of York to leave and come to the Tower for the comfort of the king his brother.

Thomas More

Thomas Bourchier put all the usual arguments to the queen, saying if she didn't give her son up it would seem as if she was deliberately provoking the hatred of the people against the Council. The young king wanted the company of his brother, and couldn't understand why he was being kept from him. It caused him anxiety, and had put into his mind the preposterous notion that he himself might be in danger. The Council would keep her sons safe, whereas here, her younger son could easily be captured and taken out of the country, and she would never see him again. And if she persisted with her womanly caprice, he was instructed to say that the Protector would take him by force. The laws of Sanctuary did not apply to her son, since he had no need of them.

She looked at him with contempt. 'I've heard all this before,' she said. If the king wanted his brother's company, he should come to her, and she would have both boys together. Her younger son had not been well, and she would not put his health at risk by sending him away. The law made the mother guardian of her children, and no one had the right to remove her son from her protection. She'd still had no word of her older son and her brother Lord Rivers – if the Council were indeed acting in good faith they should have released them by now. And her son had every right to claim Sanctuary. 'A place that may defend a thief may save an innocent,' she said.

Slowly, clumsily, the archbishop got to his knees. He pledged himself, body and soul, as surety for the prince. No harm would come to him, he swore, if she would release him. He wouldn't be before her now if he did not believe, to the core of his being, it was the right thing for her to do.

Despite herself, she was somewhat disarmed. This man had crowned her nineteen years ago and had remained loyal to her when she was slandered. He'd been named executor in her husband's original will *because of the great trust we have in him.*

It was not impossible for the Protector to get rid of an archbishop – look what had happened to Thomas Rotherham. But this archbishop was of the blood royal, descended from Edward III. It would be harder, surely, for the Protector to remove him.

But she remembered her older son and her brother, imprisoned without cause or trial. 'No harm will come to my son if he remains here,' she said.

Thomas Bourchier, Archbishop of Canterbury, did not get up. 'My lady,' he said, and his voice sounded strained, almost trembling, 'look out of the window, I beg you.'

Almost against her will she looked at the long line of armed men encircling Sanctuary, some on horseback, all in full armour. She couldn't help feeling a pang of fear.

'Do not cause bloodshed on sacred ground,' the archbishop said, and now the trembling in his voice was obvious. 'Do you want your son to be taken by force, and terrified, when he could come willingly and joyously, to take part in his brother's coronation?'

'It will only be postponed without him,' he went on, when she said nothing. 'Do you not want your son to be crowned?'

The queen expelled a long breath. Why had it come to this? Why was she so alone? Where was everyone who could help her?

'How do you propose to resist them,' the archbishop said, 'when they burst in?'

The queen could hear her own voice speaking from what

seemed to be a great distance away. 'Where is he?' it said, breaking slightly. 'Where is my son?'

He came in cheerful and smiling, as he always was, but hesitated, his smile fading, when he saw his mother's face. She motioned him towards her, put her hands on his shoulders, then on his hair and face. 'The archbishop,' she said unsteadily, 'wants to take you away from here, from me, to your brother in the Tower. To prepare for the coronation. What do you think?'

She was still holding him gently, but he looked down and away. 'I think I would like to go,' he said.

Her stomach contracted and seemed to fall. 'You would like to leave me?'

'I would like to leave this place,' the boy said. 'I'm tired of being here.'

Of course he was. They all were. The archbishop said, 'Your brother is longing to see you,' and she shot him a venomous look.

'Well, then,' she said to her son. 'Well, then.'

And so was the innocent child pulled out of his mother's arms.

Polydore Vergil

Upon the Sunday next following . . . [22 June] at St Paul's cross, being present the lord Protector and the Duke of Buckingham, with a huge audience of lords spiritual and temporal, it was declared by Dr Ralph Shaw . . . that the children of King Edward were not rightful inheritors of the crown, and that King Edward was not the legitimate son of the Duke of York as the lord Protector was . . . he then alleged that the lord Protector was most worthy to be king and no other . . . then upon the Tuesday next ensuing . . . the Duke of Buckingham came unto the Guildhall where . . . the mayor and a fair multitude of citizens were assembled in their liveries. To this assembly the duke made an oration, rehearsing the great excellency of the lord Protector and

the manifold virtues which God had endowed him with, and the
rightful title which he had to the crown . . .

Great Chronicle of London

Earl Rivers

A multitude of [troops] were moving from the North towards the
South under their chief leader and organiser, Sir Richard Ratcliffe,
[and came to] the town of Pontefract . . .

Crowland Chronicle

He received the warrant for his execution on the morning of
23 June, which was as fair a morning as any on which to receive
the news. He read through it in silence and silently handed it
back. Which made it difficult for Richard Ratcliffe to say anything
in return. Everything he could have said – about the mighty being
fallen, for instance – seemed superfluous now. He would have
preferred an argument, or even a bit of abuse. But Earl Rivers
remained calm. He went to his chair and sat facing away from the
general. So Ratcliffe bowed, and was annoyed with himself for
bowing, then went to tell the other two prisoners of their forthcoming fate.

After a moment Anthony got up and looked out of the window. One man was leading a horse across the courtyard, another
following with a shovel to pick up the droppings.

So the ordinary business of life went on.

If ever there was to be a moment of revelation, it should be
now. He had dedicated his life to the hope of it, but there was
nothing. After years of prayer and contemplation he had finally
achieved a cessation of thought. But this was not the stillness and
emptiness that preceded transcendence, so far as he could tell. It
was simply a wall, deaf-blind and insurmountable.

After several moments he went back to his chair. A servant came in carrying bread and wine on a tray, also a small parcel of paper, which Anthony had requested some days ago so that he could make his will. To this extent at least he had anticipated this moment.

He watched the servant setting out these things as though from a great distance, as though he was watching Anthony Woodville watching a servant.

The servant's movements betrayed no consciousness of either surveillance or the fate of the prisoner he served. He barely glanced up, performing his routine duties in a perfunctory, efficient way that suggested he had performed them many times before. Anthony observed a burn mark on his hand, a whitened puckering of flesh from the little finger to the wrist. He thought of asking how the servant had got it, but the moment passed, the servant nodded towards him briefly and was gone.

He opened the parcel somewhat clumsily, then held a piece of paper up and sniffed it, as he always did. It smelled of possibilities; he felt a pang of grief and loss for all the books he had yet to write, that now he would never write.

But he could write out his will.

He wrote the date, noting with satisfaction that his hand hardly shook at all. He bequeathed the land inherited from his father and from his first wife, Lady Scales, to his brother Edward, with five hundred marks set aside to pray for the souls of his first wife and her brother Thomas. He desired all his personal possessions to be given to his second wife, a young woman with modest estates in Essex. His household servants were to receive their wages for the quarter along with a black gown for mourning. He decreed that some of his land should be sold to fund a hospital at Rochester for thirteen poor folks and specified other charitable sums, such as payment for those visiting the prisoners of London. His clothing and harness were to be sold to buy shirts and smocks for poor people. Then he asked that his heart should be buried in the chapel of Our Lady of Pew at Westminster.

At this point his mind resumed its peculiar blankness and he could think of nothing further to say. He couldn't bring himself to think about his sister, or his nephews: the one who would also be executed, and the one who was in the Tower. He could do nothing for the young king now; he could not even form a prayer.

> Earl Rivers, Sir Richard Grey, and Thomas Vaughn were cruelly killed at Pontefract, lamented by almost all and innocent of the deed charged against them . . .
>
> *John Rous*

It was said of the earl that he died quickly and well, but quietly, with no words of encouragement for the other prisoners. Indeed, he barely glanced at them, merely thanking the executioner and commending his soul to God. The executioner severed the head cleanly with a single blow. It rolled across the grass, and when it stopped rolling the eyes were open, reflecting the sky. At the sight of this, young Sir Richard, who had been the most obstreperous of all the prisoners, began to weep.

The execution was witnessed by the Earl of Northumberland and Sir Richard Ratcliffe, and by the men of York, who then proceeded on their long march to London.

> Armed men in frightening and unheard-of numbers were summoned from the North, Wales and other districts . . . and on the 26th day of June, Richard, the Protector, claimed for himself the government of the kingdom with the name and title of king; and on the same day he thrust himself into the marble chair. The pretext for this . . . was . . . that King Edward's sons were bastards, on the grounds that he had been precontracted to a certain Lady Eleanor Butler before he married Queen Elizabeth, and further, that the blood of his other brother, George, Duke of Clarence,

had been attainted, so that no certain and uncorrupt blood of the lineage of Richard Duke of York could be found except in the person of Richard Duke of Gloucester.

Crowland Chronicle

Who was legally entitled to the crown and could bear its responsibilities thanks to his proficiency . . . if he were asked by the peers. On hearing this the lords consulted their own safety, warned by the example of Hastings, and perceiving the alliance of the two dukes, whose power, supported by a multitude of troops, would be difficult and hazardous to resist . . . determined to declare Richard their king.

Dominic Mancini

Then was hasty provision made for his coronation . . .

Great Chronicle of London

Margaret Beaufort

She was wading on the edge of a pond that had been dredged because some poison in it was killing the fish. But she was looking for a particular weed, which, if dried and crushed, made an effective remedy against rashes and other afflictions of the skin. So she'd put on over-shoes and a voluminous smock and was holding her skirts in one hand and a net in the other when her servant came with news.

She straightened slowly, pushing a strand of hair back into her cap, then said, 'See that there is food and wine for Lord Stanley.'

Then she returned to the house, removing her over-shoes at the door.

Stanley's glance flickered over her swiftly. But if he wanted her to dress presentably, he could give more notice of his coming, she thought. And then she thought, *he looks ill*. He was thinner; there was a scar on his cheek. But she went forward to greet him, smiling and extending her hand, saying it was an unexpected joy to see him again.

'I've ridden like the devil to get here,' he said, sitting down.

'When were you released?'

'This morning. I had to beg forgiveness and pledge allegiance to the Protector on my knees. I thought he would keep me with him.' He gave her a sidelong look. 'Thank you, by the way, for all your visits and messages of support.'

She had neither visited nor written.

'I notified your brother,' she said, 'and your son.'

Both of them knew she would do nothing to jeopardise her own son. She had already written to the Duke of Buckingham, who was the nephew of her third husband and the son of her cousin. He'd risen to such power it would be foolish not to use their relationship.

Then, in a series of unprecedented events, the Lord Chamberlain had been executed, her husband arrested and imprisoned, the late king's children declared bastards, and the Protector was now to be king.

'I didn't think it safe to come to the city,' she said. 'Isn't it occupied by armed men? But I hear your brother petitioned the Protector on your behalf – successfully, I see,' she added, smiling warmly.

Stanley made a small, disparaging noise, but she went on, 'If you'd remained imprisoned, I would, of course, have visited you.'

'Of course you would.'

She changed the subject. 'What about Bishop Morton?' she asked. 'And the archbishop?'

'The archbishop is released,' he told her. 'Dr Morton has been sent to one of Buckingham's castles in Wales.'

She absorbed this information silently as Stanley went on to tell her about his release. The Protector had come to him in the Tower, dressed in his robes of state. Stanley had got to his knees and the Protector had raised him up and kissed him on both cheeks.

'I've never been so afraid in my life,' he said.

She could see he'd suffered from the unhealthy pallor of his skin, his thinning hair. Though she couldn't remember what his hair had been like before. She didn't ask him about the scar. She wondered briefly why he had come to her, rather than his mistress or his sons.

'Apparently, I am to be steward of his household, as I was for his brother,' he said, jolting her out of her thoughts. 'We are both of us to attend the coronation. You are to carry the queen's train.'

She was so startled by this that she spoke her thoughts aloud. 'Is he mad?'

Stanley pulled his mouth down in that familiar way, and said, 'He keeps us guessing, at any rate.'

She thought furiously for several moments, then said, 'What will I wear?'

Stanley smiled at this womanly concern. 'I believe that's being taken care of,' he said. 'You are to travel to London tomorrow for the fitting.'

'Tomorrow!' she said.

'The coronation is only one week away,' he said, then, at the look on her face, he added, 'He may be mad, or madly cunning, but he's invited us to the coronation. I don't think we should refuse.'

Of course she wouldn't refuse. She'd been given the role of honour.

They would set off together, to the heart of London, which was currently the most dangerous city in the world. She would attend the new queen. The former queen would be close by, still confined in Sanctuary; the princes were still in the Tower.

Loyalty was a luxury she couldn't afford. Still she murmured, 'What will happen to them?' and he didn't need to be told what she meant.

'They say those who have left Sanctuary' – she knew he meant the marquis, and Bishop Lionel of Salisbury – 'have been in communication with other men. They've written to your son, and to Jasper. There is some talk of sending the queen's daughters secretly to them – and of releasing the princes.'

'My son?' she said. 'They've contacted my son?'

'Among others,' he said. Then he said, 'You must not interfere with this. You must let it go.'

She stood up. 'If the princesses go to my son, he should marry one of them.'

'Do not harp on that string,' her husband said sharply. 'It will do him no good, unless the prince is crowned. And he won't be.'

But she was walking away from him now, pacing. 'Men have escaped from the Tower before,' she said. 'Dr Morton escaped.'

'The princes will not escape. They've been removed to the inner quarters. No one even knows where they are.'

She turned to him. 'You could find out. As steward.'

'Have you heard nothing? I've barely been released from the Tower myself. Do you think I want to suffer Hastings' fate?'

'It's because of Hastings – and others like him – that you must do this.'

'What I must do is to stay in the Protector's favour.'

She held his gaze. 'It seems to me that it's as dangerous to be in his favour as out of it.'

'For Christ's sake! This is why I came here – to ensure you don't kill both of us with your monstrous plotting!'

'I can send money, at least,' she said.

They stared at one another, bitter, antagonistic.

'If you do,' he said quietly, 'I will not hesitate to tell the Protector.'

With an effort, she swallowed her rage. 'Why are we talking of such things?' she said. 'Come, my lord, you are tired. We must eat, and rest. Tomorrow we ride to London.'

As the day appointed for the coronation approached, Richard summoned troops to the number of six thousand into the city from his own estates and those of the Duke of Buckingham. He was afraid lest any uproar should be fomented against him at his coronation.

Dominic Mancini

Coronation

A curfew was imposed and a proclamation issued for the keeping of peace throughout London. On penalty of death, men were forbidden to stir up old quarrels, make affrays or challenges or break into Sanctuary. All new arrivals were required to make applications for lodging to the royal harbingers. No one was to harm any strangers or foreigners living in the city. Armed soldiers were stationed along every street.

On 5 July King Richard rode at the head of a procession of magnates, prelates, knights and attendants from the Tower to Westminster. He wore a doublet of blue cloth of gold and a long cloak of purple velvet furred with ermine. His queen rode in a litter wearing white cloth of gold, attended by seven ladies on horseback and five henchmen in blue. The Duke of Buckingham wore a gown of blue velvet blazing with golden cartwheels. Four thousand gentlemen of the north followed the procession.

In the Sanctuary of Westminster the former queen heard it passing and felt a strange sensation, as though her heart might suffocate. Her daughters clustered round her as if to protect her, though she knew there was nothing left to protect.

It was a great procession, one of the grandest ever seen, though it had been got together with such haste. But an animal stench of fear rose from the crowds, for armed men rode among them, obliging them to cheer.

The next morning the king and queen, wearing purple velvet and cloth of gold, walked barefoot on red cloth through Westminster Hall, led by royal musicians and heralds. The king entered the Abbey first, and the principal magnates followed, Northumberland carrying the sword of mercy, Stanley the mace, the Earl of Kent and Viscount Lovell the swords of justice. John de la Pole, Duke of Suffolk, held the sceptre, and his son the Earl of Lincoln the cross and ball. The cloth of estate was held over the king's head by the wardens of the Cinque Ports and his train was carried by the Duke of Buckingham.

A long line of earls and barons preceded the queen, who was followed by Lady Margaret Beaufort. Behind Lady Margaret came the Duchess of Norfolk, and a long line of gentlewomen. None of the former queen's sisters, not even Katherine Woodville, who was married to the Duke of Buckingham, nor Lady Strange, who was Lord Stanley's daughter-in-law, was there. Or the king's mother.

> King Edward's mother, being falsely accused of adultery, complained afterwards in sundry places to right many noble men of the great injury which her son Richard had done her . . .
>
> *Polydore Vergil*

Margaret walked slowly, carrying the queen's train. The last time she'd been here was at the christening of Queen Elizabeth's youngest daughter, Bridget. It seemed to her she was two people; one walking along the aisle of Westminster with the new queen, the other nursing dissent in her heart.

The bishops surrounded the king and queen, concealing them, and Margaret took the queen's train from her shoulders and helped her to loosen her gown until she stood naked to the waist with her husband, waiting to be anointed.

Margaret could see the queen's shoulder blades standing out painfully, a mole beneath one of them. Twelve years ago she'd married a different prince and had been widowed in the same year. Now, finally, she was queen, in all her mortal frailty.

The voices of the choir rang out as if they would burst the walls of the abbey apart. The train-bearers hurried forward to clothe their sovereigns again, and the royal couple stood together, transformed.

The procession returned to Westminster Hall, where the king's champion rode in on a white charger, and the banqueting began.

Four great tables had been set up for the bishops, the lords and the ladies, and lanterns were hung from the trees.

The archbishop, who had so recently promised the former queen that her son would be crowned, absented himself from the banquet. Lady Margaret sat next to the queen, observing the king. His face glowed in the light from the lanterns. He was solicitous of his wife, openly affectionate. He shared a joke with the Earl of Northumberland and the Bishop of London, and all of them laughed. The guests toasted him and the queen, whose smile was at once more tense and eager than her husband's. The usual excessive number of courses was served, the wine flowed. Then, to the sound of trumpets and clarions, King Richard and Queen Anne left the Great Hall and the lords and ladies were free to gather, or disperse.

The masks fell from their faces. Doubt, worry or sheer exhaustion showed in some; satisfaction and a wary hope on others. Lady Margaret, observing them, thought she would not let her own mask slip. She went home in her carriage, still maintaining that carefully modified countenance, though there was no one to see. It was part of her now; she could hardly tell where she ended and her mask began.

[After the coronation] all the attendants who had waited on the king [Edward V] were debarred access to him. He and his brother were withdrawn into the inner apartments of the Tower and day by day began to be seen more rarely behind the bars and windows. The physician Argentine, the last of his attendants whose services the king enjoyed, reported that the young king, like a victim prepared for sacrifice, sought remission of his sins by daily confession and penance, because he believed that death was facing him ... I have seen many men burst into tears and lamentations when mention was made of him after his removal from men's sight ...

Dominic Mancini

In order to release them from their captivity the people of the South and West began to ... form assemblies and organise associations ...

Crowland Chronicle

26

Chess

[The Duke of Buckingham] began to share his counsel with John,
Bishop of Ely, whom he was keeping under custody at Brecknock
Castle.

Polydore Vergil

One evening in August they sat with the board
between them. Buckingham was unnaturally silent,
and the bishop supernaturally alert. Usually the
duke would talk on the theme of himself without
tiring until the bishop had learned all he needed to know. But all
evening the duke had barely spoken.

The bishop picked up a knight. He ventured to ask how the
king's progress was going. Buckingham raised his head and said
it was going as well as could be expected. Then he lowered it
again, frowning at the board.

'He must be nearing York by now.'

Buckingham made an indeterminate noise.

'His son will be invested as Prince of Wales.'

Silence.

'You'll be attending, I suppose?'

'I don't know.'

It was possible that Buckingham had been rocked by the
recent conspiracy, which showed the strength of feeling against
the new king, in the south, at least. Or that he'd learned something new. At any rate, his usual arrogance had quite gone. He
wanted to talk, Morton felt, but didn't know how. Years of
ecclesiastical experience had taught the bishop to recognise a
man who wished to unburden himself. All he had to do was to

apply the right pressure at the right moment. So he was considering his next question carefully when Buckingham spoke.

'They love him in the north, of course. There has been a little trouble in the south, but it's settled now.'

The bishop moved his knight in its L-shaped path and said, 'I heard about the plot to release the princes.'

'Can you believe they asked me to join them?'

Morton made a surprised murmur.

'I went straight to the king, of course – I told him everything. The conspirators had their conspiring heads chopped off.'

He laughed a little hollowly, then moved his own piece on the board.

Bishop Morton considered the piece. It was so badly placed that he could not only have taken it but moved to check the queen. But he didn't want the game to end so swiftly now that Buckingham was talking. So he moved a pawn instead and murmured something about it being troubling for the king.

'The king is always troubled. He sees conspiracies everywhere – enemies, treason – he says he will not be rid of them while –'

– *the princes are alive*, Morton thought. He raised his eyes to Buckingham's. It was an ecclesiastical look, searching, compassionate. Buckingham swallowed and looked away.

'All kings have enemies,' Morton said. 'If the Crown is not inherited naturally, it is always insecure.'

'He is the natural heir,' Buckingham said quickly. 'He is his father's legitimate son.'

Morton allowed the silence to shape itself a little before saying, 'He is his father's son. But he is not heir.'

'He is heir,' said Buckingham, 'since his brother's marriage wasn't lawful.'

'Is that what the people think?'

Buckingham looked at him almost pleadingly.

'The princes,' the bishop said gently, 'will always be an obstacle to his rule.'

A shadow of an expression passed across Buckingham's face like a ghost. 'The princes –' he said.

'Their welfare must be his primary concern.'

When Buckingham didn't answer, he said, 'It must be very difficult to know what to do with them.'

Buckingham gave him a defiant, cunning glance. Then he said, 'He has not confided in me.'

'He should have confided in you,' the bishop said, then added, 'What do you think will happen to the princes, if they aren't allowed to rule?'

The look of horror passed across Buckingham's face again and the bishop marvelled that the duke wasn't more skilled at concealing his emotions. He stood up and walked away from the bishop.

'I don't know,' he said, 'we don't discuss it.'

The bishop understood that something had been said about the princes. 'Whatever happens to them, the people will neither forget nor forgive it.'

'The people,' Buckingham said disparagingly. Morton said nothing, and he went on, 'Who knows what they think – their loyalties shift like sand.'

'Not always,' Morton said. 'Though it's true, I suppose, that they have been known to accept more than one king.'

The duke looked sideways at the bishop. 'You yourself have accepted more than one king.'

'I have.'

'You served King Henry, then King Edward – you advised them both.'

'I did.'

'Did that not cause a certain – discord – in your conscience?'

The bishop looked at him steadily.

'I was faithful to King Edward, and would be faithful to his son, should he succeed him. However, if God wills otherwise – or the Protector' – he shrugged, and Buckingham watched him intently – 'well – I have already meddled enough with the world. I will return to my books and my beads.'

He smiled, but Buckingham said, 'Go on.'

After a moment the bishop said carefully, 'I would not dispute any title the Protector may claim, but for the welfare of the realm I could wish that some other person might rule. Someone with a good claim and equally excellent qualities – such as yourself.'

'I?' said Buckingham, laughing a little, so that the bishop could see the thought wasn't new to him. After a pause he said, 'I do have a claim to the throne.'

The bishop inclined his head.

'I am twice descended from Edward III.'

'Through your mother and father.'

'I am the heir of Thomas of Woodstock.'

'Your lineage is well known.'

'I'm the richest man in the kingdom. I own the most estates – next to the king.'

'And therefore the most endangered.'

Buckingham looked at the bishop.

'For if it should happen,' the bishop said, 'that the king's enemies should succeed – what do you suppose they would do to his greatest supporter?'

Buckingham's silence took on a different quality.

'If, on the other hand,' the bishop continued, returning his attention to the chessboard, 'that man were to lead a rebellion –'

'– A rebellion?'

'The people might take him to their hearts. He might gain the following that the present king lacks.'

'But – that would be treason.'

'It's only treason,' the bishop said, 'if it's against the lawful king.'

Several expressions battled for dominance on Buckingham's face.

'A rebellion,' said the bishop, 'might create a different king.'

248

Buckingham's expression altered once more.

'It's true I have support,' he said at length. 'I can command a great army.'

'You can raise the people. The present king is nothing without you.'

'He should think of that,' Buckingham said, 'before –'

'Before?'

'He – has made certain promises to me that he has not kept.'

Bishop Morton sat back, regarding the younger man. He didn't ask what the promises were. He had no high opinion of the duke's character and entitlement; certainly not as high as the one held by Buckingham himself. It was obvious to the bishop that he would not have it in him to be king. The people would never wear it. Fortunately, like most of those who aspire to power, the duke was blind to his own limitations.

All he had to do was lead him in his blindness.

'A king's gratitude is frequently short-lived,' he said, and Buckingham made a sound like a snort. 'Your king has misjudged you.'

'Misjudged?'

'He has misjudged the extent to which he needs you – and takes you for granted.'

He saw another change in Buckingham's face.

'But what can you do?' murmured the bishop, as if it were a problem in chess. 'Will you continue to serve him, even as the people rise against him and bring him down? And go down with him?'

'You don't know that will happen –'

'They will bring him down. It's a question of when. And who will lead them.'

Buckingham was visibly shaken. He began to pace. 'I could ride through my estates,' he said, 'sound out my Stafford cousins. The Herberts also –'

The bishop sat back as Buckingham developed his plans. He

would contact all the local lords. He would set off soon – tomorrow, or the next day – he could take no further action until he knew what support he had.

Lady Margaret Beaufort had written to the bishop, enquiring about the duke. He would reply that she shouldn't find it hard to exert her influence over him. He was ambitious and self-centred, yes, but he would always capitulate under the right pressure.

He looked out of the window, to where the top of the hill was bathed in a rose-gold light. The game of chess was forgotten. It would be easy for him to move one of the pieces to checkmate – so easy he could hardly be bothered. Beneath the band of rose-coloured light the sheep stood in partial shade, with bent heads, unmoving. Only man felt the need to move from his designated place; only man was therefore so fatally vulnerable.

Already there was a suspicion that [the young king and his brother] had been done away with. Whether, however, [they have] been done away with, and by what manner of death, so far I have not discovered.

Dominic Mancini

This rumour was like death to the boys' unhappy mother who still remained in Sanctuary . . . She was panic-stricken at first news of the cruelty of this thing and suddenly collapsed, lying senseless for a while. After coming back to herself she wept, howled, filled the house with her screams, smote her breast, tore her hair and overcome with such sorrow, prayed for death. She called for her dear sons, she berated herself for her madness because she was deluded by treacherous promises into letting her other son go from the asylum to his death . . .

Polydore Vergil

27

The Physician

And having in her household a certain Welshman called Lewis, learned in physic, which for his gravity and experience was well-known and esteemed among great households [the Countess of Richmond] required him to go to Queen Elizabeth not as messenger but as one who came in friendship to console her.

Hall's Chronicle

D r Lewis of Caerleon had studied medicine at Cambridge, distinguishing himself particularly in astrology. His approach to healing combined the Arabic with the Christian and the classical. He did not dismiss any method that proved its worth, and had written a treatise on the mathematics of illness: the relationship between the time taken for a fever to reach its crisis and the intensity of its virulence. He had an instinct for death, and if a patient looked likely to die would extricate himself swiftly from the case, for a doctor's fortunes were not built on corpses.

It was this canniness, as well as his manner, discreet and gravely sympathetic, that had recommended him to Margaret Beaufort. When she heard the former queen was suffering from pains in her chest she wrote immediately to recommend her personal physician, who would attend her without fee, being already in the pay of her own household.

Princess Elizabeth accepted this offer on her mother's behalf with gratitude, since there were no regular physicians in Sanctuary, just a midwife who delivered the whores of their babies, sometimes disposing of them afterwards, and an evil-faced barber who took out tonsils and appendices with the same blade with which he shaved his customers, and would, it was said, for an extra groat or two, cut their throats as well.

So, having obtained a pass, Dr Lewis presented himself at Sanctuary, taking with him a tonic prepared by Lady Margaret that contained tansy and wood-sorrel, which was, she'd assured him, an effective restorative.

The former queen's face was sallow; her greying hair straggled over the sheets. She made no attempt to move as the doctor approached.

He sat beside her and took her pulse, then tried to look into her eyes, but she turned her face away.

'My lady the countess sends her greetings,' he murmured. 'She is most concerned for your welfare.'

She looked at him, finally, and he could see the whites of her eyes were a congested yellow. 'You see what I am?' she said. 'You see what I've come to?'

'I see a grieving mother.'

Her face twisted. 'I never knew there was so much grief in the world,' she said.

The doctor bowed his head. 'Your sufferings are indeed terrible,' he said.

She looked away. 'Would that you could end them.'

'My lady, I –'

'I sent him from me,' she said, nodding. 'My own sweet son – I sent him to his death.'

'No, no, my lady,' said the doctor. 'You sent him to be safe.'

'Safe,' she said. 'He is safe now – nothing can touch him now.'

The doctor said nothing but met her gaze with his own sorrowing stare. Inwardly, however, he was alert. One part of his mission was to find out, if he could, any news about the fate of the princes.

The queen turned away again. 'How strange it is,' she said tonelessly, 'that they – while I still live.'

'But,' said the doctor hesitantly, 'as I understand it – there is no definite indication – no proof –'

'It's what all men are saying.'

'But no man knows.'

Her grip on his hand tightened. 'No one has told me anything – but I hear things – everything that men are saying comes to me. If they are still alive, why would no one tell me? It's cruel – cruel!'

The doctor bowed his head again. It was indeed terrible, he said, but if she had received no definite news, it was unwise, in his opinion, to despair. Perhaps it was not in the interests of *certain people* for her to continue to hope, and therefore she had received no assurances about her sons.

She stared at him. 'If they are still alive, where are they?' she said. 'Why has no one seen them? If he' – she could not bring herself to say the new king's name – 'has not murdered his own nephews, why does he not show them to the people as proof?'

The doctor could only point out that, if the people knew the princes were alive, they would rise in revolt to restore them to their mother, and the throne, as recent events suggested.

Her gaze intensified until the doctor thought she looked a little like the gorgon, capable of turning men to stone.

'It's not kind,' she said, 'to revive my hopes. You are no doctor if you think to torment me out of my illness.'

The doctor protested that he was doing no such thing. 'There is always reason to hope,' he said.

'What reason?'

'My lady the countess would have you know that her mother's heart grieves with you in your suffering, as the nation grieves. She says it is a great error for a king to break the hearts of his subjects, for they will turn against him – even rise against him – and look for a new leader.' He chafed her hand. 'She has sent you some of her own medicine,' he said, indicating the bottle of tonic.

The queen barely glanced at it. 'What leader?' she said.

This was the most delicate part of his mission.

'Do you remember, my lady, that before his most royal majesty your husband departed this world he had consulted with the countess on a certain matter?'

He could tell she did remember, though her expression barely changed.

'Regarding a proposed alliance between your family and hers?'

She shifted a little restlessly, but he continued: 'Your eldest daughter, the Lady Elizabeth, I believe – was there not a draft of an agreement?'

'That was so long ago,' she said.

'Yes, my lady. But the agreement still stands, does it not? And the countess' son is still there, and your daughter –'

'My daughter is still trapped here with me,' she said. 'There's no hope of us ever being released. We might as well be buried.'

'But you should know, my lady, there is much support for the young Earl of Richmond – both here and abroad – more and more men flock to his cause. It's where your brother has gone, is it not? And your son? It may even be,' he added, 'that the Duke of Buckingham will support him now.'

Her gaze turned hostile. 'The Duke of Buckingham is Satan's own supporter,' she said.

'He may be rethinking that allegiance now.'

The former queen released a long breath, as though it was the first time she'd exhaled. 'What are you saying?' she said. 'The Earl of Richmond is in Brittany – my daughter is imprisoned here. What does it matter who the Duke of Buckingham supports?'

The physician considered his next words carefully. 'If he can be persuaded to lead a rebellion here, the Earl of Richmond can return and release you and your daughters from your confinement.'

He had her attention now.

'My lady the countess wishes to know whether, in that case, you would stand by the former agreement to marry your daughter to her son.'

When she didn't reply, he said, 'Think, my lady, what it would mean – the two houses of Lancaster and York united at last.'

'But – Richard –' she said.

'I can name many nobles who will support the earl – not only your own family, but all those who still believe in the old House of Lancaster – and others who have recently turned against the new king for his misdeeds. The Earl of Richmond is the only one who can unite them all – and he is willing and eager to marry your daughter.'

'But my sons –' she said. He inclined his head.

'If your sons can be found they will be released,' he said. 'There is no question that the young earl will serve the rightful king. If, on the other hand,' he continued slowly, 'what you fear has come about, then the earl has the best claim to the throne. And if he is married to your daughter,' he went on, as she withdrew her hand, 'then your daughter would be queen. Think, my lady,' he said before she could speak, 'yourselves released from Sanctuary and your enemy overthrown. And your line and your husband's restored to the throne!'

For the first time he could see something other than despair in her, a spark of life in those eyes that were full of death. He took her hand again and pressed it, and said, 'Whatever fate has befallen your sons, you may still be the mother of kings.'

When the queen heard this her spirits raised and she besought Master Lewis to declare to the countess that all the friends and favourites of King Edward her husband would assist . . . Earl Richmond if he would take an oath that after the kingdom was obtained he would espouse . . . the Lady Elizabeth her daughter, or else Lady Cecily if her eldest daughter should not live . . . Master Lewis with all dexterity . . . concluded this enterprise between the two mothers and because he was a physician and out of all suspicion he was the common courier and daily messenger between them . . . So the Lady Margaret, Countess of Richmond

... [gave] Reginald Bray, her most faithful servant ... charge to inveigle and attract persons of nobility to join with her.

Hall's Chronicle

And she, being a wise woman, began to hope well of her son's fortune.

Polydore Vergil

28

The Countess and the Duke

Whether God so ordained, or fortune so chanced, on the road
between Worcester and Bridgnorth [the Duke of Buckingham]
encountered the Lady Margaret, Countess of Richmond, wife to
Lord Stanley . . .

Hall's Chronicle

When she heard that the Duke of Buckingham
had left Wales she decided to visit the shrine of
Our Lady in Worcester, to make an offering for
her son. She set out in the company of several
men and by sending two of them ahead discovered that the duke
was on the road between Bridgnorth and Worcester. Once she
could see his company, she rode on alone.

When the duke saw her he too separated from his men. She
drew her smaller horse beside his and looked up at him with a
winning smile. 'Greetings, nephew,' she said.

He could have pointed out she was no longer his aunt, no
longer married to his uncle, but he let it pass.

'It's a fine day for riding,' she said. 'Riding is the only way to
take the air in this weather.'

'You've come a long way,' he said, 'to take the air.'

She told him she was making a pilgrimage. 'To pray for the
harvest. And you?'

The duke said he was on his way to meet the king.

'Is the king at Worcester, then?' she enquired.

The Duke of Buckingham looked down a considerable way at
this little woman on her little horse. 'The king is travelling to Coventry,' he said stiffly. 'He's on his way to York for the investiture of

the prince. I'll meet him there. But I have some business to attend to on my estates.'

Lady Margaret observed that there was always business to attend to on one's estates. Then she added, with apparent inconsequence, that his grandfather would have been proud of him.

'My grandfather?' said the duke.

'You are so high in the king's favour – as he was in his.'

His grandfather had been high in the favour of the defeated king, Henry VI.

'And your father, too, of course – though you won't remember him.'

His father had died after fighting for King Henry in the First Battle of St Albans.

'And now you are the present king's closest advisor and friend.'

The duke didn't know why she was reviewing the complicated allegiance of his family in this way.

'He depends upon you utterly,' she said.

'I don't know about that.'

'Everyone knows it. He could have achieved nothing without you. That's why I asked you to intercede for my son.'

'I did enquire about your son,' he said, unsettled by this change of direction. 'And the king has written to the Duke of Brittany.'

'I knew it!' she said. 'When the ambassador came, I said to myself, *this is my nephew's doing.* You, more than anyone, have the king's ear.'

The duke said he was no longer sure that was the case.

'Oh?' she said. 'But everyone knows he consults you. You're his right-hand man.'

'Once, perhaps.'

'I'm sorry to hear that,' she said. 'But perhaps it's just as well.'

He looked at her.

'You wouldn't want to be blamed for his actions.'

'Blamed?'

'If what people are saying is true,' she said. 'About the princes, for instance.'

'I've had nothing to do with the princes.'

'Of course not,' she said. 'But that's what people will say. And what people say counts, as we know. *Vox populi, vox dei.*' She knew very little Latin; Alice Chaucer had schooled her mainly in French. Still, she had these useful phrases.

'Whatever they say, they are mistaken,' said the duke. 'I had nothing to do with the princes.'

She noted his use of the past tense. 'They are saying that the princes are no more.'

'I know nothing about that.'

'I know,' she said sympathetically. 'Still, it's difficult to extricate oneself from association.'

He stared at her. 'As God is my witness,' he said, 'I would never agree to such a thing.'

'That knowledge must sustain you,' she said, and did not add, *through all the trials that will come.*

The duke looked as offended as a man could. 'But it isn't *true.*'

She made a gesture of helplessness. 'It's so hard to dissuade them from what they think they know.'

'I will have it proclaimed,' he said, and she smiled at him. He had almost said, *when I'm king.*

'If you could produce the princes, that would be different.' She tilted her head at him again. 'But I see you cannot. And the people will not forgive anyone they associate with their deaths.'

The Duke of Buckingham was looking at her as if she was a monster. 'This is pure speculation, madame,' he said. 'We don't even know what's happened to the princes.'

'But if they can't be produced – well, then.' She shrugged. 'The people will give their hearts to some other prince.'

Despite himself, the duke asked, 'What *other prince?*'

'He's in exile now, but preparing to return. He has so much

support he can come back with or without permission from the king.'

'Your *son*?'

'Every day more men are flocking to his cause. They see him as their leader – as the natural heir to the throne.'

He was looking at her incredulously. Henry Tudor was of a bastard line that had been debarred from access to the throne. The duke's own mother was of that same line, but his father's descent through Thomas of Woodstock was impeccable. Also Henry Tudor had been in exile for more than half his life. No one knew him, and he had no immediate family, other than his mother, to support him.

'It was agreed, if you remember,' she said, 'that he should marry the Princess Elizabeth.'

He was momentarily distracted. But then the princess had also been declared illegitimate. 'That agreement was never formalised,' he said.

'But it has just been ratified,' she said, 'by the princess' mother.'

The duke felt a spark of outrage. 'She's in Sanctuary,' he said. 'She cannot ratify anything. There are other candidates – already in the country.'

'Do you mean yourself?' she responded swiftly. 'Do you think the people are behind you? They are behind my son,' she went on, before he could speak. 'So many families are behind him. The Woodvilles, of course, but also the Courtenays, Guildford, Daubeney, Tewkenor, Cheyney, Stonor –'

'They've made no claim for him,' he said. 'They'll want someone of royal blood to lead them.'

'My son is descended from John of Gaunt. And from Katherine de Valois. He is the nephew of Henry VI and the great-grandson of Charles V of France.'

By a renegade Welshman, he thought.

'And if he marries Princess Elizabeth he will unite the houses of Lancaster and York. Can you offer such a marriage?'

She had him there. He was married to the former queen's younger sister and, famously, had little to do with her. All the nobles who had supported King Edward would support the man who married his eldest daughter. And all those who had supported King Henry's cause would support a new Lancastrian king.

This little woman who was no longer his aunt had created a trap for him to fall into. He had even urged the king to send for her son.

'I tell you this,' she said, 'if someone else were to make a bid for the throne, then I and my son would stand between them and it like a bulwark and a portcullis. But if that person should lend his support to our cause, he would find himself well rewarded – once my son was king.'

She was so formidable in her conviction he could not laugh. It was incredible, yet even as she spoke he could feel a different vision shaping itself by the sheer force of her will. One in which he was not king, but Kingmaker, as Warwick had been. He would retain all his wealth and status and be substantially free from the pangs of kingship: the constant threat and suspicion, the burden of blame.

The countess was looking at him almost tenderly now. 'My son,' she said, 'would be overjoyed to welcome you to his cause.'

A message was sent to [Henry, Earl of Richmond] by the Duke of Buckingham . . . inviting him to hasten into the kingdom of England as fast as he could to marry Elizabeth, the dead king's elder daughter, and with her to take possession of the whole kingdom.

Crowland Chronicle

29

Plans

There were to be five separate uprisings, in Surrey, in Kent, in Wiltshire and Berkshire and Devon. The Marquis of Dorset and Bishop Lionel would raise men in Salisbury, the Duke of Buckingham in Wales and the Welsh marches.

Their armies would close like a vice on the city of London while her son landed on the south coast. By the time King Richard heard the news the capital would have been taken and the rebels would have combined to form one massive army against him. Her son would already have been proclaimed king.

Her most trusted men, Reginald Bray and Gilbert Gilpyn, had set up a network of communication all over the south. They had spread the news of the violent deaths of the princes and that their grieving mother, the former queen, had agreed to the marriage of her daughter, Princess Elizabeth, to Henry Tudor, Earl of Richmond. They'd said also that once Henry and Elizabeth were married, she would recognise him as king.

She had not agreed to this *as such*: she'd said, in fact, if her sons were alive Henry should release them and proclaim the elder one king.

But no one believed her sons were alive. London seethed and boiled with rumours as to how they might have died: walled into a secret room, suffocated, or drowned in a chest at sea.

But however they were put to death, certain it was they were departed from this world.

Great Chronicle of London

Men were stricken by this news. So many people had gathered at the gates of Sanctuary offering prayers and messages of comfort to the former queen that the guard around it had been increased again. Many more men had joined her son's cause.

So it troubled Margaret that she'd not been able to discover the truth about the princes. Dr Lewis was certain the queen didn't know, and Margaret's conversation with Buckingham had convinced her he didn't either.

The only man who would know, apart from the king, was her husband, Thomas Stanley.

Buckingham had said the king was at Coventry, so Margaret had moved her household to her castle of Maxstoke, a few miles away. She'd written to her husband from there.

When he didn't reply she wrote again. Finally, he wrote back, saying he would visit briefly, accompanied by the king's guard. He'd told the king there was some problem on his estate, but he could be there and back within a few hours.

Even as he approached she could see the strain in his posture. And in his face, as she went out to greet him as though nothing in the world was wrong. The guards were treated to her customary hospitality. They should eat and drink, she said, while she showed her husband some of the damage done by the recent storms.

Two of the guards followed them into the orchard. She spoke clearly, so they could hear. 'I'm glad to see you looking so well, my lord.'

'I'm not well,' Stanley said. 'You've put me in a difficult position.'

'I'm sorry to hear that.'

He lowered his voice. 'The king is permanently vigilant. I'm surprised he didn't come with me.'

She picked her way over a fallen branch. 'How is his majesty?'

'Much plagued by rumours of dissent.'

'Buckingham, you mean.'

'Among others.'

Gradually, she pieced together a story from the scraps of information he gave her. There had indeed been some kind of falling-out between Buckingham and the king at Gloucester. The duke had left suddenly, as though all the hounds of hell were after him.

'I wonder why?' she said, but Stanley was silent. Finally, he offered the opinion that there was some kind of dispute over an inheritance.

'But the king has been so generous,' she murmured. Then she said, 'Of course, the talk in the city is that the princes are already dead.'

She saw Stanley's face close like a vault. 'There will always be talk,' he said.

'Surely,' she said, 'the king could do something about such rumours – if he chose.'

'Such as?'

'He could produce the princes. Show them to the people.'

'He will not *show them to the people*,' said Stanley, 'while the people believe one of them is king. He would lose all his power, his majesty, overnight.'

'Surely that's better than having them believe he has murdered them?'

Stanley gave her a sidelong look. 'You know, these days, when we meet, it is increasingly like being subjected to an interrogation in the Tower.'

'Stanley,' she said reproachfully, taking his arm, 'but we meet so rarely you can't blame me for being curious. How is it to be so constantly in the company of the king?'

'Difficult,' he said. 'As I'm sure you're aware.'

Then he spoke, almost under his breath, so that although her hearing was excellent she had to strain to hear him.

At the end of July the king had despatched his servant John Green to Robert Brackenbury, Constable of the Tower, with a secret message. It had taken John Green several days to return with Brackenbury's response. Since when the king had been in the foulest temper.

'Why is that?'

'I wouldn't know.'

'But you can guess.'

'I'm not in the business of guessing,' he said.

'But the king,' she said gently, 'was upset.'

Stanley was silent. Then he said the king had flown into one of his rages, ranting that there was no one he could trust. He'd looked like a cornered animal. And since Stanley hadn't known the cause of this rage, he'd not known what to say to calm him. He could only stand speechlessly while the king ranted on, remembering the morning when his face had been slashed and he'd been dragged off to the Tower.

She gave his arm a sympathetic squeeze.

Then, in one of his lightning changes, the king had been calm again, asking in a cool and measured way who Stanley thought he could trust.

There were so many wrong answers to this that, while he knew it was unwise to pause for too long, Stanley had hesitated, before saying it depended on the matter to be entrusted.

'What if it were a matter of life and death?'

Stanley had said, 'In that case, no one.'

'No one?' the king had said. 'Not even you?'

And, uncharacteristically, Stanley had paused again. 'I was unnerved,' he said. 'I couldn't think.' The king's gaze had narrowed; he was sure he would be executed, like Hastings, there and then. Then, unexpectedly, the king had laughed and clapped his shoulder, his good humour apparently restored.

'But seriously, Thomas,' he'd said, 'who would you trust with a grave and urgent matter?'

And Stanley had come up with the name of Sir James Tyrell, who was master of the king's henchmen.

'You think so?' the king said.

Stanley had said he was a resolute man, and ambitious.

'Ambitious?'

'His hopes are high,' Stanley had said, 'but he's not rising as fast as his hopes.'

The king said that perhaps it wasn't wise to trust an ambitious man. Stanley had said that, on the contrary, he'd always found it possible to trust them, where their ambitions were concerned.

The king had considered this. Then, to Stanley's relief, he'd moved on to other things, and the subject appeared to be closed. But he had in fact spoken to Tyrell; Stanley knew there had been at least two occasions when they had spoken privately together.

'But you don't know what about?'

'No.'

'Have you spoken to Tyrell?'

'Don't you think the king would notice if I spoke to Tyrell?'

'But – Tyrell hasn't left the king? He's not been sent anywhere?'

'No.'

'Why not?'

'Perhaps the king has changed his mind,' Stanley said, 'about whatever matter it is.'

'*A matter of life and death*, he said.'

'A figure of speech.'

They were emerging from the orchard now, and the guards were catching up with them. 'These borders,' she said, 'will have to be replanted. And I must show you the little bridge.'

He had to increase his pace to keep up with her. She said, 'If you know something, Stanley, I wish you would tell me.'

'Why?' he said. 'Why does it concern you?'

'You know why,' she said. 'It concerns the whole nation, if the rightful king is dead.'

'You mustn't say such things.'

266

'Everyone is saying it. And if the people think he's done any-thing to those children, they will rise against him. They'll want a new king.'

He gave her a look of suspicion and disbelief. 'Not this again.'

'Yes, Stanley,' she said. 'My son is still in Brittany – but every day new supporters are flocking to him: the Woodvilles, the Mar-quis of Dorset – even the Duke of Buckingham.'

'Buckingham won't support your cause!'

'He already has.'

He glared at her, and she gazed back. He was no revolutionary, she knew. He had managed, over the years, to stay in favour with whichever king was in power, but substantially he had supported the House of York.

'You're dancing on the blade of an axe,' he said. 'You should be careful not to slip.'

She turned away from him, her heart thumping. But she said, 'What do you think he's done with the princes?'

'I don't know.'

'You should know. Do you think he can allow them to live?'

She thought he wouldn't answer her, then he said, 'I think he doesn't know what to do.'

'You don't think the message to Brackenbury contained instructions for him to dispose of them?'

'Dispose of them? They're not chattels.'

'They're in his way.'

'I don't think he would *dispose of them*, as you put it. I don't think his mind runs so bloodily as yours.'

'Then what?' she said. 'Don't tell me he hasn't thought of it.'

'If he has thought of it, then he has almost certainly changed his mind.'

'Perhaps it would be better,' she said, 'if it changed back.'

When she turned to him his lips had whitened, but before he could speak she said, 'What hope is there for them? He can't let them come to the throne.'

She could see from his face she was saying nothing he'd not already thought. He said, 'He could send them away –'

'To what? While they live they will be a focus for rebellion and unrest. The people won't forget them.'

'What are you saying?' he said.

'I am saying,' she said, but suddenly she found it hard to speak. She stumbled over her words. 'I am saying that – if anything were to happen to them – it would be better if it were to happen now –'

His expression was terrible.

'Than if they continued to live – in miserable imprisonment, suffering such privation – alone.'

He made an incredulous sound, but she was recovering herself. 'What can be gained by keeping them so cruelly? He should either allow them to die or – do something if it comes to it. And, in the end, you know – it will come to it.'

'My God,' he said.

'The king has issued instructions to Brackenbury that he will not carry out. He's said something to the Duke of Buckingham that has caused a rift between them. I don't think he's likely to give up – do you? I think he'll look for someone else to do it. He's already speaking to his henchman –'

'He would not ask Tyrell to do such a thing! He may have asked him to remove them, to keep them out of sight –'

'They're already out of sight.'

'– in some place where no one would even recognise them – where they could be brought up as poor people perhaps –'

'You don't think they'd remember?' she said. 'Would King Edward's eldest son not remember he'd once been king?'

Stanley was foundering. She had never seen him so unnerved. 'I – you should not speak of this –' he said. 'You shouldn't even think about it –'

'My son will have to –'

'For God's sake!' he said. 'Your son is a penniless exile. No one even knows who he is! His cause is futile!'

She spoke in a heated whisper, almost hissing. 'My son has at least as many supporters as Richard – maybe more – if the truth were known.'

'Your truth!'

'You know Tyrell,' she said. 'He was your retainer, was he not, before he was the king's? Perhaps you should speak to him.'

'I – speak to Tyrell?'

'If King Richard cannot be clear about what is in his innermost heart,' she said, 'then – you could make it clear.'

He had screwed up his eyes, trying to comprehend what she was saying. 'Are you mad?'

'Would the king not thank you?' she said. 'And Sir James? I think he would.'

She turned away from him, walking towards the fence again, and he followed her. 'Have you prayed about this?' he said. 'Have you prayed?'

She didn't answer, feeling suddenly nauseous. But he caught up with her.

'I knew you were a determined woman,' he said. 'From the first time I met you I thought, *here is a fanatic, in pilgrim's weeds*. I knew you prayed for your son as farmers pray for rain. But I did not know it would come to this. What you are proposing, madame, is a monstrous thing. You would deprive two children of their lives – a mother of her sons –'

'Have I not been deprived?' she cried in a whisper. 'I've not seen my son for *twelve years* – and before that, hardly at all. You have ten children, my lord – the queen has had twelve – I've had *one son* – and am not permitted even to see him! Am I supposed to meekly accept that? Why should others not suffer as I have suffered?'

Stanley looked as if her words were blows, striking him. His mouth worked a little before forming the words.

'If I've understood you rightly,' he said, 'you've involved yourself in a conspiracy. That conspiracy will cost many people their lives. Including the princes. You expect to draw me into it, but I'm telling you now to forget that – forget it all. I absolutely forbid you to take any further steps.'

Behind him she could see the soldiers moving towards them. 'So you'll do nothing?' she said. 'You won't speak to Sir James?'

'I'm sorry I've spoken to you,' he said. 'I will not do so again, no matter how many messages you send.'

His look had sharpened from fear to hostility. She said, 'Ah, Stanley, do not imagine that compunction will save you now. Your silence will not buy your life.'

They stared at one another as the soldiers reached them.

'Is everything well, my lady?' the first one asked.

'Quite well,' she said, without taking her gaze from her husband. 'I think we should go to eat.'

And she walked with them back to the house, feeling more shaken than she looked. She'd said too much, she thought. There was nothing to stop him going straight to the king. She'd never known what her husband would do. He might, even yet, speak to Tyrell, to encourage him to do the king's secret will. Or he might betray them all.

It wasn't the only reason she felt nauseous as she entered the house, gave her orders to her servants. She had exposed herself, or something in her that she had kept hidden, even from herself. Something that had festered through all those years of sorrow.

Somehow she got through the rest of that afternoon until her husband left, then watched him leaving with a resignation that was close to despair. Stanley would make up his own mind. She could only wait to see what would happen, what he would do.

At York Richard was joyfully received by the citizens, who of his coming made public and open triumph.

Polydore Vergil

There . . . he presented his only son, Edward, whom that same day [8 September 1483] he had created Prince of Wales and arranged splendid and highly expensive feasts and entertainments to attract to himself the affection of many people.

Crowland Chronicle

James Tyrell . . . sadly went [from York] to London.

Thomas More

30

Rebellion

Margaret

Tyrell had gone to London, but she'd heard nothing more. However, rumours of the princes' deaths were now widespread, fanned abroad by foreign visitors and dignitaries to the courts of France, Italy, Burgundy, Spain. And Brittany, of course. All those nations believed King Richard had murdered his nephews.

> Regard the events that have occurred in that land since the death of King Edward. See how his children have been murdered with impunity, and the crown has been transferred to their assassin . . .
>
> Guillaume de Rochefort, Chancellor of France

> This summer, Richard, the king's brother, had himself put in power and crowned in England, and he had his brother's children killed and the queen put away secretly also.
>
> Danzig Chronicle

Thus far, it could be said, her plans were working.

Her men were in constant communication with the rebels, taking her money to them. More money was being collected from their supporters, to be given to Henry on his return, so he could begin running the country.

At times the magnitude of this thought overwhelmed her. Her palms, her upper lip became moist; she would have to sit down.

So he could be king.

At such moments it seemed a desperate enterprise, doomed to fail. Henry, her son, would be butchered for treason, along with his supporters. She, too, would be executed, in all probability, but she wouldn't want to live. She'd staked her life on this cause because without it her life had no meaning.

There was no going back, no alternative at all.

But it wouldn't fail. She went over all the details again in her mind, searching for anything she'd missed. There was nothing; nothing more she could possibly do.

Apart from worry.

From her communications with Bishop Morton she knew King Richard was still writing to the Duke of Buckingham in good faith, addressing him as *Sweet Coz*, or, *most favoured kinsman*, so the duke had begun to feel again the pressure of allegiance, the terrible weight of treason.

He knew he would not be king, of course. He was unlikely, in fact, to rise as high with Henry as he had with Richard, since Henry had so many other supporters and advisors. The duke had said as much to the bishop, in his usual voluble and indiscreet manner; had mentioned more than once his own superior lineage.

The bishop had reminded him of the marriage between Henry and Princess Elizabeth. When the duke said the men of Northumberland and Yorkshire would never turn against Richard, the bishop had said the men of Lancashire and Cheshire were more than ready to combat them. He'd fanned the flames of the duke's self-importance, saying how vital he was to the enterprise.

Still, Buckingham was an unstable element, a weak beam. And she'd heard nothing from her husband at all.

Surely he couldn't betray her without implicating himself. And his own son, Lord Strange, who was recruiting men in Lancashire for Henry.

Of course, if she failed, he would dissociate himself from her; if she succeeded, he would claim to have supported her all the time.

She couldn't count on Stanley, as she couldn't count on Buckingham. Duke Francis would have to supply Henry's fleet and she didn't know the duke at all.

So much depended on these men and others: Richard Guildford in Kent, the Courtneys, the Woodvilles. Everything depended on their coordinated actions.

Meanwhile, King Richard continued his progress around the country, bestowing grants and honours wherever he went. He had remitted half of the taxes of the city of York, granted a generous charter of liberties to Gloucester and conferred Clarence's estates on Tewkesbury.

He courted popularity where he could.

So she teetered between anxiety and hope. She'd planned everything as far as she could; the rest was dependent on fate or chance or God's enigmatic will. She knelt for hours in her chapel, unable to pray for herself, because of the thing inside her that had turned, like a snake. Yet still she remained on her bruised knees, praying for her son, who had done nothing to deserve the misfortunes of his life; that God would favour him at last, that at least he would get his fleet.

Henry

He'd gone in person to see Duke Francis. The duke was once again unwell, and preoccupied with Parliament, but he'd listened patiently as Henry promised him the full repayment of all debts, and the title of Richmond, which the dukes of Brittany had once held, in return for a small fleet. The duke had raised him up and kissed him on both cheeks; Henry could smell the foul-sweet odour of his breath.

'You don't need to promise so much,' he said. 'Only that,

should your enterprise be successful, you will not forget your old godmother Brittany in her struggles against France.'

Henry felt the heat of relief in his face. 'I could never forget – or repay – your kindness to me,' he said.

'So,' said the duke, 'I must hope not to see you again,' and Henry felt the imminent loss of everything that was familiar to him; he was journeying into the unknown. But there was a glint of something else in the duke's eyes: speculation, or doubt.

'It's a great enterprise,' he said.

Henry said nothing.

'Who would have thought it,' the duke continued, 'when you were first blown upon these shores – a boy of fourteen?'

Henry murmured that he owed everything to the duke.

'And now – to be king? Well – it's not something to be lightly undertaken.'

Henry assured him he was not undertaking it lightly.

'Nothing will be the same for you.'

Was he trying to persuade Henry not to go?

'Everything is arranged, my lord. Many men have gathered, waiting for me.'

'You can't let them down, of course. Still, it's a strange card that fortune has turned. But what is life without chance?'

Perhaps he was reminding Henry of his own risk; that if he gave him men and money and ships, and Henry failed, King Richard could declare war on Brittany.

'I'm importuning you again,' Henry said.

'Naturally,' said the duke. 'To whom else can you turn?' He tapped his browning teeth.

In the end he granted Henry ten thousand crowns for ships and men, a further fifteen thousand to pay them, and his own naval commander, Jean Dufou, to command them. Henry knelt in gratitude, and the duke placed a hand on his head and wished him success. He hoped, once Henry was king, their two nations would be joined in perpetual amity.

'I would tell you to go in peace,' he said, 'but there will not be much of that for you.'

His gaze was unnerving. Henry bowed and left, disturbed. He had more supporters than ever, but he'd never felt so alone. So many men had come to him; Brittany had become a refuge for those who had failed in the earlier conspiracy. His household was a court of lost people, exiles, fugitives, all clamouring to be restored.

For twelve years he'd existed in a state of suspension, alternating between uncertainty, despair and a kind of lassitude. He rarely spoke English, had forgotten what England was like. If he thought of himself at all it was as a person of no place, observing everything at one remove. One day in an imaginary future he would return to a country he knew from legend. He would live a life of comparative obscurity, away from all the intrigues of court. He would not lift his head so it could be cut off.

He had never imagined he would have to return as king.

Then Richard had usurped the throne and at once had sent his ambassador to Duke Francis to encourage the duke to return the exiled Britons.

Duke Francis had reminded King Richard that he was still waiting for help from England against France.

But then King Louis had died, within months of his old enemy, Edward. He too had left his young son as king. And already there was a power struggle between the boy's sister, Anne de Beaujeu, and his cousin, the Duke of Orléans.

So Richard felt no immediate pressure to respond to Brittany's demands for aid.

For the time being, therefore, Henry and Jasper were safe and living in more relaxed circumstances than before. They were allowed to travel and hunt; they toured the countryside together and visited the market towns. Henry's allowance had been increased, since he was host to more than five hundred fugitives.

Now all this would change. His mother had written to him,

saying he should land on the south coast of England on 18 October, St Luke's Day, and he mustn't be late. Everything depended on his timing.

And so Henry, who had lived with probabilities for so long, was faced with certainties. If he failed, he would die; if he succeeded, he would be king. Either way, his life here would end.

A new life would begin, of course. But he could barely imagine it, this new life, what it would mean.

He couldn't alter anything now, at this stage. He could only make the necessary preparations to sail while the weather was fine. So the ships were rigged and men recruited.

But in the second week of October the rains began to fall. Half the market was swept away, pigs and sheep floated on flooded roads to the sea. Henry set off once and was forced to return while all the men grumbled, saying the hand of God was against them. Yet in England the revolution had already begun.

The Kentishmen be up in the Weald and say that they will come and rob the city of London, which I will prevent if I may. Therefore I pray you that with all diligence you make ready and come hither . . .

Letter from John, Duke of Norfolk, to John Paston, 10 October 1483

After another false start they had waited, but the rains had only increased; no one had known the heavens could contain so much water. The men saw signs and omens in the sky; wild riders galloping on bloody horses. Others said it was the end of the world, that God would sweep them away as in Noah's time and none of their ships was strong enough to be an ark. The most experienced sailors said the storms would last all winter. But Edward Woodville said they should sail as soon as the wind dropped.

So when there was finally a lull in the storm and a milky peace in the sky, the small fleet set out again. But soon, without warning, sky and sea churned once more. The sea turned from blue to white; the waves were like great, hissing walls.

Wind drove white foam over the sea. It rose in wings to either side of the ship, then gushed over the decks. Henry shouted for his men to battle on, but no one could hear him.

That crucial element, timing, was already lost. In England men would be waiting to crown a king who wasn't there; who would arrive, if at all, without his men, since his other ships were lost, or at least no one could see them. Still he battled on, as though the rearing sea was the embodiment of everything that had ever thwarted him. And in the morning, at last they could see land.

They established they were near Dorset but, seeing enemy ships, were forced to sail further along the coast to Plymouth.

Here there was another fleet of ships in the harbour. None of these ships bore any standard or emblem, so Henry sent out a small boat to ascertain whose they were. And the captain of one of the ships called out to Henry's men that they were from the Duke of Buckingham and had come to meet the Earl of Richmond. But because they couldn't see the duke's standard Henry's men were wary and rowed back to him. And a lengthy debate ensued.

'It's a trap,' Dufou said. The duke could not possibly have known Henry would land at Plymouth, and in any case was not supposed to meet him on the coast.

He didn't think they should land, but the thought of turning back was terrible. Almost all the provisions had run out or been swept away in the storms. No one knew where the other ships were, whether they would try to land. His men were fighting over the remaining rations. Dufou, sensing the possibility of mutiny, had two of them whipped.

'You've not waited this long,' he said, 'to destroy everything on a mischance.'

'Yes, I've waited,' Henry said. 'Since the age of four I've lived as a prisoner and a fugitive. How can I go back to that now?'

His admiral only shrugged. 'Better than death,' he said.

Henry had gazed out towards England, the promised land, which, like Moses, he couldn't enter. He didn't know where Jasper was, or Edward Woodville. He had no army to fight with if he landed, and those truly were Richard's men. Still he wasn't sure that return would be better than death.

Only he could take the decision. There was no one to advise him other than Dufou, who had nothing to gain from landing on a hostile shore.

He, Henry, had the kingdom to gain. The Crown, which a short time ago had seemed a remote possibility, seemed suddenly and painfully real.

Any one of his heroes would go ahead, even if they died in the attempt.

> Earl Henry viewing afar off all the shore beset with soldiers which
> King Richard had everywhere disposed [and seeing] none of his
> own ships within view, hoisted up sail [and returned] to Nor-
> mandy.
>
> *Polydore Vergil*

Margaret

On the appointed day, 18 October, she'd lain on the floor of her chapel until her feet were numb and she could no longer feel the side of her face. She could feel, however, the pain in each bone; the uneven curve of her ribs.

She'd used up every prayer she had but had heard nothing, either from God or her men.

Where were her agents? Where was Reginald Bray? Where was Christopher Urswick, her faithful priest? She'd stayed at Woking so they could reach her easily, but none of them had come. Which meant one of three things.

The weather was too bad for them to make their way back to her.

They had gone into hiding.

Or they'd been captured and were even now being interrogated by the king.

Because the king had found out; that much she knew. He'd mustered an army at Leicester, issued a proclamation against Buckingham, sent out many commissions of array.

The men of Kent, roused to a riotous state, had marched prematurely on London. But the Duke of Norfolk had hastily assembled his own men and blocked the Thames at Gateshead. He'd captured the leaders and interrogated them, then written to the king.

The king had marched south, with all his men.

Then Margaret prayed not to God but to His mother, Mary, who, like herself, had suffered with her son.

Hail Mary, full of grace, the Lord is with thee. Blessed art thou among women and blessed is the fruit of thy womb.

She'd had a sudden image of Henry's newborn head, almost bald, the fine veins visible, the soft spot on it pulsing.

And all her prayers turned to a single cry.

Why, why are you not helping him?

Which was no prayer at all but accusation.

When she heard nothing, she knew it was over. It was over, and she couldn't pray. She was no longer even sure she could get up.

Grasping the rail in front of her, she hauled herself upwards and stumbled towards a seat. Her head reeled. She couldn't remember the last time she'd eaten. There was a taste like ashes in her mouth.

All she could do was wait.

When Gilbert Gilpyn arrived she could see from his face what the news was.

Buckingham had been captured and executed at Salisbury. The king had refused to speak to him, despite many requests from the duke, who'd evidently thought, even now, that his eloquence could save him. He'd been interrogated by James Tyrell and in a final attempt to save himself had confessed everything, told all their plans. The rebels in Salisbury, hearing this, and seeing the size of Richard's army, had scattered.

Then the king had marched from Salisbury to Exeter. One after another the rebel forces had collapsed and their leaders had fled.

Those in Exeter had been helped by merchants to find a ship, although Thomas St Leger, the king's brother-in-law, had not been so lucky; Richard had overseen his execution himself. Then he'd sent his men to hunt the rebels down. Surrey, Sussex, Kent, Devon, Cornwall, Somerset, Southampton, Wiltshire, Oxfordshire and Berkshire were full of soldiers conducting searches and sieges, arresting everyone they could find.

She gripped the table, feeling faint. 'What about my son?' she managed to say.

Gilbert Gilpyn lowered his face. 'I believe there was some difficulty – in the Channel,' he said.

He'd not landed. There was that much, at least. He'd attempted to land twice but, seeing Richard's men all along the coast, he'd turned to sail back into exile. She could only imagine in what despair he'd given that command. Already in the south he'd been declared king. On the appointed day the Marquis of Dorset, the Bishop of Exeter and others had set out under his banner *Henricus Rex*, but had been thwarted at a river crossing by the weather.

The weather. She almost laughed. For all her planning, she could not have predicted the weather.

Gilbert Gilpyn's face was gaunt. 'What will you do?' he said, and the urge to laugh left her. 'The king knows everything,' he said.

She nodded, then crossed the room, took out some money

from her bureau and gave it to him. 'You must go into hiding,' she said.

'What about you?'

'I'll wait here.'

'My lady –'

'Where would I go?' she said. Anyone who took her in or helped her would be arrested, possibly executed themselves. Besides, there was still the weather. Gales blew, trees fell, whole houses were swept away; rain churned the roads to mud and then to streams.

She should be thankful, she supposed, that her son's wariness, the prudence that he got from her, had saved him, as it had saved him all those years ago at Saint-Malo. Yet she didn't know if he'd made his way back to Brittany, or France, or what his reception was likely to be.

What would happen to him now? What would happen to her?

She couldn't feel gratitude, only despair and rage. And the thorn of love in her soul, driving her mad with anguish.

'I'll stay here,' she said to Gilbert Gilpyn, 'and wait for news of my son.'

31

Return

The wind, which had roared in their faces like a hostile army all the way to England, blew them easily to Dieppe, where one of his other ships was waiting. Some of the men on it were wounded, others had been lost. And Dufou was more worried about the French than the English. 'We cannot stay here,' he said.

But no one could face putting to sea again.

In the end it was decided to make the long trip to Rennes overland, using what was left of his mother's money to buy provisions. But to do that they would have to pass Paris.

Dufou said they should get a safe conduct from the new king, Charles VIII, or they would certainly be apprehended and prevented from ever reaching Duke Francis.

Henry didn't know that he wanted to reach Duke Francis. After all his brave speeches, his promises? The duke must have believed he was free of them at last; now, here they were returning like beggars, needing yet more aid.

But he sent a messenger to the French king.

While they waited they were joined by another contingent of forty or so men whose ship had been swept back to Calais. More than forty had been on that ship, but he didn't want to enquire where the others were. The ones who arrived were in a sorry state, many of them injured in the storms. One, carried on a makeshift stretcher, had been battered by a falling mast, another had broken his shoulder. Three more had come down with an unspecified illness that he hoped wouldn't spread. All of them were hungry and exhausted.

There was no money for surgeons or lodgings for so many. They had to set off, camping where they could, the more able-bodied helping the rest. They looked like a pack of beggars or dogs, licking their wounds.

As they travelled slowly along the coast another group joined them. Their ship had been blown in at the Cotentin Peninsula, but fewer than half the men who'd set out had returned.

Some would have deserted, of course, as soon as they reached land; others must have drowned. Dufou said they should take a reckoning, but Henry didn't want to think about the missing. It was the first time he'd been in command of an expedition in which lives had been lost.

Dufou said he would have to get used to that. 'All leaders walk in the shadow of death,' he said.

He was right, of course, but Henry wouldn't speak about it.

The men spoke about it. They told stories among themselves of a ship that had followed them through the storms. A ship so skeletal it should not have been able to float. There were great gaps in its frame and it bore a black, tattered flag.

Others had seen a mysterious island, not marked on any map. It had appeared out of nowhere, and as they passed they could hear the ghostly chanting of long-dead sailors.

They told these stories without apparent resentment or rage. They were mercenaries, whose lives were commonly bought and sold; permanent hostages to fortune.

Henry resented them; he almost hated them for reminding him of his failure. Their stories were like gravel in his soul. God had not backed him.

Dufou was phlegmatic about this as well. 'The Gods do not communicate their whims to us,' he said, and Henry thought that was certainly true. He hadn't chosen this, any of it, just as he had not chosen these men. He'd not even wanted to leave Brittany. Circumstances had impelled him to leave, and to return.

And your ears shall hear a word behind you saying, this is the way, walk in it, when you turn to the right or the left.

But he hadn't heard, or God had tricked him, or deliberately

set him up for failure. Whatever God's purpose was, he wasn't
going to reveal it to Henry.

So he travelled with his tattered men and their stories of death.
A few days ago he would have been declared king in England.
Now he was king of beggars.

The thought of his lost Crown haunted him. He'd begun to
crave it with all the ardour of deprivation.

Eventually, his messenger returned, bringing the son of the
king's chamberlain, Henri Carbonnel, with him, and the good
wishes of the young king.

'His majesty sends his condolences,' Carbonnel said. 'He trusts
you will not despair, and will try again.'

If Henry was surprised by this, he didn't show it. He was
becoming guarded in his heart against hope or despair. Yet even
his spirits lifted when Carbonnel said he had money for their
journey. He would escort them to Brittany, where Henry could
recuperate, and try again when the weather was more clement.

He looked at Henry's troops. 'I imagine you will need reinforcements,' he said.

King of beggars, Henry thought.

'His majesty is sure your friend the duke will help you again,'
Carbonnel said.

'I can't ask him,' Henry said. He would rather walk into Hades
than ask the duke for more aid. *Perhaps the French could help*, he
did not say, and Carbonnel made no such offer.

'Give it a little time,' he said.

As they travelled together, Carbonnel told Henry that his king,
who was only thirteen, had also suffered from the ambitions of
his uncle, and was horrified by the fate of the English princes. He
would never support the perpetrator of such a crime. He was
eager, in fact, to see him overthrown.

Henry listened without comment. He couldn't speak about
the princes, whose fate he didn't know. And yet his fate was tied
to theirs. If the French king believed them dead, and murdered

by their uncle, he might support Henry. That was all he needed to know.

He was experiencing, perhaps, that hardening of the soul that follows misfortune. But his fortune appeared to be changing, because on the border of Brittany an embassy from Duke Francis met them and greeted Henry with a message from the duke that contained no hint of grievance or reproach. Henry should come to Vannes at once, he said. More of his men awaited him there.

32

Retribution

L ate in November the king entered London in triumph. The mayor and all the aldermen dressed in scarlet, and five hundred citizens in violet escorted him across London Bridge. The next morning, in the Star Chamber at Westminster, he held a great ceremony attended by all the lords and nobles of the land. He would call a parliament, he said, at which he would pass judgement on all the rebels.

Margaret considered escaping, but though the winds had died down the roads were still impassable. In any case, she had nowhere to go. The king's troops were everywhere along the coast and the border with Wales. Anyone attempting to leave the country was arrested. Richard's ships patrolled the channel, scouring it for Breton ships and attacking the coastal towns of Brittany. They brought back prisoners, for whom he demanded ransom. In London, Breton merchants were attacked and thrown out of the city. Evidently, the king wanted to make Duke Francis sorry he'd helped Henry. He was trying to force him into returning her son.

If he was sent back, Henry would be sentenced for treason. Ten men had been beheaded for that crime. She doubted Richard would be so merciful to her son.

Three men had risen around the king like a triumvirate. Henry Percy, Earl of Northumberland, the Duke of Norfolk and Thomas Stanley, who was now Lord High Constable in Buckingham's place.

Her husband Stanley, who had ridden with the king to defeat the rebels.

She'd misjudged the level of his antagonism to the new king, or his desire to save his own skin. She'd not misjudged his loyalty to her, for he had none.

It might even have been Stanley who had informed the king of her plans.

Now he had the job of meting out punishment to the rebels. Already he'd arrested Jane Shore again for her part in sheltering the Marquis of Dorset.

One of her ladies, Jane Denham, said Margaret should go to him.

'No need,' she said. 'He'll be here soon enough.'

Early in December the soldiers came. Jane Denham came to her room to wake her, but she was already awake. She'd been dreaming of her old nurse, Betsy.

'Oh, my little duck,' she said. 'What have you been up to?'

And Margaret had felt the impulse to weep on her great breasts, to be Little Peg again. Then she'd woken up. She didn't immediately move but lay feeling the impact of her dream until Jane came in.

'Oh, my lady,' she said. 'They're here!'

Slowly, Margaret sat up. She peered towards the window. The dawn sky was darkened by rain; she could make nothing out at first apart from a flash of armour here, a sword there. Then she saw an emblem.

'It's Lord Stanley's men,' she said. 'Tell everyone not to panic. My husband has come home.'

Then she stood up a little too swiftly so that she had to sit down again. Jane hurried to her.

'Help me dress,' she said.

Soon she was in the kitchen, telling her servants not to worry, her husband was here. They should prepare a bed for him, and food and drink for his men.

All the time she was thinking: *if you betrayed us I will kill you myself.*

When no one came to the door she put on her hat and cloak and went out to greet her husband.

He wasn't there.

She went to the captain of the guards and asked him where Lord Stanley was.

'He'll be here soon, my lady,' he said, not looking at her, not volunteering any other information.

'I see,' she said, looking round at all the armed men. 'Well – we're preparing breakfast. You're welcome to take some with us, if you like.'

'We're under orders, ma'am.'

'Yes?'

'We must surround the house. No one is to enter or leave.'

'I see,' she said again. 'Well – I'll send out some bread, perhaps, and ale.'

The captain said she wasn't to trouble herself on their account. 'We have our orders, ma'am,' he said.

She felt a little foolish, rain dripping from the brim of her hat. She made a remark about the weather and said if he changed his mind he had only to knock. 'You know where we are,' she said, with hardly any irony, and when he didn't acknowledge this she went back inside, taking her cloak and hat off.

Gilbert Gilpyn, who'd insisted on staying with her, came forward. 'Will we arm ourselves, my lady?' he said.

'Good heavens, no,' she said. 'This isn't a siege.'

And she went upstairs, refusing to discuss the matter further.

From her window, however, she could see that it was, in fact, a siege. More than fifty men surrounded her house. There would be no possibility of resisting them. Several of her own men had not returned from the rebellion but were in hiding, or dead. Apart from Gilbert Gilpyn, there was only a kitchen boy, a gardener and a stable hand left.

She wasn't going to resist. She'd passed through anguish and despair to a dangerous calm. She could see herself in her mirror, red-eyed and ravaged by fate. Whatever happened next, she would face it or die.

But where was Stanley?

The morning drew on and the sky lightened. In the kitchen the servants were fretting. Pots were dropped, the soup boiled over and a state of nervous apprehension prevailed. Only Margaret was calm, dressed in her formal jewellery, the heavy cross anchored around her neck, three rings on her fingers, the wimple concealing her hair and chin.

Towards midday there was a violent rapping on her door.

She stood at the top of the stairway as Stanley came in. His gaze drifted upwards and their eyes locked. He removed his hat.

'My Lord Stanley,' she said, surprised by the steadiness of her voice. 'I hope you've not been too inconvenienced by the weather.'

She didn't move as he walked up the stairs without taking his eyes from her face. But she had to step back to avoid him colliding with her at the top. He said only, 'Your room,' as he walked past her. She hesitated a little before following him, closing the door gently behind them.

'Well, mistress,' he said, facing her. His nostrils had whitened, his lips had almost disappeared. 'Despite everything I said – my explicit instructions – you went ahead with your treacherous plan.'

He walked towards her. She could feel her skin tighten, expecting a blow, but she stood her ground.

'You have achieved a great deal,' he said softly. 'The execution of the Duke of Buckingham, Thomas St Leger, and so many others. Men drowned, imprisoned, ruined – your son's cause lost.'

She lowered her eyes. Her hands were clasped together as though in prayer.

'Parliament will open soon, and the king will accuse more than a hundred persons of treason.' He was too close to her now; she could smell his breath. 'Who do you suppose will head that list?' he said.

She raised her eyes to his. 'Did you betray us, Stanley?'

He gave a short, incredulous laugh. 'I betray you? I should have done,' he said, nodding. 'That would have been the wisest course. Instead of allowing you to betray me.'

'I'm sorry?' she said. 'Are you not Lord High Constable now? Have you not been given many new estates?'

He thrust his face unpleasantly close to hers. 'You've put everything I have at risk. You may risk your own life, lady, but you will not play with mine.'

'Is that what this is about?' she said. 'Lord Stanley's determination to save his own skin?'

'I would rather save it than have you nail it to your son's mast.'

Her head felt light from lack of food; it made her reckless. 'Are you so fond of this king?' she asked. 'Have you forgotten your oath to his brother – and his brother's children?'

He wasn't known for beating women, but she knew he would like to beat her now; to see, perhaps, if she would die with her son's name on her lips.

'Do you dare speak to me of King Edward's sons?' he said.

She closed her eyes; he would not see her weep.

But he turned away from her, addressing, apparently, the far corner of the room. 'Do you know what the penalty is for treason?' he said.

She was not expected to answer, but she said, 'I suppose – as Lord High Constable – you will decide.'

'No – not I,' he said, turning back to her. 'The king, madame – the king will decide. The king you've betrayed.'

'I do not recognise him as king!' she cried. 'And for all your fine words I know that you don't either. Yet now you're his lackey – his whipping boy!'

'*Do not provoke me, mistress!*' Stanley bellowed, and she flinched. 'It's thanks to me you've not been executed already! You should be on your knees, thanking me!'

'You want me to kneel, Stanley?' she said. 'You want me to thank you for rounding up my son's supporters and executing them? If you'd given them your aid, he would surely have won.'

'When will you give up this lunatic dream? Your son will not be king – he'll be lucky to die a pauper, in exile! Why did you ever think your preposterous plan would work? How could he not fail?'

'He would not have failed if you'd helped him!' she cried. 'If you'd not been too busy grovelling before this king you despise! But at least my son is safe. He will return.'

'He will return – the king will see to that. Already he has communicated his intentions to the Duke of Brittany. Your son will return and die the death all traitors die.'

'While you, Stanley, think to line your pockets with his wealth – as well as the Duke of Buckingham's.'

'And yours, my lady.'

'What do you mean?'

His expression had changed, and he didn't answer her directly. He said, 'I have my orders.'

This is it, she thought. He would tell her he'd come to take her to the Tower.

'The king has made his decision.'

She wasn't going to betray herself, to beg him to get on with it.

'His majesty requires me to keep you under guard here,' he said, 'for the time being.'

She shook her head a little, not understanding.

'You will be kept here until Parliament meets –'

'How –' she began; but he spoke over her.

'Because of the great dishonour of attainder that will be placed upon you, neither you nor your heirs can enjoy position, wealth or estate. All your property, land, estates and wealth are forfeit to me.'

When she could speak she said, 'Oh, Stanley – you have done well.'

'And you've done ill,' he said. 'You've committed treason. You've conspired against the king and caused slaughter and ruin throughout the land. You may thank me that you're not already hanged.'

When she said nothing, he went on, 'The king requires you to beg his forgiveness, of course. And mine.'

'Forgive me, Stanley,' she said, 'for ever thinking, even for one moment, that a man might support his wife.'

'You have my forgiveness,' he said. 'Now give me your keys.'

33

Rennes Cathedral

Perhaps a thousand people were crowded into the great church: Henry's supporters and many of the nobles and clergy of Brittany. Duke Francis wasn't there, but Pierre Landais stood next to the duke's young daughter, Anne. There was Jean Dufou, his admiral, there was the Marquis of Dorset, standing with his uncle, Edward Woodville. And there, of course, was his own uncle, Jasper.

All of them looking at him.

They were waiting for him to proclaim himself king. But he had no crown. He felt its absence like a wound in his soul. Without the crown he was nothing: a failed pretender. Once Parliament had met, he wouldn't even be earl.

But it had been agreed that he should proclaim himself king before the men who'd come to him from England, many of whom didn't know him at all.

As soon as they'd reached Vannes they'd been met by Jasper and Edward Woodville, and by a sharp-faced young man who resembled Sir Edward. He was introduced to Henry as the Marquis of Dorset.

This young man, the queen's son and brother to the princess, had raised Henry's standard in Exeter and proclaimed him king. And when the rebellion had failed, he'd fled to Brittany.

Henry didn't like him.

'We can't stay here,' the marquis said, 'while the hog-king squats on the throne of England. As soon as we can, we must strike again.' His face was sharp with hatred.

'I can't go anywhere without ships,' Henry said, 'or men.'

The marquis said he had men, and the ships could be repaired. 'You should leave before you're sent back,' he said. 'Duke Francis will be reconciled with Richard any day now.'

Henry looked at him coldly. 'We need more men,' he said.

In the days that followed they came, bringing news that Bishop Morton and several others had fled to Flanders. Christopher Urswick, his mother's priest, told Henry his mother had been placed in the custody of her husband. Her servants had been dismissed, her receiver, Reginald Bray, was in prison.

All her possessions had been confiscated. She had no money, but she'd managed to send her jewellery to the King of France, to pay for Henry's safe conduct.

That explained, to some extent, his cordial reception from the French.

They were all looking at him, waiting for his response.

'Can any message be got to her?' he said.

Christopher Urswick said she wasn't allowed visitors. 'She'll be sentenced in Parliament next month,' he said. 'But I will return to England – I'll see Lord Stanley, at least.'

'We should all return,' said the marquis.

'Not until I have more men,' Henry said, but the marquis said he would wait a long time before he had as many men as Richard.

Henry knew they were expecting more from him – more response, more rage – but it was as though he couldn't feel or think. To think was to be reminded that God hadn't backed him; he'd lost many of his supporters, he was once again in exile. But the Woodvilles were waiting for him to act. He wished he could leave them out of his councils, but they were always there, the Woodvilles, impatient, aggrieved.

'I'm waiting to hear from the duke,' he said.

When the news came that King Richard planned a great ceremony at Westminster on Christmas Day, his councillors said Henry should do the same.

'Tell them about your marriage to my sister,' the marquis said.

'Do it in Rennes and maybe the duke will come,' said Edward Woodville.

Last night he'd dreamed of the crown. He was in a long dusty hall, filled with statues of kings, like the Palace of Westminster. But this place was dusty and old. All the kings from the Conqueror were there, sitting on thrones; some crumbling, others covered in cobwebs. He could see the throne he had to reach, with the crown above it but, though he set off towards it, he couldn't reach it. He thought he'd reached it, then knew it wasn't the right one. When he bumped into the last king he was horrified to feel warm flesh through the stone.

He'd woken from this dream sweating and labouring for breath.

He'd had such attacks since childhood. When he was very small, someone, not his mother, would bring bowls of steam and a poultice for his chest and sit with him until he could breathe again. As he grew older, he'd tried to manage the attacks himself; controlling his breath was the first economy he'd learned. So now he didn't give in to the impulse to fight for breath, because this only made it worse, as though God would deprive him of air along with everything else: his mother, his home, his country. He lay as still as possible, taking in what air he could, remembering his childhood, the boy he had been, and thinking how impossible it seemed that this breathless boy would be king.

Over the years he'd been many people: an infant ward and a cuckoo, a refugee and an exile. Only the Crown could bring all those people together.

And so here he was, in the cathedral at Rennes, beneath the great stone pillars, the vaulted ceiling that dwarfed them all. He had the vertiginous sense of looking down on everyone, including himself.

It seemed that all his previous selves – the child at Pembroke

Castle, the boy at Raglan Castle, the young man in exile in Brittany – were ranged behind him as he began to speak.

> Henry vowed that as soon as he had got the kingdom he would marry King Edward's daughter, Elizabeth. Then they swore their homage to Henry, just as if he had already been crowned king, promising they would sacrifice their lives [and] their fortunes rather than allow, suffer and permit Richard to reign over them.
>
> *Polydore Vergil*

Two hundred and fifty miles away, in London, Richard also spoke to his followers. Both men pledged their lives to the nation and the Crown, Richard repeating the claim of his brother's illegitimacy, the ineligibility of his line; Henry Tudor proclaiming himself king in the absence of a crown and betrothing himself in the absence of a bride.

34

Judgement

Margaret spent the dark days of January trying to reconcile herself to death, or at least to lifelong imprisonment. Yet in her heart she was not reconciled. If she had to do it all again, she would.

When Parliament began, news filtered through slowly of the many men who had been attainted and their estates redistributed.

> What great numbers and inheritances were amassed in the king's treasury in consequence! He distributed all these among his northerners whom he had planted in every part of his dominion to the shame of all the southern people who murmured ceaselessly and longed more each day for the return of their old lords in place of the tyranny of the present ones.
>
> *Crowland Chronicle*

Other men were rewarded. James Tyrell, who had imprisoned Buckingham, was given money, lands and offices; Ralph Bannister, who had betrayed him, was given Buckingham's manor in Kent.

The Act of Titulus Regius was approved, invalidating the previous reign, settling the Crown on King Richard and his heirs in perpetuity. Stanley's position as Lord High Constable was confirmed.

There was no news about Margaret. No guards came to take her to the Tower. But finally, in early February, Stanley himself arrived.

She stood before him, dressed like a nun, as he took off his hat and cloak. His expression gave nothing away. 'Perhaps we should eat first,' he said. Then he looked at her ironically. 'Or I could read you the sentence that's been passed on you?'

Do as you like, she didn't say. Despite everything, all her preparations, she felt fear like a run of cold water in her bones, but her mouth was entirely dry.

Stanley sighed, took out a scroll and began to read.

'*Forasmuch as Margaret, Countess of Richmond, Mother to the King's Great Rebel and Traitor Henry, Earl of Richmond, hath of late conspired, confederated and committed high treason against our sovereign lord the King Richard the Third in divers and sundry wise, sending messages, writings and tokens to the said Henry, desiring, procuring and stirring him by the same to come into this realm and make war against our sovereign Lord, yet nevertheless, our said Sovereign Lord, remembering the good and faithful service that Thomas, Lord Stanley, hath done and intendeth to do to our said Sovereign Lord, and for the good love and trust that the king hath in him, for his sake remitteth and will forbear the great punishment of attainder of the said countess.*'

He stopped, and she looked at him, uncomprehending. 'What?' she said.

'Did you not hear?'

When she didn't reply he read it to her again, adding, as he'd told her before, that her goods and lands would pass to him, Stanley, and after his death to the Crown. She was to be confined by him at one of his residences, *a remote and isolated place*, for the remainder of her life.

But she was to have the remainder of her life. She was to live.

She could feel a surge of blood to her face, the sensation of dizziness. She had to sit down.

Stanley was saying she was to be allowed to communicate with no one, especially her son, for the duration of her life. Or at least as long as King Richard reigned.

She couldn't believe she wasn't going to die.

'It may interest you to know,' he said, 'that at my request the king has pardoned your servant, Reginald Bray. He is to be released from imprisonment and will go unmolested as long as he has no further communication with you, or any member of your household, or person connected to you.'

When she still didn't speak he said, 'You may thank me, if you like.'

Finally, she found her voice. 'May I have a confessor?'

'Do you wish to confess?'

'I wish to have a priest with me. To conduct services, as usual. To say mass.'

Stanley sighed. 'I've already saved your life,' he said. 'I can hardly be expected to save your soul.'

That was all he would say. Except to tell her that her son was attainted, which she already knew. He had lost his estates and was no longer Earl of Richmond. But many people had benefited, Stanley said. The king was reforming many laws, especially those that oppressed the poor, and had made many grants and allowances to both merchants and clergy.

'And you?' she said. 'What has he given you?'

... lordships etc in Lancashire, Cheshire, Wiltshire, Warwickshire, Leicestershire, Bedfordshire, Somersetshire, Rutland, Oxfordshire and Wales ...

Rotuli Parliamentorum

'No more than might be expected,' he said. 'I would say you have most cause to be grateful. Have you no message for me to take back to the king?'

She was silent for a moment, trying to take it all in. She would live in permanent confinement. All her estates and wealth would pass first to Stanley, then to the Crown. Not to her son. She would not be able to communicate with him, or anyone, ever again. She looked up.

'The king is merciful,' she said.

By the end of that week she was travelling north, to her husband's house of Lathom, which was indeed remote and isolated.

It was a great stronghold surrounded by a wall two yards thick and a moat eight yards across. Nine towers were built into the circumference of the walls. A central tower, highest of all, was called the Eagle Tower. There was also the Kitchen Tower, the Chapel Tower and the Tower of Madness.

'I hope I'm not to be kept in the Tower of Madness,' she said lightly to her husband's steward, and he, according to his instructions, said nothing.

In fact she was taken to the Chapel Tower, which had a view over miles of deserted countryside. She was in the heartland of a country that had abandoned its allegiance to the House of Lancaster and now supported King Richard, as if its past had been swiftly and cleanly erased. No one from her own household had come with her; Stanley had remained in London. She could read but was not allowed writing materials. She was to live in this room, where food would be brought to her. At the end of a short corridor there was a guard.

She was alive and had been granted her life by a king who had no reason to save her. Yet it was difficult to feel grateful as the door closed on the small room, leaving her alone.

The Eagle Tower contained offices of administration; many people came and went, bringing news, carrying lawsuits, pleading cases. No one came to Margaret.

She missed news, gossip, communication of any kind, even giving instructions to her servants. She had not known before how much this had sustained her. She had a few books with her, including a Bible, but she no longer wanted to read. And she couldn't pray. God had let her down for the last time.

She was surprised, as the days passed, at how little it took to dismantle her; Margaret Beaufort, daughter of a duke, one-time sister-in-law to the king. When the serving girl didn't respond to her greeting, when she heard voices and laughter in the corridor approaching her room, then going past, when she fell asleep suddenly and woke not knowing what day or time it was, or lay awake with her heart pounding for no reason, she knew something in her was unravelling.

One day she woke and couldn't remember her name. *Margaret*, she thought. *That was my mother's name*. It took a moment for her to remember it was also her name; she'd been named after her mother. And at the thought of this, and the thought of everything she had forgotten or was about to forget, tears came to her eyes, but remained there, as if unable to fall.

That day, she didn't get up. From where she lay she could see grey clouds massing together but then parting a little to reveal the blue she'd always imagined was the blue of heaven. One of the smaller clouds surrounding this blue space was full of light, but the light dispersed as it mingled with the grey.

There was no one to make her get up, no one to comment when she left her food, to insist she washed or dressed. She supposed they would comment if she pissed herself, so in the end she had to get up. She was dully surprised by her reflection in the window, something alien glinting through its eyes.

Soon she was ill; glands swollen, throat parched and raw. She didn't know how many days she lay there, but on one of them the servant who brought her food said she had a visitor.

She looked at him blearily and didn't understand.

'Someone to see you,' he repeated.

He turned away from her, went back through the door. But she heard him speaking, then footsteps. She barely had time to push the covers back, to wrap herself in her cloak, before the door opened again.

She couldn't see his face at first, but then he put back his hood and she gave a cry of agonised delight. It was her priest, Christopher Urswick.

35

Princess Elizabeth Comforts Her Mother, the Queen

Meanwhile, Richard, hearing about the conspiracy in Brittany . . . decided on another approach so that Henry could not aspire to the throne by marriage . . .

Polydore Vergil

The former queen dreamed frequently of her husband and her sons. Sometimes they were together, standing on the other side of a wall. Everything beyond that wall was bathed in light, but on her side was deepest shade. Through a chink in the wall she could see them looking her way, unmoving, expressionless. Edward was holding the hands of their two sons.

Everything would be all right, she thought, if she could get to the other side of the wall, but though she tried, pressing her hands against the stone, there was no place she might enter, and through the next chink she could see them walking away.

Take me with you, she cried, but her voice had no sound, and she woke with her throat aching, her whole body in pain.

In other dreams she could feel the imprint of her husband's body on hers.

That, unexpectedly, was what she missed now, though she'd frequently resented it when he was alive. But for so many years her body had not been hers alone; she'd had her husband moving inside it, or an infant pressing to get out. Now she was in her forty-ninth year, her womb would not swell again; in all probability, no other man would enter her.

But the dreams were so real she could feel his lips on hers, her body lifting towards him. The yearning woke her; roused her back into the half-life she had to endure.

She'd lived in Sanctuary with her daughters for almost a year. In that time she'd witnessed the coronation of the Great Pretender, as she thought of him; the failure of one plot to rescue her sons and the bigger failure of the rebellion that would have placed her eldest daughter on the throne.

All her connections, her supporters, were either dead or fled abroad. And the Pretender was once more exhorting her to leave Sanctuary, or to send her daughters to him, as she'd sent her son. To this end, he'd sent *many grave men* to persuade her to come to terms with him.

They stood before her like puppets in some monstrous play: Surrey, Catesby, Lovell.

'Why would I give up my daughters to the man who has disposed of my sons?' she asked. And they assured her, of course, that he'd done nothing of the kind; she mustn't listen to rumours; the king would never mistreat his own nephews.

'Where are they, then?' she asked, but they could not or would not say. Instead, they repeated the king's promises. He would look after her daughters as if they were his own, restoring them to a place of honour and arranging good marriages for them. He pledged safe conduct for her remaining son, the marquis, if he would return from Brittany. For her there would be comfortable lodgings and a generous pension. She would be able to live out the rest of her days in peace at the king's goodwill.

'How am I to believe in this goodwill?' she said.

'Madame,' said Lovell, 'what possible benefit can there be if you do not?'

After a silence she said, 'You see before you a grieving mother. My life is blighted by grief, I have not one moment free from it. I've lost all my sons and now you say I must give up my daughters. I'm promised much if I do. But I've listened to promises before.'

They made further promises, together with veiled threats and subtle hints that the king would use force if necessary, but when they couldn't sway her they left.

She knew they would come back.

The guard around Sanctuary had increased again; the abbot was in trouble for his hospitality. He had already been reprimanded by the king, threatened with the loss of his office. And he was supporting them all at his own expense.

No one had known it would go on so long.

More messengers arrived from the king. Her response became desperate.

'Why can't he leave me alone?' she demanded. 'What harm am I doing him? I have no friends, no influence – what hope do I have?'

'No hope,' they assured her, 'not while you remain here.'

In between their visits she fell into a profound melancholy. Not even her youngest daughters could cajole her out of her despair.

She'd received many messages from the common people of London, passed through the gates or thrown like paper missiles over the walls. Many of them asserted in poor writing that for them she was the rightful 'kyng' of England and promised her that one day she'd be restored. Others contained messages of hope about her sons, who were still alive, they said. Some claimed to have seen them being rowed away from the Tower to a ship that had sailed for France or Burgundy. Or disguised as serving boys in the kitchens of this or that great house.

My brother's wyf nos a woman of hir vylage that dos foster poer children and has taken recently into hir care ii boies abowt xi and ix yeres. Very fare they are and lyk to his blest majesty as cud be . . .

These messages at first fed her hope, then were like an opiate for her pain; now they only aggravated her despair. So she continued in a life that was more like a dream than any of the dreams that visited her, from which she was increasingly reluctant to wake.

But one day the abbot's servant came to her, saying that the Lord Chancellor himself, Bishop Russell, had come to see her.

She received this news with a hollow dread, knowing it presaged some crisis; that the king's patience had given out at last. Bishop Russell had taken over as chancellor from Thomas Bourchier, who had persuaded her to give up her youngest son. She didn't want to see him, but she didn't have the power to refuse. So she kept him waiting half an hour, because even in her distressed state she would not appear before anyone unkempt. Her eldest daughter helped her to dress her hair and put on what jewels she had.

When she entered the Jerusalem Chamber finally, he greeted her with a thin smile, and said he trusted she was well.

'As well as I can be,' she said, sitting down.

'The winter chill –' he said, then stopped at the look on her face. 'Well, madame, I will come to the point. His majesty wishes you to release your daughters immediately.'

'I'm sure he does.'

'It's no longer appropriate for them to be here.'

'I see nothing inappropriate about it.'

'They are not criminals. They're in no need of protection from the law.'

'Not the law, perhaps.'

'Then from what, my lady?'

She laughed, without any humour.

'No, my lady,' he said. 'You must speak plainly. The king desires it.'

'Plainly?' she said. 'In the past year I've lost my husband, my brother and my sons. Is it any wonder I should prefer to keep my daughters?'

Lord Russell pressed his fingertips together. 'But you see, my lady, that's precisely why you should let them go.'

She waited.

'You want to keep your daughters safe, but they're not safe

here. The king won't be patient for ever. If he has to send in his guards, your daughters will be taken directly into secure custody, since you've defied his command. No one will ever see them again.'

She started to speak, but he continued. 'If, however, you send them out willingly, they will be kept at court, where they will be visible to all. The whole court will see how they're treated by their uncle. I myself will watch over them – and many others who have their interests at heart.'

The queen rose suddenly, as if she would accost him, but instead she turned away. Then she looked at him and said, 'Less than a year ago another chancellor stood where you are now, making the same promises. I listened to him – and I never saw my sons again.'

The chancellor looked down at his fingertips. 'The situation is different now,' he said.

'How?'

'I mean, now that your sons aren't here.'

'What do you know about my sons?'

'Nothing,' the chancellor said quickly. 'I only know they're not here.'

'But where are they?'

He began to protest, but she said with tears in her eyes, 'Oh, if you know something – anything – about my sons, don't keep it from me. Tell me, for pity's sake – have you no mother?'

The chancellor strove to rescue the conversation. 'I would tell you if I could, my lady,' he began, but she turned away from him with a passionate cry. After a pause he said, 'I wish –' then he stopped and started again. 'I only meant that your daughters pose no – difficulty to the king. It would not be in his interests to harm them in any way. And what life do they have here?'

The queen was silent. It was true her daughters posed no threat to Richard, after his Act had made them illegitimate. Still, there was the question of her eldest daughter's betrothal to

Henry Tudor – that must aggravate him like a stone in the shoe. Yet he could hardly risk any more scandal.

'Many of us,' Russell said, 'care deeply about your daughters' welfare. I, for one – Lord Stanley, for another –'

Stanley. Her husband had given him custody of their eldest daughter. But Stanley had helped to suppress the rebellion against Richard; he'd imprisoned his own wife. She couldn't trust Stanley.

'I can assure you,' the chancellor said, 'if you give up your daughters it will not be to the king's protection only, but to the care of everyone at court.'

The queen pressed her hands to the sides of her head, then covered her face.

'I beg you,' he said, 'don't let it come to force – and imprisonment.'

She expelled a long breath through her fingers.

'I'm sorry if I've distressed you,' he said. 'I would not for anything have added to the burden of your grief. I came in the hope of helping you, if anything – and I will come again.'

She shook her head.

After further protestations, he left. The queen made her way back to her seat. She felt winded by the force of her emotion. And trapped. She could see no way out of this situation.

There was a tap on the door and her eldest daughter came in. She hurried to her mother at once, sat on a little stool in front of her and clasped her hands, then kissed them.

'*Maman*,' she said, gazing earnestly into her mother's face. The queen closed her eyes. 'What is it?' the princess said. 'What did he say?'

'Nothing that hasn't been said before. That I should give you up – send you away from me.'

'What did you say?'

'What do you think I said?'

The princess said hesitantly, 'But do you think we *can* stay here?'

The queen opened her eyes. 'Do you agree with him?'

'Of course not,' her daughter said. 'It's just – we've been here so long – and there's nothing we can do – nothing we can achieve –'

'What do you expect to achieve?'

'At court,' her daughter said, 'we can keep our eyes and ears open – we can listen to what's being said.'

'What do you think will be said?'

'I don't know, *maman*, I just think – someone must know – have heard something – about my brothers,' and her eyes filled with tears, but the queen made no move to comfort her.

'Whatever they know,' she said, 'they will keep to themselves.'

'People talk,' said her daughter. 'They whisper – behind closed doors.'

'Then how will you hear them?'

'I will listen,' the princess said. 'I'll talk to people – make friends.'

The queen looked at her daughter, so pretty; so apparently without guile. 'Do you want to go so much?'

'*Maman*,' the princess said, resting her cheek against her mother's hands.

'I don't want you to go.'

'Then we won't,' said the princess. 'We won't go anywhere without you. You should come with us.'

'I don't think the invitation is extended to me.'

When her daughter didn't answer, she said, 'I can't let you go. How could I know you were safe?'

The princess said, 'Lord Stanley would look after us. And we would write to you. Whenever I hear anything I'll let you know.'

The queen felt as if her heart and lungs were constricted by a tight band.

'He would have to make certain pledges,' she said at last, 'publicly – before everyone.'

I, Richard, by the Grace of God, King of England, in the presence of my lords spiritual and temporal, promise and swear on the word of a king that if the daughters of Dame Elizabeth Grey, late calling herself Queen of England, will come to me out of the Sanctuary of Westminster ... then I shall see that they be in surety of their lives, and also not suffer any manner hurt by any person ... by way of ravishment or defiling contrary to their wills, nor any of them imprison within the Tower of London or any other prison, but that I shall put them in honest places of good name and fame and ... every one of them give in marriage to some gentlemen born ... and over this that I shall yearly content and pay for the said Elizabeth Grey, during her natural life ... to John Nesfield, one of the squires of my body ... to attend upon her the sum of 700 marks ...

Proclamation of Richard III at Westminster, 1 March 1484

In April the king's only son, Edward ... died in Middleham Castle after a short illness ... You might have seen his father and mother after hearing the news at Nottingham ... almost out of their minds for a long time with the sudden grief ...

Crowland Chronicle

36

Princess Elizabeth Comforts Her Aunt, the Queen

'**E**dward, Edward!' she cried.

Her ladies, Mary and Sofia, tried in vain to get the queen back into bed. 'My lady – you'll catch cold.'

'But where is he?'

The older of the two ladies shot a despairing look at Elizabeth. She dropped to her knees beside the queen. 'He's not here, my lady – look,' she said.

She attempted to put her arms around the queen's shoulders, but the queen shook her off. 'He is here somewhere – I know it.'

Elizabeth made a show of looking under the bed. 'He isn't here, see?'

The queen sat back on her heels, rubbing her sleep-encrusted eyes. 'Why can't I find him?' she said, her voice cracking.

Elizabeth glanced at Mary, who shook her head. Sofia left quietly.

'If you get back into bed, I'll look for him,' she said.

The queen clutched her. 'You'll find him?'

'I'll try.'

'But you must – you must find him – he's just a little boy!' She covered her eyes again, taking long, grieving breaths. 'I don't know why he isn't here –'

Elizabeth and Mary together tried to move the queen back into bed. 'Come, my lady,' Elizabeth said. 'You remember how it was when you were small – playing hide and seek – you would get tired if no one came looking. If you get back into bed,' she said, pulling the cover back, 'he'll soon be tired of waiting.'

Between them they manoeuvred her under the covers. 'But he

will come back, won't he?' she said, and Elizabeth repeated, 'He'll get tired of hiding.'

She sat on the bed and attempted to pull up the neck of the queen's chemise, which had fallen open to reveal the ridges of her breastbone and the brownish stub of a nipple. She could hear the doctor coming.

His voice could be heard from one end of the palace corridors to the other.

'Now, then!' he boomed. 'What's happening here?'

Queen Anne didn't take her eyes from Elizabeth's face. The lids were so swollen they were almost shut, but the queen would not fully close her eyes.

'Don't leave me,' she whispered.

'I won't leave you,' Elizabeth murmured, then louder, 'Look, here is your doctor – come to make you well again!'

The doctor checked the queen's pulse, her urine, then gave her another dose of the medicine he feared would be too strong for her. It contained a very strong opiate, he said, which might be too powerful for her delicate constitution. But in the days since the news of the prince's death he'd increased the dosage steadily.

The queen drank with only a little encouragement, then sank back, still holding Elizabeth's hand.

'You'll stay with her?' the doctor asked.

'I will.'

'That's good. If she wakes again you may give her a little more. Not too much – it can be dangerous in the wrong quantities – but I don't think a little more will do much harm in the circumstances.' His laugh, by contrast with his speaking voice, was surprisingly soft, almost girlish. Then he sighed. 'These things take time,' he said. He looked back at the queen, whose breathing had changed. But her eyes were still not shut. Through the slits it was possible to see crescents of white.

'It's hard for a mother to lose a child,' he said. Elizabeth looked at him with dislike. What did he know about it? About the grief of her own mother, who had lost so much more than this queen? But she said, 'I'm sure she'll sleep now. And if she wakes I'll give her a little more of the potion.'

The doctor looked as if he would say something else, though Elizabeth wished he wouldn't. But all he said was 'Well – I'll leave you to it. You know where I am if you need me.'

He left Elizabeth sitting by the bed, still holding the queen's hand. And an hour or so later it began again.

'Edward – Edward, my son!'

'Ssssh, my lady – don't distress yourself.'

'But where is he – bring him to me!'

'He's not here, my lady – he's at Middleham Castle, remember?'

'But I want him with me!' Despite Elizabeth's efforts, she crawled from between the sheets and knelt on the bed. 'Why has he left me?' she cried.

'Hush, my lady – you'll wake everyone up!'

'Bring him back to me!'

Elizabeth climbed on the bed with the queen. 'My lady – you know I can't.'

'Why – what have you done with him?'

'Sssh, now,' Elizabeth said, smoothing back strands of the queen's hair. 'You'll make yourself ill.'

The queen pressed her fingers to her mouth. 'I wasn't with him,' she said. 'He must have called for me, but I wasn't there!'

'He knows you loved him,' Elizabeth began, but the queen put one finger on her niece's lips. 'Can you hear him calling for me?'

'No, my lady – it's only the palace guard.'

'No – there – do you hear?' She scrambled to the edge of the bed, listening. When Elizabeth put her hands on the queen's shoulders she could feel them shaking. 'What kind of a mother sends her child alone into the dark?' she said, and began to wail, clutching the bed cover.

'I have one son – *one* – and God has taken him from me! Have I not lost enough? Must I suffer every misfortune there is?'

The princess could, of course, have pointed to her own misfortunes, or to the fact that her mother, who had until recently been queen, had lost her husband, her brother and three sons in that year alone. But not while the queen was rocking herself into a frenzy on the bed.

'God can't have him! He's mine – he's all I have!'

'He's not all you have – you have your husband, the king. And the nation.'

But the queen knocked her hand away. 'Why – why did He not take me?'

Then she was howling, mouth wide open, a strand of spit spooling from her upper to her lower lip.

Sofia hurried back into the room and the three of them got the queen back into bed and administered more of the dangerous medicine. Finally, she fell asleep again. But she wouldn't let go of Elizabeth's hand.

This preference for her eldest niece had shown itself almost as soon as Elizabeth arrived at court.

In the early days of March the five daughters of Elizabeth Woodville had left Sanctuary surrounded by guards. Elizabeth had felt considerable turmoil at leaving her mother, and at the prospect of meeting her uncle. She'd thought perhaps she couldn't bear it, after all that had happened, filled as she was with her mother's aversion. Then she'd thought she could bear it: she wouldn't even have to look at him, she would keep her eyes lowered modestly when they met.

But in fact she'd walked boldly up to the king and queen, looking at them both. The king stood, smiling stiffly; the queen had looked nervous, if anything. The princess had dropped into a perfect curtsy and then risen, smiling radiantly at the king.

She saw his eyes startle, then look again.

'I don't know how to thank you, dearest uncle,' she'd said, 'for your hospitality and compassion.'

His eyes became wary, but there was something else in them; a different light.

She'd seen little of him after that, until they were told they were to go on progress with him and the queen. By the end of that week they'd set off, travelling north.

And the queen had begun to single her out from her sisters.

They'd travelled from town to town, which had so wearied the queen that she had to be carried in a litter. And she wanted Elizabeth to sit with her. Whether it was because she was easy to talk to, less flighty than Cecily, who would be fifteen that month and was already flirting with the courtiers and even the men-at-arms, or simply because she was only a few years younger than the queen, she didn't know, but the queen plainly preferred her company.

It meant that Elizabeth was isolated. She couldn't be her mother's eyes and ears, as she'd promised to be. Between reading aloud to the queen or helping to dress her hair, she hardly found a moment in which to write.

She'd not learned anything about her brothers. The queen's chatter was inconsequential, even inane. She did learn, however, that the reason they were accompanying the king on progress was that he feared another invasion from the Great Rebel in Brittany as the weather improved. Elizabeth, of course, was betrothed to that great rebel, but the queen said that would be rearranged. 'We'll find a better husband for you,' she said, patting Elizabeth's knee. And Elizabeth, who had been betrothed four times now, only bent her face dutifully over her embroidery.

Of course, if he couldn't have her, Henry Tudor was pledged to marry one of her sisters, so the king would have to arrange marriages for all of them. As soon as they arrived at Nottingham, the queen said. When Elizabeth asked who the king might choose, the queen was vague. Some respectable gentleman or other, she said. Elizabeth tried to imagine her life on a farm somewhere, away from court. 'You are the eldest,' the queen said. 'You must be married first.'

Elizabeth couldn't write any of this to her mother, or say that she found the new situation almost as confining as the old, for who knew whether or not her letters would be intercepted?

Our uncle keeps us safe, she wrote, *and spares no effort to protect us.*

She'd also learned that the king did not keep company with the queen unless they came to some public place, where they would stand side by side. Of course, the queen was delicate and frequently ill, with a headache or some nervous indisposition, and Elizabeth was familiar enough with royal marriages to know there was often no time for intimacy. Still, she thought he might do more than send a nightly enquiry about the queen's health. Because the queen was fretting – anyone could see that. She was pining for the company of her husband or her son. They were travelling to Middleham, she said frequently, to see her son.

But the king was prodigiously busy. He had a reputation for unstinting labour, often working through the night. He was reforming all the laws of the land.

He taught others to exercise justice and goodness . . . so that they should see the countries where they lived well-guided and that no extortions were done to his subjects.

Great Chronicle of London

In Cambridge he made grants and endowments, saying English universities should shine like a beacon throughout the world.

On my faith I never liked the qualities of any prince as well as his. God has sent him to us for the welfare of us all . . .

Thomas Langton, Bishop of St David's

Of course, her mother would not like to hear that the king was preoccupied with dispensing justice and remedying wrong. She didn't like to hear him referred to as king at all, but she knew her daughter's letters would be read.

I expect we will see more of his majesty at Nottingham. I will write to you again from there.

But when they got to Nottingham the king was permanently in conference, and the talk was all of defence, fortifications, improving the courier system, increasing the arsenal of the Tower and importing gunpowder. He was marshalling all his forces against invasion.

The queen became more fretful. She wanted to see her son, who wasn't well, she said. He had some childhood malady and would doubtlessly recover soon. 'But I should like to go to him,' she said. 'If only his father were not so obsessed with protecting the realm!'

It was not until 20 April that the news came. The five princesses could hear Queen Anne bellowing like a demented beast in her room. When the king tried to see her she drove him away with shrieks and blows. She wouldn't see anyone except for Elizabeth, whom she wanted to keep with her at all times.

So the former princess attended the grieving queen. She'd had so much practice at consoling the afflicted that she did it well, not addressing the queen's pain directly, nor drawing attention to her own, but attending to practical details, smoothing the bed covers, combing her hair, encouraging her to drink when she wouldn't, and to eat, and sending for the doctor when necessary. She knew by instinct as well as experience that grief should be greeted as a guest.

Only when the queen lapsed into fragmentary unconsciousness did she have time to write: one single letter in the two weeks following the tragic news. *You will have heard by now of the lamentable death of the prince,* she wrote. *The king and queen are distracted by grief.*

She could imagine her mother's pleasure on reading this. It would not have escaped her, as it had not escaped the nation, that the young prince had died on the anniversary of her husband's death. Already people were saying that this was the hand of God. Other, darker rumours suggested that the curses of the former queen were finally bearing fruit. Which was not good, of course, because it revived all the old allegations of witchcraft.

But there was barely time to consider how to phrase these things before the queen was awake and calling again for her son like a lost bird. There was no indication that time, or anything else, would cure her.

Elizabeth was sympathetic, of course, but she couldn't help contrasting the queen's hysteria with her own mother's fortitude. The present queen seemed by nature weaker; constitutionally brittle. It was one of the mysteries of life that some people had to bear so much more pain than others.

Only once did the queen refer to Elizabeth's own troubles. In a rare moment of lucidity she said she was grateful to the princess for staying with her; she could not bear to be consoled by those who didn't know what grief was.

Elizabeth was instantly alert. 'I share your grief, my lady,' she began.

'I know you do,' said the queen. 'Your brothers were the same tender age –'

Elizabeth's throat constricted suddenly, and by the time she could speak the queen's eyes were vague again. 'It is the sins of the father,' she said, and the fine hair on Elizabeth's arms, the back of her neck, stood up.

'I'm sure his majesty can have committed no sin worthy of such misfortune,' she said, and just for a moment the queen's eyes focused sharply.

'I meant my father,' she said, and her eyes clouded over once more, then swam with tears, and there was nothing for it but to soothe her back to sleep.

Elizabeth felt disturbed by this. She could neither sleep herself, nor finish the letter she'd begun. Her thoughts were restless, unsettled. *What am I doing here?* she asked herself, but could find no answer. In the last year her world had changed so completely she felt like a ship cast adrift on a stormy sea.

At last she fell into an uneasy doze in which she dreamed of her brothers, that the elder of the two was leading the younger one away from her. She felt she had to stop him, to bring them back. So she called out to him – 'Edward!' – and in the same moment the queen woke, calling, 'Edward! Edward!'

And the princess brushed her tears away with the heel of her hand and rose to attend the queen.

Not long after the death of the prince the young Earl of Warwick [son of the Duke of Clarence] was proclaimed heir apparent in the royal court . . .

John Rous

[Richard] sent hand-picked messengers to the Duke of Brittany who in addition to the great gifts they brought with them, promised that Richard would give him all the annual income from the estates of Henry and the other English nobles who were staying with him if he would henceforth keep them in strict custody. The messengers . . . could not negotiate this with the duke for that he had become feeble by reason of sore and daily sickness, wherefore Pierre Landais, his treasurer . . . answered that he would do as King Richard required . . . However . . . John Morton, Bishop of Ely who lived in Flanders, being notified of that practice by his friends in England, gave intelligence to Henry of the plot and advised the earl that he should get himself and the other noble men out of Brittany into France . . .

Polydore Vergil

37

Flight

Five miles out of Vannes, Henry's guide veered off the road, while the rest of his company went on to Rennes. That way, when Landais sent his soldiers after them, they would follow Henry's men, rather than Henry himself. Another contingent, led by Jasper, had set off two days ago. Jasper had told everyone he was going to Rennes to visit Duke Francis, who was ill. Before he got to Rennes, however, he would turn off the road and gallop towards the French border. Henry would meet him at Angers, where the French court currently was.

That was the plan. Landais' agents would by now have realised that Jasper had not arrived in Rennes. In all probability, they would have set off after him. That was why Henry was taking a different route. One that depended on this young man.

His guide, who'd said his name was Joncis Tristyard Gondyvar Perrinele – *but you can call me Perrin* – led Henry into woodland, where all paths seemed to disappear. He dismounted in a small clearing, and Henry did the same. Then Perrin handed him a soft bundle.

'Your clothes,' he said, as Henry looked at it doubtfully. 'You cannot travel as king here, eh?'

The bundle contained woollen leggings, a pair of weather-beaten boots, a shirt and a short cloak. The boots were muddy, the shirt stained and the cloak stank of something Henry thought might be shit.

'They are good clothes,' Perrin said, seeing the look on Henry's face. 'I wore them when I was a groom in Duke Francis' stables.'

He turned his back, tending to the horses, while Henry reluctantly began to pull off his clothes.

Edward Woodville had said Perrin was an invaluable scout. *Knows every tree in the forest, every stone in the road.* That was why he'd been chosen to accompany Henry now, on a route which, hopefully, Landais' men would not know.

Henry didn't know it either, and he didn't know Perrin. Also, he didn't trust Edward Woodville. He had no reason to believe that Perrin would betray him, or lead him miles out of his way into unknown countryside; all the same, he didn't like getting undressed, unbuckling his sword, in his presence.

Perrin turned to him smiling broadly as he finished.

'Now you are the servant and I am the master,' he said. 'I will call you Henri. No, don't thank me,' he said, as Henry started to speak. 'Maybe I can wear your crown when you are king.' And he turned with a short laugh, leading the horses away.

At some point, Henry would undoubtedly have to reprimand him. But for now he was dependent on his goodwill.

'Where are you going?' he asked.

'To water,' Perrin answered. 'A horse must drink, no?'

There was this edge to everything he said, but if Henry pulled him up for it he would probably deny it. Or shrug, because what could Henry do? He didn't know the area. All he could do was follow Perrin, like any servant, and hope he wasn't being taken to a trap.

He'd had his doubts about this plan, even though he'd helped to devise it. Given such short notice, such urgency in the message from Flanders, it was the best they could do.

Almost a year had passed since his catastrophic attempt to invade England. Most of the former adherents of Edward IV and the Woodvilles were with him now, together with members of his mother's household and the sons of those who'd died or been executed in the Great Rebellion. Dispossessed by attainder, they were intent on regaining their fortunes and status. Many of these brought their own retainers with them. John Harcourt arrived from William Hastings' household with a small army of his own.

Weekly, almost daily, their numbers grew. They treated the château in Vannes as a court, addressing Henry as 'sire'. They didn't mix with the local population, who endured all this with their customary stoicism. Henry had forbidden his men to fraternise, to indulge in any kind of drunken revelry, so as yet there had been few complaints or trouble. But he couldn't keep so many people in suspense for ever. They all felt the weight of inertia, of enforced passivity. So he'd applied repeatedly to the French for aid, and Anne de Beaujeu had replied charmingly, promising nothing. But in April an embassy had arrived from France promising to help Brittany against the English attacks, and as a consequence six ships were being prepared for Henry's fleet.

Then Henry heard that Elizabeth Woodville had surrendered her daughters to King Richard and was preparing to leave Sanctuary herself.

'What is she doing?' he demanded of the marquis, who looked thoughtful.

'I imagine she's doing what she's been told to do,' he said. 'The king has pledged to arrange their marriages.'

'Elizabeth is betrothed to me.'

Now the marquis looked hostile. 'They could hardly stay there for ever. We should have gone back for them. As I told you.'

It was pointless to go over the same ground again. Henry couldn't risk another failure; another voyage in winter.

He'd heard nothing from or about his mother. Before Richard's Parliament he'd expected at any moment to hear news of her execution. Then, finally, he'd heard that she'd been spared attainder but would remain in captivity. All her goods, her houses and her lands – all Henry's inheritance – had been given to his stepfather, Lord Stanley. He'd saved her life, and taken her fortune.

The people who came to him from his mother's household told him she was 'kept very straitly'. She couldn't write or talk to anyone. For the first time he could remember, she was not directing his affairs. He felt the loss of that keenly; she'd always been there, guiding and supporting him, urging him to return. Losing her was like a ship losing its rudder.

He couldn't say this, of course; he had to be seen to be acting alone. Yet there was so little he could do. He sent many letters into England, Wales and France, and waited for replies.

Then the news came that King Richard's heir had died. Other than Richard himself dropping dead, it was the best news they could possibly have received. The passing of the little prince was marked by a celebratory feast.

'Bless him, wherever he is!' the marquis cried. 'He could have done us no greater service than this!'

It was not right, of course, to celebrate the death of a child, but Henry didn't stop them. They'd had so little to celebrate, and now the French might finally help.

But Richard was trying to conclude a truce between England, France and Brittany. On 8 June, all hostilities ceased though Anne de Beaujeu still wrote sympathetically to Henry.

Sympathy wouldn't get him back to England. The strain of waiting pulled equally on his nerves, his heart, his hopes. Sometimes he thought he would die still waiting.

That summer a man was sent to Brittany, bearing a message for Henry. He didn't find out what that message was because the man had landed in Normandy by mistake and was captured by the French. Who'd treated him gently once they realised he was not one of Richard's agents. He'd told them King Richard was hoping to revive the old claim of England to the throne of France and was even now planning to invade.

Henry considered this unlikely, since Richard's resources had been depleted by the Rebellion and by handing out rewards to his supporters. However, this news impeded the truce. In England the two squires who'd sent the messenger were arrested. One of them, Collingbourne, had penned a scurrilous rhyme about King Richard, which had been pinned to the door of St Paul's Cathedral.

The cat, the rat and Lovell a dog/ Ruleth all England under a hog.

It was not hard to work out that the cat was Catesby, and the rat Ratcliffe, and the hog Richard himself. So for this witticism Collingbourne was sentenced to death.

Then Catesby himself had arrived in Brittany. He'd gone straight to Vannes, where Henry's household was, and offered at the shrine of St Vincent Ferreri in the cathedral.

You can see me, he seemed to be saying, *and I can see you.*

While Catesby was negotiating with Pierre Landais, Christopher Urswick travelled four hundred miles from Antwerp, to say Bishop Morton had discovered the secret terms of the truce. Landais had agreed to imprison Henry's entire party and return them to England.

Christopher Urswick had obtained a safe conduct for Henry to go to France. His followers couldn't accompany him. Henry could hardly leave the country in secret, taking his whole court with him. So the plan had been devised.

It had its flaws, since Landais would undoubtedly arrest his followers as soon as it was discovered that Henry had left. Also, Henry was wandering through the Breton countryside with this unknown squire.

They'd reached a small stream, and Perrin led the horses to drink, filled a small flagon himself, then handed it to Henry.

'Your wine, sire,' he said, bowing.

There was that mocking tone again. But Henry drank and wiped his mouth. 'Now what?' he asked.

'Now we walk.'

'And then?'

'Then we ride.'

Henry thought of asking whether Perrin was being paid by Landais. Over his shoulder, Perrin said, 'I hope you're a good rider – we'll have to go fast.'

'I can ride,' Henry said, though in fact he was not used to sustained hard riding.

'It will take us ten, maybe twelve, hours to reach the border.'

Henry said, suspiciously, he didn't think the border was so far away.

'Not by the usual route,' Perrin said. 'But then, we're not going by the usual route. Only I know the route.'

'I hope you know it well.'

'I know all routes well,' said Perrin. He continued to lead his horse over ground so rough that it could hardly be called a path, and Henry was forced to follow.

As the trees thinned, walking became easier. Soon, without a word to Henry, Perrin got on his horse and set off at a fast trot. Hurriedly, Henry climbed on to his own horse, hoping the ground was better than it looked, that his horse wouldn't stumble.

He was jolting in the saddle. The jolting rattled his teeth, and when he leaned over the horse's neck he banged his nose so that his eyes blurred with tears. The long mane streamed into his face as Perrin increased his pace to a canter, then a gallop.

After about a mile, Perrin slowed his horse. Then, after another mile, they galloped again, and so they went on – galloping, cantering, galloping – until Henry thought they must stop or he would fall off. His back hurt, and his thighs; even his arms felt the strain from holding the reins more tightly than he should. He would not call out to Perrin, would give no indication that he couldn't keep up, even though the distance between them was increasing. He suspected Perrin was testing him, or trying to prove he was the better man.

Then, just as he thought he couldn't stand any more, they came to another patch of woodland with a stream and Perrin slowed down to let Henry catch up.

'Out of practice, eh?' he said, and before Henry could reply he dismounted by the stream.

Henry slid from his horse, feeling a sharp pain in his groin. He wondered if he'd pulled a muscle there, because it hurt to move.

He could only lie on his back and pant. Even his ribs were hurting. He could feel the sweat cooling on him in the night air.

He could smell the grass and hear faint rustling noises through it. He could hear the trees stirring in the darkness. Further away, he could detect the mossy scent of the stream; the horses' necks would be bent over it, their sensitive nostrils flaring and quivering.

'Next time we'll gallop further,' Perrin's voice said, unexpectedly close.

Henry's hand shot out, gripping his ankle and jerking so that Perrin fell backwards with a surprised yell. Then Henry was on top of him, thrusting two fingers into his throat, under his chin.

'Who's paying you?' he said. He jabbed his fingers upwards.

In the moonlight Perrin's eyes were wild and white. He writhed and swore in Breton. 'What the fuck?' he said.

'Don't think you'll take me to Landais,' Henry said. 'I'll kill you first.'

'Him!' Perrin spat. 'The Great Maggot – I do nothing for him!'

Henry released his grip a little. 'Who are you working for?' he said.

'Get the fuck off,' said Perrin, but Henry maintained his hold. It was a hold he'd learned from wrestling with the brothers at the Tour d'Elven.

'If I push my fingers now,' he said, 'I can snap your windpipe, thus.' He pushed a little. Perrin choked.

'Go on, kill me,' he said. 'Then what will you do? How will you find your friends? They are waiting for you, no?'

'How do I know you'll take me to them?' Henry said.

'Where else would I take you?' said Perrin. 'I'm not working for anyone apart from myself. And all I want is to be rid of you.'

'Rid of me?'

'Yes – you! All of you foreign leeches holding court in our country! Eating and drinking – paying no taxes – doing no work – who do you think you are?'

'I think I am king,' said Henry.

'And I'm the Virgin Mary. King of England – here in Brittany! You need to go and bleed your own country dry! For me – I cannot see you go quickly enough – that's why I'm taking you to France. Of course,' he said, 'you're welcome to find your own way there.'

Cautiously Henry released him and he scrambled backwards, rubbing his neck.

'Your duke has supported us, all this time –'

'Yes – at our cost!'

'– and I'm grateful. He would not want you to betray us now.'

'Everyone knows the duke doesn't rule this country any more. The Great Worm rules, and makes his own deals. I say Brittany should be for the Bretons. We don't need your foreign courts.'

Henry shook his head. 'You think I want to be here?' he said. 'Do you think I've not longed, every day, to go home? I've spent thirteen years in exile. Why do you think I risked everything to invade my own country?'

'You didn't even land. How many more times will you come crawling back to us – for us to support you like a king?'

Henry saw the hatred in his face. 'Not many more,' he said quietly, 'if Landais rules.'

Perrin's expression changed. 'I'm not taking you to Landais,' he said. 'I'm taking you to your friends – and to France.'

Henry sensed he was telling the truth, that he could trust his hatred of Landais. 'Then we should go,' he said, although all his body was hurting. After a moment Perrin nodded.

'OK,' he said.

Henry climbed on to his horse with some difficulty as his guide set off at a slower pace this time. He felt once more the thrust and pull and rhythm of his horse which set the world in motion.

Perversely, Perrin seemed more conciliatory now. He pulled his horse up beside Henry's.

'So –' he said. 'Your father was king?'

Henry shook his head. 'My uncle,' he said.

'But he had no sons?'

'He had one son – who was killed.'

'What was your father?'

'He was half-brother to the king.'

'Not this king?'

'No.'

'But if the king had no other sons, then your father should have been king?'

Henry didn't want to explain the years of dynastic strife. 'My father died before I was born,' he said.

'Ah – mine too,' said Perrin. 'And my mother is also dead.'

'My mother is alive,' said Henry, thinking, with a tinge of melancholy, that he would like to see his mother again.

'So – you will fight a great battle,' Perrin said, 'and kill this king. And hope no one comes to kill you.'

He had a way of putting things, this squire.

'When I'm king,' said Henry, 'I'll try to rule well. So no one will want to kill me.'

'That's what this king thinks – no?' said Perrin. Then he said, 'I would not like to be king,' and Henry replied that, in all probability, he wouldn't have to be.

'No,' said Perrin. 'But my claim is nearly as good as yours.'

He smiled, to show he was joking, and the edge seemed to have gone out of his smile. Henry didn't smile back, but he relaxed. They rode until the starlight faded and a mist rose from the earth and gathered above a lake, where the horses drank again. Then they rode once more, and Perrin said they would soon be at the border.

But then he got off his horse and pressed his ear to the earth. 'Men are coming,' he said.

'What men?' Henry asked, and Perrin looked at him with scorn.

'I do not know *what men*,' he said, 'only that there are several of them. We should ride.'

He got back on his horse and set off, Henry following after. The jolting movement began again; there was no time to worry about holes in the ground or obstacles underfoot. Everything beneath him was moving rapidly, unevenly. His back felt bruised.

Then all at once the jolting smoothed into a rippling motion. The grass flowed back like the horse's mane, the moon sailed with them. Henry's horse was running with all his might, his hooves pounding to the beat of Henry's heart. Finally, at the crest of a hill, they could see the roofs of a town below. Perrin reined in his horse.

'That's the border,' he said. 'Your friends will take you to Angers.'

Henry looked at him. 'The French will not let a Breton cross the border,' Perrin said. 'You'll have to go on without me. But you're lucky – they won't let Landais' soldiers in either!'

He tugged the reins of Henry's horse. 'Ride hard, my friend!' he said, and Henry was off, without even thanking him, riding for all he was worth towards France.

This Peter the treasurer ... once he understood that Henry was departed, sent out horsemen every way to bring the earl back to him. The horsemen made such haste that there was never anything more nigh than overtaking the earl [who] arrived at the French border scarcely more than an hour before their arrival ... [where they were turned back by the French]. But the Englishmen who remained at Vannes when they knew Henry was fled ... were in despair of their safety. However ... the Duke of Brittany, taking it in evil part that Henry was forced to fly and being for that cause very angry with Peter ... called unto Edward Poynings and Edward Woodville giving them money and commanded them to conduct all the Englishmen to the earl, who having received all his retinue [in France] was wondrously glad.

Polydore Vergil

[William Collingbourne] was put to a most cruel death on Tower Hill where, for him was made a new pair of gallows upon which, after he had hung a short season he was cut down alive and his bowels ripped out of his belly and cast into the fire, and he continued to live until the butcher put his hand into the bulk of his body, and said in the same instant, 'O Lord Jesu, yet more trouble,' and so died to the great compassion of many people.

Fabyan's Chronicle

38

The Princess and the King

In December the Lady Elizabeth with her four younger sisters . . .
attended the queen at court at the Christmas festivals . . . at Westminster Hall.

Crowland Chronicle

She had stayed in the great stronghold of Sheriff Hutton
all summer with her sisters, the young Earl of Warwick
and the king's own bastard children, in order to protect
her from the Tudor and from the men of the court,
until a husband was found for her.

But, preoccupied by the death of his son, by negotiations with
the French and the Scots, by increasing defences until all England
resembled a fortress, the king did nothing until three events
prompted him.

The first was Henry Tudor's defection to France. The exiled
earl was now known to be openly in league with the French.
From Calais Lord Dinham had written that the border wasn't
safe. And the truce was delayed again.

The second was the escape of the Earl of Oxford from
Hammes. In October Richard had made arrangements for that
earl to be transferred to the Tower so he couldn't be rescued by
the French. William Bolton was sent to escort him to England,
but Bolton's men were attacked by a force led by James Blount,
Constable of Hammes, and John Fortescue, who had become
reconciled to the earl during the years of his captivity. They
overcame Bolton's men and took the Earl of Oxford to join
Henry Tudor near Paris.

Henry, meeting the earl was overcome by great happiness that this man of such nobility and skill in warfare had by God's will been freed and come to him at such an opportune time.

Polydore Vergil

Then there had been the execution of Collingbourne, at which the crowds had wept openly, so it seemed the people were not for him but for his rebels and traitors.

At this point he wrote to Elizabeth Woodville to say that her daughters would spend the Christmas season at court, where *certain arrangements* could be made.

Yet still he didn't know who to choose.

He'd recently named the Earl of Lincoln, who was the son of his sister and John de la Pole, as his heir, rather than Clarence's son, the Earl of Warwick. This was because Clarence's son was witless, people said. The king, having kept him company on one long journey, had changed his mind about the succession. But the Earl of Lincoln and his brothers were already married. In any case, he wouldn't want his nieces so close to the throne.

Several other courtiers were either married or unsuitable, so a darker thought had flickered like a shadow across the king's mind.

The queen showed no signs of recovery.

Neither the society she loved nor all the pomp and festivity of royalty could heal the wound in the queen's breast for the loss of her son.

Crowland Chronicle

Her illness had progressed, if anything, and they spent little time together. It didn't seem likely he would produce another son with his wife. If his wife were to die, he would be the most eligible man at court.

He dismissed this thought, of course, because of the legal and moral complications. It would cause a great scandal. Even if he could bribe the pope heavily enough, the people would never accept it.

Although it wasn't expressly forbidden in Leviticus. The Roman Emperor Claudius had married his niece Agrippina. And had Parliament not declared that Edward was not his father's son? In which case he was not full uncle to his niece.

It would be the ultimate triumph over his adversary. There was already a powerful faction in the country which supported Elizabeth as heiress to the throne. And if the former princess proved to be as fertile as her mother, then the people would soon be won over. If they were to have children, it would solve so many of his problems.

Also, she was beautiful. He remembered the moment she'd risen from her curtsy, smiling at him. He was no less susceptible to beauty than his brother, although more restrained.

So apartments were prepared for the five daughters of Elizabeth Woodville, and a generous allowance allocated for their wardrobes.

> They were received with all honourable courtesy by Queen Anne, especially the Lady Elizabeth, who was ranked familiarly in the queen's favour . . . as a sister.
>
> *Crowland Chronicle*

Even in the few short months since they'd last seen her, she'd grown much thinner. Her cheeks were sunken and yellow beneath the paste applied to them, which couldn't disguise the dry patches, or the sores around her lips. Her eyes seemed larger, her hair more sparse and, from time to time, she was racked by bouts of coughing that seemed as though they would break her ribs apart.

No wonder the king had turned from his corpse-like bride!

Yet she seemed touchingly pleased to see them. She embraced them all, subjecting each of them to her clammy touch and the unmistakeable odour of ill-health. 'Now we will be gay again,' she said. There was a feverish glow in her eyes.

When the king saw his niece the idea that had started as a calculation in his mind caught fire. It seemed to him that some new aspect of her loveliness was revealed to him with each change in the angle and quality of light. When she danced, all his breath seemed to stop in his throat.

He began to seek her out.

She was reserved with him initially, but he took that reserve for modesty. She was not like her mother! Or like the other court ladies, vying for his attention, because already it was rumoured he would have his marriage annulled in order to beget more sons.

Whenever he met his niece he would greet her in the customary way, by lifting her chin and kissing her on the mouth. She didn't resist him, she was as compliant as a subject must be towards her sovereign, but he could feel her distancing herself from him. Which only made him long to kiss her more. Soon all his courtiers were commenting on the frequency of these chance encounters, and the regularity with which the king insisted that his niece should sit with him, his hand brushing her thigh.

The young Elizabeth could not be insensible to these advances. Even though she'd spent so much time in Sanctuary, and before that had been guarded jealously by her father (who was as strict about his daughters' virtue as he was liberal with any other woman's), still she'd been brought up at court, with its intrigues and infidelities, its secret assignments. She'd breathed its heady perfume of desire and power. She was not unmoved by the attention of the most powerful man in the country, but she was troubled by it, because of their close relationship and because of what everyone said had happened to her brothers.

So she wrote secretly to her mother, hinting at the situation she dared not express. Elizabeth Woodville spent a long time staring at this letter, then at the wall, before replying, *Give nothing until you have something in exchange.*

But by the time this message reached her daughter, the king had already contrived to meet his niece alone.

The lady who attended her had mysteriously disappeared. All her sisters were otherwise engaged. She wasn't accustomed to walking around the palace unaccompanied, and so, mystified, she hurried along the dark corridor to her room.

Her uncle stepped out from the shadows. Before she could curtsy, he reached out, lifting her chin, and pressed his lips to hers.

It was not a kiss from a king to his subject or from an uncle to his niece. Elizabeth felt her heart begin to hammer as though she was afraid, and maybe she was afraid, yet also she felt a sense of her own power over this man who was king, and knew that she must not now, of all moments, get it wrong.

'Your grace, I –'

'Don't be so formal.'

'Shall I call you uncle?'

A shadow crossed his face and she knew she must retrieve the situation.

'I – was just going to my chamber.'

'To your bed?' His fingers moved from her chin to a tress of hair that had escaped its net. 'What will you dream of, Elizabeth? What is it that you dream?'

I dream of my brothers, she could have said, because she did dream of them regularly. They stood facing her, holding hands. Or sometimes they faced away from her, which made her cry.

Perhaps he wanted her to say she dreamed of him, but she said nothing as his fingers moved from her hair to her collarbones, tracing them. She allowed her eyelids to droop. She was thinking furiously, *what would my mother do?* She'd put off her father for three whole years.

'Do you dream, my lord?' she said, looking at him from beneath her eyelids. He flinched slightly, then recovered himself.

'I do now,' he said. 'I dream of a young, beautiful girl.' His fingers moved to the neckline of her gown, without quite touching her breast. She stood very still.

'How is her majesty the queen?' she said. The fingers stopped.

'You reproach me,' he said, and she said no, quickly, but he withdrew his hand.

'You are right to reproach me,' he said. 'My dear wife is very ill. Perhaps she will not recover. Certainly she will bear me no more children. And a king must look to the succession. And a man must look to his bed.'

She could feel his gaze on her; there was no point pretending she didn't understand him.

'Sire, I –'

'You don't think of me in that way, perhaps. I'm not to your taste.'

She hastened to protest, but he interrupted her. 'I'm so much older than you. I'm not handsome. No' – he stopped her again – 'don't flatter me. Don't speak to me in the language of the court. Not to me. We are more to one another, you and I – we can speak from the heart.'

She was silent.

'We're not so different, either,' he continued. 'We've both lost people who were dear to us. Dearer than anything in the world. We are both essentially alone.'

She held her breath. Did she dare ask him about her brothers?

'One grieving heart responds to another,' he said. 'One spirit cries out for fellowship. Whatever the world might say.'

He was looking at her with such a wounded expression that despite everything she felt a pang of compunction. 'Your son,' she murmured. His face contracted briefly.

'Yes,' he said. 'And to all intents and purposes, my wife. And – I too have lost my brothers – as you have lost yours.'

Her heart was pounding hard enough for her to feel the pulse of it in her ears. 'I think of them all the time,' she said, her voice catching.

'As I do,' he replied, but his face was in shade.

'If only I knew –'

'What happened to them?' He moved to one side of her. 'What do you think happened to them?'

'I don't know.'

'But what do you think?'

He was playing games with her, surely. She turned to face him, but his expression was sombre, even melancholy. 'I know what's said about me,' he said. 'I've heard the rumours. You've heard them too, I think. There will always be rumours, like the poisonous air in a well. They don't matter to me. What matters to me is what you think.'

She stared at him speechlessly.

'Do you think I'm capable of such a terrible crime?'

'I could never accuse your grace –'

It was the expected response, but in that moment, gazing into that sensitive face, an alteration occurred in the former princess. She believed him: he could never have murdered his nephews, her brothers.

He saw the shift in her, the dawning of faith. He took her shoulders as if to draw her to him.

'But –' she whispered.

'Yes?'

'It's hard to know –'

'It is hard,' he agreed, drawing her closer.

'If I only knew –'

He was stroking her shoulders so that the gown slipped from them a little. 'But you can believe,' he said. 'If I asked you to, would you believe in me?'

'Yes,' she said, and he kissed her, then buried his face in her neck.

'Would you love me,' he said, into her hair, 'as I love you? I love you as I have never loved anyone before, Elizabeth. Elizabeth – tell me you will give your love to me.'

She felt paralysed by warring impulses. 'Whatever your grace commands,' she said, stumbling a little over the words.

He released her at once. 'Commands?' he said. 'Command you? No.' In a swift movement he had replaced her gown on her shoulders.

'Sire –'

'No.'

'I don't know –'

'Then we'll wait,' he said, 'until you do know. You will come to me of your own accord, or not at all.'

He wasn't angry any more; his voice was tender. His finger moved around her lips. Then suddenly he was gone. She was alone in the dark corridor.

She hurried to her room, let herself in, pressed her back to the door. Her flesh felt tender and exposed where he'd touched it; her face was hot. She felt the full force of her conflicting emotions, and that deep sense of disorientation so easily confused with love.

Many things are not written in this book, of which I grieve to speak, although the fact ought not to be concealed that during this feast of the Nativity, far too much attention was given to dancing and gaiety and vain changes of apparel presented to Queen Anne and the Lady Elizabeth, the eldest daughter of the late king, being of similar colour and shape; a thing that caused the people to murmur and the nobles and prelates greatly to wonder thereat. It was said by many that the king was bent either on the anticipated death of the queen taking place, or else by means of a divorce, for which he supposed he had quite sufficient grounds, on contracting a marriage with Elizabeth whatever the cost, for it appeared that no other way could his kingly power be established, or the hopes of his rival be put to an end.

Crowland Chronicle

39

The Queen and the King

[The king] complained [of his wife's barren condition] to Thomas Rotherham, Archbishop of York, recently released from custody, and said the same to his friends. Then he arranged for an anonymous rumour to circulate about the death of his wife the queen . . . when the queen heard that the horrible rumour of her death was widespread among the people she thought she was ruined and sadly went to her husband . . .

Polydore Vergil

She walked past the guards, who did not know what to do about this trembling, agitated woman. She didn't falter when told that the king her husband was very busy with important business; she mustn't go in.

It seemed she would be too frail to push open the heavy doors, but when she leaned on them they gave. And the king, who was talking to a few of his closest councillors, glanced up briefly, then looked again.

She advanced towards him like a wraith. Sparse hair unkempt, eyes glittering, she stared at the small assembly of important men.

'Are you conspiring?' she said. 'Are you conspiring to kill me?'

The king began to rise. 'My lady,' he said, 'you're not well.'

'No, I'm not well,' she said. 'Thanks to you.'

'You shouldn't be out of bed,' he said, stepping towards her. She moved away from him.

'Why?' she said. 'What don't you want me to hear?'

'Where are your ladies? Where's your doctor? Why have they abandoned you like this?'

'I've been abandoned by no one but you,' she said. 'Do you think I don't hear what people are saying?'

He had almost reached her, but she held up her hands to ward him off.

'You shouldn't listen –' he began; but she spoke over him: 'You think because I'm closeted away in my rooms I can hear nothing – see nothing?'

Her voice rose, and so the king raised his. 'You're distressing yourself for no reason. Come – let me take you to your room.'

'You think I haven't heard you will put me away – or worse? That your wife is barren and will not serve? That you're only waiting for me to die?'

The lords around the table looked studiously away from the king and queen; they did not glance at one another.

'Enough, madame,' the king said. His face was cold. 'Do you not see I'm busy here? You must go back to your room. Let me take you.'

She backed away from him again as he reached out to her. 'Yes – you would like that,' she said. 'To take me to my room, where I'm out of sight. But not to my bed. How long since you have taken me there?'

The king glared at his councillors, who did not look back.

'You're not yourself, my lady,' he said in a low voice with an edge like steel. 'Or you would not embarrass yourself in this way.'

'I'm not embarrassed – you're embarrassed,' said the queen. 'Because I'm speaking the truth. Who does keep you company in bed?'

The king spoke with a cold fury. 'These are the phantoms of a disordered mind.'

'There's nothing wrong with my mind,' she said, 'or with my heart – except that you're breaking it. What have I done to you that you should treat me so?'

'Anne – dearest,' said the king, though the fury was still in his eyes. He stepped forward and the queen stepped back, bumping into William Catesby's chair. The knock was not hard, but it caused her evident pain. She stumbled a little, and William Catesby stood up.

'My lady, you've hurt yourself,' he said. At the same time the king moved to take hold of her, but she shied away from them both.

'Stay away from me!' she cried. 'Would you dispose of me here and now – in this chamber?'

But the king had already caught her, drawing her swiftly into his arms.

'Come, my lady,' he murmured into her hair. 'This is not seemly – you shouldn't distress yourself. Let me take you back now, to your room – come with me, hmm?'

He pressed her close so that she seemed to fold into him and, half carrying her, he led her across the room.

> Sweetly kissing and consoling her, telling her she should be of good cheer.
>
> *Polydore Vergil*

Her feet dragged across the floor. At the door he spoke in low, peremptory tones to the guards, but at that moment one of the queen's ladies, Sofia, came running along the corridor. Clearly, from her expression, she thought she was in trouble, but the king spoke to her calmly enough, telling her to take the queen back to her room and to make sure she slept well. She was to give her extra medicine if necessary.

And he watched Sofia with an impenetrable expression as she led the queen away, before returning to the room where his councillors were; where he had so many pressing things to discuss.

News had been brought to him from across the sea that . . . his adversaries would, without question, invade the kingdom during the following summer . . . A few days later the queen began to be seriously ill and her sickness was then believed to have got worse because the king was completely spurning his consort's bed . . . what is there left to tell? Towards the middle of March, 1485, on a day when a major eclipse of the sun took place, Queen Anne died.

Crowland Chronicle

Those men who objected most strongly to his marriage [to his niece] and whose opinion the king rarely dared oppose were Sir Richard Ratcliffe and William Catesby. These men told the king to his face that if he did not deny any such purpose before the mayor and the aldermen of the city of London the northerners in whom he placed the greatest trust would all rise against him, charging him with the death of his queen . . . in order to satisfy his incestuous desire for his kinswoman. Furthermore they brought forward more than twelve doctors of theology to state that the pope had no power of dispensation over such a close degree of consanguinity. It was thought by many that these men and others like them put obstacles in the way through fear that if Elizabeth attained the rank and dignity of queen it might be in her power to avenge the death of her uncle Anthony and her brother Richard upon those who had been the principal offenders in the affair . . .

Crowland Chronicle

40

Elizabeth Pleads Her Case

She sought him out. When he put her off, saying he was busy, she waited outside his chambers. Though the guards denied her access, she wouldn't be sent away but waited meekly with her hands clasped, her head hanging down.

As soon as the king came out she hurried forward to speak to him, breaking all the rules of court. 'Your grace, I've hardly seen you.'

She couldn't help but notice the light in his eyes dying as he looked at her.

'I'm busy,' he said. 'As you can see.'

'My lord is working too hard. It's past midnight. I've been waiting for you for hours.'

William Catesby looked to the king, to see how he would respond to such familiarity, but he only said, 'You shouldn't wait. You should go to your room.'

'But then I wouldn't see you at *all*,' she said, and Catesby said, 'Your majesty – shall I have her removed?'

But the king indicated with a small gesture that this would not be necessary, then he said gently, 'I keep unsocial hours. You should go to sleep.'

'I don't sleep well,' she said. 'I have bad dreams. That you've forsaken me.'

The intimacy of this caused his councillors to fall back with a scandalised air, except for Catesby, who remained sternly at the king's side. The king took his niece by the arm and steered her away.

'What are you doing?' he said.

'I – wanted to see you,' she faltered. 'I haven't seen you for weeks –'

'For a good reason.'

'What reason?' she said. 'You said you loved me – we should never be apart. And now you won't even come to my room!'

'You know I can't.'

'You are king,' she said bitterly. 'You could come if you wanted.'

'You know that's not true.'

'You swore you loved me! You said I would be your queen!'

'A man may say much,' he said. 'A king may do little.'

'Yes, he can – if he is truly king!'

His grip on her arm tightened. 'Are you saying I'm not truly king?'

'No!' she said. 'I only want to be with you as before.'

'That's not possible. Not now, not ever.'

She dashed a tear from her cheek. 'Have you deceived me, then?' she said, giving him a look of piteous reproach.

It was hard not to feel tender when she looked at him with all the wounded ardour of young love. Not uncalculated, no, but it was not a mature calculation; she was still too transparent for that.

She was crying freely now. 'I gave you my heart, and you swore you'd given me yours. How could you have deceived me?'

He saw he would have to be cruel.

'Perhaps you should return to your mother with the news that her plans have come to nothing.'

She gasped as if he'd struck her, but he went on: 'You cannot stay here, importuning me like any woman of the streets. If you cannot act becomingly I will have to send you away.'

'I won't go!' she cried. 'If you send me away you'll kill me!'

'Do not distress yourself; you'll be perfectly catered for. I'll arrange a match for you in Portugal or Ireland – the Earl of Desmond, they say, is looking for a bride.'

She tugged her arm free. 'Oh, sir,' she said, 'you do me too much honour.'

And she walked rapidly away.

He watched her for a moment, feeling a pang of regret but glad at the same time that she had taken command of herself and not collapsed into helpless weeping.

Certainly he would not return her to her mother, where the two of them would conspire together to renew their bargain with the Tudor. He would have to come up with a different plan.

And so she was transferred to the London home of her guardian, Thomas Stanley.

In the first few days she suffered an agony of remorse and shame. It seemed to her that her heart must be broken, though it was difficult to distinguish it from her pride. She'd lost, at a single stroke, her first love, her matrimonial prospects and the Crown.

The king did not come to see her before she left. She wasn't allowed to attend the queen's funeral in case she made a scene. And Stanley wasn't at home. He'd remained at court, locked into his secret councils with the king.

It was like being in Sanctuary again, except that, in theory, she was free to come and go. But where could she go? She could hardly wander the streets alone. And here she didn't have the company of her mother.

Her mother would have to be told, if she didn't already know, that her daughter had been banished; had suffered the ultimate humiliation. Her mother, if anyone, would know what she should do next. So she wrote quite sparingly of her misfortune, only adding at the end that she was *utterly wretched*, but remained her dutiful and obedient daughter.

Then, while awaiting her mother's reply, she wrote to certain lords at court, including Lord Stanley and the Duke of Norfolk, begging them to intercede on her behalf with the king.

But the only message she received was from the Countess of Richmond, mother of the exiled earl to whom she was still, ostensibly, betrothed. It asked for her assurance that she would keep faith with her son.

The countess had obviously heard the rumours about her and

the king. She would have expected a stern rebuke, a withdrawal of association. Yet the countess had written to her in a friendly and sympathetic way, enquiring about her health, reminding her in so many words that she was still the most valuable asset to their cause.

No one else had written or responded to her letters.

In some corner of her heart she'd hoped the king might write to her, expressing his regret at his treatment of her, perhaps confessing his secret love. But there was nothing.

Yet still she hesitated to reply to the countess. It would be a great risk; tantamount to allying herself openly with the enemy of the king.

She decided to wait until she'd heard from her mother.

But the next day she heard that King Richard had made a public denial of her.

In the Great Hall, in the presence of many of his lords and other people, [the king] showed his grief and displeasure and said it never came into his thought or mind to marry in such manner, nor was he pleased or glad at the death of his queen, but as sorry and as heavy in heart as a man would be.

Mercer's Company Records, 1485

She wept on her bed at this news. But perhaps there was more of her mother in her than she'd realised, because her tears were soon replaced by a calm, cold feeling that was almost a stupor. There was no point weeping when there was no one to witness it, and every point in working out what must be done.

Let him punish me, she thought suddenly, savagely. Let him martyr me if necessary, and see what the people thought of that! Whatever happened, she was not about to be foisted off on some foreign earl. At least if she stood by her contract to Henry Tudor, there was a chance she would still be queen.

So she wrote to the countess, saying she'd never wavered in

her loyalty, whatever the countess might have heard. She was most willing to be married to her son, there was nothing that her heart longed for more, and she would be grateful if that message could be conveyed to the Earl of Richmond.

She received an immediate response. The countess was glad to know her feelings and would be happy to pass on such a message. But perhaps Elizabeth could write to her son herself, if her guardian agreed? It would be better, after all, if Lord Stanley knew she was writing.

Elizabeth was nonplussed by this message. It seemed to be submitting her to a test. *If you are serious*, it seemed to say, *you will state yourself openly*. But surely the countess knew, better than anyone, that Stanley was close to the king?

Was she suggesting Elizabeth should attempt to draw Lord Stanley into collusion with her, thus co-opting him indirectly into Henry's cause? She would have tried this herself, no doubt, and failed.

So Elizabeth was to be the instrument of the countess. She was to be the one who would take the risk, because it was a risk. Stanley could take the information directly to the king.

She was annoyed by this, of course: the assumption that she must be desperate and friendless enough to allow the countess to use her in this way. But she couldn't give up the idea of a betrothal that would spite the king, and she had to act soon, before he married her to someone else. And she did want to see her guardian, Stanley. He was ignoring her, which stung. She determined to write to him again, reminding him that she was her father's daughter, that the late king had entrusted Stanley with her welfare.

While she was waiting for a reply, she heard from her mother. But there were no words of sympathy; the letter expressed, in the coolest terms, her disappointment. *Bear with your failure as you can*, it said. And it went on to say that the king had offered many inducements to Elizabeth's brother the marquis to return home, and she was urging him to comply.

The princess was dismayed by this letter. Where was all the sympathy, the maternal concern? Her mother seemed to be saying that Elizabeth had failed her and she would look to her remaining son, her firstborn, for support.

She raged inwardly at the tone. How many times had she been her mother's confidant and comforter? She could almost feel her heart hardening in her chest. But it seemed prudent to wait to see Stanley before she made any response.

This time, unexpectedly, he replied. He would call in to see her briefly one evening at the end of the week.

When he arrived he went straight to his room without greeting her. He didn't dine with her; food was taken up to him. But she received a message saying she could present herself to him in an hour.

As she waited her mood sank. Stanley would not be on her side, he wouldn't act on her behalf. In all probability, he resented her being there. Even so, she dressed herself carefully, and went to him looking pale and meek.

But Stanley wasn't moved by young, pretty women. 'So,' he said, 'I hear you've been busy.'

'I – have written –'

'Many letters, yes. That was unwise of you. But then you've acted unwisely in many respects.'

She wouldn't be rebuked by him. 'I didn't know what else to do. I have no friend at court – no one to turn to – nowhere to go!'

'On the contrary,' he said, 'I hear you can go to Ireland. His majesty is already arranging it.'

'I will not go to Ireland,' she said sharply. 'I'm already betrothed, remember? To your stepson.'

'You seemed to forget that easily enough.'

'I did not forget,' she said. 'Most bitterly do I remember my lost hope. That's the message I would like to send him – if you let me.'

'Why would I do that?'

'You're his father. And my guardian.'

'I'm the King's Steward,' he said, as if he thought her a fool. 'What makes you think I would betray my lord?'

And he began collecting together the papers on his desk, as if the matter was settled.

But she wasn't ready to give up. 'Look how he treats me,' she said, drawing closer to him. 'I'm sent away from everyone, treated like a prisoner – when I'm the daughter of a king. I should be queen!'

'You should be careful who you say that to,' he observed.

'I say it to you – because my father trusted you to take care of me.'

He turned away from her so she couldn't see what he was thinking.

'He trusted you with my welfare,' she said, 'and this – *this* – was not what he meant, or imagined.'

'He did not imagine that you would go whoring after your uncle,' he said, and she flinched.

'As God is my witness, that isn't *true!*' she said.

He turned back to her. 'No?' he said. 'But you've allowed people to think it is true. I hardly know which is the more regrettable. Or disgraceful.'

It took her breath away that he should talk to her like this. 'Why won't you help me? All I want is to send a letter to my love.'

'What makes you think he would want you now?'

She lifted her chin. 'Because I am my father's daughter,' she said. 'Without me, he cannot be king.'

Stanley sighed and closed his eyes. 'He can't be king,' he said. 'He's not even an earl any more. He is a penniless exile. And I am Constable of this country – my job is to defend it against him. You're asking me to risk everything in order to act on your behalf?'

She brushed a tear away swiftly with the heel of her hand. 'If you had acted on my brother's behalf,' she said, 'we would be spared all this. Because he would be king.'

A lightning change flickered over his face and for a moment she feared she had gone too far. But he walked away from her, towards the window. He didn't say anything for several moments, and she didn't dare to speak. Then he said, in a peculiar, altered tone, 'In any case, what makes you think that I can get a message to the exiled earl?'

'Everyone knows it,' she said, 'except for the king.'

'Do you threaten me?' he said, turning back to her.

'Not at all. I merely want you to ensure any message I send will be safely delivered to the Earl of Richmond, and not to the king.'

Stanley gave her a long, appraising stare. 'You've been writing to my wife,' he said.

'It's her dearest wish that any division between her son and myself should be healed,' the princess said.

'I'm sure it is.'

'So may I write my letter?'

Stanley glared at her. Then, unexpectedly, he laughed quietly, shaking his head. He began to gather his papers again. 'Ay, do,' he said. 'And I will read it. That's all.'

'But –'

'That is *all*,' he said, turning on her a glare of such ferocity that she could only drop a swift curtsy as he left the room.

While Henry Tudor stayed [in France] the rumour came to his ears that King Richard ... had decided to marry Elizabeth the daughter of his brother, and to marry off Cecily, Edward's other daughter, to some unworthy no account. This ... cut off all hope of achieving their plan from his followers, and it pinched Henry to the very stomach ...

Polydore Vergil

41

Pinched

He was fitting an arrow to the bow when the messenger came. He took the shot anyway, and everyone applauded, even though he missed. It was a good shot, they said, caught by the wind. He walked away from them, ostensibly to look for the arrow. There was a peculiar feeling in his stomach and his mouth was dry.

So much had depended on being able to unite the houses of Lancaster and York. Now, when they heard that Elizabeth of York would marry her uncle, the Woodvilles and all those who'd been loyal to Edward IV would desert him.

But more than that, something turned in his stomach, that this woman, who was to have been his, had betrayed him for an incestuous passion.

It was worse than when he had discovered that Yvette had been passed on to him by the Rieux brothers, well used. He had dwelt on reports of the princess as *fair* and *lovely* and *good*.

His councillors were catching up with him, anxious to discuss the matter.

He must write again, they said, to all his supporters in England, urging them not to support this marriage. He should write to the French king before anyone else told him the news. Then he should summon all his followers to convince them this was not necessarily a setback.

Henry nodded, half listening. His followers were not fools, and neither were the French.

The news sent ripples of delight through the French court; speculation as to whether any children from such a union would be born with two heads. Outwardly courtiers were sympathetic to him, knowing he'd been betrayed, but the sympathy came always with a little twist of the knife: *You are better off without that one, eh? If you married her now you would be sharing your bed with your own uncle* . . .

And so on. Henry took this affably, as he must: the permanent petitioner, the supplicant, smiling, cap in hand.

His councillors said he should sign his letters as king from now on. Now that the title of earl had been taken from him, the only title left to him was king.

He felt a nervous superstition about doing this. No previous claimant to the throne had used the title before they were crowned; there was something almost blasphemous about it. But his followers needed to know they were not following a dispossessed earl.

He wrote to several noble families, but few responded. It seemed nothing would go well for him since his promised bride had betrayed him, since he'd prematurely claimed the status of king.

But perversely, the French seemed prepared to accept his claim. He was of the House of Valois, of course, but also he suspected that they enjoyed the sense of having an English king in thrall.

Richard had extended his truce with Brittany by seven years. The duke had promised to offer no further support to 'Richard's rebels', so the English king was preparing to send archers to them at last. The French government saw this as a direct threat. It was a topic of concern for the forthcoming Parliament, which was to meet in Rouen that May. The French king had promised he would raise the issue of aid for Henry in the form of money, ships and men.

Henry was used to promises. Yet that April, he and all his entourage were invited to travel with the French court to Normandy for the opening of Parliament. Henry's councillors were jubilant – this surely was the sign they'd been waiting for, that the French would keep their word. Henry, however, could not shake the feeling of impending doom; as though he'd eaten something his stomach refused to digest.

Nonetheless, they prepared for the journey. Horses were groomed and caparisoned, armour polished and the flag of *Henricus Rex* taken out.

And at this crucial moment, the Marquis of Dorset disappeared.

It was a full day before anyone realised. It wasn't unusual for the marquis to go off on his own, or with a small party of men. He was bored with Montargis, he said. He got restless when the weather changed, and needed to go hunting or drinking.

And Henry was distracted, on that same day, by a messenger from Lord Stanley's household who brought a letter from the Lady Elizabeth containing a gold ring.

The messenger told Henry that Richard had formally repudiated Elizabeth in the Great Hall of St John's in Clerkenwell. He'd denied he'd ever had any plans to marry his niece.

And so she's written to me, Henry thought.

'This is great news, sire,' John Fortescue said, and the Earl of Oxford agreed. Only Jasper was silent, glancing at Henry's face.

'King Richard has sent the lady to Lord Stanley's house,' Riseley said. 'He's had no further communication with her. It's said he will marry Joanna of Portugal, and the lady herself he will marry to the Duke of Beja or the Earl of Desmond.'

Of course, all his councillors said he must write back without delay. And announce that the marriage would go ahead as planned. The French would have to be told the rumours about the princess were false; Henry was once again the unifier of Lancaster and York. That should stop them making their jokes about two-headed babies.

Edward and Richard Woodville and the Marquis of Dorset should be told at once.

All this time Henry had stood in silence, without reading the letter or putting the ring on his finger. Now he said, 'Where is the marquis?'

No one had seen him. But they weren't unduly concerned because of his habit of disappearing. Henry sent a messenger to his rooms, but they were empty. His uncles, when summoned, did not know where he was, but they were sure he would be back in time for the evening meal.

Henry scanned their faces for signs of duplicity and found none. They were delighted, as Henry must be also, by the news about their niece. And that it had arrived before the French parliament convened.

Henry nodded, hardly listening. He sent two of his men to question the manservants of the marquis, reasoning that it wasn't possible, in such a closely guarded environment, to leave without being seen. They returned with the intelligence that three of his retainers were also missing. And a young groom had said the marquis had taken his horse to be re-shod in a nearby village. They'd gone to the village accordingly, and the people there said the marquis had taken the road to Flanders.

Henry was not surprised. He'd never trusted the marquis. But since he knew everything about them, all their plans, he was forced to act.

Although it was late, he sent his herald to alert the French king of this defection and to plead for permission to pursue the marquis through French territory.

When permission came, he despatched John Cheyney and Matthew Baker to look for the errant marquis, who might already be in Flanders or on a ship to England.

In fact they found him in an inn barely seventy miles away, distracted by a game of dice.

'If you come with us now,' John Cheyney said, 'I will pay your debts. If not, I will tell that nice fellow there' – he nodded towards a large and grotesquely scarred gentleman – 'you are unable to pay them.'

The marquis protested, but they stood firm and at last he was persuaded to leave.

By the time they reached Henry, he was sober enough and somewhat surly. Henry greeted him cordially, raising him up and kissing him on both cheeks. 'You should write to your mother,' he said. 'Tell her you won't be leaving after all.'

The marquis did write to his mother, apprising her of the new situation between the princess and Henry – which was how Henry learned that Elizabeth had been taken back to the fortress of Sheriff Hutton. So it seemed as though the long shadow of the king's suspicion had fallen on Stanley at last. Henry didn't know whether there would be further retribution against his mother, but there was nothing he could do about that. He had to travel to Rouen with the French court.

On 14 April the two courts made their ceremonial entrance to Rouen. In the great cathedral there Henry made an offering, which was solemnly recorded by the canons as if he was king.

At the same time, Bishop Morton travelled from Flanders to Rome, where he asked for a papal endorsement of Henry Tudor's challenge to Richard III, who had jeopardised his relationship with the papal see, because no pope could be seen to endorse incest.

When Parliament began on 4 May, King Charles finally asked for aid for Henry Tudor, *our Valois cousin, who has more right to the English throne than any man living.* Parliament granted Henry forty thousand livres, and permission to recruit men in Normandy.

So once again he made preparations to invade England. Ships were rigged, his men pinned notices to the doors of churches and inns advertising payment for all those who would join this noble cause, and a small stream of volunteers began to arrive.

And yet the feeling of dread persisted.

He had not responded to the letter from Elizabeth. He'd sent a message to his mother via her priest, telling her the engagement was still on, but sent none to his betrothed.

Trust no one: that was the essence of what he'd learned in his twenty-eight years. The previous kings Henry VI and Edward IV had trusted the wrong people, which had destroyed them. He would not make the same mistake. Certainly he wouldn't trust his future wife; this unknown female who came from an enemy camp; who had already betrayed him.

So it was with a return of the bad feeling in his stomach and chest that he sat down finally to write, to thank her for her letter and assure her that nothing had altered between them; that he would cherish the ring she'd sent him with all his heart.

In England rumours grew daily that those in rebellion against the king were speeding up plans for their invasion of England. The king, however, being in doubt as to where they intended to land . . . took himself to the north shortly before Whitsuntide. He left his chamberlain Lord Lovell near Southampton to deploy his fleet [and] keep a faithful watch on all parts of that region . . . Shortly before [the invasion] Thomas Stanley, steward of the king's household, had received permission to cross into his native Lancashire to see his home and family from whom he had been absent a long time, but he was not permitted to stay there unless he sent his eldest son, George, Lord Strange, to the king at Nottingham in his place . . .

Crowland Chronicle

42

Meeting

All spring Margaret had felt afflicted by melancholy at the death of the queen. It surprised her; she should have been pleased. But there was the fear that the king would marry his niece, which would deal an irretrievable blow to her son. And the queen had been so young, less than one year older than Henry. She was stricken by the thought that Henry might die before she could see him again.

On the day of the funeral she'd prayed dutifully for the queen's soul, remembering her as a little girl, the youngest in a household of children, always struggling to keep up. Yet not defeated, or petulant, her little face bright with the expectation that she would eventually catch up with all the bigger, older children around her.

She didn't know why she found this memory so poignant; Queen Anne had been another obstacle between her son and the throne.

But such a short, sad life! She had endured the loss of everyone close to her: her son, her sister, her father and, if the rumours were true, her husband, in the process of becoming queen.

Who would remember her? Perhaps not even God would remember this tragic queen. Surely by now there would have been too many lives for Him to think about; too many faces passing through His mind. All those similar features: eyes, noses, mouths, passing from one generation to another. She herself sometimes had difficulty remembering names, and she was only in her forty-second year. So God, who existed in eternity, must be eternally thinking, *I'm sure I've seen that one somewhere before.*

It was a blasphemous thought, and one she shouldn't be thinking as she knelt in prayer. She should pray instead for the whole world, because surely He'd not forgotten that.

She'd reached, she believed, an accommodation with God. She was forced to believe in Him, or at least to accept the framework of belief, but she'd stopped expecting Him to act on her behalf. He in turn, she assumed, had stopped expecting her to surrender her will to His. She continued to take mass, of course, and fast regularly. She had impressed the household of Lathom by her piety.

So much so that the conditions of her confinement had been gradually relaxed. She was visited by her priest and permitted writing materials. As the spring drew on, she was even allowed into the gardens; accompanied, of course, at all times.

The staff had begun to consult her about expenditure, or illness. Gradually, she'd begun to run this household as her own.

She'd created a garden, clearing a strip of land and transplanting herbs from the kitchen garden. She'd sent for seeds from Woking. So now she had a border of Nigella, or love-in-a-mist, its blue, overlapping petals fading to white at the centre. In each flower head was a tangle of filaments, containing seeds which could be used as a spice like pepper or ground to a paste and mixed with honey, then applied to the skin to soothe afflictions such as her third husband, Henry, had suffered. Also, they could be made into a tea, which was said to be beneficial for the lungs.

Now, at the end of July, this border was like a ribbon of sky beside the green lawn.

In a spirit of scientific enquiry she'd collected the seeds, pressed the flowers, separated the ovary and pistil for further examination. In another life she could have been a surgeon, peeling back flesh from muscle, separating ligament from bone.

They would say of her, perhaps, that she'd liked gardening. She'd created several, and missed them all.

When she thought like this she felt as though she might weep, but one of the great virtues of gardening was that it could lead your mind away from its concerns. Here by the gate the climbing rose was already overgrown and would need to be cut back, carefully, because it was still in bloom.

Soon she was so absorbed that she was startled when a voice spoke behind her.

'I thought you'd be here, forcing nature into doing something else it doesn't want to do.'

Her skin leapt, and all the little pulses beneath it raced, but she gave no sign of this. She straightened slowly.

'Lord Stanley,' she said. 'I wasn't expecting you.'

'Really? You have issued your summons regularly enough.'

'And you have ignored them,' she said, smiling.

'I'm here now.'

'So I see. It's good of you to come.'

'It is good of me to come,' he agreed. 'I see you've been busy.'

'Don't you like it?'

'I liked it well enough before. But I suppose it's a rule of nature that one cannot leave a woman in any place and expect to find it unchanged when one returns.'

She didn't want the conversation to take an unpleasant turn almost before it had begun. She wiped her hands on her smock. 'You must be tired after your long journey,' she said. 'Shall we go in?'

Without waiting for him to reply, she led the way towards the house, entering by a side door near the scullery where she could slip off her over-shoes and smock. In the kitchen she gave instructions for some refreshments to be served in a room adjacent to her own, then led him upstairs.

By the table she paused, and didn't know how to go on.

'So,' she said faintly. 'How is life at court?'

Stanley pulled out a chair and sat down. 'How is the king, you mean? And what does he know about your son? Let me save you the preliminaries,' he said, as she started to speak. 'You've summoned me here because you think I'll give you information.'

'Not only that,' she began.

'No,' he said. 'You also want to know whether I'll support him.'

She closed her eyes briefly. 'I'm concerned only about his welfare.'

'Yes,' he said. 'Every conversation we've ever had in the course of our marriage has been about your son's welfare.'

'Do you blame me for that?'

'No, but I blame you for your many attempts to inveigle me into your schemes.'

She sat down, facing him. 'I've not deceived you, Thomas,' she said. 'I think you've always known that my son's interests have been my primary concern.'

'Yes,' he said. 'You've been admirably candid about that.'

She returned his gaze steadily.

'I have to admire your singleness of purpose,' he continued. 'Indeed, you are a model for other women. Lady Margaret – beacon of unflagging hope and enduring determination. Obdurate as any martyr. If they cut you open they would find your son's name printed on all your organs.'

'Perhaps you would have preferred your name?'

'Heaven forbid, I'm not suicidal yet.'

She made a move as if she would rise. 'I see you've made this long journey just to insult me.'

'Not at all. I've come to tell you to leave me out of your plans.'

'I'm sorry?' she said.

'Do you think the king doesn't know you're sending me messages? Do you know how much pleading I had to do in order to come here? In the end he would only let me go if I left my son behind as hostage.'

'George,' she said.

'Yes, George. What do you think that means?'

She thought for a moment before she answered. 'I think,' she said, 'you have come, anyway.'

He leaned back. She was a clever woman. When he was away from her he sometimes underestimated that.

'The king needs someone to muster his armies in the north,' he said.

'Is that what you're doing?'

'I told him I would rally the forces, yes.'

'But then you came here, to see me.'

'To tell you to stop,' he said. 'Stop trying to draw me into your schemes. Because once more, madame, you've put me and mine in danger.'

'That was not my intention.'

'No?' he said. 'Then why continue to write?'

She didn't answer, and he said, 'What kind of position do you think you're putting me in? You've put both me and my son at risk.'

'I'm sorry –'

'Yes,' he said, 'I'm sure you are. Sorry your husband is not the complete tool you would have made him. Not like your last one. You sent him off to his death cheerfully enough. Even though he'd done everything a man might reasonably do for you.'

Outrage bristled in her, but she wouldn't give him the argument he wanted.

'And then you selected me,' he said. 'For excellent reasons – proximity to the throne, influence, wealth and status. And the ability to summon large forces of my own.'

She lowered her eyes in that irritating way she had, as though in prayer.

'Is there anyone who is not expendable to you?' he said. 'Your husband? Your servants? The king?'

It seemed as if she would speak, but he carried on. 'The king's sons – the princes and heirs to the throne? Do you want to hear what happened to them? No – I see you do not.'

She'd started to rise, then she looked at him with an expression so chilling it would have frozen another man. 'Is that why you're here? To ask me to defend myself to you? I'm afraid you've had a wasted journey, my lord. Because I will not do that – not now, not ever.'

'No,' he said, 'I was not expecting that from you.' Then as she turned to leave he said, 'So you don't want to hear about your son?' and she paused, without turning round.

'You don't want to know if he's set off yet, and with how many, and what support he has, and what plans King Richard has made against him? Or,' he added, 'whether or not I will betray him to the king?'

She turned, finally, with an altered expression. 'Will you?'

'I've not decided yet. I can tell you,' he said, as she turned back towards the door, 'that he will set off tomorrow, or the next day, with fewer ships than he had hoped for, and fewer men. A few *beggarly Bretons*, as the king describes them. The French king has discharged all his undesirables on this errand – all his petty thieves and whore-mongers, his horse-cobblers and beggars, and even his lepers he sends on this escapade with your son. And if the weather is fine and the right breeze blowing, they may even land. And there, on the south coast, they will face the biggest armies that this realm has at its disposal, the most experienced generals, the greatest ordinance. And be slaughtered to a man.'

She was very pale. 'You paint a vivid picture,' she said. 'But if you would muster your men for my son instead of Richard – you could change that picture. Don't tell me you enjoy being kept under the king's watch at all times. Do you not want a better situation for yourself, Stanley?'

'Don't presume to tell me what I want – what I should do!' He rose and came towards her. 'I, madame, have spent my entire career avoiding the petty quarrels of kings and dukes – each of whom was keen to see Stanley's blood spilled on their behalf. You expect me to join in this battle on the losing side – give up my life and the life of my son for the woman who calls herself my wife and her renegade son whom I have not yet met? For this I should give up my place as the king's most trusted advisor?'

She was looking at him with disconcerting sharpness. 'It seems to me you've already given up that place,' she said. 'You can't return to Richard after this – do you think he doesn't know the game you've been playing? Why else would he keep your son? If Richard wins – as you seem convinced he will – you can't seriously think he will reinstate you. But if my son wins, Stanley – you'll be father to the king.'

'So you would have me trade my son for yours?'

She looked at him with an indescribable expression 'You have other sons.'

He made an incredulous sound that might almost have been a laugh, then shut his eyes and tilted his head back. 'Bravo, lady,' he said. 'That is the best yet.' Then he opened his eyes and directed on her the full hostility of his glare. 'I do have other sons,' he said. 'And you may be sure of one thing. If by some remote chance it seems as though your son will win, then I will support him with all my heart. Until then – I'm with the king.'

They stared at one another. There were other things she might have said, but it seemed as though all words ended here. She'd known well enough when she married what the deal would be. Her husband would act according to his nature, and she to hers. She held his gaze a moment longer, then said, 'Perhaps you will accompany me to the hall, where we can eat a proper meal.'

As she led the way she told herself she'd done what she could. Her men were all over the country, renewing the network of support from the earlier failed rebellion.

Perhaps she shouldn't have spoken to her husband. Stanley would never join the losing side, and he clearly believed her son would lose. Henry had so few men, and the south coast was heavily patrolled. Yet she would not despair. For one thing, she didn't think Stanley would inform the king while there was any chance at all her son might win. And for another, Henry would not be landing on the south coast, but in Wales; which, so far as she knew, was not defended at all.

43

Voyage

Then Henry, thinking that speed was of the essence so that his friends would no longer hang suspended between hope and fear, after he prayed to God for success and prosperity, sailed from the mouth of the Seine on 1st August 1485 with only 2000 soldiers and a few ships.

Polydore Vergil

As a child he used to wonder about the world that existed underwater; a world in which clouds and trees hung upside down, and instead of birds there were the sly, shifting shadows of fish. On hot days he'd wanted to shed his clothes like so many layers of skin and slip into that other world. Would fish swim through the trees there and cows plant their hooves in a liquid field?

That was what he used to think when he was a child, lying on his stomach and peering into some pond or stream. He remembered a woman who might have been his nurse pulling him back, afraid he would fall in.

That was a long time ago, at Raglan Castle.

Now he was returning to Wales, crossing a much bigger stretch of water. All around him the blue sea crumpled and bulged.

It had to be Wales, though the journey was longer and the overland route tortuous – who knew how many men they would lose along the way? But the south coast would be patrolled as before, and at least Wales would give them the advantage of surprise. He would need that advantage.

Before they sailed he'd assembled his troops. They'd stood before him, ramshackle, scurvy and maimed. Even his French commander, Philibert de Chandée, a natural enthusiast, had gazed thoughtfully at the ground, while the Earl of Oxford had observed that the French must be liberating themselves from such men. When Henry spoke to them they barely responded.

There had already been three revenge killings, a fight in a brothel leading to the deaths of two more men, and no fewer than fourteen attempted escapes. The evening before their departure the air sweated like an elderly harlot and many hundreds of them had run riot through the inns near the port. Chandée said hopefully that he was sure some of them would return. And Jasper had given a short despairing laugh and walked away.

Henry looked at his French commander. 'Can it be done?' he asked, and Chandée shrugged.

'When the dough rises the bread must be baked,' he said.

Henry didn't need to be told that he couldn't back out now. Chandée clapped him on the shoulder. '*Courage, mon ami,*' he said. 'Only death is worth the dice, eh?'

But a message had come from the Welsh lawyer, John Morgan, that Rhys ap Thomas, the most powerful man in Carmarthenshire, had committed himself to Henry's cause. Because of the prophecy that one day a Welshman would rule Wales.

They called him the new Arthur. All through the valleys the bards were singing of his return:

When wilt thou, Black Bull, come to land? How long shall we wait?

Lewis Glyn Cothi

Meanwhile his troops were comparing him to William of Normandy not because they saw him as a conqueror but because they saw him as French. His army was mainly French, and no one in England had heard of him.

That night he sat on the bay, watching torchlight flicker in the black water. He heard a dry cough behind him.

There was no need for the cough; he would have known his uncle's footsteps anywhere. A moment later his head appeared in the water.

'Perhaps you should get some sleep,' he said.

Henry did not reply to this. There was almost no need for words between him and his uncle; they were like a long-married couple. Jasper said, 'What are you thinking?' and Henry replied, 'I was trying to remember my mother's face.'

Jasper nodded, then he crouched beside his nephew, his hands dangling between his knees. After several moments, he said, 'I want you to know that – whatever happens – whatever comes of this – I would not have it any other way.'

In the last year, Jasper had taken on a withered look. How old was he? Henry wasn't sure. But with a leap of imagination he saw for the first time that his uncle could have had a different life. He could have raised his own family and lived in his own home.

All this had been denied him, because of the necessity of looking after his nephew; the impulse of loyalty towards his brother and his brother's son.

Henry did not embrace his uncle or squeeze his hand. He looked down at the water, where both their reflections were deposited like alternative selves. They sat together in silence, listening to the rhythm of the lapping waves.

Not all the men returned. But in the last hour more arrived; discharged soldiers from a nearby military base, which, combined with the mercenaries from Brittany and a contingent of Scots under the command of Bernard Stewart, Lord of Aubigny, came to more than two thousand men. They set sail from Honfleur with a fair, southerly wind.

Edward Woodville, commanded one ship and the Earl of Oxford another. The Marquis of Dorset had been left behind as security for the money he'd borrowed from the French, though he'd protested vigorously about this. As they sailed they encountered no opposition, no patrolling fleet. After six days, for the first time for so many years he was within sight of his native land.

This was a Sunday, the seventh day of August. Henry disembarked, aware of all his men watching him. His foot sank in the wet sand which closed over his print. Because it was the Lord's day, he knelt at the water's edge. He lifted a handful of sand and sang:

Judica me Deus, et discerne causam meam.

His voice was swallowed by the air, mingling with the cry of the gulls and the hissing of the waves. But he leaned forward and kissed the sand and made the sign of the cross. Then he stood and strode quickly up the beach, leaving his men to the great work of disembarking, the unloading of weapons and armour and food with which any invasion must begin.

44

Prayer

Intermittently, Margaret heard news. She heard that Henry had landed in Pembrokeshire, close to the place of his birth, and had been greeted by the men of Dale. King Richard had stationed his soldiers in Dale that year, but by miraculous good fortune had withdrawn them only a few days before. So it was safe for Henry and his men to camp there. About fifty of the men of Dale had joined him, which wasn't many, but it was a beginning.

From there he'd moved to Haverfordwest, a fortified town, but no one had resisted him; in fact, a delegation of townsfolk had been sent to welcome him, and the officer, Arnold Butler, declared that the town would serve Jasper Tudor, its natural lord. At the same time they heard that Rhys ap Thomas had changed his allegiance back to Richard.

It was incomprehensible; Rhys had talked loudly of liberating his people from the English king. However there was nothing to be done. They could only continue to march north, to where John Morgan, the lawyer, was mustering men in Cardiganshire.

They had to avoid the lands belonging to James Tyrell, William Herbert and Thomas Vaughn, so they stayed near the coast.

In Cardigan they heard that Richard Williams, steward of Haverfordwest and King Richard's agent, had set out secretly to Nottingham to warn his sovereign that the enemy had arrived.

When he heard of their arrival the king rejoiced, or at least he pretended to rejoice, sending his letters everywhere to say that the day he had longed for had now arrived when he could easily triumph over such a wretched company ... Meanwhile, he dispatched terrifying orders in a host of letters to all the counties

of the kingdom . . . with the threat that, after victory had been
gained, anyone who might be found in any part of the kingdom,
not to have been present in person with him on the battlefield
could hope for nothing but the loss of all his goods, his possessions and his life.

Crowland Chronicle

It was not unexpected. Henry's army could hardly have travelled through Wales without someone notifying the king. Henry
sent out his own letters to all the lords on the route towards
Cheshire, telling them to meet him there. And to Rhys ap
Thomas, promising him the lieutenantship of Wales if he would
come to Henry's aid.

After only five miles they heard that Walter Herbert was travelling towards them from Carmarthen with a mighty host. Henry
had to round up his men to prevent them from fleeing and send
out scouts to investigate the area, but there was no sign of any
army. The only troops who approached were with Richard Griffith and John Morgan of Gwent, who had come to join him. This
pleased Henry greatly since Griffith was on friendly terms with
Rhys and said he would send Henry's message to him. Fifteen
miles east of Cardigan, Einion ap Dafydd Llwyd sent food and
drink to them and pledged his support. By 12 August they'd
reached Aberystwyth, where the town and garrison surrendered
to Henry without resistance.

It was almost too easy. But at Aberystwyth Henry took the
great risk of writing to his stepfather, telling him of his route
through the mountain passes of mid-Wales to Welshpool and the
Shropshire plain. He would cross the River Severn at Shrewsbury
and hope to meet Stanley there before marching towards London. There had been no word from his stepfather. Once they
were through Wales they would be on Stanley territory, and no
one knew whether it would be hostile or not.

Needless to say, Stanley didn't reply.

Henry sent more letters, to the Kynaston family, hoping if not for support then at least for their neutrality as he passed their lands; and then he'd spent one night with the bard Dafydd Llwyd at Mathafarn.

Dafydd Llwyd cared nothing for the dynastic struggles of the English, only for the liberation of his own people. But Henry was welcomed to his wooden hall, high in the mountains, and in the morning many other bards had formed a circle around Dafydd's Hall, chanting:

'*Harri a fu,*
Harri a fo,
Harri y sydd,
Hiroes iddo.'

Henry who was, Henry who will be, Henry who is, long life to him.

And all the men stamped and cheered.

Then they went on to cross the valley of the Banwy.

No other invader had attempted such a journey. It was only thirty miles, but through some of the most rugged mountain passes in Wales. The journey was exhausting, but it meant Henry could reach Welshpool undetected. Here more men came to join him. Rhys Fawr ap Mareddud came from Conway with two hundred men and cattle, so that all the company could feast. And Henry was presented with a white horse, because all the prophecies said the new Arthur would be carried to victory on a white steed.

And then, on the evening of 16 August, Rhys ap Thomas came. Henry met him on the high ridge overlooking Welshpool, and Rhys said King Richard had demanded his son from him as hostage, so he had been afraid to come. But he had a thousand men with him now, and could call on a thousand more.

Henry didn't trust him. Margaret wouldn't have trusted him

either. After some hard bargaining, Henry told Rhys he would offer him the stewardship of South Wales, under Henry's rule. Rhys had argued, because Henry had offered him all Wales. But if Rhys had come sooner, Henry said, that offer would stand. As it was, he had to offer rewards to those men who had supported him.

Henry thought Rhys would not agree to this new deal, but the next morning, unexpectedly, he'd knelt before Henry, offering his sword. Then he'd turned with his arms raised and a shout had gone up from his men.

And so on that day Henry had left Wales with an increased company, and pressed on to Shrewsbury, where he hoped to meet his stepfather. But Shrewsbury, having received orders from King Richard, closed its gates to him. Henry and all his army were locked outside.

That was the last news she'd heard. She didn't know where Henry had gone from Shrewsbury, whether another town had let them in. She had no idea whether or not he'd managed to meet with Stanley or whether her husband would support her son.

She did know Richard had summoned people from all over the country, and was moving his great army towards Leicester, to prepare for imminent battle. So any day now, Henry, inexperienced as he was, would fight the biggest army that could be mustered in England, under its most experienced general.

Panic and sickness gripped her at the thought, but there was no point. Either her son would die, or he would live: that was all.

If he lived, he would be king.

If he died, she had to hope it would be swiftly and cleanly, on the battlefield.

If he was taken captive, he would suffer the punishment for treason. He would be partially hung then tied to a scaffold for dismemberment. His bowels would be ripped out of him and burned, his member cut off while he was still alive. As the originator and instigator of the rebellion, she could be made to witness it.

She would take poison first. She'd not studied plants for so long without learning the means to put herself to sleep quietly and skilfully.

It was suicide, of course: the ultimate sin. She could not be saved if she committed suicide, according to St Augustine. Like her father, she would not be saved.

Perhaps that was why she couldn't pray.

So many mothers would be praying that day; the sounds of their prayers like the whirring of countless insects. Which of them would God listen to? Or had he grown deaf, as well as forgetful, in His great age?

She had an image of Him cupping His great ear in His almighty hand.

She could only kneel in her chapel, with her head on her clasped hands, thinking these blasphemous thoughts.

It would be her fault if her son didn't succeed, because she couldn't pray.

If she ended her life, would that not be a desertion of her son?

Perhaps she would be able to get a small phial to him, containing the same poison she would drink. That would be suicide and murder. But they would face divine judgement together.

She would look God in the eye and say, *you didn't help.*

She wasn't good enough to pray. She wasn't good at all. She was being punished for the sins that had accreted to her, like limpets covering a stone or fungus over the rotten stump of a tree. Stiffly, she got up.

Today or tomorrow, or the next day, her son would face a battle, for the nation and the Crown. Everything depended on it. Whatever happened next, the world would change for both of them, and for England.

And she, Margaret Beaufort, could only wait. There was nothing else she could do.

45

Detour

Henry had retreated four or five miles from Shrewsbury and camped on the banks of the Severn. The next morning, he'd sent conciliatory messages to the bailiffs, saying that if they were admitted to the town he and his men would pass through quietly, causing no damage or injury to anyone. They would respect the oaths of loyalty the townsmen had taken to King Richard.

Still they wouldn't let him in.

If he was denied access to Shrewsbury, he would have to make a lengthy detour and it was possible that other border towns would follow its example.

His men were restless, and he was preparing to turn round when a messenger arrived from William Stanley, his stepfather's brother, who was overlord of Shrewsbury. He had told his messenger to order the bailiffs to open the gates. This he did by wrapping a message around a stone and throwing it over the walls.

After a lengthy pause the portcullis was raised. And the chief bailiff lay on the ground, because he'd said Henry's troops could pass through Shrewsbury only *over his belly*. So they all stepped over him.

The other bailiffs escorted Henry through the town. As agreed, the troops didn't halt in Shrewsbury but camped on a hill near Newport. And the next day they made their way to Stafford, where William Stanley himself came to meet them.

This was the first time Henry had seen his step-uncle; a broad man with narrow eyes. He came with a small retinue of men, but not with Henry's stepfather. They greeted one another warily and Henry said he'd hoped to see his stepfather by now.

William Stanley said his brother was even now approaching Leicester.

'Leicester?' Henry said; but William only shrugged.

'There have been developments,' he said.

As soon as the king had heard of Henry's arrival he'd sent messages to Stanley, summoning him. Stanley had replied that he was ill of the sweating sickness. He'd also sent a secret message to his son George, who was still in the king's custody, to say that he should *slip away from Nottingham when he could*. George had made a bid to escape but had been captured by the king's soldiers and interrogated. He'd confessed at once, telling the king that he and his uncle, William Stanley, and his cousin Sir John Savage had plotted to join Henry Tudor. But he'd sworn, even after some mistreatment, that his father had no part in it.

'Is that true?' Henry asked. William Stanley raised his hands and let them fall again to his side. 'It's true he confessed,' he said. 'Even though I don't think the interrogation was unduly severe. My nephew is no hero,' he said.

The king hadn't killed George, because then he would have no hold over Stanley. Instead, he'd made him write to his father, explaining the danger he was in and begging him to come at once to the king with all the forces he could muster.

'So Stanley's going to Richard,' Henry said.

'Not if you get to him first,' said Sir William.

'It's out of my way.'

'I would advise a change of route,' Sir William said. The king was still at Nottingham, waiting to see who would join him, but he would leave soon. 'If you go towards London now, he will intercept you.'

Henry looked at him narrowly, suspecting a trap. 'I'll consult my men,' he said.

He turned aside and sought Lichfield, where he passed the night outside its walls. Early in the morning of the following day he entered the city and was honourably received. Three days earlier, Thomas Stanley had come to that place accompanied by a little less than five thousand men. Learning of Henry's arrival, he went to the village of Atherstone to wait there for him, for he feared that if he openly sided with Henry, Richard, who so far did not completely distrust him, would kill his son George . . .

> Although Henry's forces were increasing wherever he went, still he was in no small anxiety . . . concerning Thomas Stanley. And he was informed that . . . nothing was stronger than Richard's army. And so . . . he halted on his march accompanied by only twenty armed men, to deliberate what to do . . . His army arrived at Tamworth [and] he gloomily followed at a distance . . . and when night fell he lost sight of its tracks . . . Then he secretly went to Atherstone where the brothers Thomas and William Stanley were encamped.
>
> *Polydore Vergil*

He approached the scouts, who were alarmed, thinking some spy from Richard's army had come. He had to lay down his arms before they would take him to the camp.

Two men looked up as he drew near. The one sitting with William Stanley could only be his stepfather. He could see the similarity between them, though his stepfather's face was longer and narrower. It seemed to narrow further as he looked at Henry, but William Stanley greeted him genially enough.

'Ah, nephew!' he said. 'We were just talking about you!'

Nephew, Henry thought.

Thomas Stanley rose swiftly for a man of his years. 'Good to meet you at last,' he said.

Henry took Stanley's hand. He was perhaps fractionally taller than his stepfather, who did not bow. The rules of precedence were not entirely clear; this was his stepfather, but Henry was his king. Unless, of course, Stanley was still loyal to Richard.

'This is an unexpected pleasure,' Stanley said. He led Henry towards a seat and Henry followed, thinking, *so this is the man who keeps my mother prisoner.*

'I can't stay long,' he said. 'I must rejoin my men. We're camped three miles away.'

'We know,' said William. 'We saw you arriving.'

And Stanley said, 'It's not a very large company.'

'It could be increased,' said Henry, looking at him.

William said, 'Richard has left Nottingham now – he's heading towards Leicester.'

Henry didn't ask how he knew. 'How many?' he said.

'Eight – maybe ten thousand,' William said carelessly. 'He's still waiting for the Duke of Norfolk and the Earl of Northumberland. And John de la Pole.'

'How many men do you have?' Henry asked.

William had almost three thousand with him, Henry's step-father nearly five.

'And you?' Stanley said.

But Henry thought he must know, if he'd seen them arriving. 'I'm also waiting for reinforcements,' he said. 'They should come tonight.'

'Let's hope so,' Stanley said.

If the Stanleys joined Richard, as he was expecting them to do, Henry was hopelessly outnumbered.

'I came to see if you would send some of your men to march in my vanguard,' he said.

Stanley looked thoughtful. 'That's one possibility,' he said.

'Is there another?'

'I was thinking we would view the field first.'

See who's winning, Henry thought.

'It's good to have an overview,' William said. 'That's what went wrong at Tewkesbury – no one could see anything. The Duke of Somerset was taken completely by surprise. Two hundred spearmen won the field that day.'

He'd forgotten, apparently, that the Duke of Somerset was Henry's cousin. William Stanley had fought against Lancaster that day. Henry didn't remind him. He couldn't afford to fall out with either of these men. But he was tired of the prevarication, the refusal to commit.

He started to speak, but a messenger arrived.

'King Richard has been joined by the Duke of Norfolk and the Earl of Northumberland,' he said.

William Stanley's eyebrows raised. 'Better late than never,' he said.

Henry had written several letters to the Earl of Northumberland, hoping for his support. Now he'd joined Richard.

The atmosphere had palpably changed.

'If our forces combine, they will still be enough,' Henry said.

'It's not only a question of numbers,' Stanley said, 'but of experience.'

Did they want him to beg? 'I must ask you to commit yourselves,' said Henry. 'I have to consider how to deploy my men.'

'That can be decided when we see the lie of the land.'

'I would still like you to send some of your forces with me tonight.'

It was foolish to press them, and the fractional pause before William's answer underlined his error. 'Not tonight,' he said. 'Our men are tired, they're sleeping. We can send some across in the morning.'

He was furious with them, and bitterly disappointed, but he mustn't show it. He rose abruptly to leave, then looked directly at Stanley.

'It rests with you now, father,' he said, and for the first time Stanley smiled his vulpine smile.

'I think it rests with the king,' he said. He didn't say which king he meant.

Henry made his way back to where he knew his own men would camp that night, cursing himself for wasting his efforts, for showing his inexperience so clearly. The Stanleys would act in their own interests, as they always had; they were little more than soldiers of fortune. They wouldn't tell him anything but would allow him to wonder, to face Richard's great army still wondering.

He would have to tell his men that Richard was on his way.

His breath became laboured; he could almost feel the small airways in his lungs constricting. A sweat broke out on him; he felt as though he was breathing through soup. *Not here, not now*, he prayed. He could not fall ill before the battle; he had to be fit and well, and prepared to die.

His army was distraught over the sudden absence of its commander [but] then as the sky grew light Henry returned . . .
offering the excuse that . . . he had been outside the camp to
receive some welcome news from certain secret friends . . .

Polydore Vergil

46

King Richard Prepares for Battle

On Sunday 21 August the king left Leicester amid great pomp
and wearing his crown, together with John Howard, Duke of
Norfolk and Henry Percy, Earl of Northumberland, and other
prominent lords, knights, esquires and an enormous throng of
the common people. The number of men fighting on the king's
side was found to be greater than had ever been seen on any one
side in England . . .

Crowland Chronicle

He had shaken off suggestions that he should sleep
and instead paced the contours of his camp, waiting
for news. The Duke of Norfolk had camped in
Leicester itself; Lord Stanley, he'd been told, was
approaching from the west and his brother with him. The Earl of
Northumberland had arrived late, bringing a fraction of the men
he'd hoped for and his apologies. His men were already weary, he
said. They needed to rest. They should form the rearguard and be
the last to leave the town.

Or the first to flee, Richard had thought, but he'd agreed, showing no suspicion.

John Paston had been summoned, but hadn't arrived yet. John
de la Pole, Duke of Suffolk, hadn't come either, although his son
was there, eager, doubtlessly, to be king if Richard was killed in
battle. Robert Brackenbury was also late; Rhys ap Thomas had
defected and taken other Welsh chieftains with him. Other men
had deserted when they could.

But he would fight with what he had. He had taken up position outside the town, on Ambion Hill. His army stretched

across it, four hundred feet above the plain, so he had a wide view.

By late afternoon the invading army could be seen pitching tents on lower ground. Reports said his own army outnumbered the Tudor's by at least three to one, that the Welsh rebels and Breton mercenaries were an ill-paid, untrained rabble, likely to desert.

But there was the unresolved question of the Stanleys. From his position on the hill, he could see them arriving, taking up position, keeping their distance from him and from the Tudor. Thomas Stanley had not responded to his messages to come at once, directly, to his king.

At dusk, lights began to glow like so many fireflies, from the Tudor's camp to the south and the Stanleys' to the south-west, and his own. He sent another messenger out and received a prevaricating reply.

Something, somewhere just out of sight, was troubling him. When he looked quickly over his shoulder it wasn't there, yet he could see it flickering in the corner of his eye.

But he'd not got where he was by giving in to premonitions or apparitions. He had what he'd always had: his courage, his vigilance, his obsessive regard for detail. So he paced and watched, scoured the terrain and waited, and paced again and watched.

He could taste the night air, feel its smoky texture on his skin. He felt fiercely alive, as if there were enough life in him for six kings. Only when his chamberlain, Viscount Lovell, suggested he should save some of his strength if he was going to fight in a few hours did he return to his tent. He didn't expect to sleep; all the nerves and muscles of his body were tense.

He took ill rest at night, lay long waking and musing, sore wearied with care and watch, rather dozed than slept, troubled with fearful dreams.

Thomas More

In one dream he sat on a chair which was like a throne but fixed to a wheel. It rolled to the edge of a precipice, and on the other side of this precipice sat his nephew, Edward, the boy king, on a similar throne.

The boy said nothing but looked at his uncle, and the older king spoke first.

'How is it with you, nephew?'

Afterwards he couldn't remember precisely what his nephew had replied. Because he'd suddenly seen more people standing behind his nephew: his other nephew, and their father his brother, and his own father, Richard, Duke of York. And his wife, Anne, and his other brother, George, and William, Lord Hastings.

It was only a dream, but he woke from it with the taste of death in his mouth.

Viscount Lovell came to the tent to wake him, though it was still dark, and saw he was already awake.

'Did you sleep well, my lord?' Lovell asked, and he murmured that he'd had bad dreams.

And instantly regretted it, because that news would fly through the ranks as only rumour could.

'What dreams, my lord?' Lovell asked, and he summoned enough wit to reply it was nothing – only what might be expected before battle.

But as his chamberlain moved around his tent assembling his armour he remembered more details.

How is it with you? he'd said, and his nephew had said something – what was it? – in reply. That he would know soon enough?

He rose slowly as Lovell brought his armour to him. His neck felt stiff and his shoulder ached. Viscount Lovell adjusted the straps, but he made him take it off again, and moved his arm back and forth before Lovell strapped him into it once more; tightly enough to hold him upright.

'Bring me my crown,' he said, but Lovell hesitated.

'You don't want to lose it, sire.'

'Why would I lose it?' he said, then he remembered that in his dream he had lost the crown; it had fallen down the sheer cliff side.

He said, 'This day I will live or die King of England.'

Lovell brought him the crown and adjusted it over his helmet. For a moment they looked at one another, eye to eye, and Viscount Lovell seemed disturbed by what he saw. But Richard only said, 'Let the troops know I'm ready.'

He wondered briefly where his son had been, in his dream. He hadn't seen his son. Then he went outside to see his councillors and to check on the progress of his camp.

His chief men were gathered round the entrance to his tent: Richard Ratcliffe, William Catesby, John Kendall, his secretary, and others. He stooped to leave the tent and put out one hand to secure his crown. As he straightened he noticed the looks of concern on their faces, which told him how he must look to them in the greying light.

. . . his face, which was always drawn, was deathly and drained of colour.

Crowland Chronicle

But he told them that, if he appeared pale, it was only because he'd spent the night going over the battle plans they'd made.

'Is Lord Stanley here?' he asked, but no one answered.

'Brackenbury has arrived,' Catesby told him.

He could hear the sounds of his camp stirring: the faint chink and clash of armour, horses whickering and stomping.

His nephew was just behind his shoulder. Almost, he asked the watching men if they could see him: his nephew, the child king. Then he recovered himself and looked again at their strained and wary faces. There was something he'd been meaning to tell them, he said.

He declared that the outcome of that day's battle, whichever side won the victory, would destroy the kingdom of England . . .

Crowland Chronicle

The words would not come out as he intended. Certainly they were not the words usually spoken by a king to his generals. He tried again, but he was interrupted by a squire.

The young man, who had a crop of spots on his chin, said there were no chaplains in the camp to say divine service.

'Why not?' he asked, and the young squire blushed and said that he believed some men had left.

'Left?' he said, looking at his generals. Richard Ratcliffe said he believed some men had, in the night, gone over to the enemy. 'Walter Hungerford,' he said, 'and Bourchier, and some others. Possibly the priests went with them.'

'Shall I look for someone who can say mass?' the squire said. 'The men don't want to go to their deaths unshriven.'

At this, Richard smiled a terrible smile. But he took the young man by the shoulder and told him to have no fear. If their quarrel was God's, they needed no priestly supplications; if it were not, such prayers were idle blasphemy.

The squire started to say that in any case he should look for the priests, when another messenger came from Norfolk to say he was ready to march, and Richard smiled round at his generals with that same, terrible smile.

'At least one of my generals is ready,' he said. 'We cannot have him marching alone.'

As they dispersed to see to their men, he sent the young squire to fetch his horse, a white charger like the one his father had given him many years ago. He told his secretary to send a final message to Lord Stanley, summoning him to come at once, if he valued the life of his son. Then he looked out over the terrain.

The thought came to him that all this land had once belonged to Lord Hastings, whom he'd had executed, who had appeared in his dream.

Day was dawning, grey and warm. He could feel a light sweat on his upper lip, an ache in his troubled shoulder. He adjusted his crown, then his visor, resisting the urge to look behind him. They were all there: his nephews, his brothers, his father, his wife, the old king, Henry VI, and his wife, Margaret of Anjou, and their son, the prince.

Good, he thought. Let them judge him.

Further away he could see the opposing army, moving like so many locusts across the valley. He could see the two camps of the Stanley brothers, several thousand red jerkins beneath their banners. If they joined the Tudor, his own army would be outnumbered. He could see his messenger returning from their camp. He waited while the messenger repeated Stanley's words: *I have other sons.*

He nodded, then issued his command: that Lord Strange [son of Thomas Stanley] should be beheaded on the spot . . .

Crowland Chronicle

Then he got on his horse and prepared to lead his men down the hill.

47

Henry Tudor Prepares for Battle

He'd spent the night in his inn but woken before dawn, labouring for breath. All his muscles were contorted, his feet chafing one another, pushing the sheets. Sweat covered him.

He could breathe in tiny amounts but couldn't release it; his lungs wouldn't release the air. His heart was hammering. He would die here, in this room, before the battle.

How could he be king if he couldn't breathe?

He attempted, using every last drop of will, to relax his muscles. Gradually, the tension eased. He lay limply on top of the bed, concentrating on one breath at a time.

He was already too exhausted to fight.

His generals had told him he shouldn't fight. They had persuaded him to stay out of the battle, but in full view of all his men. He had objected to this at first, not so much because he wanted to fight, but because of how it would seem to his own men and to the enemy. The last king to have stayed out of a battle was his uncle, Henry VI, who had no reputation as a warrior, or a king.

But they were all agreed; Jasper, the Earl of Oxford, de Chandée, because of his inexperience in warfare. He'd taken part in only one battle when he was a child and had been protected from the actual fighting. Also, it was important for his troops to know where he was, and that he was alive. And thirdly, because he had no heir. If Richard was killed the Earl of Lincoln would take his place, but if Henry was killed the battle was over, and lost.

His generals had taken over with their plans, virtually excluding him. As he lay on his bed now, coaxing air into his constricted lungs, he thought that once he was king he would no longer be ruled by his lords. He would call on them as little as possible. He would suppress them, in fact, even if it meant making great changes in his realm.

Once he was king.

To get to that moment he had to kill the existing king. A man he'd never met but whose fate seemed irretrievably linked to his. And had been linked, according to philosophy, since the dawn of time, because the king existed in the Eye of God, throughout eternity.

But if God knew who it was, he wasn't telling Henry.

On this day everything would change; he would become king or he would lose his life. These restricted breaths might be the last he ever took.

The sky was pale now; still with a few faint stars. He remembered lying in the forests of Wales all those years ago considering what it meant to be, to have a soul that would guide him through his life. He had never found that out, or whether the story of his life had already been written. But he had the sense of himself *going through the motions*, as if acting a part in a play. He didn't know what the end was, but he did know, suddenly and clearly, that whatever the outcome, even if he became king, he would lose his life; he would surrender it to the Crown.

With that thought, strangely, his breathing became more regular; he could feel sweat cooling on his face. He was prepared to sacrifice his life to the Crown.

It was still early, but he wouldn't sleep again. He got up and dressed himself, on what might be the last morning of his life.

His men were not awake yet, but he tended the horses. Their solid presence, the warmth of their breath, calmed him.

He could see the opposing army on the hill above the plain. They formed the longest line he'd ever seen.

Gradually, his camp woke. A messenger came with news that some of Richard's men had deserted him for Henry. Someone had pinned a note to Norfolk's tent that read, *Jack of Norfolk be not bold, for Dickon thy master is bought and sold.*

And John Howard, Duke of Norfolk, had ripped down the note and torn it up, but not before most of his men had seen it. Then he'd sent a message to Richard to say he was ready for battle, and he'd delivered this message to his squire in a loud, clear voice, so that all would hear he was not a man to be shaken by such a trick.

Henry went to see the men who had come to him. They knelt before him; he raised them up and kissed them. He could see them taking in his French manner, his accent. He assigned them places in his army then sent a final message to his stepfather, asking him to join him on the battlefield.

The opposing army began to move.

> Richard . . . led all his army out of camp . . . He stationed the archers in front like a wall and placed Duke John of Norfolk over them. After this came the king himself with a choice company of soldiers . . .
>
> *Polydore Vergil*

As they moved down the hill Henry could make out the arms of the Earl of Surrey, who led a flanking wing of horsemen and infantry, and Lord Ferrers, moving his own flank into position on the other side.

Lord Ferrers, his guardian's brother, with whom Henry had often stayed.

As each contingent swung into place, a shout went up from Richard's men.

> The leader of the vanguard was John, Lord Howard. Another lord, Brackenbury, was also in command of the vanguard which had eleven or twelve thousand altogether . . .
>
> *Jean de Molinet*

The light cannon were drawn up on carts and chained together into a phalanx that no army could pass. Behind these came the heavy guns, the bombards, trundling slowly into position, where they would fire stone balls down on Henry's men. Many of the foot soldiers had guns.

Four of Stanley's knights rode into Henry's camp with two hundred men, no more, to swell his vanguard. They said the rest of Stanley's men would come in their own time.

And so his vanguard was woefully small, and not well equipped, though the Earl of Oxford, who led it, was an experienced general. The right wing of cavalry was led by Gilbert Talbot and the left by John Savage. French, Breton and Scottish contingents made up the central body of the army, and Henry's uncle, Jasper Tudor, brought up the rear.

He'd not been well, Jasper; the long march through Wales had taken it out of him. He looked old. It was in consideration of this that he'd not been given a more prominent position. He hadn't argued about this but allowed younger men to take the lead. As he passed Henry they exchanged one glance, and Henry knew with a shock of recognition that his uncle did not intend to leave the field that day. Either they would win or he would die. Jasper Tudor had had enough of exile, and his fugitive existence.

The Earl of Oxford, with a large force of French as well as English troops, took up his position opposite . . . the Duke of Norfolk . . .

Crowland Chronicle

Henry's vanguard moved slowly to the field, avoiding the marshy ground on the right. The Earl of Oxford rode back and forth, keeping his mercenaries in line. He passed close enough to Henry for him to see the severe lines of his face. But then their eyes locked and the Earl of Oxford smiled. In that moment Henry knew that he, too, would not want to survive this battle if they lost; he would not go back to imprisonment or execution. But the moment passed and the earl rode on, shouting orders, and it was the turn of John Savage and Gilbert Talbot to manoeuvre their men into position.

Henry's own men, in the reserve, kicked out the fires and packed what was left of the food.

The Battle of Bosworth: 22 August 1485

There now began a very fierce battle between the two sides.

Crowland Chronicle

The cannons blasted and Norfolk's archers opened fire. Gilbert Talbot's men completed their deployment under a hail of arrows.

Henry stood a few feet behind his standard bearer, a young man called William Brandon, who had come to him in Brittany after Buckingham's rebellion. He would have a good view of his army being destroyed.

He would pitch in, of course, if he had to. He would lead a small troop of men-at-arms, archers and billmen. But they would not join in the fighting unless it was necessary.

If it became necessary, he was already lost. But it would be better to die in the field than afterwards.

The cannons fired again, and Norfolk led his men in a direct charge.

He could see Oxford's banner and hear him shouting as Norfolk's men thundered towards him. The sight seemed to have thrown Oxford's men into confusion. Their lines broke, and John Savage's wing was fatally exposed.

Oxford shouted again and, though Henry could not make out the words, his officers took up the shout. Gradually, men gathered round the banner. He could see them forming into a wedge, facing Norfolk's men.

Guns cracked and cannon balls punched through the ranks. Beneath a storm of arrows Oxford's men waited and did not give.

The lines bulged and a surf of axes, swords, spears rose as the two sides collided. Oxford's troops moved slowly forward and Norfolk's line bent backwards like a bow.

It was impossible to see who was gaining ground.

Oxford shouted again and the shape of his troops changed, thickening once more into a wedge.

Henry could see Norfolk's men pause, bewildered by this manoeuvre; there was a momentary lull in the fighting. Then Rhys ap Thomas' men charged and John Savage joined in.

Miraculously, Norfolk's line began to crumple and break.

John Savage charged again, driving the duke towards the Earl of Oxford. And a shout went up – Norfolk was down – struck by an arrow in the throat.

His men started to retreat. Henry could just make out the Earl of Surrey, Norfolk's son, fighting furiously over his father's body.

Then Richard himself charged with a mass of infantry, obliterating the green of the hill. There was no sign of the Earl of Northumberland.

The Earl of Northumberland who was on the king's side . . . ought to have charged the French but did nothing except to flee, he and his company, and to abandon his king, Richard, for he had an undertaking with the Earl of Richmond, as had some others who deserted him in his need . . .

Jean de Molinet

The Stanleys remained poised like eagles to the side of the battlefield.

Another shout went up – Lord Ferrers was down. Henry's heart hammered as though it would burst. He couldn't see the king.

And then he did.

Riding out like thunder from the flanks of his army, with only a small body of men, heading directly towards Henry.

Later it would be said that he *stood his ground*. As the king thundered towards him, hacking his way through Henry's troops, he remained near his standard of the red dragon.

He saw William Brandon's stance change. The muscles in his neck tightened like cords. One man fell, then another before the king, whose axe rose and fell in a flashing arc.

A third man went down, then a fourth. He drew ever closer, impossibly, through all the men who stood in his way.

John Cheyney was down, that *mighty man*, toppled like a great tree. Richard's axe came down again and another man fell.

Henry had never seen anything like it – this small, wiry man wielding his axe as though possessed. No one could stop him.

> Let me say the truth to his credit; King Richard bore himself like
> a gallant knight and despite his little body and feeble strength . . .
>
> *John Rous*

He was shouting – his mouth was moving – but Henry couldn't make out the words. The meaning, however, was clear.

It was death, his death coming towards him.

He couldn't have moved, even if he'd wanted to. For a moment he felt dizzy, as though he was spiralling upwards, out of himself. Almost as though he was leaving his body before the death blow came.

There were only three, then two men between them. For the first time he drew his sword, though it would be useless against an axe.

He didn't have an axe.

From the corner of his vision he could see something red pouring down the hillside, as though the hill itself had opened an artery and was streaming blood. He had no time to make sense of this, for the second man was down, brought to his knees then toppled by a great blow from the king's axe, driving through his helmet.

Now only William Brandon stood between Henry and the king.

He saw Brandon's shoulders quiver and flex as he tried to bring the standard between him and the king.

Richard knocked it sideways with a single blow. The great arc of his axe swung again, and Brandon buckled and screamed, but did not fall. Until the king struck again and he did fall, toppled to the side. And Henry's gaze locked with Richard's.

He looked into his enemy's eyes. Saw that absolute intent.

Richard came forward, raising his axe.

And was struck by a blow from behind.

He didn't turn, Henry always remembered that; he would not be deflected from his purpose. Another blow struck him on the shoulder, and still he strove forward, to end this battle once and for all.

And then he was surrounded by William Stanley's men, in their red jackets.

More and more men came, and Richard was driven backwards into the marsh. Then his horse was down, Richard himself was down, but somehow, impossibly, he was picking himself up.

In the thick of Stanley's men, King Richard fought on: shouting again and again that he was betrayed.

John Rous

His crown rolled off, his helmet was driven into his skull and it was no longer possible to see him through the press of fighting men.

King Richard received many mortal wounds, and like a spirited and most courageous knight, fell in the battle and not in flight.

Crowland Chronicle

King Richard was killed fighting alone and manfully in the thick-
est press of his enemies.

Polydore Vergil

Someone passed in front of Henry, bending forward and pris-
ing the standard from William Brandon's dead hand. He lifted it
up and grinned at Henry, teeth pale in his soiled face. When
Henry could see beyond him again Stanley's men had withdrawn
a little, and there, between them, lay the body of the king.

'The king is dead,' someone said. Henry couldn't believe it;
could not believe he had not been the one who'd died.

He took two or three steps forward and gazed down at the
body of his enemy.

The king's eyes were open, staring upwards, emptied now of
their rage and intent. Yet they seemed to contain an accusation
meant only for him.

So you succeed, they said.

Blood had soaked into the ground around him; there were
clumps of hair and teeth. One of his fingers still twitched, as if
reluctant to let go even in death.

Henry felt light-headed, as if his knees wouldn't carry him. He
must not faint now. He stood before all these men, who'd won
the battle for him, and felt as if he should have something to say
but could think of no words at all. He took another step forward,
prodded the former king's body with his foot and moved his lips.

'Let him be seen,' he said.

One of the Welshmen stuck [King Richard] with a halberd, and
another took his body and put it before him on his horse and carried it . . . as one would bear a sheep.

Jean de Molinet

And Richard, late king, body despoiled to the skin and nought
being left about him so much as would cover his privy member,

was trussed behind a pursuivant called Norroy as a hog or other vile beast.

Great Chronicle of London

As soon as Richard's men saw their king thus they began to surrender, one after the other.

Henry moved on to higher ground, where he could see his generals. The Earl of Oxford was pursuing those of Norfolk's men who were trying to escape, but de Chandée and Gilbert Talbot were making their way towards him and, behind them, his uncle, Jasper, who had not been killed but was on foot, walking towards Henry and frowning in concentration.

And behind him came the two Stanley brothers, with identical, speculative smiles on their faces.

Thomas Stanley was carrying something. It took a moment for Henry to realise it was the crown.

Battered and muddied, but still recognisably the precious crown that, as the Spanish envoy had once noted, was worth a hundred and twenty thousand pounds.

Lord Stanley approached his stepson, holding it and smiling.

At the last moment he turned and held it up, so the mass of armed men on the field could clearly see it.

And a great shout went up.

Still smiling, Stanley turned back to Henry, and Henry suppressed a moment of recoil. However late, the Stanleys had saved the battle, and his life.

He stepped forward, removing his helmet, and knelt.

The flesh of his scalp moved under the crown. It slipped a little, and Henry lifted his hand to hold it on.

As he stood, Stanley shouted, 'God save the king!'

And the soldiers cried God save King Henry, God save King Henry! And with heart and hand uttered all the show of joy that might be.

Polydore Vergil

Still he couldn't believe it. He stood before them all, the living and the dead, wearing his dented crown.

Jasper was smiling at him, with tears in his eyes.

As the shouting died down, Henry knew he must give thanks to God so it would be clear to everyone it was no whim of fortune that he'd won the kingdom and the nation but Heaven's judgement.

And so he held up his hands and began to pray.

And thus by great fortune and grace . . . won this noble prince the possession of this land, and then was he conveyed to Leicester the same night and there received with all honour and gladness.

Great Chronicle of London

48

Consequences

Reginald Bray's man galloped through the gates. As soon as she saw him, his colours, the flag borne behind him, she knew.

Her heart seemed to stop. It seemed as if the whole world had stopped.

'Oh, my lady,' someone said. 'You're so pale.'

Her legs would not carry her; someone was helping her to a chair. She sank into it, acutely aware of the weakness of her body. *I should have eaten*, she thought, *I should have slept*. She needed to be strong, for him.

But the messenger was here, falling to his knees.

'It's true, then?' she said, before he'd spoken, and 'Is it true?'

'It is a most glorious victory,' he said.

'Oh, my lady!' someone said; and someone else said, 'The Lord be praised!'

Margaret pressed her fingers to her mouth, afraid that the fluid rising from her stomach to her throat would spill from her lips.

'Your son is in Leicester,' the messenger said, 'where they have received him with all joy and gladness. Tomorrow, or the next day, he will ride to London, to be received there as their king.'

There were tears in her eyes but she didn't weep. 'And – Richard?' she said.

Henry ordered the dead king to be placed in a little hermitage near the place of battle and had him covered from the waist downwards with a black rag of poor quality, ordering him to be exposed there three days to the universal gaze.

Diego de Valera

She nodded. 'How – how many?' she asked, meaning how many had died.

'I don't know the precise number, my lady,' the messenger said. 'The count was still being taken when I left. But his majesty your son wanted me to come to you without delay. I can say there were many more fallen on Richard's side than on ours.'

His majesty your son. She could not stop nodding. 'Thank you,' she said. 'Thank you.'

There was so much to do, so many arrangements to be made. Margaret's days passed in a kind of blur.

Another messenger had arrived from her son, to say he was indeed preparing to set off for London and it was his dearest hope that she would join him there.

From this messenger she'd learned the details of the battle. Her son had been saved by the intervention of her husband and his brother, who had remained out of the battle until the last moment. Richard had almost reached Henry before William Stanley's men had surrounded him and cut him down.

This detail caused nausea to rise from her stomach.

A moment later, everything would have been lost.

Her son's life, the fate of the nation, hanging on a hair. Each time she thought of it she felt weak, as though she might have to sit down.

She had to remind herself that they had saved her son's life. Richard had been cut down by their men. As soon as he was known to be dead, men had thrown down their swords and submitted to the new king. Her son, Henry.

Again, the feeling not of triumph, but sickness. Perhaps she was in fact ill.

Stanley had placed the crown on Henry's head.

This made her mouth twist into a smile. Stanley, claiming his moment.

The battle had lasted less than two hours, but more than a

thousand had died, mainly on Richard's side, and many more had been taken captive. A few had escaped, including Viscount Lovell and William Catesby. Though Catesby had been captured and hanged in Leicester.

Other key supporters of the House of York were dead. John Howard, Duke of Norfolk, and Lord Ferrers, Lady Herbert's brother, who, together with Lord Herbert, had imprisoned Henry's father so long ago.

She remembered him bargaining over the price she should pay to have her son back, fourteen years ago, in a London inn. And now he was dead, as Lord Herbert was dead. Edmund, her Edmund, was avenged at last.

Ratcliffe and Brackenbury were dead, which was good, because Henry would not have to deal with them now.

Stanley's son, George, had not been killed, though Richard had ordered it. It seemed his men had disobeyed him, or been distracted. George, miraculously, had survived.

The Earl of Northumberland had stayed out of the battle and had then submitted to Henry, who had taken him temporarily into custody. Others hadn't turned up at all. Her first husband, John de la Pole, had not turned up. Even though his son was Richard's heir. She could not imagine what had led him to stay out of battle. Perhaps he was just tired of fighting. As they all were.

This should be the last battle. England could not survive many more. But it had made her son king.

The thought was so wild and impossible that when it came to her she felt a fierce, exultant joy.

That was how she was: at one moment full of joy and zeal, writing to her son, making arrangements to move her whole household to London; the next overpowered by the sheer magnitude of it and disbelief that it had happened at all. It was a dream. She would wake up and find out that Richard was still king after all.

She had to remind herself it was true. The last Plantagenet king was dead. Her son was the first Tudor king.

And then she would feel frightened, because no one knew him. He had so little support.

Richard had failed, not just because of the Stanleys but because of all those who'd deserted him. Their disloyalty had sealed his fate.

Her son could not depend on anyone's loyalty, because who was there to support him, apart from his uncle and herself? The Stanleys and the Woodvilles couldn't be trusted, the Welsh chieftains would support their own cause and all the mercenaries would go back to Brittany and France.

There was the Earl of Oxford, of course, but it was better not to put faith in anyone. Look what had happened to the previous kings.

Henry had so little family. The Beaufort males were all dead, there was no one left from the House of Lancaster, and no more Tudors as yet.

He would marry, of course, and soon, to Elizabeth of York. The papal dispensation would have to be applied for immediately. And the Act of Titulus Regius, which had declared all the heirs of Edward IV bastards, would have to be revoked.

There were other Acts to consider. The one of 1397, for instance, that had declared the Beaufort line legitimate, should be reaffirmed by Parliament. The later statute, debarring them from the throne, should be suppressed. Any slurs on the legitimacy of the Tudor line would also have to be suppressed. New genealogies would be created.

As soon as he could, her son should go on progress around the country, so that everyone would recognise him as king. And he would need to suppress the private armies of the lords, take away their power to lead uprisings against him.

Edward IV and Richard III had both tried this and failed. Her son would have to succeed.

She wrote to Henry, expressing her heartfelt joy at his success, enquiring about his health and urging him to send for his future bride, Elizabeth, as soon as possible. He wrote back assuring her he was well. He'd already sent to Sheriff Hutton for Elizabeth, and for her cousin, the Earl of Warwick.

Clarence's son. Something would have to be done about him.

And the Earl of Lincoln, wherever he was. No one should start reviving these alternate claims to the throne.

With this messenger her son had sent a gift: the book of hours belonging to Richard III. It had been found in his tent after the battle.

It was stained and battered, a small but eloquent reminder of her son's victory. She ran her fingers over the slightly roughened texture of its binding and felt the nausea again.

It wasn't her fault.

Men had turned from him because of what they thought he'd done.

Because of what he had done, she reminded herself. He'd taken the throne from his nephew.

Whatever else men thought was hardly her fault.

It had to be done.

She had a momentary impulse to throw the book away, but then she knew she would keep it, with the one she had from Margaret of Anjou. The doomed king with the doomed queen. And the one from her father, who had also been doomed.

She couldn't read it now; she had to go to bed. Tomorrow she would go to meet her son in London.

He would arrive before her and she would meet him there. They would spend a few days in Woking, which was the only place they'd ever spent time together. In the space of a few days they would have to catch up on everything they'd missed.

She'd seen so little of him since his infancy. And now, after all they'd gone through, he was king.

There was that wave of disbelief again.

Only when she saw him, held him, took her place as his

advisor as he began the great business of running the country, would she believe.

That night, as she drifted in and out of sleep, she remembered all the people who'd died since the wars began. Her mother, who had died too soon to know her grandson would be king. Her father, whose face she couldn't see. Would he have taken his life if he'd known?

Alice Chaucer with her books, the Duke of Suffolk with his map. How the world had changed since then!

Betsy with her great shaggy eyebrows and dimpled face. Who had been there in the hour of her son's birth. 'Who'd've thought it,' she said, 'and him just a scrawny scrap! No one even thought he'd live.'

'I knew he would,' Edmund said, and there he was, tall and brave in his prison cell. 'He had to live, as I had to die.' And Owen Tudor stood with him, proudly, because his grandson was king.

There was her third husband, Henry, looking at her with his wary smile. 'At least it wasn't for nothing,' he said.

Behind him was the Duke of Buckingham, whose death might justifiably be attributed to her; then her Beaufort cousins, Lord Herbert and Lord Ferrers, the Earl of Warwick. Prince Edward stood with his mother and father, Margaret of Anjou, Henry VI. The old king looked wise and knowing, not at all foolish or mad.

'I told you he was the prince who would come after me,' he said.

And there also was King Edward with his two sons, one of them wearing the crown.

She started awake, her heart racing. Was she dying, that these people were coming back to her?

She couldn't afford to die, not now. She had to remind herself she had won; her son had won.

But at what cost?

It had cost her, and so many people, everything.

She should not be lying here, thinking this; she should be pleased; she should be overwhelmed by joy. But a cry of agony came from her soul: *what cost, what cost, what cost?*

For a moment she was afraid to open her eyes in case all the people were still there, thousands of them pressing into her room. But then she pushed back the bedclothes and got up.

There on the table was the book of hours.

Finally, she sat down and opened it.

Though the cover was slightly damaged, the frontispiece was fine. An image of the Annunciation of the Virgin.

The mother of God knelt at a desk that was draped in scarlet. On her head was a wreath of flowers, because she was Queen of Heaven. Her hands were uplifted in prayer and a prayer book was open before her. The angel Gabriel knelt at her side, looking up at her in adoration. He held a long scroll that contained his sacred announcement: *Behold the handmaid of the Lord.*

In that one moment, her life, and the fate of the world, had changed.

As Margaret turned the pages she could see that Richard had written in it in tiny, contorted handwriting. On the first page he'd written *hac die natus erat ricardus rex anglie iijus apud foderingay anno domini mcccclij*. Though she had so little Latin, she could translate this much: 'On this day was born Richard III King of England at Fotheringhay in the year of Our Lord 1452.'

The feeling of sickness returned.

She thought of his mother, Proud Cis, whose last son had been killed. Only yesterday she'd rebuked one of her ladies for speaking disrespectfully of the duchess, who was the mother of kings. Who'd prayed for her son as Margaret had prayed for hers.

But Margaret's prayers had been answered. After all her disbelief, her doubt. So many people had been killed in the war of succession, the battle for the throne, but her son had won.

She felt a kind of terror at the thought of it. God, in whom she'd stopped believing, had answered her prayers. She could not afford ever to doubt Him again.

There was Richard's prayer in his little book: *Free me thy servant King Richard from all tribulation, grief and anguish in which I am held, and from all the snares of my enemies.*

He had prayed, as she had, but God had answered her prayers. And now her son would face the tribulation, grief and anguish of kingship. But she would help him, if God spared her.

God would spare her, surely. He would not visit her sins upon her son. Everything she'd done was because he'd been taken from her and she'd had to fight to get him back. How could she have done otherwise?

She would atone; she would be a model of piety, like the Virgin Mother. No one would ever doubt or question her faith. She held the small book that had belonged to Richard III to her heart and pledged herself to God: *Behold the handmaid of the Lord.*

Darkness, and silence. It wasn't possible to know whether God would forgive or spare her. Richard hadn't known, or her father, or any of the people who had died. It was a condition of life that it was lived blindly, in ignorance. *Lord forgive us, for we know not what we do.*

But the Lord had come down conclusively on their side. Surely that was evidence that she was forgiven? That she could start again. They would make a new England, ruled by piety and good management, not warfare.

Behold a king shall reign in righteousness.

When she opened her eyes there was the small book, scuffed and stained, like Richard's last testament, *his mortal remains.* She flicked through the pages once more, past his date of birth, his sad prayer. He had written in it, as she had written in those other books, and now his writing was hers.

She felt a rush of horror at the thought of her own writing; her own Secret Chronicle. All of that would have to be destroyed. Or changed, because it was always possible to alter what had been written. Glancing down at the former king's handwriting once more, she picked up her quill and methodically, thoroughly, scoured out Richard's name, replacing it with her own. *Margaret R.*

Which stood for Richmond, of course, but also for Regina, or queen.

About the Chronicles

chron-i-cle: A factual written account of important or historical events in the order of their occurrence.

England has a rich and varied tradition of chronicle writing. Most early chronicles were written by monks and associated with the great monastic houses, which often had a designated chronicler. The monastery of Crowland provided a chronicle with continuations that conclude in 1486. These may not have been written by a monk, however, but by a bishop or lawyer who was staying in the monastery.

By the fifteenth century, the monastic tradition of chronicle writing was in decline. A new group of chronicles came from the towns. These civic narratives were all written in the vernacular, and most were centred on London – *The Great Chronicle of London* and *The Short English Chronicle* were written at this time. We do not know the authors of these, but Robert Fabyan's *Concordance of Hystoryes* was published in 1516 as *The New Chronicles of England and France*. Fabyan was a London draper, sheriff and alderman and, while his work begins in antiquity, it contains many events that he witnessed during the course of his life.

In the reign of Edward IV, William Caxton brought his printing press to England. As a result, there was a greater variety of chronicle writing than ever before, and several histories commissioned by noble houses. John Rous, for instance, was a historian and antiquary who spent most of his life in service to the Yorkist dynasty and, in particular, the earls of Warwick. The *Rous Roll* contains a family history centred on the life of Richard Beauchamp, 13th Earl of Warwick, and a predominantly Yorkist version of the conflict between Lancaster and York.

It could also be said, with some justice, that the Tudors used this new technology to considerable effect, rewriting their own histories and genealogies.

Polydore Vergil, Italian cleric and Renaissance humanist historian, came to England in 1502 and was encouraged by Henry VII to write a comprehensive history of England – an *Anglica Historia* – which was not finished until 1531. He has sometimes been called the 'father of English history', and his epic work marks a shift in historical writing towards the 'authorised version' that could be printed and widely distributed throughout the known world. Thomas More, also a humanist scholar, wrote *The History of King Richard III* in English and Latin during the early part of the reign of Henry VIII, when he was under-sheriff of London. Both these accounts, therefore, can be said to have been influenced by the Tudor version of events.

Edward Hall (1497–1547) was a lawyer whose most famous work, *The Union of the Two Noble and Illustre Families of Lancastre and Yorke*, commonly known as *Hall's Chronicle*, was published a year after his death. It begins with the reign of Henry IV and ends with the death of Henry VIII, casting the Tudors in a favourable light.

It should be noted that none of these chronicles is contemporary. They describe events retrospectively, relying on earlier sources, and are judiciously partisan.

Other accounts of the period are written by foreign emissaries. These include Jean de Waurin, a Burgundian soldier and diplomat who served both Duke Philip the Good of Burgundy and his successor Charles the Bold, and Philippe de Commines, who wrote his memoirs at the court of Louis XI of France. Georges Chastellain was a Burgundian chronicler and poet who wrote *Chronique des choses de mon temps* for Margaret of Anjou, and Jean Molinet, also a Burgundian poet, was his secretary, who continued

Chastellain's chronicle after his death. Mancini, an Italian poet, was sent from the court of Louis XI to report on English affairs. The *Milanese State Papers* is a collection of ambassadorial letters sent mainly by Milanese envoys in England, France and Burgundy to successive dukes of Milan.

In this period, an increasing number of records were kept – rolls and files in the Public Records Office, government records such as the *Rotuli Parliamentorum* in the Chancery archive, and local records such as the Coventry Leet Book or the York Civic Records. Also, the first collections of private letters survive – circa two hundred and fifty from the Plumptons of York and more than a thousand from the Pastons of Norfolk – which provide an invaluable glimpse into the daily lives of people caught up in the 'intestinal conflicts' and political turmoil of the period.

None of the chronicles can be said to be definitive. They are partisan, contradictory and unreliable in certain respects, but also vivid and readable accounts of a tumultuous period of English history. The chroniclers' approach to writing, and to history, is very different from that of the contemporary historical novelist; the chronicles convey the spirit of the age without resorting to interior perspective or reflection. It seemed to me that the different approaches were complementary, and might usefully be brought together.

Acknowledgements

Nine years ago I set out in faith on this project, without knowing whether it would ever be published. I have met some amazing people along the way whose interest, encouragement and practical help have been invaluable. I have neither the time nor the space to thank everyone, but I am truly grateful. Special thanks are due to Anna Pollard, for her reading, support and careful attention to the family trees; to Ben also, for technical support and further work on the family tree; to Terry and Dot Devey-Smith for their wonderful hospitality in Brittany, and for taking me to so many places associated with Henry Tudor; and to the staff of Chetham's Library, as ever.

I also want to thank my agent, Charles Walker, for taking these novels on in their embryonic form and for seeing so clearly what I wanted them to be; and his assistant, Chris, for his enthusiastic support of them; and Juliet Annan and the rest of my editorial team at Penguin, for their patience and unstinting efforts in nurturing them through to maturity.

LIVI MICHAEL

SUCCESSION

In this first book of Livi Michael's Wars of the Roses trilogy, two remarkable women cunningly work the strings of succession . . .

Margaret of Anjou is young, beautiful, French and wildly unpopular when she marries England's ill-fated Henry VI. After the English are banished from France, civil war erupts. Margaret becomes a warrior queen, fighting for her husband's right to be king and her son's position as his rightful heir.

Meanwhile, heiress Margaret Beaufort is born into a troubled inheritance. Fiercely sought after by courtiers, by the age of thirteen she has married twice and given birth to her only son, who will be the future king of England. But then he is taken from her. . .

'Has the colour and power of the best of the chronicles she uses' *Sunday Times*

'Portrayed beautifully, honestly' *Historical Novel Review*